The Tyburn Waltz

Books by Maggie MacKeever

The Tyburn Waltz
Vampire, Bespelled
Waltz With A Vampire
An Extraordinary Flirtation
Lover's Knot
Love Match
Cupid's Dart
Lady Sherry and the Highwayman
French Leave
Our Tabby
Sweet Vixen
An Eligible Connection
Strange Bedfellows
Lady Sweetbriar
A Notorious Lady
Fair Fatality
The Misses Millikin
Jessabelle
Lady Bliss
A Banbury Tale
Lady in the Straw
Lord Fairchild's Daughter
El Dorado
Outlaw Love
Caprice

The Tyburn Waltz

Maggie MacKeever

Vintage Ink Press
Los Angeles

Copyright © 2010 by Gail Clark Burch

Cover based on the portrait of Louise Augusta, Queen of Prussia, painted by Elisabeth Louise Vigee LeBrun, 1801. Original located at Schloss Charlottenburg, Preussischer Kulturbesitz, Berlin.

Corner design elements courtesy of Istockphoto/ Angelgild

ISBN: 978-0-9826239-3-0

Library of Congress Control Number: 2010930364

First Printing: November 2010

This book is an original publication of Vintage Ink Press. For further information contact www.vintageinkpress.com

Printed in the United States of America

With many thanks to those
who have walked these roads with me.

Prologue

London, 1810

The grim smoke-blackened walls of Newgate Prison rose stark against the sky. Since early on this Monday morning, the crowd had been gathering round. When the great deep bell of St. Sepulcher's tolled the appointed hour, unlucky Odo Cockbain would be led out through the Debtor's Door and up a short flight of steps onto the gallows, there to deliver what was expected to be a passable dying speech, which the poor brute was no doubt practicing even now, before he was hanged.

Men, women, and children, highborn as well as low, congregated in the streets and on the rooftops. The more affluent among them commanded seats at the windows overlooking the gallows. Mingling with the spectators were vendors of barley broth and taffity tarts, tea and coffee and ginger beer and patent nostrums involving hog's lice; broadsheet and ballad sellers, shoplifters and pickpockets and merchants; drunken lordlings that had passed the night celebrating in the tavern across the way.

Making his way through the throng was a neat little man in dark coat and trousers, white linen, plaid vest, and carefully polished shoes. On his nose perched wire-rimmed spectacles, on his thinning hair a black bowl-shaped beaver hat. Pritchett had more the appearance of a clerk than a Bow Street thief-taker, save for the gilt-topped baton tucked under one arm. He paused to buy a bunch of lavender and a meat pie wrapped in greasy paper before continuing down the cobbled street, past the gallows and up to the great barred gate.

A nod, a coin, and Pritchett followed the leather-aproned turnkey into a rambling maze of yards, staircases, wards and ways so dark and dim that candles were necessary even in the daylight. The stench of unwashed flesh and excrement, sickness and death, was so noxious that it made a man's eyes sting. The few windows faced inward, and were heavily barred with strong iron.

Down dismal passages they walked, through heavy oaken iron-bound gates that swung open and slammed shut again behind, past filthy cells where prisoners were manacled to chains stapled in the floor, lying in the fetid dampness with no covering and perhaps a rotting corpse for company until the deceased's relatives dredged up enough money to buy its release. The turnkey paused by the men's common yard, where an elaborately staged 'prize fight' was underway behind a door fashioned from thick bars of wood. The brutal thud of fist against flesh, the crunch of bone, the howl of shouting, bragging, cursing spectators... 'Twas one way to dissipate energies that otherwise sought release in riots and disturbances. Let the brutes crack each other's nappers, and damn any nonsense about who drew first blood.

Pritchett prodded the turnkey with his baton. The man led him to a private cell. Pritchett pulled another coin from his pocket. The turnkey unlocked the door.

The cell was small and close and clammy, empty of furnishings, the smell of urine strong enough to gag a mule. The walls oozed moisture. Rats and mice burrowed in the filthy straw. The turnkey's candle illuminated a small ragged figure huddled in a corner of the tiny room.

Pritchett stepped into the chamber. The turnkey set down his candle on a narrow shelf. The heavy door swung shut behind him. The prisoner scrambled to his feet.

In addition to his Bow Street staff, Pritchett was armed with his prized Manton pistol—octagonal barrel with two white metal lines inlaid, engraved breech and lock, rounded chequered butt—not to mention his own handy bunch of fives. Unlikely he would have to use either his pistol or his fists. This scrawny mite must measure under five feet tall and weigh less than seven stone, a considerable amount of that muck clinging to his person. In tattered furze breeches and ragged shirt, he looked like someone could have stuck him on a stick to scare off crows.

The felon was staring at his dirty feet as if he expected his toes to detach themselves and go crawling toward the unlocked door. Pritchett raised the lavender to his nose, and inhaled. "In the interest of saving time, I'll tell you what I know. You were caught on the day sneak. If snatching a set of silver teaspoons wasn't bad enough, you had about your person a diving hook and picklock, as well as a ginny to open the grate. You've no money for easement, and by now your belly is as empty as if your throat was cut." With the head of his baton, he tilted up the prisoner's chin. "You've me to thank for your private accommodations. You see, I know that you're no boy."

She met his gaze because she had no choice, her own eyes a startling vibrant blue surrounded by long thick lashes and an arch of dark eyebrows. Her nose was straight above a stubborn mouth, her face heart-shaped, her short curly hair matted to her head with dirt.

Dirt, and Pritchett didn't care to think what else. She stank like rotting fish. He breathed deeply of his lavender. She jerked her chin away and suggested what he might do to her backside.

"More likely I'll plant my boot there." Pritchett handed her the meat pie and watched her cram the pastie whole into her mouth, wondered how long it had been since she last ate. The wrists and ankles that protruded from her ragged clothing were alarmingly thin.

Pritchett had no stomach for this business. But business it was, and once it lay behind him he would go home, clean his clothes with potter's clay or chloride of soda, and put it from his mind. "You are well and truly caught, young Jules. There's a very real possibility that you might dance the Tyburn waltz for your sins, or at the least be sent to the hulks, providing that you don't die of gaol fever first."

The girl scowled at him. "Go tip a pike."

Pull a cat's tail, and she would scratch. "Howsomever, I'm here to tell you that you can't hang twice."

The meat pie was devoured, the paper licked clean, and the girl's attention all for him. "Mayhap you aren't aware that countless crimes are punishable by death or transportation," Pritchett added. "Including the theft of property worth more than five shillings from a shop."

"May'ap instead of 'angin' you'll jaw me to death," she snarled, displaying teeth that were white enough, the two front ones slightly overlapped. "Cut the cackle and get to the 'orses. You ain't 'ere for the pleasure of me company."

Pleasure had nothing to do with Pritchett's presence at Newgate. He kept a prudent distance from the girl's clever hands. Miss Jules could slip a ring off a gentleman's finger, or a banknote from his pocket, without her victim noticing anything more than the usual jostling of a crowd.

She could also, in the normal way of things, lift a set of silver teaspoons as easy as water rolling off a duck's back. "How old are you, lass?"

"Old as me tongue and a little older than me teeth."

One meat pie had not been sufficient to disarm her. Pritchett was tempted to give the baggage a good shake. "If I had a dog with no more wit than you, I'd hang him. As *you* may hang without my help. Answer me, girl."

She narrowed those amazing eyes at him. "Ten and four, near as I can guess."

He had merely been curious. Pritchett stuck the lavender in his lapel. "Your luck is in today. If you're willing to put yourself in my hands, on behalf of a certain benefactor, he'll see you released from gaol."

"What's a benny-factor?"

"A gentry cove."

Hope, followed by resignation, flashed across her expressive face. "Odds are this swell of yours is lookin' to take a tumble-in."

Pritchett was not often astonished, but his jaw dropped open now. "A *what?*"

"A tumble-in. To dab it up. That's 'ow it is with the nobs. From a Mayfair mansion to a bare mattress in the corner of some rathole, and soon enough the poor doxy is sellin' 'erself on the street 'til some cully does for her or she dies of the pox. If I must dance, I'd rather 'twas at the sheriff's ball."

This raggedy snippet foreswore the blanket hornpipe? Pritchett almost smiled. "When the Cap'n wants a tumble, he won't be tossing up the skirts of such as you. Yes, I know you're not wearing skirts at the moment, but if you was."

Jules chewed on her lip. Pritchett wondered if the girl had ever owned a skirt. "Is he queer in the attic?" she asked.

That was an excellent question. Pritchett had wondered the same thing. "As I see it, you've two choices. You can go along with the Cap'n and sleep on clean sheets with a warming pan in your bed. Or you can take your chances in the common ward. How long do you think it will be before someone discovers you piss without a pizzle? Maybe an old whore could stand the business, but not a young pullet like yourself. And all that's before you go out of the world by the steps and a string."

Impossible to escape his meaning. Jules paled beneath her dirt. "What's your Cap'n want with me?"

Though it was unlikely he meant to give this ragamuffin a tumble, whatever Cap'n Jack intended wasn't likely to be good. Pritchett reminded himself that no one so frail and fragile as she seemed would have survived long in London's cruel streets. The Cap'n's private business was none of his affair.

Still, Pritchett's conscience pricked him. "I'd be lying if I said I knew his purpose. But I'll give you fair warning, as should know: dare the Cap'n and be damned."

Came a moment's silence while Jules mulled over his proposition, her eyes fixed on the floor while she idly poked one toe into the stinking straw. "A Bow Street man would turn on his own mother if there was a reward."

The girl spoke the truth. "It's not likely you'll have any better offer, and that *is* the way of it, lass."

She raised her eyes and studied him; thrust out one grubby paw. "Done then, and may the devil take you if you're gullin' me."

Gingerly, Pritchett took her hand in his and shook it. He tried not to think what unspeakable substances might be accumulating on his glove.

Chapter One

Death's unavoidable, let's have a drink.
— Seneca the Elder

"More," she murmured. "Harder. Faster." Ned eyed the breasts swaying before him, laved one rosy nipple with his tongue. The bedstead creaked beneath them. Lilah was racing hell for leather. He thanked God she didn't have a riding crop.

He took firmer grip on her slender hips, thrust upward into her, again and again, at a spanking good pace. She gasped and moaned and rode him like the well-seasoned equestrienne that she was. Their bodies were slick with sweat, their image faintly ludicrous in the mirror hung above the bed. An ignoble end for the fifteenth Earl of Dorset: asphyxiated while taking his pleasure amid a whore's tumbled sheets.

Ned couldn't die yet. His cousin had been clear about the reproductive duties of an earl. He reached down and slid his fingers into Lilah's damp curls. A skilled caress, and then another. Her body tensed. One more deft manipulation. She shuddered, and groaned. As did he. She collapsed upon his chest.

Moments passed, before she stirred, and slid off him. Ned opened his eyes. Lilah made a pretty picture, posed provocatively beside him on her crimson satin sheets. Her long, thick chestnut hair fanned out on the pillow. Her lavender eyes, as they met his in the mirror, held the cynical expression of one who had no illusions about the world.

Ned sat up and reached for his waistcoat. "I've brought you something. You won't insult me by refusing it." While it was the custom for patrons of Lilah's establishment to give her girls a present—which was then passed along to their employer who in turn shared with them a small portion of its worth—Lilah seldom accepted such tokens for herself. He dropped a string of glittering gems on the sheet.

Lilah held the bracelet up to the light, contemplated the quality of the stones, fastened it on her wrist and admired it again. "I wouldn't dream of insulting you. Or your excellent taste. Thank you, Ned."

"You know I would be happy to do more." He began to dress.

Lilah propped herself up among her pillows to better watch her guest pull on his clothes. The fifteenth Earl of Dorset—to her forever mere Ned Fairchild—was all graceful hard-muscled strength, with broad shoulders and narrow hips, thick auburn hair and eyes a woman might drown in, were she so short of sense. His face was saved from beauty by a slightly aquiline nose and a more-than-slightly wicked month. "Since you are so eager to be of service, you may go downstairs and tell me if my new French chef is worth the fortune I am paying him," she said.

The moment for any serious conversation had passed. Ned smoothed his hair and gave his cravat one last twitch before he stepped out into the hall.

The Academy was doing a brisk business this evening, its elegant apartments graced with gentlemen in formal attire, women in gowns as fashionable as any worn by ladies of the *ton*. Ned strolled through the supper room, assured himself that Lilah's French chef lived up to his reputation; spared a brief glance into another chamber where an enactment of the Tahitian Feast of Venus was underway. This highly imaginative tribute to the anthropological researches of Captain Cook featured live sex acts performed by South Sea Island 'maidens' and a dozen well-endowed athletic youths. Flower-wreathed dildos added a whimsical touch.

Ned had seen it all before. And done it, like as not. Once with considerably more enjoyment than now. Everything had changed, and not for the better, since he'd become a bloody earl. He collected his hat and greatcoat from a servant. Perhaps a brisk walk might clear the cobwebs from his head.

King's Place was a seemingly insignificant alley near the royal palace. Almost all the houses here were dedicated to pleasure, their interiors designed by the likes of the Adam brothers, decorated with furniture in the elegant styles of Sheraton and Hepplewhite. Liveried servants were *de rigueur,* as well as expensive carriages, for the residents confined their perambulations to St. James's Park. Ned pulled up his coat collar and set out for a stroll.

He had not far to travel, though far enough that a more prudent man might have chosen not to go afoot. The streets were dark and empty save for the watchman in his box, the occasional carriage that emerged wraith-like from obscuring mist made up of equal parts coal smoke and river fog. A skinny dog snarled at Ned as it slunk into an alleyway. Moodily, he kicked at a pile of rubble, half-wishing that some thugs would try and interfere with him so that he might break their heads.

No one interfered, alas, and at length he reached his destination, an ancient brick structure perched near the river on the north side of the Thames. The old house pleased Ned, for it stood as far beyond the pale as he. Wakely Court had been the ancestral home of his grandmother's family, all now deceased. The ramshackle building stretched three stories above the street, was adorned with turrets and gables and a forest of tall rectangular chimneys, bay and mullioned windows with tiny jeweled diamond panes set in designs of ornamental lead.

Light shone from a great many of those windows, despite the lateness of the hour. Ned approached the front door.

That great portal creaked open to reveal a glum-faced individual of middle years and impressive girth, his old-fashioned livery splotched with damp. "I believe you will find Mistress Clea in the library, my lord," said Tidcombe, as he took Ned's hat and coat.

Ned mounted the stair. Although she refused to accept it, Clea at fifteen years of age was not altogether grown up. He wondered what excuse she would have, this time, for being out of bed so late.

Candles blazed in the library, illuminating a ceiling with huge molded beams supporting lesser timbers, the spaces between filled with plastered lath; a chimneypiece featuring Bacchanalian revels complete with nubile maidens and satyrs and a large quantity of grapevines; heavy oak furniture embellished with intricately carved animals and flowers.

Dusty draperies hung at the windows. Moth-eaten tapestries adorned the paneled walls. Countless books lined the old shelves, rested tipsily on the floor alongside maps of the world, a calculating board with counters, and a perpetual almanac in a frame. The library was Ned's favorite chamber. To its clutter, he had added a huge pewter inkstand and an excessively ugly statue that he had brought back from his travels and given place of honor on the old desk.

The first thing Ned noticed as he stepped into the brightly-lit room was that one window lacked a curtain. Second was the aroma of spilt brandy that hung heavy in the air. Third was his sister, perched on the chair behind his desk. She glowed with excitement. Dirt smeared her muslin nightdress, and one pretty cheek. Cobwebs bedecked her mahogany hair.

Ned folded his arms and tried to look stern. "What was it this time? Virgil? Apuleius?"

She twinkled at him. "Juvenal. But I was asleep! A noise woke me. I think it was Cerberus." Wakely Court's most recent tenant had left behind a full complement of servants—Tidcombe the butler, and the housekeeper, Mrs. Scroggs; several maidservants, two named Mary; a number of footmen, chief among them James—and also a pug-nosed, pop-eyed, nasty-tempered little dog.

Ned glanced warily around, found the beast sprawled amid a tumbled stack of books, resembling nothing so much as a dirty mop with stubby legs. If Cerberus lacked the three heads generally accorded the guardian at the gate to hell, he had more than enough teeth, as displayed now with a curled lip, and a snarl.

The snarl was directed not at Ned, but at the fireplace. Ned turned in that direction. "What the deuce?" he inquired.

Clea beamed. "I've been on the fidgets for fear you wouldn't return home in time, and I might fall asleep, and she might escape. That is why Bates has the firearm. I told him he might trust me to guard her, but he said you'd have his head."

Bates, the grizzled batman who had been with Ned in the Peninsula, was indeed holding a firearm. "You would have, sir, and that's a fact," he said.

Drawn up close to the fireplace was an armchair. Seated in the armchair was a slight figure bound with cords. Ned's window cords, if his eyesight did not deceive him. "Would someone please explain?"

"I caught a housebreaker!" crowed Clea. "Or Cerberus did, because he tripped her. And then I pulled the curtain down, and knocked her on the head."

Ned looked at his decanter, which lay empty on the carpet. "Couldn't you have used the inkstand, or the globe?"

Clea waved off his objections. "A housebreaker, Ned! I knew you would like it of all things."

Ned would have liked it better if his good smuggled French brandy had not been splashed about the room. Now that he had decided he wasn't cup-shot, he could have used a drink. "Why is she so damp? Why are *you* so damp? Where are her clothes?" The housebreaker was clad in nothing but the velvet drape, so far as he could tell. She was a little bit of a thing, and looked not much older than his sister.

"Her clothes were beyond dreadful." Clea sounded as prim and disapproving as if she cared about such stuff. "I decided she should have a bath. Bates and Tidcombe helped. And James. That is, they helped until we realized she was a girl! She had on boy's clothing, and though her breeches were beyond dirty, it was an excellent idea. Think of trying to climb a drainpipe in skirts! She must have got in the house that way. After we discovered she was a female, it was Mrs. Scroggs and the Marys and me. And Bates. But everything was proper. Bates looked at the ceiling while he held the gun."

Clea might believe Bates had looked only at the ceiling while in a naked female's presence. Ned was skeptical. He glanced at his batman. Bates had the grace to blush.

"Her garments were nastier than she was underneath them," added Clea. "I think the grime is part of her disguise. And a prodigious clever disguise it was, because it fooled us all."

The housebreaker did not appear gratified by Clea's approval.

Impossible to tell the color of her hair under its grease, but her blue eyes shot angry sparks.

Ned moved closer to the captive. "Why is she gagged?"

"Bates said her language wasn't fitting for my ears. What's a gundiguts?"

A gundiguts was a prim pursy fellow. "Tidcombe," said Ned.

Clea nodded, satisfied. "And a bundle-tail?"

"Mrs. Scroggs, no doubt." That worthy was both short and squat.

Clea clapped her hands together. "I am furthering my education! Nickninny I knew, and lobcock. What about gingambobs?"

Ned opened his mouth and closed it, appalled at how close he had come to discussing testicles with his sister. Bates cleared his throat. Behind her gag, Ned could have sworn the housebreaker smirked.

He appropriated the pistol. "You've had enough educating for one evening. I'll deal with this now."

Clea bounced indignantly in her chair. "But *I* caught her!" she wailed.

"Yes, and a good job you did of it." Ned pulled his sister to her feet. "Now go back to bed."

She shot him a reproachful glance. Her lower lip quivered. Her shoulders slumped. Unmoved, Ned turned her toward the doorway. "Bates will escort you to your room."

The batman was no more eager than Clea to be dismissed. "You might want to think again, sir. That one's a she-demon. Precious near took a bite right off me arm."

"And I might not!" retorted Ned. "The chit's no bigger than a minute. Hardly a danger to a great strong fellow like myself. Or maybe you think that since I resigned my commission I've gone soft?"

Only a crackbrain would think that. If he no longer fought the French, the lieutenant still rode and boxed; indulged in all the sports so beloved by gentlemen, and some others that were not. Even dressed by the finest tailors, he retained the air of the adventurer he recently had been.

The lieutenant additionally had an air of wishing to punch out someone's daylights. Bates didn't care to volunteer. "I'll be seeing Miss Clea to her chamber, sir," he said, and ushered that reluctant damsel from the room.

Ned waited until the door clicked closed behind them before he turned back to the prisoner. He found himself curious to see the rest of her face.

He reached for her. She tensed. "Behave yourself," said Ned. "Or I won't remove your gag. Before you try and bite me, you might remember that I may yet turn you over to the constable." Gingerly, he untied the sodden material and pulled it from her mouth.

She grimaced. "Bugger and blast."

Her voice was light, oddly appealing. "Tsk! Such language. What were you doing in my house?"

The straight little nose twitched. "'Twas a misunderstanding. I was just passing by."

"And dropped in for a spot of brandy? You're not a good liar. I think I will untie you. You'll recall that I have the gun."

She eyed the pistol. "Ain't likely to forget, am I?"

Her hands were tied in front of her. Wisdom dictated that he leave them safely bound. Surprisingly elegant hands they were, the fingers slender and graceful.

Ned set aside the firearm, unfastened the cords that secured her ankles, rubbed the soft flesh where the bonds had chafed. Her bones were small, delicate, finely formed. She cursed and tried to kick him. He experienced an absurd impulse to pick up this defiant scrap and hold her safe from the world.

Well, why not? If he could hardly hold a housebreaker safe, he could certainly still hold her. Ned untangled her from the chair; scooped her up, drapery and all, and sat her on the desk. The fabric parted, revealing one smooth and slender shoulder, and the curve of one plump breast. Older than he had thought her, he decided. She clutched at the curtain and scowled.

Here was a female unimpressed by title and position. Ned trailed one finger down her soft cheek. "Tell me your name."

She turned her head and bit his wrist; at the same time planted her bare foot in his groin. Abruptly, Ned released her. "Point taken," he said and then cursed, because she grasped the ugly statue in her hands and aimed it at his head.

Caught off balance, Ned stumbled backward. The thief scooted off his desk. He grabbed for her, caught handfuls of the curtain. She brought the statue down, hard, on his skull. Tangled in dusty draperies, Ned crashed to the floor.

He lay there for a moment, staring at the ceiling. Cerberus waddled forward, and stuck a cold nose in his face.

The dog's breath was unpleasant. Ned pushed him away. Cerberus made a noise that sounded suspiciously like a snicker, and flopped down on the hearth.

Slowly, Ned sat up, clutching his sore head. He'd not soon forget his last glimpse of the housebreaker, scrambling mother-naked out his library window, clutching his ugly statue in her hand.

Damned if he'd enjoyed anything so much since he departed the Peninsula. When Bates returned to the library, he found his master holding a bloody handkerchief to his head, and laughing like a loon.

Chapter Two

Be careful about starting something you may regret.
— Pubilius Syrus

Julie slipped through the stage door. The theater's resident feline rubbed against her ankles with a welcoming *meowr*. She picked up Ophelia and pressed her face against the cat's soft black fur.

A clutter of theatrical necessities was piled up willy-nilly. Julie skirted scenery and props, a classical doorway with roses creeping up it, a full-scale flying machine drawn by a dragon and complete with clouds; kept her eyes peeled for a glimpse of one of Drury Lane's resident ghosts, her favorite Charles Macklin, who in a previous century had killed a fellow actor in an argument over a wig. The theater had burned down since—plumbers repairing the roof had gone off and left their fires burning—and had been rebuilt, but the ghosts remained. Instead she encountered scene shifters and painters and carpenters, and other corporeal backstage personnel.

Beyond the stage lay the dressing rooms, one for ladies and one for gentlemen. Julie found Rose alone in the ladies', standing among the dressing tables and wig stands, gazing somberly into a looking glass. She was a woman of determinedly indeterminate age, with warm hazel eyes and fiery red hair and ordinary features that were able to change chameleon-like from joy to sorrow in an eyelid's blink. Her slender, graceful figure was nicely set off by a high-waisted leaf-green gown.

Julie walked up beside her friend, surveyed her own reflection. Today she was merely another female come from market, her shawl around her shoulders, and her basket on her arm.

She set down the basket. Ophelia pounced. Julie pushed the cat aside, retrieved the statue, set it on the dressing table in front of Rose. The bizarre figurine head of a hippopotamus, legs and arms of a lion, tail of a crocodile, swollen belly and human breasts—was no more appealing in the brighter light of day. "The fencing cove in Rat's Castle said it wasn't worth its weight in metal, whatever that might be, and I should take it from his sight. I'd hoped to do better. You should see the inside of that old house. Dusty and creaky and full of useless stuff. Not what one would expect of a gentry ken."

"Language," Rose said automatically. "And you shouldn't have broken into a gentleman's residence. No, or any other. What if you were caught? Oh, this is all my fault!"

"Gammon!" retorted Julie. "You didn't send me there."

"No, but I might as well have." Rose glanced from the statue back to her mirror, her expression morose. Handsome—and more important, wealthy—admirers weren't as plentiful as once they had been, when Rose was young and pretty, and believed the world well lost for romance.

Not that Rose wasn't still attractive, at several years past forty, due to diligent applications of *Pommade de Seville* and a Wash of the Ladies of Denmark and Virgin Milk; as well as discrete recourse to Pearl White Powder and rouge. And not, certainly not, that she had given up on romance. Rose fell in love with appalling regularity and predictably disastrous results, due to an unfortunate weakness for handsome rogues. For all her heart was forever being broken, it was generous. As a result, her pockets were most often to let.

"Oh, Jules," Rose sighed. "I wish you didn't have to go."

As did Julie. It was that imminent departure that had inspired her foray into the sneaking budge; she had hoped to filch something valuable to tide Rose over while she was away. Which just went to show that one should stick to one's own skill, and thereby avoid being first clapped into Newgate, and then running bare-arsed through the streets. Fortunately, like many another young thief before her, Julie had learned to make her way quickly among the warren of courts and alleys and lanes that lay between the rookeries and London's fashionable West End.

Her school had been those streets. She had progressed from a ragged cherub perched on a doorstep holding two grubby packets containing some residue of tea and sugar, sobbing that she'd been robbed and dared not go home; to a dirty scamp begging a bite from strangers and later stealing from shop-windows and stalls; to finally a pilferer of pockets so deft as to be a force of nature, like the tide that swept up items from one location and deposited them elsewhere.

She touched the ugly statue, wondered if it had meant something special to its owner. Julie was sorry to have taken it from him, in that case. She scolded herself for this mawkishness. There was no place for regret in her line of work.

Rose meanwhile was scolding Ophelia, who had attempted a foray among the makeup pots and jars. She snatched up the cat and put her on the floor. Ophelia leapt back onto the dressing table. Rose swatted at the contrary creature. Her eyes were suspiciously damp.

Julie pretended not to notice. "It's not forever, Rose."

"We don't know how long it will be." Rose unscrewed the top of a ceramic jar. "Or what will happen afterward."

Julie didn't want to think about afterward. "I'll not be that far away."

Rose screwed the lid back on, and pushed the jar aside. "It won't be the same. We've been playing at make-believe. Now things are about to become all too real. I'm afraid for you. The Cap'n . . ." Rose's voice trailed off.

No one knew the Cap'n's true identity, save perhaps for the Bow Street Runner Pritchett, who served as his mouthpiece. Some whispered he was of noble birth. Whatever his origins, the Cap'n was the center of a vast network of profitable nefarious enterprise. Rose was but one of countless unfortunates who'd been caught in his sticky web, in her case result of having been so foolish as to keep locks of hair, each labeled with the name of the paramour to whom it had belonged, accompanied by letters that were equally enlightening, and consequently left open to blackmail.

Which only further convinced Julie that love turned one's brain to pudding. "Maybe," she suggested, "I'll catch the eye of some rich swell."

"Don't think it!" Rose said fiercely, tears forgotten as she launched into a tirade. Wasn't she herself a fine example of what happened when a girl set her feet on the road to ruin, bedazzled in her instance by an attractive young scoundrel who had deceived her into thinking he was a wealthy gentleman? Bread and cheese and kisses. Bachelor's fare.

Julie recalled the eye she'd caught last night, and wondered what might have happened if she hadn't fled. She had thought the earl was going to try and kiss her. What a queer thing it had been to be held on his lap. Julie had never sat on anyone's lap before.

Yes, and she'd not do so again until hell froze over, gentlemen's laps not being for such as her, so she'd best put the surprisingly pleasant memory out of her head. "In other words, if someone flashes his ivories and expects me to hitch up my skirts I'm not to tell him his brains are in his ballocks. Don't fret yourself, Rose. I promise butter won't melt in my mouth."

Rose picked up a hairbrush. "Remember what I taught you. Don't put yourself forward. Don't raise your voice. Adopt a conciliatory manner at all times."

Julie extricated Ophelia from among the clutter of cosmetics. The cat draped over her shoulder and batted lazily at her curls. On Cap'n Jack's orders, Julie had endured a caper merchant (dancing master); could now employ the break-teeth words (King's English) of a young lady and properly use a muffling-cheat (napkin); had in fact had so many new notions stuffed into her idea-pot (head) that sometimes she feared it might burst. After spending the past four years being trained to play the part of a pretty-behaved female, Julie would much rather be a sow's ear than a silk purse.

But her friend was in a fluster. "I was bamming you, Rose."

"You shouldn't be bamming me, any more than you should try and swear the devil out of hell." Rose had received a more than adequate education before her slide down the slippery slope to ruin. "You must stay always in character, and think in proper terms, to avoid making a misstep. Young ladies are supposed to be, well, ladylike." She abandoned her lecture to throw her hands up in the air. "This is a mad scheme!"

Julie privately agreed. "Mayhap I should let that swell set me up nicely, so that we may lie in clover, and bid Cap'n Jack go and be damned."

Rose shook her head. "Don't think you may outsmart the Cap'n. I know of one girl that had her face slashed, and that's not the worst I could tell."

Julie needed no warning. Cap'n Jack could have had her clapped back in irons anytime these past four years.

A knock came at the door. Rose was required onstage. She grimaced at her mirror—

"O! now forever
Farewell the tranquil mind, farewell content!"

Then squared her shoulders, transformed herself into gentle Desdemona, and sallied forth so that Othello might smother her beneath the bedclothes.

Julie picked up the ugly statue. She dared not leave it behind to incriminate Rose. Too, she had developed a fondness for the thing, reminder as it was of the brief glimpse she'd had of another kind of life. Not the bathing part—she'd gotten over her horror of baths these several years past—but the closeness between young Clea and her Ned. Blood kin, they were, from the look of them; and fond enough of each other, which from what Julie had observed of the world, was often not the case.

She shoved the statue into her basket. It was foolish to become attached to things, for there was always someone bigger, quicker, more clever, to snatch them away. Even more foolish was becoming attached to people, for the same applied. Julie didn't need to be warned about the consequences of disappointing Cap'n Jack. She was less afraid of what might be done to her than what might befall Rose.

Julie set that worrisome notion aside as she left the dressing room. She inhaled deeply of the familiar scents of candle wax and lamp oil, unwashed bodies, dust and wood. Drury Lane was huge, seating three thousand bodies in boxes and galleries and pit. The newly rebuilt theater additionally boasted a grand circular saloon with rooms for refreshment at each end; Doric columns and Corinthian pilasters; an arched ornamented ceiling with a turret light. The interior was colored gold upon green, with rich crimson relief. She wondered what it would be like to watch an entertainment from a private box.

Julie didn't know much about the *ton,* save what had been taught her, which was concerned largely with how to flimflam them; and that the nobs could so easily be gulled made her think them pig-widgeons to a man. She exempted from that harsh judgment her gentleman acquaintance of the night before. That one had been no pig-widgeon, even if he had been careless enough to let her escape. Julie's thoughts kept returning to him, and his pretty face. Although 'pretty' wasn't the right word, and 'handsome' not close. His eyes had been green as emerald glass, or maybe genuine gemstones; she had no experience with the real article. Yes, and wasn't she becoming as big a pudding-head as Rose. Maybe it was something that happened to a female's brain when she reached a certain age.

She was eighteen now. Or thereabouts. Julie had no one to tell her when she'd been born. Or where.

The actors had gathered on the stage, which was so large they were dwarfed by its immense space. Between the pedestal lamps and the curtains on each side were massy columns of verd antique, the gilt capitals supporting the arch over the stage, in its circle the arms of his majesty. Julie stepped into the wings, where she and Ophelia, who had followed her, might watch the action without being in the way. The huge auditorium made subtlety next to impossible—a person seated in the back row of the Two-Shilling Gallery was one hundred feet from the stage door—and the rehearsal was perfunctory at best.

Because the footlights created a large cluster, 'the rose', an actor moved to the bright spot each time he had an important speech, then moved three steps to the right or left to make way for the next speaker. So as not to inhibit gestures, they spaced themselves arm's length apart. It was curious to Julie that some players must punctuate a speech by the shaking of a finger, or the clenching of a fist, or plopping arms akimbo on their hips; speak with their profile turned to the stage, as Mr. Sowerby was doing now.

Mr. Kean spotted Julie, and winked. She smiled back at him. There were those who ridiculed Mr. Kean's small stature and gruff voice, but the actor had taken the town by storm in *The Merchant of Venice* earlier this year. Now he was daring to portray Iago as a careless cordial villain. Mr. Sowerby's Othello was considerably less compelling. Rose was so absorbed in the complexities of her character that she was deaf to all else.

Ophelia rubbed against Julie's ankles. She bent to stroke the cat. Come tomorrow Julie would make her own debut as an actor, her stage the West End.

Chapter Three

Hyde Park was more than usually crowded this sunny afternoon, a good portion of the city's population having ventured forth in hope of glimpsing Czar Alexander of Russia, Emperor Frederick William of Prussia, or any of the generals and field marshals, princes and barons and dukes that accompanied these august personages. All the world was in London, now that hostilities with France had drawn finally to an end. All during the past month, distinguished visitors had flocked to the capital.

Everybody who was anyone rode and drove around the Ring, the ladies driving in their *vis-à-vis*, the gentlemen mounted on glossy thoroughbreds. They made a dazzling spectacle of silks and laces, brass-buttoned blue coats and leather breeches and highly polished top boots. Since Lord Dorset refused to promenade, he and his sister had drawn up their mounts under a shady tree.

Clea was in high spirits. She was wearing a brand new riding habit of pale green that complimented her eyes and a matching gold-banded cap that perched atop her mahogany hair. In the midst of much confusion, she sat her pretty dappled mare with considerable skill. Ned's white gelding, Soldier, didn't care for London crowds. Nor did Ned, but Clea had pleaded to discover what all the uproar was about.

"Look," she said, and pointed. "There's Kane." As powerfully muscled as his huge black Arabian stallion, Lord Saxe had a handsomely rugged face, tousled too-long dark hair, and sleepy brown eyes that had been variously likened by his legion of admirers to whiskey, amber, honey and (more prosaically) burnt caramel pudding; and an apparently irresistible air of having just left a well-sated lady behind in a rumpled bed. His progress was not speedy. Every female in the vicinity strove to put herself in his way.

Kane reached them at last, and immediately treated Clea to a lazy, bone-melting smile. "You look as fine as fivepence today, Miss Fairchild."

She dimpled at him. "Do you think so, Lord Saxe?"

"Have I not just said so?" Kane winked. "You cast all the other ladies into the shade."

Ned supposed he should mind that his sister was flirting with a rakehell. However, she had been flirting with this particular rakehell since she was three years old. "Platoff is so provoked by all the fuss that he's reluctant to go out of doors."

"As Russian is the only language Platoff speaks, I don't wonder at his resolution. Our visitors are all sick to death of the way they are followed about. Even the horses of the Czar's escort have had their tails plucked for souvenirs." During the past few weeks, Kane had seen more of the Allied Sovereigns than he wished.

"And the Grand Duchess?" inquired Clea. "How do you find her?" Grand Duchess Catherine of Oldenburg, favorite sister of the Czar and whispered by some to be his evil genius, had arrived in March, whether on a diplomatic mission or to snare an English husband had not been determined yet.

"She is capricious. Whimsical. Her Highness delights in stirring up trouble, especially where the Regent is concerned. Poor Prinny set up her back at their first meeting." The lady's reaction to Kane had been quite the opposite, which was how he had become an unofficial escort, his assignment less to protect the Grand Duchess from her admirers than to protect innocent bystanders from her. "But what woman is not capricious at times? Catherine lost her husband to typhoid not so long ago. Her nerves were shattered by the burning of Moscow. If as a result she can tolerate neither music nor the Regent, we can make allowances, I think."

Clea tilted her head and studied him. "You like her."

"I like all the ladies." Kane arched a lazy brow.

Clea arched an eyebrow back at him. "'Keep thy hook always baited, for a fish lurks ever in the most unlikely swim.' I am reading Ovid. *Ars Amatoria.* Don't tell Ned."

As if Ned didn't already know. Clea had a much broader understanding than most damsels her age, her brother's feelings about education being that beyond the basics she should study whatever she wished. He wondered, not for the first time, if he had done Clea a disservice by dragging her around the world with him after their parents' death.

His misgivings were not eased when she asked Kane, "What's an abram mort?"

"A madwoman."

"And gingambobs?"

Kane regarded her with amusement. "Who have you been talking to, brat?"

"We caught a housebreaker. That is, *I* caught her. Ned let her get away."

"Her?"

Ned protested, "I didn't let her escape, exactly. I have a lump on my head."

He wondered how his housebreaker had fared. Ned felt a wee bit guilty at sending her off unclothed. Though it was hardly his decision that she should go scampering through his window. He smiled as he recalled the view.

The expression in Kane's brown eyes was not lazy now. "Was anything taken?" he asked.

Clea shrugged. "That ugly old statue of Taweret."

In case Kane didn't understand, which was unlikely because beneath his practiced indolence Kane was very shrewd, Ned added: "The ugly statue of Taweret that was sitting on my desk. Head of a hippopotamus, legs of a lion, tail of a crocodile, human breasts and swollen belly—*that* Taweret."

"Tsk!" said Clea. "Think what Cousin Hannah would say if she knew you were discussing breasts and bellies and fertility goddesses in front of me."

Kane frowned. He did not admire Cousin Hannah. "Taweret.

How curious," he said.

Curious indeed, agreed Ned. Why, of all the things in Wakely Court, had the thief made off with that particular item? Unless she had been sent for it specifically, the theft made no sense. But who could know what the thing was? Everyone involved with Joham Sandoval was dead.

Or so they had believed.

Ned had been one of Wellington's Exploring Officers, agents who moved behind enemy lines, discovering troop movements and gathering strategic information, risking constant exposure and death. If he had not been able to spare his sister the sight of dead horses and shattered homes, sick and wounded soldiers, he *had* spared her knowledge of men like Joham Sandoval.

Happily unaware of the grim tenor of her brother's musings, Clea craned her head. "Speak of the devil," she remarked.

Ned followed his sister's gaze. The devil—in this incarnation, the Dowager Countess of Dorset, mother of the previous and much lamented earl—was wearing a startling bonnet trimmed with tufts and rows of ribbon and large clusters of flowers, all in shades of deepest mourning.

Her skeletal, black-gloved hand beckoned. "You'd best go and do the pretty," said Ned. Clea touched her heel to her horse's flank and rode ahead.

The men followed at a distance, stealing a moment's privacy. "We need to retrieve that artifact," Kane said.

"Agreed." Ned was looking forward to encountering his little thief again. He surveyed the crowd. The population of London had increased some two hundred thousand with the arrival of the Emperor and the Czar, resulting in a scarcity of both milk (the cows frightened out of the Green Park by constant huzzas) and clean clothes (the washerwomen busy working for visiting royalty). "Spies, do you think?"

"My dear." Kane was sardonic. "I should think, everywhere. Apropos of which, Castlereagh charges me to ask if you have grown bored with civilian life." There was no more time for conversation. The dowager's carriage loomed just ahead.

The carriage, and its occupant, had seen finer days, the former in need of a fresh coat of paint, the latter in need of some color in her thin cheeks, some dye to hide the grey that liberally streaked her hair. Lady Dorset inspected Ned, and sniffed. Then she turned her gimlet stare on Ned's companion, who promptly treated her to his most seductive smile. The tiniest of twitches briefly animated the dowager's features, confirming Ned's private conviction that there wasn't a woman alive who could refrain from smiling back at Kane.

Lady Dorset bowed. Lord Saxe tipped his hat. A polite conversation regarding the weather ensued.

The dowager, along with the rest of London, had questions about the Royal Guests, which as soon as politely possible she was quick to ask. "Speaking of whom," remarked Ned, as he looked into the distance where plumes and cuirasses could be seen dancing among the trees.

"Charming as is the company, I must excuse myself." Kane winked at Clea. "'*Video meliora, proboque; deteriora sequor.*'"

The Dowager frowned after him. "Eh?"

Clea was also watching Kane. "'I see the better way, and approve it; I follow the worse.'"

The Dowager turned her frown on Clea. "Saxe will never make a tolerable husband. And you should be wearing mourning, miss."

"Clea is too young to think of marrying anyone." Two sets of eyes fixed incredulously on Ned. "Well, isn't she?"

This absurd question was deemed unworthy of an answer. "Kane is ineligible, based on his forays among the fleshpots?" Clea demanded of their cousin. "Fiddlestick! And while I'm sorry for your loss, Cousin Hannah, I won't wear mourning for someone I never met. I don't see the point of dressing in black, at any rate. You're either sad or you are not, whatever colors you wear, and whatever colors a person wears will hardly make a difference to the dead."

Hannah's jowls quivered. "You are a great deal too outspoken, my girl! Moreover, young ladies shouldn't know about fleshpots."

"Yes, but I wasn't a young lady until recently," Clea pointed out; reasonably, her brother thought. "I have gone overnight from being a soldier's sister to a female of good breeding who might anticipate making an advantageous match. Or so you have said."

"And so you might." Hannah squinted at Ned. "Were your brother not so neglectful of his duties. Had he a proper way of thinking. Did he not leave you to your own devices while he goes about his—" this said with the utmost disapproval— "worldly pursuits."

She made Ned sound the worst of scoundrels, which he was not, although he did bear responsibility for his sister's awareness of flesh-pots. He was tempted to toss the old bat into the Serpentine. Bat-tossing being conduct unsuitable for an earl, Ned reminded himself the dowager was grieving the loss of her son, not that she'd been any joy to be around even before tragedy struck. "Cousin, I assure you that I strive to conduct myself with the utmost propriety and prudence at all times."

"What a clanker!" hooted Clea. "You are almost as good a liar as Kane."

"And *you*," Hannah announced, "are impertinent!"

"Yes, I am," Clea admitted, without a trace of shame. "If I am to form an eligible connection, you will have to take me in hand."

Hannah said, suspiciously, "What brings about this sudden change of heart?"

"It is not so sudden. I have decided I would like to have children, in which case I believe it is customary to get married first."

Hannah blanched. Ned sympathized.

Came a commotion in the park as Platoff, the Hetman of the Cossacks, appeared on the scene alongside two attendants armed with long spears, followed by the hugely popular Marshal Blücher and his splendid mustachios. The crowd went wild when the Czar arrived, mounted on a beautiful horse, dressed in a scarlet uniform, and sporting a large collection of feathers on his head. "We will speak further of this, miss!" promised Hannah, before she commanded her coachman to join the mêlée.

Shouts and curses and excited voices rang out as the Royal Equestrians, preceded by the Duke of Kent, galloped over the green to Kensington Garden. The crowd attempted to follow them through the private gates. Boots were dragged off in the crush, and the Master of the Horse thrown to the grass, and Marshal Blücher backed up against a tree.

Ned was more concerned with his sister. "What are you up to, puss?"

Clea treated him to a dimpled grin. "It's you who doesn't want me made into a pattern-card of respectability. I don't mind. We *are* respectable now. More or less."

The instincts that had kept Ned alive behind enemy lines were all shrieking 'danger' now. "I'm expected to believe that suddenly you wish to live a dull, boring, and unexceptionable life."

"You needn't look at me as if I am a traitor." Clea patted his hand. "Is it so strange that I want to have pretty dresses, and to go to parties and be admired?"

"I admire you," Ned protested.

"You're my brother, silly. I'm not going to marry *you*."

She wasn't going to marry anyone at any time soon, because any young cawker who looked lustfully upon Ned's sister would have his liver carved out and fried. "When you marry, you'll become your husband's property. He may beat you if you don't do as he commands."

"As if I'd marry anyone who would beat me. Just because. . ." Clea shot him a guilty sideways glance. "I'm sorry, Ned."

"I didn't beat Bianca." And the vixen certainly hadn't lived under his thumb.

Clea had already changed the subject. "I *do* want to marry, Ned, someday. I may be but fifteen, but that is not too young to start to prepare. Hannah will prose and preach at me and I will largely ignore her, but she's the only one who can arrange my come-out, and so we must make use of her." She grinned, thereby transforming herself from a young girl on the verge of womanhood to an urchin of perhaps twelve. "We won't tell Hannah that I've decided to have a dazzling career as an acknowledged beauty, with dozens of gentlemen dangling at my slipper-strings, and writing me silly poems, and going off to shoot themselves when I cast them aside."

Soldier took exception to the crowd, or his master's mood, and made his displeasure known. Conversation lapsed for a moment as Ned brought the gelding back under control. "There'll be no dangling until you are twenty years of age. Maybe thirty. Better forty. This is what comes of letting you read Ovid. I should lock you up until then."

Clea ignored this brotherly foolishness. "And while Cousin Hannah is fussing over me, thereby being distracted from her grief, which anyone must agree has been permitted to go on far too long, you'll be left free to go about your business." Her mare shifted nervously, and she took firmer grip on her reins. "Hannah is prodigious high in the instep. I wonder what term our housebreaker would have for her. It is very awkward to keep thinking of that girl as 'our housebreaker'! I wish we knew her name."

Ned intended to know the girl's name. He intended to learn all there was to learn about their thief. Once he knew, he would—

Well, that depended, didn't it, on whether she was an innocent, or no.

Chapter Four

A liar better have a good memory.
— Quintilian

Enter, stage right, Miss Julie Wynne. Impoverished young lady from York. Hopefully no one would recognize the street urchin in this unexceptionable young female disguised in a serviceable dark gown and cloak, standing on the front step of a tall brick bow-windowed townhouse in Grosvenor Square. Julie stared at the door-knocker, which was fashioned as the head of a lion, and wished that she might turn and scurry back where she belonged, which wasn't among these fine squares and wide flagstone pavements, but rather the dirty streets and ill-lit alleys and tenements of the East End. Since she could not, Julie took firmer grip on her battered portmanteau—property of Rose, who in the course of her chequered career had done considerable traveling—and raised her hand.

The door swung open. A superior individual in immaculate livery gazed at Julie down the length of his long nose. "Lord Ashcroft is expecting me. I am Miss Julie Wynne."

"If you will follow me, miss." Julie was given no time to admire the entrance hall with its grand stone staircase, but ushered post-haste into the study and left there to cool her heels. Since there was no one to see her, she allowed herself to gawk. Walls hung with gilt-bordered flock paper. An organ—at least she thought it was an organ—with gilt pipes. Plate glass windows draped with green damask silk; Aubusson carpet and a great deal of some dark, rich-looking wood. Had Julie had the good luck to break into a house like this, she and Rose could have lived in clover for a long time.

Julie strolled around the room, estimating the cost of things—

the pierced steel fender with its hand-sawn design of birds and animals was especially fine, though a person would be hard-pressed to escape through a window carrying such an item tucked under her arm—due not to any innate acquisitiveness but as an adjunct to her craft. She studied a pair of pewter candlesticks, and a colorful japanned urn. Thirty china figures perched on the marble chimneypiece. Julie was fingering a goat being attacked by a dog when a noise made her turn.

Her first impression was a blaze of color: double-breasted long-tailed claret-colored coat worn over two astonishing silk waistcoats, the first bright pink with an overall pattern, the second plain rose; pale buckskin pantaloons, highly polished Hessian boots, a dazzling white shirt and intricately tied cravat. Her second impression, once her eyes had become accustomed to all this man millinery, was that the wearer of the clothing was of medium height and build, not an out-and-outer but not soft-looking either, with sandy hair and grey eyes and a cheerful sort of face, a smattering of freckles on his nose.

Julie was only guessing about the cheerful part. The gentleman didn't look the least bit happy at the moment. "You're not going to steal the silver plate, are you?" he asked. "Murder us in our beds?"

Murder was hardly Julie's business, and Pritchett had made it clear there was to be no filching, save at his command. "No, my lord, to both." She curtsied. "You must be Lord Ashcroft."

"I must be, mustn't I? though I'll allow as I'd rather not." The viscount looked about his library with a furtive air. "Damned if this ain't an awkward business. Don't suppose I should ask how you got into this fix? I'll lay odds you *are* in a fix or you wouldn't be here. If you don't want to tell me, I don't mind! Wouldn't want to be vulgarly inquisitive, would I? Myself, I've been drawing the bustle too freely and fell behindhand with the world. Tried to repair my fortunes—well, who wouldn't?—and damned if it ain't true that it's never wise to bet against a dark horse!" He clasped his hands behind his back and began to pace. "You'll say it was stupidly done of me. I admit I may have been a trifle disguised."

If ever Julie had seen a pigeon ripe for the plucking, one stood before her now. "More like you were as drunk as a lord."

"But I would be, wouldn't I?" The young man paused in his perambulations, looking perplexed. "Mean to say, I *am* a lord. Maybe a viscount ain't as grand as a duke, but it's nothing to sneeze at."

Definitely a pig-widgeon. "Drunk as a wheelbarrow, then."

Lord Ashcroft couldn't argue, or he *could* have but there was no point in it, for he had definitely been cup-shot. At any rate, to make a long story shorter, he had in the natural course of such things next found himself talking of securities and credentials with Messrs Howard and Gibbs, best of the bloodsuckers—here he begged pardon; he had quite forgot he was talking to a young lady—moneylenders, that was, though she wouldn't know of such beings! And he'd thought he had things in good order until he received the unhappy information that someone known as 'Cap'n Jack' had bought up his vowels. "And even if I *could* come down with the derbies, the Cap'n won't accept them, and so I must flop around like a fish on his hook."

Julie, too, had almost forgot she was a lady, so fascinated was she, not by the viscount's account, for London was awash with spendthrift young gentlemen determined to gamble away their inheritances, but by the viscount himself.

"And if Maman finds out …" He shuddered in his shiny boots.

"What would your mama do?"

"Have a spasm. At the least."

"So what if she did?"

Lord Ashcroft rolled his eyes toward the ceiling. "Maman in her palpitations ain't a pretty sight. You're to take the place of her companion, Mildred, who went to Oxford Street to match a length of ribbon and never came back home, in case you don't know. A queer thing, that. Not you not knowing, if in fact you don't, but that old Milly should take French leave. Maman is in a taking about it. I don't see why that should be, since she didn't like the woman above half, but Maman can be pecky sometimes." He paused for breath. "Do *you* know this Cap'n Jack? I don't think I want to be told what he has in mind."

Julie found herself feeling sorry for this foolish fribble, caught so firmly between his mama's foot and the Cap'n's thumb. "I know that he is dangerous. You must do as you're told."

"As if I didn't always." Lord Ashcroft resumed his pacing. "Except when I wagered more than was in my pocket, but everybody does! Thing is, I've never been a *nacky* one, and now I'm in the devil's own scrape. Maybe I should just put a period to my existence. I don't see otherwise how I'm to get clear."

The viscount acted as if the weight of the whole world rested on his shoulders. Julie set out to persuade the unhappy young man into a less fatalistic frame of mind. All would turn out for the best, she assured him (and without the slightest belief in her own words) if he only gave it time, because time was the healer of all wounds and—

Julie thought of her mentor, and murmured:

"The time and my intents are savage wild
More fierce and more inexorable far
Than empty tigers or the roaring sea."

Romeo and Juliet had been a trying experience, for Rose had been deemed too old for a Juliet, and relegated to play The Nurse.

Lord Ashcroft stared at her with admiration. "That's the dandy! I'll leave it to you to fix it up all right and tight. Dashed if you ain't the answer to a fellow's prayers."

He expected *she* would haul his coals out of the fire? Julie added knock-in-the-cradle to her list.

Before Julie could disabuse the viscount of his delusions, the library door opened, and a woman floated into the room. She was very pretty, in an ethereal antique fashion, draped in pale lilac cambric and a lacy shawl and a fetching French lace cap.

The otherworldly aura faded when her eyes lit upon Julie. "What is this?" she inquired. Again, Julie curtseyed. She felt like a jumping-jack.

Impervious to nuances, Lord Ashcroft beamed. "Look what I have brought you, Maman. A new companion to take poor Milly's place. Her name is Julie Wynne. She is a parson's daughter. Related to Babbington. And she promises that she will fix us up all right and tight. Miss Wynne, this is my mama, Lady Georgiana. I'll leave you two alone to get to know one another." With a nod and a bow and a flick of his elegant coat tails, and the air of a man who hadn't a care in the world, he stepped out into the hall.

The viscount's mama resembled her son in looks, though her hair was a darker shade, and no freckle would dare pop out on that aristocratic nose, and she didn't look at all carefree as she arranged herself gracefully in a chair. "Fix us up all right and tight?"

Julie fought an impulse to fidget. "I didn't say that."

"I didn't imagine that you had. What a good boy my Tony is, to be always thinking of his mama. And if you have ambitions in that direction, Miss Wynne, you may abandon them at once."

"No, my lady. I mean, yes, my lady." Julie eyed the rings on Lady Georgiana's fingers; estimated their value; reminded herself that she wasn't a knuckler now, but a respectable female.

"Do sit down, Miss Wynne! If I must continue staring up at you, my head will begin to ache. I do not enjoy a strong constitution. Well? Have you nothing to say?"

What? That she wished she might be elsewhere? "No, my lady," Julie murmured.

Lady Georgiana sighed. "This is like trying to make conversation with a post. I can see that you are a perfectly correct young person wearing a dreadful dress. Tell me what else there is to know about yourself."

Her ladyship wanted conversation? Very well. Julie took a deep breath, put herself in the role, as Rose had taught her, and became the orphaned daughter of a country parson, left destitute in the world. She spoke of tithe dinners, and raising funds for charitable institutions; of providing soup for the villagers during hard winters, and clothes and blankets; of bars of soap boiled up in the rectory, and helping to operate the Penny Bank and the Clothing Club. She explained how annoyed her papa had been when the singers were told not to sing the Responses in the Common Service, but had the impudence to do so anyway. Told of the young lady who, after two months of Bible study, could do no better than tell him that on

Palm Sunday Jesus went up to Heaven on an ass.

Lady Georgiana interrupted. "Was your papa an Evangelist?"

If she said he was, would she be turned off? Julie didn't dare. "Papa believed that the Church was as gentlemanly a pursuit as any other, and that a lack of religious conviction in no way interfered with his overall supervision of parish affairs."

Georgiana wasn't interested in ecclesiastical lessons, which was fortunate, because Julie had come to the end of Rose's reminiscences, or those of Rose's reminiscences that were suitable in this instance to relate. "You are not in mourning, I hope, Miss Wynne. A companion who is in mourning would be of no use to me at all."

Again temptation reared its head. Julie stamped it down. "Papa died some time ago, my lady. He was meticulous about visiting the sick, and contracted a putrid sore throat. I have been living with a relative. She married recently, and there is no longer a place for me in her household."

"You are too attractive," said Lady Georgiana. "Your looks would be a consideration with me also, were my son in the petticoat-line. Who did Tony say you were related to? Babbington? I don't believe I know a Babbington. Not that it matters, because I need someone, and here you are. You appear amiable enough. I hope you have good sense."

If she had good sense, reflected Julie, she would never have got caught swiping silver teaspoons, and thus wound up in Newgate, and come to the attention of Cap'n Jack. Lady Georgiana hadn't waited for an answer, but continued to think out loud. "You won't have a dowry, so you can't expect to wed. And no one with your looks could hope to be hired on as a governess. Plus, you are too young. I'm not certain you are not too young to serve as my companion, but perhaps you may amuse me. Very well! I will expect you to provide me with company and conversation, help me entertain guests, and frequently accompany me to social events. In return, you will receive board and lodging and an allowance. My son will have arranged all that."

Julie opened her mouth to explain that Lord Ashcroft had done no such thing, but Lady Georgiana had already forged ahead. "I suppose you have been seldom in society. We shall change that, providing that you know how to conduct yourself without putting me to the blush. You will see the Czar—he is considered very handsome!—and the King of Prussia and brave Marshal Blücher. They will not deign to notice you, but you may admire them from afar." She embarked upon a frivolous, gossipy sort of conversation concerning the most illustrious members of the *ton*. Julie, who didn't wish that anyone should admire her, and hadn't the slightest interest in whether Princess Charlotte did or did not marry the Prince of Orange, decided that Lady Georgiana was as feather-headed as her son.

Lady Georgiana frowned. "You are positively Friday-faced. I do not care to have dismal countenances about me, for I am sensitive to that sort of thing. I must insist that you be cheerful at all times, Miss Wynne."

'Pecky', the viscount had called his mama, and she did indeed resemble a bad-tempered chicken. "Yes, my lady," Julie murmured.

"Lud, I see that you may soon 'my lady' me to death! You may have the privilege of addressing me as Georgiana when we are alone. And I shall call you—what was it? Judith? Jennifer? Ah, yes, Julie. What an ordinary name. Do you play the organ, Julie? The harp? Perhaps, sing?"

Julie did none of those things and so she explained, adding for good measure that neither could she paint with watercolors, nor sew a straight seam. "Then how are you to entertain me?" Lady Georgiana inquired.

Julie, well rehearsed for this question, allowed that she played a fair hand of cards.

"Excellent! You may refresh yourself, and shortly we will have some tea and a hand of piquet." Lady Georgiana rang for a servant to take Julie to her room.

Not the stiff-rumped footman answered the summons, but a cheerful snub-nosed maid. "Here you are, miss," she said, as she opened the door of a bedroom on the second floor. "Shall I unpack for you?"

Most certainly, she should not. Julie didn't want anyone else's nose turned up at her 'dreadful' gowns, which the dealer in used clothing had sworn were straight off the back of a duke's daughter fallen on hard times. She sent the servant away, closed the door and leaned against it, and let out a great breath.

She had done it. She'd passed the first test, without shaking her finger or clenching her fist or propping her hands on her hips.

Julie wandered around the room, marveling that she was to have so much space to itself. There was a dressing table decorated with festoons of flowers, and an oval looking-glass; a deep wardrobe in which her meager belongings would be drowned; a corner washstand; a tallboy four feet wide and six feet high, the top drawers far above her head.

The bed had a canopy. Julie wondered if anyone had ever died as result of a canopy's collapse.

Rose's battered portmanteau looked as out of place as Julie felt. She paused by the window, looking down into the garden, wondering what Rose was doing at that moment, wishing that she could discuss the afternoon's events with her friend.

Was this what it felt like to be homesick? Julie had never had a real home. She walked over to the bed and poked the mattress. Pritchett had said when they first met that she would sleep alone with a warming pan in her bed. Julie heaved the portmanteau onto the coverlet and began to unpack.

Beneath her personal belongings lay the queer-looking statue. Julie sat down on the mattress, wished she might ask the statue's owner what the ugly thing meant.

He would have made a pretty pirate. A dashing highwayman. She wondered if he ever thought of her, the way she thought of him.

It wasn't likely. Julie flopped over on her back. Maybe it would be for the best if the canopy did cave in and crush her in her sleep.

Chapter Five

The great thing is to know when to speak
and when to keep quiet. — Seneca the Younger

Lord Dorset was privileged—or not, in his opinion—to be present at the grand entertainment hosted by his Regent for the Allied Sovereigns at Carlton House, the once-modest two-story mansion that Prinny had, at monumental expense to the nation's unappreciative taxpayers, transformed into a palace worthy of an oriental potentate. The visitors marveled at the Entrance Hall with its porphyry columns and cornices adored by Etruscan griffins; the Throne Room with its canopy of helmets and ostrich plumes, walls curved with painted mandarins and fluted yellow draperies, peach-blossom ceilings and canopies of tassels and bells. Carlton House was pronounced—by the guests, not the unhappy taxpayers—not only the finest house in England, but the rival of Versailles and St. Cloud. Ned pronounced it damned hot.

"Be grateful you weren't at dinner," retorted Lord Saxe, to whom this complaint had been voiced. Kane was in an uncivil mood. The only member of the dinner party able to communicate in all three of the languages represented, the Grand Duchess had made not the slightest effort to ease any of the conversation. Kane had been strongly tempted to bash her over the head with a gold serving plate.

Thought of head-bashing brought him back to the current conversation. "You weren't able to learn anything more about the artifact?"

Ned had not. Discrete inquiries had uncovered no information about either the missing statue or his thief.

Sandoval was dead. Ned had seen the body. Why this renewed interest in the statue? Did someone wish to step into the brigand's boots?

The crowd inched forward. The men advanced a step further along the circular double staircase. "Campbell reports that Napoleon vows to from now on live like a justice of the peace," said Kane. Colonel Sir Neil Campbell, one of Ned's fellow Peninsular War veterans, had been made British Commissioner on the island of Elba and was consequently experiencing the monotony of exile. "Call me a pessimist, but I think it unlikely the Emperor is occupied with nothing but his island, his house and cows and mules. Castlereagh believes Elba too small to contain the Emperor's ambition, and dangerously near the French coast." Skillfully, Kane edged away from a female bent on plucking at the sleeve of his dark blue evening coat. "He also thinks the Czar must be half mad. Pulteney's has erected a temporary structure where ladies are admitted by ticket to witness him arrive and depart from his hotel chamber. Instead of being annoyed by the intrusion, Alexander smiles and bows and shakes their hands." Ned contemplated giant bronzes of Chronos with his clock and Atlas bearing a map of Europe on his back, and reflected that lunacy was not confined to Russian royalty. He glimpsed their host, sporting a scarlet coat lavishly ornamented with gold lace. Prinny was speaking with a slender and very animated lady. Ned nudged Kane, who pulled a wry face.

While Kane went off to curb the Grand Duchess's mischief-making tendencies, Ned made his cautious way toward the Conservatory. London's dark streets might hold few terrors for a man who had spied his way through the Peninsular War, most often in disguise, though being caught out of uniform behind enemy lines would have seen him immediately shot as an enemy agent or hanged; but the drawing rooms of the *ton* was terrain treacherous as he had ever traversed.

The Conservatory was not so much an adjunct to a palace but a miniature cathedral, its nave and aisles formed by clusters of carved pillars, with stained glass windows and a fan-vaulted ceiling. At the west end, a low wide Gothic door led out to the gardens. Nearby, as he had anticipated, Hannah was holding court.

The dowager glimpsed him, and frowned. Ned made his way to her side. Hannah looked him over, but found nothing to criticize in his appearance, and therefore merely grimaced. For his part, Ned thought she resembled a crow dressed up in black sarcenet and crape.

"I've a bone to pick with you," said Hannah, briskly dispensing with civilities. "You had best give your sister over to me before she is wholly ruined. A young woman who speaks Latin! What were you thinking to allow that? Moreover, it is unsuitable for her to reside in a bachelor household."

Had Hannah gotten to know him and disliked him, Ned might not have minded, but she hadn't bothered to get to know him first. "Clea has been residing in a bachelor household since she was nine years old. She has for all practical purposes been managing that same household for almost as long. It was never 'unsuitable' before."

Hannah sniffed. "It's always been unsuitable, but then no one cared. Now, however, you are the earl. Matters have changed."

With that, Ned couldn't argue. If he weren't an earl, he wouldn't be wandering around Carlton House, staring at old china vases and imperial dragons while his cousin shouted incivilities in his ear. Hannah hadn't shown the slightest interest in Ned's sister before he succeeded to the title. Now she wanted to drag Clea off and teach her how to properly hold a teacup. That Clea wanted the same thing was beyond his comprehension, but it seemed she did.

Hannah gave Ned's arm a sharp pinch. "You have an obligation to the family. Think of your sister, if you won't think of me. Consider what would become of Clea if you was to suddenly become deceased."

Ned had no intention of suddenly becoming deceased, but the previous earl probably hadn't either, unless it was to escape his tiresome parent. "I'm hardly the last of the line. The title is in no danger of dying out."

"The title came to *you!*" snapped Hannah. "Heaven only knows where it might end up next. I'll see to your sister's come-out on one condition: *you* shall speedily choose a companion for life."

The suggestion became no less appalling with repetition. Still, Hannah had a point. With the title had come properties, and with properties tenants. Countless other people were depending on Ned to do as he should.

Hannah clamped her hand vise-like on his arm. "At least you may begin to survey the field." Without giving Ned an opportunity to retreat, she steered him around the room, introducing him to one young lady and another, in between explaining their pedigrees.

The first damsel glanced away in pretty confusion. The second favored Ned with a giggle and a smile. What did one talk about with young ladies so ignorant of the world? He and Bianca had done little talking. Not that Bianca had been an innocent.

And not that Bianca would have made a proper earl's wife. "They're barely out of the schoolroom," protested Ned.

Hannah awarded him an impatient glance. "You'll want a young wife. So you may mold her to your taste."

Ned thought of the young women in London's countless brothels and the men who had molded them and wondered, where's the difference? Nonetheless, he smiled and nodded and said everything kind and civil to Hannah's countless candidates, who were all very proper, and very boring also. He clenched his jaw to stifle a yawn.

"Don't look so forbidding!" scolded Hannah, then hissed out a breath as the person she liked least in all the world stepped into her path. The flibbertigibbet was fitted out for the occasion in a froth of heliotrope satin and white crape, trimmed with lace and knotted beading and gossamer net, a Grecian scarf around her shoulders, and blue satin slippers on her feet. Her hair was arranged in ringlets and knots. Draped about her person was a profusion of pearls.

Said Hannah, not quite beneath her breath: "Mutton dressed as lamb." Added Ned, quickly: "Lady Georgiana. You take my breath away."

"You are too kind, Lord Dorset." Fluttering skillfully darkened lashes, Lady Georgiana tapped Ned's arm with her carved ivory fan. "Hello, Hannah. I am surprised to see you here. Oh, but your poor William was acquainted with the Regent, was he not? A pity you couldn't join us at dinner. Prinny had in front of him at the table a basin of water with a temple in it, from which a stream meandered the entire length—two hundred feet, my dears, if an inch!—bordered with moss and aquatic flowers, spanned by four fantastic bridges, and filled with frolicking silver and gold fish."

"I hear the Regent hung his portrait set in brilliants around Marshall Blücher's neck." Hannah sounded as if she might have had a frolicking fish stuck in her throat. "Blücher knelt at his feet."

Lady Georgiana gently fanned herself. "I vow dear Prinny changes the furniture so often one can scarcely find time to catch a glimpse of each new arrangement before he has replaced it with another. The present state of things is unusually fine. Have you noticed the chandelier in the Crimson Drawing Room?"

Hannah bared her teeth. "I've noticed that you have a new companion. What happened? Did you wear the last one out?"

Ned had been so enjoying the hostilities—Georgiana and Hannah were bitter rivals, Georgiana holding the advantage because she was a lady by birth and Hannah merely by marriage, as result of which Hannah was determined to topple Georgiana from her throne—that he had scarce paid attention to anything else. Now he looked around. Georgiana had indeed acquired a new attendant, a small slender creature clad in a pale yellow gown that didn't suit her bright gold hair. The girl was staring at a luster of glass and ormolu that resembled a shower of diamonds, the bauble probably costing between two and three thousand pounds. The expression on her face put Ned in mind of soldiers in the midst of battle, shocked immobile by carnage and cannon fire.

"She's newly come to town," explained Georgiana. "Miss Julie Wynne from York. We have notified Bow Street that Mildred has vanished into thin air." The girl started, blinked, stared down at her gloves.

Hannah and Georgiana resumed hostilities, and Ned made his way to Miss Wynne's side. "A dreadful crush, is it not?" he said.

"I suppose." She spoke so softly that he barely caught her words.

Was the girl shy? Ned studied her bent head, which afforded him only a glimpse of the straight line of her nose and the plumpness of her lips and the rosy color rising in her cheeks. His eyes drifted lower to the bosom of her gown. Clea, who had taken to poring over fashion magazines by the hour, would have called the dress a 'Corset frock', the bodice lacing across the front like a corset, the sleeves short and full.

Damned if Miss Wynne didn't seem familiar. Ned couldn't think why. A man wouldn't soon forget those bright willful curls. They looked as if they'd been repressed with a stern hand and were merely waiting for a moment's inattention so they could burst free.

She said, "You are staring at me, my lord."

"So I am. My apologies. I was struck mute with admiration for your curls."

She shot him a sideways glance, so quick he hadn't time to note the color of her eyes. "Gammon," she said.

Gammon? Ned's mood further improved. "Not one for idle conversation, are you, Miss Wynne?"

She flushed but refused to look at him. "Like you say, I have no conversation. I don't mean to be rude."

Ned thought she meant to be precisely that. Had she dared, the chit would have shoo'd him away. It was a novel experience. Most females wanted him to stay.

"Dorset!" Hannah beckoned. Ned excused himself. The dowager was no doubt wondering why he was talking to a mere companion, such creatures being—in the opinion of the Hannahs and Georgianas of the world—far beneath the notice of a gentleman as exalted as himself.

The encounter with her archrival had but briefly distracted Hannah. She drew Ned's attention to the next eligible on her list, this one a trifle bran-faced, granted, but it didn't signify, for she was a biddable female and wouldn't cause a moment's unease. Alternately, the dowager suggested an acknowledged beauty prone to temper, but she doubted Ned would like that.

Would he not? Temper sprang from passion, and Ned liked passion well. An alliance with a temperamental beauty would be infinitely preferable to marriage with a good biddable female.

What was he thinking? Infinitely preferable would be no marriage at all. The earl required an heir, however, and to the devil with the wishes of mere Ned. Perversely, he imagined the next young lady without her clothes.

Without her clothes?

Ned abandoned Hannah in mid-sentence, and shouldered his way through the crowd. He found Lady Georgiana admiring one of Prinny's earlier efforts, a Chinese room with walls of painted glass that gave the visitor a disconcerting impression of being trapped inside a lantern. Trailing after her, laden down with vinaigrette and hartshorn and now a Grecian shawl, the rooms having grown too warm for even the languid Lady Georgiana, was Miss Wynne.

As if she felt his attention on her, the girl glanced directly at him. Vivid blue eyes locked with green.

Chapter Six

If Jupiter hurled his thunderbolts as often as man sinned,
he would soon be out of thunderbolts. — Ovid

The Strand was largely empty now of the humanity that crowded along its length by day, from the bewigged barristers of the Temple and the Courts to the curiosities and freaks of Fleet Street. Julie slipped by booksellers and printing houses, repairers of 'Umbrellas &c', purveyors of fine spirits and tea. She attracted no attention in her shabby clothing, a cap pulled over her bright hair, dirt smeared on her face.

Noises echoed eerily through the thick sooty fog, the sounds of distant revelry, argument, debaucheries the nature of which Julie could only guess. Moisture dripped off the brim of her cap and trickled down her chin. She ducked deeper into the shadows as a watchman passed by on his rounds, listened to the clatter of the night-soil man's cart wheels on the cobblestones, inhaled the smell of wet animals and decaying garbage and the stench of the Thames.

Rose's lodgings were in Russell Court. Julie slipped around the corner of the building, shimmied up a drainpipe, crept along a ledge; crouched outside a third-floor window and peered in. Rose sat in a large winged armchair, writing in her journal by the light of an oil lamp. In her ruffled muslin wrapper, her hair loose around her shoulders, she appeared much younger than her actual years. Snoozing in her lap was Ophelia, the Drury Lane cat. Julie tapped on the glass.

Rose started, and her pen skittered across the page. Her eyes widened when she saw Julie perched on the ledge.

She set aside Ophelia, hurried to the window. "Jules! What's wrong with using the front door?"

"I didn't want to be seen." Julie scrambled across the sill. This way no one might remember that Mrs. Scarron had been visited by a grubby boy in the wee hours of the night. Rose closed the window against the damp.

Her journal lay open. Julie sneaked a peek, but reading didn't come easily to her, wouldn't have come at all had Rose not seduced her with children's tales. The actress had been offered a handsome sum by a Fleet Street firm to publish her memoirs, but had refused it out of loyalty to those with whom she'd shared the experiences that would have made her autobiography profitable. Too, without the letters and mementos that had been stolen from her, Rose was fuzzy on some of the details.

Julie took off her sodden cap and jacket and backed up to the fire. "You brought Ophelia home with you?"

"I was lonely. Ophelia is good company." As if the cat understood the compliment, it began to purr. Julie regarded the bottle sitting on the table beside Rose's book. Rose followed her gaze. "Pritchett stopped by."

Pritchett had probably brought the gin. Like Satan tempting Christ on a mountaintop. At least, Julie thought that was where Satan had tempted Christ. "It's none of my affair."

That it was not. Rose turned away. Her reflection in the pier-glass strongly indicated that she was in need of fresh cucumber juice to rejuvenate her skin. Followed by water in which spinach had been boiled. Finished off with twenty pounds of strawberries and two of raspberries crushed and thrown into a bath.

"Stop frowning," advised Julie. "Or you'll get lines between your eyes. You've told me so often enough."

Rose didn't have lines, did she? With her fingertips, she smoothed her brow. "I want to know what you've been about."

What Rose wanted was a wealthy protector, so she didn't have to fill her empty evenings with Bow Street Runners and Blue Ruin. Julie met her friend's eyes in the glass. "Pritchett mustn't learn any of what I'm about to tell you," she warned. Had Cap'n Jack known of Julie's previous encounter with Lord Dorset, she wouldn't have met him again in the crowded rooms of Carlton House, because her neck would have been broke first.

"As if I would." Rose picked up the gin bottle, and held it to the light. "It wasn't but a nipperkin, Jules."

It had been rather more than a nipperkin, unless Pritchett had drunk half the bottle. Which was also none of Julie's business, as Rose would be quick to point out. "I left Lady Georgiana tucked safely in her bed. Where the viscount might be is anybody's guess. I have to be back at Ashcroft House before they realize I'm gone."

Rose thunked the gin bottle down on the table. Some things shouted into the silence even when left unvoiced, especially when accompanied by reproachful glances and primmed lips. Julie thought Rose had been drowning her sorrows in company with Madame Geneva.

Maybe she had been, and if so whose business was it? "I should be safely abed myself," Rose snapped. "Instead of sitting up late and reading, which everybody knows leads to crow's feet around the eyes, and fretting about a blameful chit who is wet behind the ears. Yes, and what *are* you doing here?"

If Julie was wet behind the ears, it was due only to the rain. "I'll tell you when you come down off your high ropes."

Rose uttered several pithy comments about ungrateful ragamuffins as she paced the floral-patterned carpet, navigating her way between mismatched pieces of furniture and cases displaying her bibelots, among them a fine collection of theatrical figurines and an even more remarkable compilation of love-tokens, most memorable a minuscule Cupid drumming on a pair of breasts. Any of those items might have brought her a fair sum of money, but Rose would go without a month of dinners before she considered pawning a memento of some lost love. Julie thought of her own stolen statue, and wondered if its owner felt similarly.

Rose sighed as she sank back into her chair. Ophelia jumped into her lap. "If you must have it, I was trying to draw information from Pritchett, though I might have more luck pulling teeth from a hen. I don't think he has any notion what Cap'n Jack intends."

Julie was less certain. Bow Street officers were very skilled at looking after their own skins.

Rose added, "He was in momentary expectation of something, but I don't know what. Tell me about these people you're staying with."

Julie did know what Pritchett was expecting. Alas. She moved away from the fireplace, her backside having grown quite toasty as the room filled with the stench of steaming wool. "Lord Ashcroft is a noodle. Lady Georgiana is sensitive to the dismals and forever quacking herself. I'm supposed to entertain her, though she doesn't know how I may do so when I have no conversation. She says it is disobliging of me not to be more interesting."

Rose snorted. "If she only knew."

"In that event, Lady Georgiana would drink from all fifteen of the medicine bottles on her bedside table, her favorite being Bateman's Pectoral Drops. She too is a gamester, and better at it than her son. I play at cards with her, and she wins."

"You must let her, then."

"She cheats." Julie wriggled her toes in the old boots, which were much more comfortable than what she thought of as her proper lady shoes. "Lady Georgiana has dragged me into every shop in Oxford Street and through a tedious procession of afternoon calls. I've drunk enough tea to float the British Fleet. Oh, and we went to Carlton House."

"Carlton House!" Rose sat up so straight that Ophelia extended claws to avoid being bounced off her lap. "Tell me all, you wretched child."

"The pillars were hung with thousands of lanterns. The screen that separates the house from the street was silhouetted by topaz and scarlet flares set between palm trees. Inside . . ." Words were inadequate. "It was like something from a fairy tale."

"Did you see the Distinguished Visitors?"

"Ordinary folk dressed fine." Julie grinned as Rose looked shocked. "Lady Georgiana likened the Czar to an angel. He was handsome enough, I suppose. The ladies were strutting like crows in a gutter to get his attention. I've never seen anything like that house."

"I don't think there *is* anything like it," Rose said dryly. "The Prince Regent has expensive tastes."

So he did. Julie gazed at the painted village scene, one of Rose's most prized possessions, which hung upon one wall. She had counted over a hundred pictures on the walls of Carlton House, in just the rooms she had been privileged to inspect. Of those rooms, Julie had been most impressed by the Armory, the palanquin of Tippoo Sahib, and the dagger of Genghis Khan, which was perhaps not surprising in a young woman who went about with a knife tucked in her boot.

"It doesn't seem right," she concluded, "that one man should have so much."

Of course it didn't seem right, reflected Rose. Julie had no more than the clothes covering her back, and those were on loan. "The man who owns all that will one day be king. Sooner than later, if his father keeps talking to oak trees in the park."

Julie hadn't been impressed by her Regent. "He is very fat."

"Spoken with all the disapproval of one who's never had an opportunity to overindulge. Time will smooth the edges of your critical faculties, my girl; and Prinny was handsome once. What else?"

What else, indeed. "Lord Dorset was at Carlton House."

Sometimes, despite the long-term consequences, nothing but a frown would do. Rose asked, "Did he recognize you?"

"I think so. I can't be sure. I thought it was all up with me, but then he walked away." And thus far no representative of the law had come knocking at the door.

"Hmmm." Unless she was mistaken, and Rose was seldom mistaken about such matters, Julie's cheeks were flushed beneath her dirt. "What is Dorset like?"

How to describe the earl? Julie didn't try. "He said he felt as if we had met before. If he hasn't placed me yet, he will soon enough. Maybe I should just hop the twig."

"Language," scolded Rose. "In any event, you couldn't hop high enough. I wish we were well out of this business."

"If wishes were horses, pigs would fly." Julie reached into her pocket. "I don't think I got that right."

Rose threaded her fingers through Ophelia's soft fur. "It's *when* pigs can fly. Which will be never in our life."

And never in her life, thought Julie, was when she'd be done with Cap'n Jack. She opened her hand and spilled its contents onto the tabletop. Lilacs, mauves, deep purples glittered in the lamplight. Gold-set amethysts in the form of a large cross. Ophelia reached out an inquisitive paw.

"Carlton House, I presume." Rose nudged aside the cat, picked up the brooch and held it closer to the light. "A pretty thing, but not worth the risk of stealing it. I wonder what the Cap'n is about."

Chapter Seven

Going to hell is easy; it's coming back that's hard.
— Virgil

Had Julie been inclined to guess Lord Ashcroft's whereabouts, she might have predicted he would be somewhere amidst like-minded gentlemen, engaged in games of chance at White's perhaps or Brook's, Boodle's or the Cocoa Tree. London boasted numerous establishments the purpose of whose existence was parting young gentlemen from their blunt.

She wouldn't have been far off the mark. Tony was passing his evening at the Argyll Rooms in the Haymarket, where a masquerade ball was underway. He was not a happy man.

Tony had nothing against the Argyll Rooms, which were fitted up in a splendid style with gilt lamps and Corinthian pillars and an extraordinary number of scarlet draperies. He especially didn't mind the card chamber, where he'd whiled away no little time trying to catch the smiles of fortune by risking a few pounds he could ill afford to lose.

He no longer graced the card room, however, having been removed therefrom in a most discourteous manner. Currently he was sulking in the oblong grand salon. Tony cared no more for masked revels than for gaming with people he didn't know, having already had the unpleasant experience of seeing on the gallows a fellow with whom he'd tossed the dice not that far in the past. If his opinion had been asked, and as usual it hadn't, Tony would have said that his eviction from the card room was akin to locking up the stable after the horse had taken it in its head to bolt.

Above the entrance to the grand salon, on each side, were

three tiers of boxes, ornamented with elegant antique bas-reliefs and enclosed with richly molded gold scrolls. Over each box hung a circular bronze chandelier with cut-glass pendants. The women present here tonight were as scarlet as the draperies, for no respectable female would dare set foot within these walls. Tony watched without enthusiasm as the dancers took their places, and the fifty-piece orchestra embarked upon a deafening waltz. He wasn't one for the ladies, or either the not-so-ladylike, due to the influence of his mama, which was enough to put any man off the opposite sex.

"You'd think Maman would be grateful I brought her someone to keep her company," he said to his companion, "but no. She demands to know what has become of Mildred, though she didn't like poor Milly above half. Come to think of it, so do I. Want to know, that is." He paused to consider. "Or maybe I don't, because I'll wager it's nothing good. Yes, and you needn't say that it's my little habit of making wagers that's put me in this predicament because I already know that. Thing is, I don't think I can stop. Miss Wynne says I'm a pigeon ripe for the plucking and that at the rate I'm going, I will soon be bald. Which may be true—I'm not saying it ain't—but it's hardly kind of her to say so when she's living under my roof. I ain't normally one to kick up a dust over trifles, mind you, but to be told to take a stranger into my household and swallow her with good grace is the outside of enough. And furthermore, I'm not sure she *can* fix it up all right and tight, even if she said she could."

If Jules could have fixed anything up right and tight, reflected Pritchett, to whom these comments were directed, she would have long since done so. As he listened to the viscount's laments—Try as Tony might (and he *did* try, half-heartedly), money ran through his fingers like water. Just the other day he had gone to Tattersall's to look at horseflesh and ended up buying a Thoroughbred. Tony didn't need another Thoroughbred. He didn't *want* another Thoroughbred. But he had one, all the same— Pritchett observed the crowd. The regular pay from the Police Office being less than enough to support a family, most Bow Street officers supplemented their income with blood money and rewards. They were free to take inquiry work for anyone who could afford them. Some earned a guinea a night standing in theater lobbies and keeping a sharp watch out for miscreants.

Pritchett was paid more. He had long since amassed sufficient funds to withdraw from the business, were he not caught in the Cap'n's net.

As was Lord Ashcroft caught. No matter how hard the viscount might try to sconce the reckoning, it would nonetheless be paid. Pritchett had scant patience with his fellow prisoner, who was a startling vision in cream kerseymere breeches, a fifteen-guinea embroidered waistcoat in a virulent shade of green, and a corbeau-colored coat with covered buttons; and who had indulged more than was prudent in the grape.

"I thought I was bad off when just the gull gropers had me in their talons," the viscount continued. "It's up all with me now, or it will be if Maman finds out. You'd know what I mean if she ever rang a peal in *your* ears. There's never the least use disputing with her, for she always has the best of it, and if she thinks she don't, she flies off the hooks. It's more than flesh and blood can stand. Yet she *is* my flesh and blood, and so stand it I must."

Lord Ashcroft had more to stand than a peevish mama. "Miss Wynne suits?" Pritchett interrupted.

"A monkey would suit," retorted Tony, "if it could trail along after Maman like a tantony pig and carry her falderals and listen to her complain. Which is what I'm doing, isn't it? Complaining, I mean."

Yes he was, and there was precious little point in it. Pritchett said, "Talking won't pay toll."

Maybe it wouldn't, but Tony saw no reason why he shouldn't complain, if he was so inclined. "Tell me this: why me? It ain't like I'm the only punter to be a trifle scorched." He gazed wistfully in the direction of the card-room. "I would have come about if that damned fellow hadn't shoved in his oar."

Why the viscount? Expedience, perhaps. Cap'n Jack wasn't one to let an opportunity pass.

Tony was still bemoaning his ill luck. Pritchett would never understand the fascination of risking something valuable in the hope of winning more. But why *should* he understand? Gaming was the vice of the wealthy and high born.

Pritchett strolled around the perimeter of the crowded room. With the end of the French wars, officers fresh from continental battles were rushing to the tables, playing hard and raising stakes.

He did not go unnoticed. Some observers saw merely a neat, fastidious little man with thinning hair and spectacles, for his Manton pistol was not on display, nor his gilt-headed baton. Others knew exactly what he was. Pritchett had a reputation, and it wasn't for fair dealing. Aspiring criminals gave him a wide berth.

Tony trailed behind him, talking all the while. "Lower your voice," Pritchett interrupted. "You never know who may overhear."

Tony stopped, mid-sentence, and moved closer. "Is he here?"

"Is who here?" Pritchett asked.

Tony looked nervously over his shoulder. "Cap'n Jack."

Pritchett suspected that the Cap'n was indeed present, result of the small hairs on the back of his neck standing up as if to salute. "No one can say when the Cap'n will put in an appearance. He has eyes and ears everywhere."

"Don't want to see him," muttered Tony. Or hear him or even know about him. I'd blow out my brains out except Maman would really cut up stiff in that event."

Pritchett sighed. "Go home, Ashcroft."

Tony's thoughts had been heading in a different direction, specifically the card room. "But it's early yet."

"Home," repeated Pritchett. "Go."

Tony was too well trained by his mama to argue with orders issued in so authoritative a tone. "I may not be a *downy* one," he said with dignity, as he turned away, "but that don't mean you may try and bamboozle me. I'll lay odds you know more about this business than you are willing to say."

The viscount would lay odds on a fly crawling along a windowpane. Pritchett followed Tony through the crowd, watched to see that he headed for the exit and not toward the card room, though it was no skin off Pritchett's nose if the young fool dug himself in more deeply than he already had.

He felt the menace hovering behind his right shoulder. It drawled, "I would be very displeased if you were to develop scruples at this late date."

"I was just protecting your investment, sir." Pritchett had no desire to turn around. "Ashcroft will be of no use to anyone if he blows out his brains."

The voice was smooth and dark and dangerous. "You did not tell me Dorset spotted the girl at Carlton House."

The girl, the viscount, the thief taker. Pawns each one of them, being set in place for some specific purpose, which Pritchett doubted was the pilfering of some society matron's jewels. "I didn't know. The earl will be wanting his statue back."

"The earl will also want to know why she took it," said the Cap'n. He was briefly silent. Pritchett held his breath.

"As do I." The voice was thoughtful. "Dorset may prove to be of use."

Pity Dorset, then. "You asked to be notified when the house in Curzon Street was ordered opened up."

"So I did."

Came a cool breeze at Pritchett's back.

He exhaled. Dare the Cap'n, and be damned.

Chapter Eight

No one is able to flee from love or death.
— Pubilius Syrus

All was quiet within the library of ancient Wakely Court, save for the occasional rustle of a page and the snuffle of the dog, sneezing and snorting being among the beast's myriad unpleasant traits. Clea was buried in Ovid, while Ned mulled over the recent dispatches from his friend, Colonel Sir Neil Campbell, whose exile on Elba was being enlivened by the hoards of British visitors flocking to view the Corsair holed up in his den, the passport office considering curiosity a sufficiently good reason for visiting the island, and Napoleon being not averse to conversation that not only relieved his tedium but also kept him abreast of events in mainland Europe. Cerberus lay on his back in a patch of sunlight, inviting a belly scratch, at which point the unwary scratcher would probably find his hand bit off.

The room looked even shabbier in the daylight, and no less untidy. Ned noted that the drapery had been put back in place. He found it far less fetching at the window than when wrapped around his thief.

The statue had not been similarly restored. Ned contemplated the empty spot on his desk where the thing had stood. Thanks to Hannah, he had precious little time to deal with stolen artifacts or light-fingered lasses or Portuguese *bandidos*. He'd thought himself done with the latter, and wasn't certain he was not.

Clea glanced up from her book. She was reading Ovid's *Metamorphoses* today. Ned wondered what his sister meant to transform herself into. "You're engaged with Hannah this afternoon?" he asked.

"I am. We are interviewing singing teachers. You may join us if you wish."

"Thank you, but I would rather have my toenails pulled out."

Clea wrinkled her nose. "I wish I could say Hannah improves upon acquaintance, but she does not. She certainly has a bee under her bonnet about you marrying."

That she did. A whole swarm of bees. A veritable hive. Everywhere he went, there was Hannah, thrusting yet another marital prospect under his nose.

Ned was up to his elbows in females. He might have enjoyed this surfeit of damsels in another circumstance, but these young ladies were uniformly dull.

A frown marred Clea's brow. "You won't marry to suit her, will you? I am perfectly able to see what's going on right beneath my nose. Hannah has told you she will oversee my come-out on the condition that you wed some properly blue-blooded milk-and-water miss, and so you are leading her a merry dance. Which is all well and good as long as you don't trip and stumble smack into parson's mousetrap."

Next he would have Clea trying to select his bride-to-be. "Don't concern yourself, puss. Hannah can't force me to do something I don't wish."

"Stuff! Of course she can. *I* don't particularly wish to learn to sing, but Hannah insists." Clea closed her book. "And so, like the sirens encountered by Odysseus, I shall lure sailors to their doom."

Ned leaned back in his chair and regarded his sister. Clea was wearing a simple muslin gown. On the chair beside her lay a green sarcenet pelisse and a straw hat bedecked with yellow flowers and a green ribbon. Her hair had been fashionably cropped and styled in the current mode to cluster in ringlets around her face.

Already Hannah's influence showed. Ned supposed he shouldn't be regretful when it was what Clea wished. "I promise you," he said, "that I shall allow myself to be nibbled to death by ducks before I marry where I don't please."

Clea studied him in turn. "I've been thinking of Portugal."

Bianca, she meant. "I haven't," said Ned, and it was almost true.

Clea shook her head. She loved her brother dearly; and while she meant to make a career of breaking hearts herself, she didn't wish a similar fate for him. That he should break hearts was fine—or if not fine, it was what gentlemen *did*—but she didn't care to see him have his own heart broke.

Ned believed her too young to know about such things. He sometimes was absurd. Bianca's parents might have turned a blind eye to a casual flirtation—where better to hone a senhorita's suitor-trapping skills than on a dashing military officer?—but, like other upper-class Portuguese families, were firmly opposed to their daughter marrying a British husband due to religious differences.

The obvious solution would have been to elope. Wellington, however, had made it clear that officers who misbehaved in such a manner would be placed under close arrest and handed over to the local authorities.

None of this would have stopped Ned if he had really wanted to wed Bianca. Clea wished she could be certain her brother knew that he had not.

Came a tap on the door. Cerberus opened one eye and growled.

Tidcombe hovered in the doorway. "Lord Saxe—"

"Is right behind you," said Kane, following close on the butler's heels. A pained expression on his face, Tidcombe bowed himself out of the room.

Kane was dressed for riding in a blue coat with brass buttons, leather breeches, and gleaming top boots. "I suspect your butler doesn't approve of me."

Neither did Cerberus. The dog launched himself at Kane's riding crop and engaged it in a tug-of-war. Clea rose, clasped Cerberus around his middle, and deposited him on the carpet some distance away. Being somewhat partial to females, the dog merely snapped at her.

"Tidcombe approves of none of us." Ned propped his booted feet on his desk. "He finds us too informal for his taste. We should send him to Cousin Hannah so that she may show him the error of his thinking. You look tired. It must be from all that racketing around with the Distinguished Guests."

Kane shot him a look. "The Czar can't arrive anywhere without a hysterical ovation. There are never less than ten thousand people waiting outside the Pulteney Hotel to gawk at him. He has apparently made a private resolution to do none of the things that Prinny expects, instead demanding to meet Whig leaders and defending liberal views, all of which might be less disturbing were the man not the most powerful leader in Europe." Alexander and his sister are indefatigable sightseers. Thus far they had viewed the Abbey and Westminster; the Tower and the British Museum; the Royal Exchange and the docks. Kane dreaded to discover what further excursions lay in wait.

He watched Clea resume her seat. "You are stylish today, brat."

"Am I not?" Primly, Clea smoothed her skirts. "Cousin Hannah is turning me into a young lady."

Ned propped his booted feet on the edge of his desk. "Clea has decided to make an advantageous match. She wants to have offspring, you see. As well as a dazzling career as an acknowledged beauty with dozens of gentlemen dangling at her slipper-strings, and writing her poems, and going off to shoot themselves when she casts them aside."

Kane's eyes crinkled with amusement. "That's all right, then."

Clea looked indignant. "You don't think I can?"

"I've no doubt of it." Kane awarded her his lazy, heart-stopping smile. "Still, I would hate to see you grow up too soon. There are dozens of proper young ladies out there, *chérie*, but there's only one you."

Clea was for once without words. Her cheeks turned pink.

Again a tap on the door. Tidcombe entered the room, bearing before him a calling card on a silver tray. "You have another visitor, my lord."

"We are popular today." Just to be annoying, Clea snatched up the card. "Sabine? You left Sabine waiting in the hall?" With a flurry of skirts, she ran from the room.

Tidcombe gazed heavenward. "Mrs. Sabine Viccars, my lord."

"So I gathered," Ned said dryly. "Clea will show her in." Tidcombe departed, doubtless in search of the bottle of medicinal spirits he kept hidden for all-too-frequent occasions such as this. Kane looked mildly interested and Ned added, "Sabine was with us in the Peninsula. Her husband died during the fall of Badajoz." During an unforgettable moonlit night made brighter by the immense fireballs the French hurled over breaches on which they had fixed obstacles made of razor-sharp swords, along with exploding powder barrels and an endless barrage of shells.

The carnage had been appalling. The morning after the siege, Wellington had wept to see so many of his finest men destroyed.

Kane glanced at the doorway. "Your young lady claims to be an impoverished gentlewoman from York?"

"I suspect that 'claims' is the operative word."

"Thus far we've found no Wynne family living in Yorkshire. Further inquiries are being made." Kane contemplated the old globe. "Damned careless, don't you think?"

Clea returned, bringing with her a stunningly beautiful woman in her middle thirties, fine-boned and as fair as if she had wandered into this world from some otherworldly realm. Her figure was pure perfection, her features patrician, her eyes a stormy gray. Silver-gilt hair made a startling contrast with dark lashes and brows.

Ned rose to his feet. "Sabine. Welcome home."

"Home?" Her voice was husky. "It's been a long time since England was that to me."

Ned performed introductions. Kane and Sabine both gave excellent impressions of being politely unimpressed. In Sabine's case, it might even have been true. Countless officers had sought to court her after her husband's death, for no attractive woman was long left without a husband during a campaign.

Which brought Ned back to the question of why she was here, now. "We're delighted to see you. I'd heard you were in France."

"It's raining Englishmen in Paris." Sabine settled in one of the ornate carved chairs and regaled them with a description of Louis XVIII's arrival in Paris. An escort of fourteen carriages. Doves released into the sky. "A swarm of adventurers and troublemakers of all sorts besiege the Tulieries. Everyone is relentlessly gay."

Clea, as she had informed her brother, was an astute young lady; and Sabine was not in the habit of making idle social calls. "Look at the time! I don't want to leave you, but I must. Proper young ladies always keep their word." She bent to kiss the older woman's cheek; snatched up her pelisse.

Kane smiled lazily. "'*Te de aliis, quam alios de te suaviust fieri doctos,*'" he said.

"It is better to profit by a horrible example than to be one? Never fear. For you I shall always be a brat." Clea crammed the straw bonnet on her head, and sauntered out of the library.

"A proper young lady?" said Sabine.

Kane awarded her his practiced smile. "Clea wishes to break hearts."

"Of course she does. She is fifteen. But you are safe, I think." If Kane's smile was heart-melting, Sabine's was sufficient to poleax any gentleman not already stunned speechless by her looks. Kane was far too seasoned a warrior to go down under a single blow, but he did almost blink.

Ned knew Sabine far too well to insult her with the offer of any beverage as mawkish as tea. He brought out the Madeira and three glasses and poured. "What brings you back to England? You don't seem delighted to be here."

Sabine raised her glass. "England holds many memories for me, not all of them happy. I had hoped to speak privately with you, Ned."

"In other words, I am *de trop.*" Kane made no move to take his leave.

"Further introductions are in order," said Ned, distracting his friends from their antagonistic concentration on each other. "All the world must know by now that secret agents are prone to pseudonyms. Therefore, if I may: Sabine, meet the Raven. Kane, say hello to the Swan. Sabine is one of Wellington's most valued secret weapons. Kane has been in the employ of the British government since he reached his majority."

The Swan and the Raven regarded one another without enthusiasm. Kane was first to speak. "I've heard of you."

"And I you." Sabine returned her attention to Ned. "As you said, England was once my home. Now that the war has ended, is it so odd that I might wish to come back?"

Not odd, but Ned didn't know that he believed her. "I sense another hand in this."

"Castlereagh had hoped that if the Allied Sovereigns were in London and away from all the Paris schemers, Alexander might prove easier to deal with." Sabine noticed the ugly dog crouched at her feet, reached down to give him a scratch. Such was her charisma that, instead of biting her, Cerberus merely snarled and drooled. "I'm told it has not served."

"You think you may succeed where diplomats have failed?" asked Kane.

Sabine straightened. "It's not what I think that counts."

Chapter Nine

What you didn't hope for happens more often
than what you hoped for. — Plautus

Julie was trying to do as she should. The problem was: according to whom? Lady Georgiana would have been horrified to see her creep along the upper hallway of the French ambassador's residence. Cap'n Jack would have been equally dissatisfied to learn that she had not.

The strains of distant music followed her. Julie had learned various country dances, the cotillion and the quadrille, her dancing master having possessed the patience of Job and a healthy fear of the consequence should he fail in his task. She hummed the tune, pirouetted in the middle of the hallway, and wondered what it would be like to dance with someone who didn't reek of garlic and stood more than five feet tall. It wasn't likely she'd find out. As a mere companion, Julie was expected to fade into the woodwork.

Well, she was fading now. Julie had left Lady Georgiana holding forth on the unfortunately frog-like appearance of the Prince of Orange.

The third door on the left, Pritchett had told her. Julie counted carefully, glanced before and behind to make sure she was alone before turning the knob. The door was unlocked, as Pritchett had promised. She stepped inside.

Candles burned on the mantle. A fire blazed in the hearth. Julie closed the door behind her and wasted precious seconds just looking around.

There was a patterned carpet on the floor, and expensive paper on the walls. Two gilded chairs covered with straw-colored satin had been drawn up near the fire. In one corner stood a wardrobe with matched oval panels, and by the window a bureau cabinet with an arched top. The huge high bed with its domed tester and draperies of richly fringed blue damask was big enough to accommodate Noah and the entire contents of his Ark. Nearby was the mahogany writing desk that had brought her here, strewn atop it a number of items that would light up the eye of any fencing cove.

Julie's own eye brightened. She clenched her fists. It had taken a great deal of time and practice to become the skilled operator that she was. Yet now she was meant to meekly follow instructions and keep her hand in, so to speak, by filching a required item here and there. That the selection of those items made no sense to her mattered not at all, as Pritchett had informed her when she asked.

Yes, and she'd best get on with it, hadn't she, before Lady Georgiana decided she'd scarpered like her predecessor and raised a rowdy-do. Julie left the pretties where they lay and slid open the left-hand desk drawer. Hidden in the furthest corner, as she had been told it would be, was a gentleman's stained leather glove.

A strange thing for the French ambassador's wife to have as a keepsake. Julie picked up the glove and wondered what story lay behind it, and how Cap'n Jack had found it out.

The door snicked open behind her. Julie spun around, nudged the drawer shut with her hip, thrust the stained glove behind her back.

Lord Dorset closed the door and leaned against it. "Have you lost something, Miss Wynne?"

Her heart, which had jumped right out of her chest to flop about somewhere on the floor. Julie reminded herself to breathe. Ever since their last meeting, when the earl had looked her smack in the eye, she had been half-expecting him to pop up like some genie from a bottle and clap the sheriff's bracelets on her wrists. When he had not, she dared hope that she was safe. Now his gaze met hers again, and she knew that she'd been wrong. Eyes as green as emeralds, yes; and as cold.

He frowned when she didn't answer. "I'm waiting," he said.

"Um? That is, you startled me, my lord." It wasn't entirely due to shock that her heart was thumping like a drum. Tightly fitting black pantaloons made it clear his lordship had no need of padding. An excellently cut coat showed off his broad shoulders and lean waist. His skin was golden from the sun, his cheekbones strongly sculpted; he was blessed with an arrogant nose, a firmly chiseled jaw, and a mouth that promised pleasure so potent as to make a maiden swoon.

The earl looked every inch the gentleman in evening dress, and at the same time thoroughly uncivilized. He also looked impatient. Julie added, "I was looking for the ladies' withdrawing room. I must have taken a wrong turn."

His green eyes were intent on her. "You must have taken the wrong stair."

A vision popped into Julie's head. Of herself at the sheriff's ball. Dancing the Paddington frisk, the Tyburn jig.

How to escape? The window was too far away to reach. Pretty Ned stood smack between her and the door.

Julie searched about for something with which to defend herself. Nothing on the desk was of sufficient weight. A pair of stout silver candlesticks stood on the bureau. She shifted in that direction, just a little bit.

He moved quickly toward her; caught her shoulders before she could bolt. Julie tried to kick him, but the earl blocked her with his body, and she found herself trapped between strong thighs.

With one arm, he held her fast against him; with the other he plucked the glove from her hand. Julie sighed. "I don't suppose you'll believe I found that on the floor."

"I'd sooner believe the moon is made of molasses." He inspected the glove more closely. "*I* don't suppose you'd care to explain."

Julie shook her head. She was rendered mute by the sensation of being held so close. Lord Dorset smelled not of garlic but starched linen and leather and something she could only describe as male. He stood nearer six feet tall than five. She wondered what he would do if she asked him for a dance.

He set her away from him, still gripping her firmly, and looked her over from head to toe. Julie had the queerest sensation that he could see right through her disguise—pale green dress with puffed sleeves and a rounded neck and a short sash tied in a bow behind; shift, corset and petticoat; stockings and slippers and long gloves— to the imposter underneath.

He exhaled, and it was as if the coldness left him. "What am I to do with you, Miss Wynne?"

Miss Wynne? Who was Miss Wynne? So overwhelmed was Julie by his lordship's proximity (and the notion he might see her corset) that she forgot she had acquired a last name. She wriggled, inadvertently brushing her breasts against his arm. The sensation was surprisingly pleasant. "Um?"

The earl's expression suggested he might be experiencing some sensations of his own. "You can no longer deny that we have met before."

He underestimated Julie. "I *don't* deny it. We met at Carlton House, my lord."

"We met prior to that, my girl, and I have the knot on my head to prove it. Was it necessary to hit me so hard?"

Julie disliked being so deceitful. "I didn't—"

"Let me refresh your memory." He released her. "Ugly statue with the head of a hippopotamus, tail of a crocodile, legs and arms of a lion?"

A very ugly statue, and yet he hadn't called a constable. Julie stole a quick glance at the hall door. "You followed me," she said.

"I came here tonight for you. I knew Lady Georgiana would attend. I arrived in time to see you flitting up the staircase." The earl turned the glove over in his hands. "I believe that I shall call you Julie. The fact that I know you to be an impostor—and yes, I *do* know it; you're no more a parson's daughter than I am the king— surely puts us on informal terms. And in turn you must call me Ned."

She must call him a thatch-gallows, thought Julie. She didn't mean to do so out loud.

So overset was she, however, that she did exactly that. "For you to cast aspersions on my character," the earl retorted, "is like the pot calling the kettle black."

"I'm not the one carrying around a pilfered glove."

"Yes, but I'm not the one who pilfered it. Speaking of which—"

Julie was on the verge of suggesting to her companion what he might do with his questions when she heard the door latch snick. Before she could as much as blink, 'Call-me-Ned' had caught her up as easily as if she weighed no more than a flea, carried her to the tall wardrobe, and closed them both inside. "Fortunately for you, sunshine," he whispered, "chivalry is not dead."

His breath stroked warm against her cheek, feathered through her curls. It felt better than she'd ever dreamed breath could. He smelled faintly of brandy, and Julie wondered where he had been before he came here.

Looking for her, she reminded herself. Which proved a person should be careful what she wished, for she had caught the interest of a swell.

His arm was tight around her, like a band of iron holding her imprisoned against his body. His hand was splayed flat across her ribs, his thumb only inches from her breast, her back warm and toasty where it pressed against his chest.

Lord Dorset was perfectly at ease with their situation. Perhaps he had hid in a wardrobe before, cocooned by a crush of muslin and silk and inhaling stale perfume. Her own heart was pounding fit to burst.

He must surely feel it. The scoundrel was probably used to females responding to him this way. No question he was a favorite with the ladies. Certainly he showed no reservation in manhandling *her*. Julie didn't mind. Being held like this was better than a waltz. Better even than sitting on his lap.

And wasn't she betwattled, crouched here in the darkness thinking moonish things while disaster waited outside the wardrobe door?

Someone was in the bedroom. Julie heard the sounds of movement, the slide of a drawer. Impossible to tell if the intruder was female or male. As Julie waited to be discovered, her heart crawled up into her throat.

The outer door opened again, and closed. She strained her ears, heard nothing.

Julie stirred. Ned breathed, "Be still."

She waited, grateful for a few moments' respite before the piper must be paid.

He opened the wardrobe door; stepped into the room; made sure it was empty, and then held out his hand. Julie untangled herself from the abused apparel. Mme Morel's abigail was going to have fits.

The earl extricated her from the wardrobe's depths, but did not let her go. "You would have been caught," he said.

And didn't she know it? "I wasn't doing anything wrong. My lord." Julie tried to withdraw her hand from his.

"As I've already told you, we're way past 'my lord'." Instead of releasing her, as a gentleman would have done immediately he realized she wished it—or so Julie presumed; she had scant true knowledge of the breed, save Tony, who one could scarcely count —Lord Dorset (as she thought of him rebelliously) pulled her with him toward the door. He looked out into the hallway. "Come along."

Julie dug her heels into the carpet. "Come along where?"

"Where do you think? I'm taking you back where you belong."

He meant to betray her. Julie had regretted bashing the handsome young lordling with his statue. Now she wished she had hit him hard enough to break open his traitorous skull.

She glanced frantically around. The candlesticks were out of reach. "Wait. You don't understand."

"I understand that the longer we linger here, the greater the chance that we'll both end up in the suds. I will lay it out for you: you're a common thief, Miss Wynne, albeit a lovely one. A series of small thefts have plagued the *ton* since you arrived on the scene. An amethyst pendant. A chrysoberyl bracelet. A turquoise and pearl brooch. Now we may add to the tally a stained leather glove."

A number of thoughts chased themselves through Julie's brain as she listened to this speech. Astonishment that a fine gentleman should think her pretty. Regret that he had gone back to calling her Miss Wynne. Dismay that she'd forgotten about the stained glove.

She shivered. He frowned. "Are you cold?"

"A goose walked over my grave. About that glove—"

"We need to discuss this, but not now." He drew her with him down the hall.

Julie tried, unsuccessfully, to wriggle out of his grasp. "You're all about in your head if you think we may have a proper conversation over tea and biscuits in Newgate."

"Who said anything about Newgate?"

"You said you were taking me back where I belong."

"You think you belong in Newgate, hardened criminal that you are?" To her astonishment, he smiled. "I'm taking you back to the ballroom, Miss Wynne. Escorting you myself, so that you don't get lost again."

The chatter of voices, the strains of the orchestra grew louder. They rounded a corner and were swept up into a throng of ladies wearing splendid gowns and jewels, gentlemen in excellently tailored trousers and fine frock coats.

Ned raised his voice. "You are aware, I'm sure, that York has a rich Roman and Viking history, result of being capital of both the Roman province of Britannia Interior and the Viking kingdom of Yorvik. I am eager to hear your impressions of The Shambles, Miss Wynne, and Clifford's Tower."

What impressions Julie would have liked to share with the earl, she dared not, as he well knew. She contented herself with a speaking glance.

"We must talk," he said, more softly. "Meet me in Hyde Park tomorrow at dawn. The northeast corner. Where the Tyburn gallows stood."

Tyburn. Gallows. Julie felt herself blanch. "Clunch," he added. "If I was going to inform on you, I would have already done so. Don't say you can't steal away, because I know otherwise."

He *wasn't* going to betray her. "You don't know the time of day, my lord."

He smiled at her rebellious expression. "I know what you've forgotten: I have the glove."

Chapter Ten

Use the occasion, for it passes swiftly.
— Ovid

Hyde Park was nigh deserted at this early hour, save for those few hardy gentlemen like Lord Dorset who enjoyed a brisk gallop at dawn. Ned met none of his acquaintance, nor had he expected to. Now he and Soldier waited, at the northeast corner, where the Tyburn Triple Tree had stood until it was removed for obstructing the highway.

Ned imagined the gallows might well have done that; it had been a huge triangular construction capable of hanging twenty-four prisoners at once, eight on each horizontal beam. Convicted felons were released from their chains and put on a cart, often seated on their coffins; taken to St Sepulchre's church to receive nosegays of posies, driven down Snow Hill and across Fleet Ditch, then back up to High Holborn. Accompanied by hangman, peace officers, constables and an ever-growing festive crowd, the procession would arrive at last at the gallows, there to watch the condemned prisoner suffer a slow agonizing death. As if it weren't indignity enough to jerk and thrash about at the end of a rope, a proceeding that might go on a considerable time if someone wasn't inclined to pull on the poor bastard's legs or beat on his chest to hasten death, his clothes were then stripped off and given to the hang-man, who also peddled body parts, hair and blood, and pieces of the fatal rope. Because the procession to Tyburn had grown more and more unmanageable, executions were moved to Newgate prison in 1783.

Ned saw Julie, in the distance, walking toward him. Golden

curls peeped from beneath the hood of her dark cloak. He felt a queer clutch in his belly at the notion that such a vivid creature should hang. No doubt remained in his mind that she was behind the recent thefts.

Fortunately for Miss Wynne, Ned was no longer in service to the Crown. Yet he could hardly let her go on as she had been. How he was to prevent her, he hadn't determined—arranging that they meet on this particular history-filled corner had been his first step in that direction—but prevent her he must, if not for her own good and the good of all the noble ladies whose jewel boxes she threatened, for his own peace of mind.

She hadn't tried to run, and he gave her credit for it. Ned had set his batman to watching Julie after they met at Carlton House, a task that Bates was finding more onerous than he had anticipated he might.

Julie came to a stop in front of Ned, looking as if she wished him to perdition. He leaned down: "Give me your hand." Warily, she obeyed. Her grip was surprisingly strong. She wasn't wearing gloves.

Ned pulled her up on the saddle in front of him, settled her sideways across his lap. She squeaked and clutched his arm. At Ned's signal, Soldier moved forward. Julie sat stiff as a post.

The hood of her cloak had fallen back. Her body was warm against his chest, his thigh; her soft curls brushed Ned's chin. "Relax. You're safe," he said.

Julie remained rigidly silent as they rode diagonally across the park to the Serpentine, the lake created by the damming of the Westhaven River at the request of George II's wife. To the south was the bridle trail known as Rotten Row, so favored by the *ton*. Ned guided Soldier toward the wide path on the north side of the lake. There was no lack of wildlife in the vicinity: rabbits and squirrels, geese and swans, the occasional fox.

Ned swung Julie down from the saddle. She looked up at him. "I've never ridden on a horse before."

"You surprise me," Ned said gravely as he also dismounted. "What did you think?"

"I think your horse is very tall and I was afraid I might fall off. Does he have a name?"

"His name is Soldier. Turn over your hand, palm up." Ned reached into his pocket for a lump of sugar. "Now hold it out to him."

She obeyed. Soldier snuffled and delicately removed the sugar lump from her palm. Julie smiled. "His skin is so soft."

Her skin would be softer. Ned decided he must discover just how soft it was. After he discovered why she had stolen his statue, and the rest.

Julie stepped back. "I shouldn't be here. Say what you mean to, because I don't have long."

Ned tucked her hand through his arm and held it fast, both for the pleasure of touching her, and in case she took it in her mind to leave. "Then I shall remind you that I know there is no Julie Wynne from York. What's your real name, sunshine?"

"Why do you call me that?" She tried to tug away from him, but he held her fast.

"Because sunshine is yellow, like your hair."

Julie scowled. "So is sulphur. How would you like it if someone called you grasshopper because your eyes are green?"

Ned laughed. She delighted him. "I paid you a compliment. In response you should flutter your eyelashes and simper and say 'oh, la, my lord.' No, I don't wish you to do that! Has no one ever paid you a compliment before?"

"Why should they?"

Leaving Soldier to follow behind and sample the vegetation, Ned drew her beside him along the path. "For any number of reasons. A compliment is an indication of esteem, respect, affection, admiration. A sincere compliment lifts the spirits not only of the person who receives it, but he who pays it as well. So when I tell you that your hair is the loveliest I've ever seen and your eyes the most extraordinary, I'm expressing my admiration for you, and at the same time making myself feel good."

The recipient of Ned's compliments wrinkled her nose. "What you're doing is emptying the butter dish over my head."

She was quick and clever, and not easily caught off-guard. Ned tried a different approach. "I've noticed you don't wear jewelry."

"That's a puzzle to you? Not all of us *have* jewelry, my lord."

"Is that why you stole some? I question your taste. Topaz would suit you better. Amber. Jade. You are full of life and color, not prim and pastel. I would—"

He didn't finish the thought; she kicked him in the shin. Ned felt no pain, due to the thick leather of his boot, but the act took him by surprise.

He released her. Julie demanded, "Are you offering me a slip on the shoulder, then?"

She was all puffed up and fierce, like a flustered banty hen, and the sight of her ruffled feathers made Ned smile again. "Come down off your high ropes. I was doing no such thing."

Julie bristled even more. "I know I'm not the sort of female to become a gentleman's fancy-piece, nor do I wish to be, but it's not kind of you to point it out."

Now he'd hurt her feelings. Had she not already done it for him, Ned might have kicked himself. "You misunderstood. I think you may not have quite grasped the concept of compliments."

"Oh, so now I'm a slowtop." Julie plopped her hands on her slim hips. "Let's see if I've got this right. If I was to say that nothing I have filched has been as pretty as your eyes, it would be a compliment. And if I was to say you're a cod's head, it would not."

She thought his eyes were pretty? Ned reminded himself that the purpose of this conversation was not flirtation, but theft. "We were discussing your name."

"*You* were discussing it. I already know what my name is. As you would know also if you had been listening. Are you going to give me back the glove?"

Some country parson's daughter? Ned thought not. "Will you give me back my statue?"

"It must be worth something to you."

"If you didn't think so, why did you steal it in the first place?"

"I never said I *did* steal it, did I?"

"You didn't need to say so, since we both know you did. Do you still have the blasted thing?"

"Maybe and maybe not. Do you have the glove?"

"Maybe and maybe not."

She huffed out a breath. Ned could almost see the ideas flitting through her mind. "What does it mean, your statue?" she asked.

"What makes you think it means anything?"

"You want it back."

"It might be of great value."

"Not according to the fence– Um. The appraiser I consulted."

If she had tried to fence it, she had no notion of the thing's true purpose. "The statue is a representation of Taweret, the Egyptian goddess and protective deity of childbirth. She was popular among ordinary Egyptians as a protectress. Pregnant women commonly wore amulets bearing her image." He awaited a reaction. Most young ladies of Ned's acquaintance—or of his acquaintance since he had become an earl—would be beyond embarrassed by the mere hint of pregnancy.

Julie's eyes widened. Ned wondered if she was at last going to disappoint him, which might not be a bad thing, but she said, "Have done. I'll trade your statue for my glove, and we can pretend we never met."

Ned didn't care for this proposition. "It *is* my statue. And it's not your glove."

She ignored the distinction. "Did you bring it with you? The glove?"

"Did you bring the statue? I thought not. My dear, I'm not a flat."

"And I'm not your dear!" she snapped. "Nor will I be, so you needn't try and turn me up sweet."

"Turn you up sweet?"

"Your sort doesn't call my sort 'dear' unless you've mischief in mind."

Ned choked back his laughter. He had already offended her once today. "'My dear' is in the nature of another compliment," he said, with as much solemnity as he could muster. "It means I like you. Tell me why you need the glove."

She looked as if she wanted to throttle him. "It's not me as needs it or I'd say keep the thing! But have it I must, or I *will* be in Newgate, and what will become of your precious statue then?"

Ned wasn't sure the statue wouldn't be safer with her. No one would think to search for the blasted thing in Niddicock Ashcroft's house.

Safer, providing she stayed out of Newgate. "The glove isn't the only thing you've stolen. Did you do it for a lark?"

Ducks squabbled behind them, splashed and quacked. Julie glanced at the pond. "For a bloody *lark*?"

He had offended her again. "Do you need money? Perhaps I can help."

She rolled her eyes. "You can't go around asking people like me questions like that. We'll always say yes. Since all the money in the world won't change anything, you may keep it. I wouldn't take anything from you, at any rate."

This young woman grew more and more a novelty. "Why not?"

"Because if you was to give me money, you'd have bought me, and I'm not for sale. What's the time?"

Buy Julie? Ned should have been appalled at the suggestion. Instead he recalled what she had looked like in a state of nature. He had seen the rear view clearly, and was curious about the rest.

He pulled out his pocket watch, an ornate piece that had once belonged to his maternal grandfather. Julie craned her neck to look at the dial. "I have to go." She turned away.

Ned caught her wrist. Julie stumbled against him and he caught her up against his chest. It was like clutching a rainbow. Her warmth sizzled through the combined thicknesses of coat and cloak.

She felt like heaven and smelled like jasmine. Ned was proud that he remembered how to speak. "If you try to cut and run I will be very cross."

Julie squirmed. He held her tighter against his body, distracted himself from her intoxicating closeness by counting the leaves on the tree branch overhead.

She went limp in his arms. "Are you threatening me, my lord?

Most men would hit a woman and think nothing of it. I'd expected better of an earl."

As distraction, these remarks were considerably more effective than leaf counting. "Someone has hit you?"

She stared at him. "What world do you live in?"

"The same as you." Ned gave in to temptation, and trailed his fingers across her soft cheek.

Julie jerked away. "Why did you do that?"

"Because I wanted to."

"Do you always do what you want, my lord?"

"If you don't stop calling me 'my lord' I will take drastic measures." Reluctantly, Ned released her. "We're not finished with this conversation, you know."

"I didn't think we were." Julie awarded him a glance brimful of mischief. "Ned." He watched her saunter down the path until she passed out of his sight.

It wasn't that late, surely? If Julie got into trouble with Lady Georgiana on Ned's account, he would have to make amends.

Ned reached for his timepiece, found his pocket empty. The minx had filched his watch.

Chapter Eleven

They come to see; they come that they
themselves may be seen. — Ovid

Featherbrain, said Julie to herself. *Cabbagehead.* Why oh why had she picked the pocket of an earl?

She had nibbled the ticker of a gentry cove, and trusted that he wouldn't see her hobbled for it, which was as paperskulled a gamble as any Tony had ever made. And this after Ned had said he liked her, and complimented her eyes and hair, which made her wonder now if he needed spectacles. When she considered her looks, which wasn't often—or *hadn't* been often before she met Lord Buccaneer and started noticing her appearance—she thought merely that her bright curls made her too easily recognized, hardly a good thing for someone on the sneak.

Bottle-head stupid, that's what she was. Pretty Ned had held her close, and her brain had melted, and she'd given in to impulse.

She'd wanted to impress him, Julie admitted. *Why* she wanted to impress him was something she didn't care to think about.

She concentrated on her surroundings. The entertainment being offered this evening at Covent Garden Opera was *The Grand Alliance,* followed by *Richard Couer de Lion,* a story Julie liked well. Feigning blindness, the troubadour Blondel sought to find his imprisoned master, King Richard, who managed to be reunited with Marguerite of France barely in time to prevent her becoming a nun.

The playbill hardly mattered, as the Allied Sovereigns had promised to attend. More attention was being paid to the royal box than to the stage. As early as five o'clock an immense crowd had battered down the inner doors and barriers in front of the pay box, with the result that countless people gained admission without pay-ing for their seats. The decorations of the theater were damaged in the stampede and many ladies' dresses torn. The audience settled in and grew progressively more unruly as they waited for the spec-tacle to begin at eight o'clock. A wit in the gallery diverted them for a time with a demonstration of his skill at whistling.

Lady Georgiana reached over and rapped Julie's knuckles with a pierced horn fan. "Stop air-dreaming, miss!"

"Yes, my lady," Julie murmured.

Lady Georgiana was not deceived by this meek tone. She frowned at Julie before returning her attention to the stage. Her ladyship was the epitome of elegance this evening in a lavish gown of orchid Italian crepe trimmed with floss silk and lace. A fortune in jewels was woven through her curls.

A poor family could live several lifetimes on the proceeds of those gems, mused Julie. While Tony could (and doubtless would if his mama didn't have a stout lock-box) lose them all in one night of play.

The theater was elegant, having three circles of boxes, with a row of side-boxes above them, on a level with the two-shilling gal-lery. The box fronts were perpendicular, each circle supported by slender reeded pillars in burnished gold, the seats covered in pale blue. The circular ceiling was painted to imitate a cupola, in square compartments, with a light relief; the panels grey in color with wreaths of honeysuckle in gold. Romantically lit by patent lamps and elegant chandeliers, everything looked very grand.

Julie felt grand herself, sitting in this private box, wearing a gown of pale pink crepe and a lace shawl. She might have felt she dressed up pretty, had not Lady Georgiana taken pains to tell her she did not.

Covent Garden had burned down in 1808, reopening the next year to the Old Price riots, which ended with the cost of admission not being raised. The theater's history was rich with famous names: Charles Macklin, David Garrick, Peg Woffington; John Philip Kem-ble and his sister Sarah Siddons; William Henry Betty, 'The Young Roscius', who at twelve years of age was earning one hundred pounds a night. Being in a theater made Julie long for Rose. She wondered if Covent Garden had a resident cat.

Intermission came, and with it a flock of visitors. Julie withdrew into the shadows at the rear of the box. Softly, she hummed the song King Richard had composed for Marguerite:

"O Richard! O my king! The universe forsakes thee—"

"You are familiar with the play, I see," came a lazy voice from behind her. "It was banned during the troubles in France, due to its favorable depiction of royalty."

Julie started, spun around. Lord Dorset arched an eyebrow. "I didn't mean to frighten you, Miss Wynne."

If he hadn't meant to frighten her, he wouldn't have snuck up on her like a cat preparing to pounce. "You're drawing attention to me. Lady Georgiana won't like that."

Ned nodded toward the front of the box. "I brought my cousin. Lady Georgiana is too busy insulting Hannah to heed us."

Julie glanced over her shoulder. Lady Dorset was wearing inky black taffeta lavishly ornamented with satin rouleaux, topped off by a turban with ostrich plumes.

Lady Georgiana wafted her fan. "Prinny has commissioned Thomas Lawrence to paint portraits of the Allied Sovereigns. Despite the fact that he is rumored to have been a lover of Princess Caroline, dear Thomas is all the rage. I, naturally, have already had my portrait done."

"Naturally." Hannah's nose twitched. "I hear that the Czar has insulted the Regent by saying his current flirt is 'mighty old'. Lady Hertford is your age, is she not?"

"We will leave the ladies to their pleasantries," said Ned. "I want a word with you, buttercup."

Sunshine. Buttercup. Poppycock. "So you shall have it, my lord greenbean." Julie brushed her fingers over his white Marcella waistcoat, felt the fascinating strength of his body through those several layers of clothing. "You have a smudge."

He caught her hand and held it against his chest. "Are you

aware that your eyes change color with your moods?"

Julie wondered what color her eyes were now that she was practically panting due to his proximity. "Is this more of your flummery?"

He moved her hand away, released it. "No, simply the truth. Were I to compliment you, I would say that you are bold as a brass-faced monkey. How dared you steal my watch?"

Julie peeked at Georgiana and Hannah, who were now arguing politics, one taking the Tory point of view, and the other the Whig, not from any strong conviction but to cause annoyance and thereby entertain themselves. "Are you certain your watch is missing, my lord?"

He reached into his pocket, pulled out the watch. "Clever girl."

"*That*, I did for a lark." The box was growing steadily more crowded as people came to pay their respects, and to gossip, and be seen. Julie searched for an innocuous topic of conversation, one that didn't have to do with items stolen and brought back. "Why is your horse named Soldier?"

"Because he was one, as was I."

Julie recalled a certain ugly statue. "Did you do your soldiering in Egypt?"

The earl folded his arms across his chest. "One might think so, might one not? But, no. I was in the Peninsula."

He was a soldier who had seen serious action, then. "Cuidad Rodrigo? Badajoz? Salamanca?"

"I cashiered out after Badajoz. You've done some traveling of your own."

What nonsense was this? "I've never been away from London."

"You forgot Yorkshire."

So she had. Probably because her fingers still tingled from where she'd pressed them against his chest. Heaven forbid she ever touched him without layers of cloth between them. She'd expire on the spot.

He was waiting for her comment. Julie said, "Lady Georgiana would hardly hire a companion who grew up in St Giles."

He leaned closer to her. "And did you grow up in St Giles?"

"I'm just saying." Much more than she should. "Ask me no more questions, my lord. I can't answer them."

"You were to call me Ned."

His voice was low, his breath warm against her cheek. The intimacy of the moment caused Julie to come over queerly faint.

She stepped away from him. Ned gazed out over the theater. "Niddicock doesn't accompany you tonight?"

"Niddicock spends as little time as possible with his mama. Do people really call him that?"

"It suits, does it not?"

It did that. "There's no real harm for Tony, for all his tongue runs twelve score to the dozen. I have to have that glove. Please, Ned."

He glanced at her. "It's so important to you?"

"More than you can imagine." Cap'n Jack might be present. Watching her. Wondering why she hadn't fulfilled his last request.

Ah well, if she wound up back in Newgate, she would no longer have to tolerate Lady Georgiana's jobations and whims. Julie had a horrid suspicion that she might have spoke that last thought aloud.

Voices rose behind them. Newcomers had entered the box. Julie turned away from Ned's quizzical glance. A dark gentleman, a pale woman, and—

Clea came quickly toward them. "Cousin Hannah says a lady should never be alone with a gentleman for any length of time, lest she be compromised."

"I don't want to know that you know what's involved in being compromised." Ned said, looking appalled.

"Then I shan't tell you." Clea smoothed her white skirts. "Am I not a picture? Fine feathers make fine birds. I'm not sure I wouldn't rather be a pigeon than a peacock, but we shan't tell Cousin Hannah that." She inspected Julie. "Who are you?"

Ned caught Julie's hand and tucked it through his arm. "Miss Wynne, this is my sister Clea, who has yet to learn her manners. Clea, say hello to Miss Julie Wynne from York."

Clea cocked her head. "Have we met before, Miss Wynne?"

"I don't think so, miss," Julie spoke gruffly, in an attempt to disguise her voice.

Ned chuckled, confound the man. "Have you a frog?"

Frog? What about a frog?

"In your throat."

"It's the theater," Clea said helpfully. "We are all breathing each other's air."

Ned spoke to his sister. "You haven't met Miss Wynne unless you have been to Yorkshire. She is the daughter of a parson, now deceased."

"How sad," Clea said. "I'm sorry for your loss."

The young lady's gaze was entirely too shrewd. Julie turned away. The newcomers—Lord Saxe and Mrs. Viccars—were speaking of the recent announcement in the press that Wellington, en route from Paris to Madrid, had been waylaid on the road with his two aides-de-camp and murdered, news that had mercifully been proven false. The lady was wearing a celestial blue gown with long sleeves and a deep flounce of lace. The gentleman was so handsome that no sensible female would trust him out of her eyesight. Lady Georgiana patted around her person in search of quizzing glass, handkerchief, mirror, snuffbox or smelling salts. She saw Julie standing with Lord Dorset, and beckoned imperiously.

"I warned you," muttered Julie. "She'll give me a rare trimming, and it will be all your fault."

"Allow me." Ned urged Julie forward. "My apologizes, Lady Georgiana, for monopolizing Miss Wynne. We were discussing mutual acquaintances in Yorkshire." As he spoke, a buzz swept through the theater. The audience rose from their seats to cheer. The Distinguished Guests had arrived.

They entered not from Bow Street or Covent Garden, but by way of a private staircase through the royal entrance from Hart Street. The sovereigns were in uniform, their hair worn plain in the modern fashion, Prinny the only one of the party with powder in his curls. Generals Chernichev and Bülow attended their monarchs; the Czar and the Emperor of Prussia and the minor princes shared the Regent's box. Lady Georgiana pointed out Prince Augustus of Russia, the black sheep of his family, with whom Princess Caroline was currently entranced; Prince Frederick of Prussia; Prince Paul of Württemberg; thin pale Francis of Austria with his long face and his tendency to go about in the greatest possible state. The audience lined up with their backs to the stage in hope of getting near enough to shake someone's hand. A special anthem was sung, followed by "God Save the King", repeated twice.

Julie paid no attention to either Lady Georgiana or the Allied Sovereigns, or even the ostracized Princess of Wales, who during the spirited singing had entered another box. Clutched in her left hand, where Lord Dorset had tucked it, was the stolen glove.

Chapter Twelve

*Neither will the wave which has passed by be called back;
nor can the hour which has gone by return.* — Ovid

Weak morning sunlight streamed through the library windows, past the dusty draperies, across the shabby carpet, alit at last on the ancient desk. Behind it, the current earl of Dorset lounged in breeches and a loose linen shirt. Opposite him, Lord Saxe was sprawled in a carved chair.

Kane's expression was incredulous. "You gave her the glove."

To the usual clutter on the desk had been added a coffee urn. Ned poured more of the strong dark liquid into his cup. "It will be interesting to discover what she does with the damned thing."

"And you will know that how? Ah, the inestimable Bates. I can see him now, skulking about London in the young lady's wake."

Ned smiled wryly. "The vocabulary of the usual young lady doesn't contain 'bugger', I suspect."

"Don't be so certain."

"You grow jaded, my friend."

"What I'm growing is exhausted. Diplomacy is more wearying than debauchery." Kane held out his own cup for a refill. "Princess Caroline mistimed her entrance last night. She had meant to arrive separately from the monarchs, and receive her own applause. The princess is so upset at her exclusion from all functions honoring the royal visitors that she's hounding Liverpool for permission to leave the country."

Ned had little interest in the Regent's estranged wife, who was more beloved of the general populace than was her husband, due less to any merit on her part than to Prinny's vast unpopularity. His thoughts returned to Julie's stolen glove. He hadn't taken it with him to the theater with the intention of returning it—or he thought he hadn't—but had found himself moved by her distress.

Or maybe he had simply been fuddle-brained with lust. Ned hadn't felt Julie put back the watch. He *had* felt her clever fingers tiptoeing down his waistcoat, and had damned near had her up against the wall.

"Am I boring you?" Kane regarded his friend with a jaundiced eye.

Ned stared into his cup. "The stains on that glove were blood. Which makes me wonder whose blood was spilled, and when, and why the damned thing was in the possession of the French Ambassador's wife."

Kane contemplated the contents of his own cup. "It makes *me* wonder what a blood-stained glove has in common with pilfered jewelry and an Egyptian statue. You are protecting a felon, I think."

"We don't know that she is a felon." Rather, Kane didn't know, because Ned hadn't informed him of Julie's 'back in' Newgate. He wondered if she was aware of that revealing slip.

And then he wondered if the slip might have been deliberate.

"Have you considered," said Kane, with the eerie empathy that made him so proficient at both philandering and politics, "that this girl might be deliberately rousing both your curiosity and your protective instincts?"

Julie posed no real threat, surely? Ned didn't suspect her of involvement in anything truly vicious; she wasn't up to weight for that sort of thing. Or so he sensed, and Ned's nose for mischief hadn't thus far steered him wrong.

Except in the instance of Bianca. "There is that," he muttered.

"I'm glad you admit it. You'll let me—"

"No. We play this out my way."

Kane might well have argued—he was certainly in a mood to argue, since tact forbade him voicing his opinions to the privileged individuals who were making him wish to tear out his hair—but a section of the bookshelf swung aside, and both gentlemen tensed.

Clea stepped through the opening, Cerberus at her heels. Ned let his pistol slide back into its drawer. "Found another secret passage, have you, puss?"

She looked more her usual self this morning, with cobwebs in her hair and dirt smudged on her face. "A hidden staircase," she said cheerfully. "It leads to an attic I hadn't seen before. I found these marbles as well." She set her lantern down on the desk.

"One assumes," Ned said to Kane, "that the previous owners of Wakely House were either involved in questionable activities or politically inept. There are secret passages, hides, and concealed staircases everywhere."

To Cerberus's way of thinking, there were intruders everywhere. The dog's temper was already exacerbated by explorations of hitherto-unknown and very dirty spaces, and the additional irritation of finding a strange male on his turf (or perhaps not entirely strange; Cerberus dimly recollected the previous instance of the riding crop) was more than he could tolerate. The dog crouched, wriggled his hindquarters, and with a blood-curdling howl, attacked.

A spirited contretemps ensued. At its conclusion, Kane nursed a damaged boot while Cerberus sat sulking in a far corner, and Ned had laughed himself into stitches, and spilled his coffee as well.

Clea smoothed the pages of the fashion magazine she had snatched up to dissuade the defender of the turf to withdraw his teeth from Kane's tall leather boot. "Do you think I should purchase false bosoms made of wax?"

Ned choked on his last gasp of laughter. "You should not."

Clea plopped down on the carpet and set out her marbles. "I wasn't asking you, silly. Kane's the expert in such things."

"A hit, a palpable hit," that gentleman remarked, with no small degree of irony; Ned was hardly a stranger to the foibles and frivolities of the fairer sex. "As a general rule, brat, gentlemen don't like to be deceived."

"But what if one is a trifle deficient in that area?"

"One is only fifteen and need not despair just yet."

"Are you certain?" Clea peered down at her chest.

Only someone who was watching closely would have seen Kane's lips twitch. "It is quality not quantity that counts."

Ned propped his feet up on the old desk. "Is this what I have to look forward to? Conversations about bosoms?"

Clea added, "And bums. I'm not certain—"

Kane smiled outright. "Your bum is fine. Trust me on that." Ned dropped his head into his hands.

Clea placed a marble on the second knuckle of her forefinger, positioned her thumb behind it, and gave it a flick. "Don't be so dreary, Ned. It isn't like you are unacquainted with female body parts. I am growing older, and I must discuss these things with someone, and I don't think Cousin Hannah counts. Now, are we playing marbles, or are we not?"

Ned removed his boots from the desktop. Kane took off his coat. The carpet was rolled back, and charcoal from the hearth used to inscribe a circle on the old wooden floor. An interval passed in the pleasant pastime of marbles, during which Clea contrived to knock her opponents' missiles into the far corners of the room. Cerberus crept closer to encourage the players by means of whuffs and snarls.

Came a tap on the door, and Tidcombe entered. Sight of the gentlemen in their shirtsleeves, and the young lady in her dirt, all three sprawled in the most undignified manner on the floor, caused him to stop dead in his tracks.

"I told you it was unnecessary to announce me." Sabine stepped around the butler to enter the room. At sight of the pretty-smelling lady, Cerberus wagged his stump of a tail. Stiff with disapproval, Tidcombe withdrew.

Sabine untied her cloak. "Who's winning the game?"

"I am, of course." Clea scooped up her marbles and clambered to her feet with an agility envied by every other person in the room. Cerberus recalled that he was sulking and withdrew to do so in the shadow of a stack of books. "What do *you* think about false chests made of wax, Sabine?"

"I've already told her that gentlemen aren't so shallow as to judge a young lady on the bounty of her bosom." Kane brushed dog hair and dust off his breeches and reached for his coat.

Sabine observed the play of manly muscles as the baron

donned his jacket. "Nonsense. Of course you are. I feel I should point out that wax is prone to melt."

"So in the midst of passion," Clea reasoned, "one's bosoms might start to slide down one's chest. I can see that might throw a damper on romance." Kane laughed. Ned groaned.

Sabine emptied the coffee urn into Ned's abandoned cup. "I promise, Clea, that you will break whatever hearts you wish without resorting to false body parts. Not that there is any harm in the use of artifice." Ned wondered what had brought Sabine to them at this early hour. She looked as if she'd had less sleep than Kane.

"Speaking of artifice, I have been thinking of Don Miguel." Clea glanced at Kane. "Don Miguel Sanchez, one of the *guerrilha* chiefs. He had a marvelous curled moustache of which he was exceedingly proud. He usually wore a pelisse reminiscent of the 16th Dragoons, along with an immense hussar cap that had the Eagle of Napoleon reversed, and a brace of pistols tucked into a gaudy red sash. One might never see a more verminous set of rascals than Don Miguel and his men."

"They were the worst nightmare of every French convoy commander," remarked Sabine.

Kane lounged deeper in his chair. "One of your swains?"

"Not mine. Don Miguel had a fondness for Clea. He considered it barbaric that Ned dragged her through a war."

"It would have been more barbaric if he'd left me behind," Clea said, with feeling. "I might have fallen into Cousin Hannah's hands. And anyway, it was not so bad as all that. Remember the winter we spent in Frenada? Frenada is a grindingly poor Portuguese village," she added, again for Kane's benefit. "The better sort of inhabitant had a two-level dwelling, the ground floor reserved for livestock. Somehow Francis obtained lodgings large enough for the three of us to live in comfort and sometimes entertain a few guests—since Ned was frequently gone on Wellington's business, I spent much of my time in Iberia with Francis and Sabine. We had a roast goose and plum pudding for dinner that Christmas, and singing afterward. The officers of the Light Division performed Shakespeare's *Henry IV* in a ruined chapel on the outskirts of town."

Clea was right. It hadn't been all hardship, admitted Ned. There had been cards and impromptu musicales and fox hunting in the traditional manner on the Biera highland. Even Wellington occasionally left off deciphering letters and reports of guerilla agents and exploring officers, pouring over maps and plotting enemy marches, to ride out from his farmhouse headquarters. And then had come Badajoz and forty-six hundred allied casualties, over eighteen hundred of the dead and wounded belonging to the storming parties of the Light and 4th Divisions, Francis Viccars among them.

"I have vowed," remarked Sabine, "never to eat rabbit again."

She was more slender than when Ned had last seen her. The clever cut of her dove-grey gown couldn't disguise how thin she had become. When the reminiscences wound down, Kane said, "Clea, if you wouldn't mind—?"

"Just fancy. There is something I must do elsewhere." Clea walked toward the door. "I could eavesdrop, you know."

"But you won't."

"I won't. But being proper is sometimes a dead bore."

"'*Di pia facta vident.*'"

"The gods see the deeds of the righteous?" Clea pulled a face. "All in all, I think I would rather be bad."

The door closed behind her. Sabine waited briefly before she crossed the room, opened the door, inspected the empty hall.

She closed the door and leaned against it. Kane stretched out his long legs in front of him. Sabine regarded his damaged boot. He said, "Cerberus is blind to my charm. Unlike yours. Apropos of which, the Czar is cutting a swathe through polite society—and probably impolite society as well, but no one speaks of that—and ladies are falling at his feet like ripe plums."

Sabine walked to the window. "It is not in my nature to fall."

Kane looked skeptical. In Ned's opinion, Sabine spoke the truth. She and her gallant Francis had seemed less like lovers than friends.

She stood at the window, gazing out. Cerberus emerged from behind his stack of books to pad across the carpet and sit down beside her, pausing to growl at Kane en route. Sabine bent to stroke the dog's ugly head. "Last night at the opera. Who was that girl?"

Neither Ned nor Kane had any doubt of what girl she meant. "We are most sure of who she *isn't,* which is one Miss Julie Wynne," explained Kane.

"Ned said she's from Yorkshire."

"Ned was merely attempting to disarm Lady Georgiana. Miss Wynne is a mystery. Why do you ask?"

Sabine picked up her cloak, reached into the pocket and withdrew a miniature in a gilt frame. "You will be discreet?"

Kane's patience was wearing thin. "Who in all London might better understand discretion than the Swan, the Raven, and the Fox?"

Ned studied the portrait. A young man gazed back at him with amused arrogance. A young man with stunningly blue eyes, a dark arch of eyebrows, and guinea gold curls.

Sabine drew her cloak around her, as if suddenly chilled. "His name was Julian Faulkner, and he was Lord Carlyle's eldest son."

Chapter Thirteen

*It's stupid to complain about misfortune
that is your own fault.* — Pubilius Syrus

London was a city of illuminations, in honor of the peace that had yet to be signed. Shop windows displayed transparencies with lights burning behind them, each in competition with the next. Covent Garden Opera showed Britannia trampling on Napoleon with Elba to be seen on the horizon. Ackermann's, the print shop in the Strand that had been one of the first to have its premises lighted by gas, featured an especially fine rendition of the Corsican attacked by Death. The Gaslight Company in Fleet Street had erected a tree of laurel leaves with a profusion of blossoms, each a jet of the marvelous new flame. The town was half mad with festivities and fireworks and frigates firing on the Serpentine.

Cobbled streets were thronged with traffic, every imaginable conveyance from iron-rimmed wheels to leather-shod feet. Street sellers worked their way through the crowd, hawking all manner of goods from hot eels to lavender for use in the linen-press.

Julie didn't dawdle to look in the shop windows, as on another day she might. Cap'n Jack would want his glove. He'd want to know why she hadn't made it available to him immediately it was stolen. Julie had to make up some Banbury tale. She didn't want the Cap'n to come within a mile of Ned.

For that matter, she didn't want the Cap'n within a mile of her either, and it made her shiver to think she wouldn't know if—or when—he was. He could be following her that moment. He could, if he wished it, sneak up behind her and slit her throat. Julie glanced over her shoulder but saw nothing more suspicious than a grizzled bellows-mender with his tools in a bag on his back.

A bellows-mender who was oddly familiar. The man stepped into a pastry shop, and Julie decided she must be wrong. She had no time to be starting at shadows. Lady Georgiana was in a rare taking today, and Julie must be back before she woke up from her nap.

The streets grew increasingly narrow, this close to Drury Lane. Julie side-stepped a donkey cart piled high with firewood, and then a broom-vendor; swiped an apple from a market-cart and tucked it into the pocket of her cloak. Without practice her abilities would wither away, and then where would she be?

Inside the theater, rehearsals had begun. Everyone was tiptoe-ing around backstage. The Distinguished Visitors were to grace the theater with their presence. Mr. Kean had traded his part of Iago for that of Othello, and consequently Mr. Sowerby's nose was out of joint.

The scene underway did not require Desdemona. Julie found Rose in the ladies' dressing room, contemplating her reflection as with a pair of small steel pinchers she removed a stray hair from her chin. Ophelia was snoozing among the makeup pots.

Rose whirled away from the looking glass, grabbed Julie's el-bow, and gave it a good shake. "Where have you been? Pritchett has been plaguing me. He said I'm to tell you that you must watch your step."

Julie *was* watching, wasn't she? Every step she took, and every word she said. For the most part. Except when in the presence of a certain earl. Surely she hadn't—had she?—said 'back in' Newgate. Silently, she handed over the glove.

Rose frowned. "*This* had Pritchett in a dither? I don't under-stand."

"You must tell him that I couldn't get away before."

"I must, must I?" Rose set the glove on her dressing-table. "And the truth is that—"

"Dorset caught me and pinched the glove himself."

"Oh, Lord." Rose plopped down on a bench. Ophelia sniffed the glove, decided it wasn't worthy of her interest, and resumed her nap.

"I cobbled it," sighed Julie. "Someone almost caught the both of us, and we hid."

Rose looked no less horrified. "You hid."

"In a wardrobe." Julie had been thinking about that wardrobe ever since, and how she had enjoyed being held so close. The earl was strong enough to lift her right off her feet, and warm to the touch, and she wished that she might see him without his clothes.

Yes, and then what, pudding-head? "I'd have been nabbed sure as winking if it hadn't been for Ned."

Rose elevated her eyebrows, remembered that such movement led to lines marring the forehead, and lowered them again. "'Ned'?"

"He says we've gone far beyond 'my lord'. I've been thinking, Rose. If Cap'n Jack is a gentry cove, why does he need me for this business? Wouldn't it be simpler for him to do the thing himself?"

"That's for him to know." Rose looked quickly around, assured herself the Cap'n couldn't be hiding in a suit of armor, or under a powdered wig. "If Dorset took the glove from you, how did you get it back? Tell me you didn't steal it from him!"

"No. I stole his pocket watch. A right nice ticker it was. Real gold."

Rose groaned. Julie grinned. "I gave it back."

"You gave his watch back to him."

"I figured if I gave him back the watch, he'd give me the glove. And I was right, wasn't I?"

All about in the head was what Julie was, if she thought Rose would be put off. Rose demanded to have the whole of the story, and in the proper order, from beginning to end. Therefore she heard about the rendezvous in Hyde Park, and how the earl had taken Julie up on his horse, and managed to make only minimal interruptions, such as, "'Buttercup'?"

"It was in the nature of being a compliment," Julie explained gravely. "You know all about compliments, Rose. Ned was a soldier. In the Peninsula. That queer statue came from Egypt. It's a fertility goddess, he said."

Rose did know about compliments. She also knew a great deal

about the sort of gentlemen who made compliments to ladies, and thought, *Oho.* It was one thing for Rose to have a fondness for a rogue; she was—though she had not set out to be—a woman of the world.

Julie was not, nor did Rose intend for her to be. "Dorset said a lot to you. I wonder what you said in turn."

"What else? That I'm Miss Julie Wynne from York. Which he knows I'm not." Julie picked up a makeup pot.

The girl had never before shown any interest in cosmetics. Rose snatched the pot away. "And how does he know that?"

"He had inquiries made, I guess. Are you worried he'll find out who I really am? That's not likely, Rose."

Of course Rose was worried. It was in the nature of rogues to know more than they should. "We've strayed from your story. You stole Dorset's watch in Hyde Park. Then what?"

Obediently, Julie related her adventure at Covent Garden (which, she assured Rose, didn't hold a candle to Drury Lane) or at least the gist of her adventure, how Ned had sought her out, and spoke with her, which put Lady Rumption in a snit. "I understand why her previous companion ran off."

"If run off she did."

Julie met Rose's eyes in the mirror. "You think—"

"I think it's better not to think about such things. Dorset knows that you stole his statue, yet he hasn't given you away."

"He says he won't peach on me, and I believe him." Ophelia rolled over and Julie stroked the cat's furry belly. "He gave me the glove because I said I had to have it. You must swear to me that you won't tell Pritchett about him, Rose."

"As if I would." It wasn't really a vow, Rose told herself. And even if it was, vows could always be broken, and in Rose's experience often were. "What *did* you do with the statue?"

"I have it with me in my room at Ashcroft House."

Telling, that. "You won't give Dorset the statue because you think that if you do you won't see him again."

Julie felt her cheeks redden. "Have you been at the gin? Lady Georgiana has already told me that I needn't think I may make a conquest of an earl."

Her ladyship had the right of it, so far as she went. Titled gentlemen married unworldly damsels who knew what forks to use at table and naught of real life. Left to her own preferences, Jules would eschew cutlery altogether in favor of her fingers. If Dorset wanted the girl, it would be as his paramour.

Rose had done her best to warn Jules against such folly. Alas, Rose knew—none better—that good sense went flying out the window when romance came knocking at the door. "I'll wash my hands of you, my girl, if you go tossing your bonnet over the windmill."

Julie rolled her eyes. "I think you must have windmills in your head."

Rose remained unconvinced that bonnet-tossing wasn't in the offing. "Do you think your fine earl can protect you, Jules?"

He already had protected her, reflected Julie. "I think I need to know more about Yorkshire."

Herself, Rose needed to know more about this unpredictable gentleman, and she knew just the person who could find out. While she debated how many of these new developments she should share with Pritchett, Rose armed Julie with further information about bell-ringers and morning prayers, the etymological history of the name 'York', and in addition a few pithy proverbs. Wakened from her nap by all this chatter, Ophelia yawned and stretched and took herself off to resume her slumber in a far corner of the room.

A knock came at the door. Rose was required onstage. She locked away the stained glove and went off, as Desdemona, to deal with a fateful glove of her own.

Julie wandered through the theater and back out into the street. She pulled the apple from her pocket and wiped it on her sleeve.

Rose considered herself a Terrible Example. Julie considered her worth a hundred Lady Georgianas with their pills and potions, their meaningless lives. Rose brought pleasure to hundreds, maybe thousands, with her turns upon the stage. Lady Georgiana couldn't claim to provide that much misery.

The two of them believed she'd taken a fancy to the earl, and maybe she had. What of it? Julie well knew that fancying something and thinking she might have it were two different things.

The cobbles were thronged with traffic, every imaginable conveyance from iron-rimmed wheels to leather-shod feet. Street sellers worked their way through the crowd. Julie passed by a beggar with his leg doubled under at the knee to simulate a lost limb, his mouth frothing with foam produced by eating soap. As she bit into her apple, she felt a prickle of awareness, as if someone's eyes rested on her.

Julie ducked into the doorway of an apothecary's shop. Over the counter, for some unknown reason, hung a stuffed crocodile.

A grizzled bellows-mender shambled past the doorway. He met Julie's gaze.

No wonder the man had seemed familiar. She'd seen him last at Wakely Court, when Miss Clea had insisted that she have a bath. Bates hadn't been dressed as a bellows-mender then. She stuck out her tongue.

Dashing earls. Stolen statues. Bloody hell.

Julie slipped out the back door of the shop into a maze of alleyways and courts and interlocking back yards where any thief worth her salt might give pursuers the slip. She *was* a thief, and must not forget it, no matter how many social functions Lady Georgiana dragged her to, or how many dashing earls told her they admired the color of her curls.

Chapter Fourteen

Any man can make a mistake;
only a fool keeps making the same one. — Cicero

"Pay attention!" Lady Georgiana rapped her knuckles on the table. Tony gazed at his cards. The most interesting, and most difficult, part of piquet was choosing what to discard. In this instance, it made no difference. Tony wouldn't have been surprised to learn his mama had an entire deck of playing cards tucked into the long sleeves of her dress. He held no face cards.

Lady Georgiana chose her own discards, then returned to the topic she had been discussing before her son's inattention threw her off the track, to wit her hired companion's predilection to desert her post and amuse herself with rascally earls.

"There was more than one?" asked Tony, amazed and also grateful that he'd managed to wriggle out of escorting his mama to the theater that night. If only he had managed to escape the house before she'd caught him today.

She ignored his interruption. Her ladyship had much to say about the danger posed to innocent females by gentlemen of Lord Dorset's sort. Or not-so-innocent females, for that matter. Ruinous entanglements were mentioned, and squalid intrigues, flattering overtures and amorous vagaries. Though he thought she was making a great piece of work about nothing, Tony withheld comment. If his mama must ring a peal over someone, he'd rather it was Julie than himself.

Georgiana threw down her cards. "I trust I know how many days are to the week! Ring for more tea."

No wonder his mama's health was fragile. She had consumed

gallons of the stuff already, and devoured a plate of digestive biscuits as well. "I don't want tea," Tony protested.

"You will have some," retorted his fond parent. "Nonetheless."

The morning room was a pleasant if overly feminine chamber, with an assortment of brass-inlaid rosewood furniture, an upholstered sofa and armchairs, and pretty blue and white striped paper on the walls. In one corner perched a harp with an elaborately carved wooden frame. Tony skirted a low bookcase and tugged on the bell pull.

Georgiana resumed her grievances. A lady's companion was required to be well bred and well educated, to possess a spotless reputation and steady nerves. She was expected to display a meek and modest manner in both her action and her dress, as well as in her speech. Unless Georgiana's ears had deceived her (and if so it would be for the first time), she had heard Julie say 'bloody hell' just yesterday.

"I say 'bloody hell'," Tony protested. "So do you. Said it when you was told Lady Dorset had been at the British Museum. Heard you myself."

"That dreadful, dreadful woman. How dare you mention her?" Hannah had contrived to be present when Czar Alexander and his sister visited the British Museum; had conversed with the Grand Duchess about a colossal marble foot, supposedly once attached to an Apollo, donated to the Museum by Sir William Hamilton.

Georgiana continued on for several moments, speaking of serpents clutched to her bosom and snakes in the grass. Uncertain if she was talking about him or Julie or Lady Dorset, Tony strolled around the room and sat down at the harp. He tilted the instrument back to rest against his shoulder, and placed his hands on the strings.

The music, as always, filled him with contentment, which lasted but briefly, until his mother fluttered her handkerchief. "Let us have something less lively, if you please. This energetic sort of music is wearing on my shattered nerves. Naturally, you get your musical ability from me. Your dear papa couldn't carry a tune."

Tony's dear papa had been more interested in carrying on

with dollymops than in anything musical, unless a great deal of liquor was involved, a circumstance which had led to his fatal tumble down the back stair of a house of low repute; and the main thing Tony had got from his mama was a monumental headache. Wondering if he was ever to be allowed to leave the morning room, he abandoned Turlough O'Carolan in favor of a dirge.

The harp sang sweetly beneath his fingers. Tony saw to it that the instrument was kept in tune. He had wanted to study music further, but his mama nipped that notion in the bud. Gentlemen hunted and boxed and gambled, said she. They didn't go around plucking harps. This particular gentleman wondered if, had he been permitted his music, he might not be in a cleft stick now.

"I asked her to read the *Morning Post* to me," Georgiana brooded, "and she stumbled over every other word."

His mama must mean Julie, Tony decided; Lady Dorset hadn't been at Ashcroft House today. That he knew of, at any rate. Why she might wish to be, he couldn't imagine. Tony didn't wish to be at Ashcroft House himself.

A maidservant appeared in the doorway and curtseyed. "You rang, my lady?"

"Fetch some tea," said Georgiana. "Tell Miss Wynne that her presence is required." The maidservant curtseyed again and allowed as she would be happy to inform Miss Wynne of her ladyship's request, except that Miss Wynne wasn't in the house.

"Not in the house!" echoed Georgiana. "I sent her to her room."

"That's as may be, my lady, but she didn't stay there long. Went out, she did." The maidservant had never had the nerve to disobey an order, and was therefore happy to snitch on one who had. "Alone."

"Alone? No one accompanied her?"

"Very stealthy she was, my lady. Crept out the side door. I happened to be by the window or no one would have seen her go."

"You mean you happened to be dillydallying." Georgiana might spend considerable time rubbing shoulders with prince regents and kings (if not Grand Duchesses at the British Museum), but she knew how things went on below stairs. Just this morning she had perused a most instructive handbook addressed to female servants, which told them on one page how to preserve their virtue, and on the next how to preserve fruit, and on the third urged them to refrain from coughing, scratching, whistling and blowing their noses in the presence of their superiors.

Perhaps she should present the volume to Julie, who clearly needed instruction in how she should behave. Or, more specifically, in how she should *not*. Georgiana vented her spleen on the hapless maidservant. By the time the girl went off to fetch the tea tray, she was practically in tears.

Georgiana revisited her primary sense of grievance. "A lady's companion is required to sit quietly and unobtrusively and be at her employer's beck and call, not go off without permission. I hope you aren't paying too generous a salary."

So much for the soothing effects of music. Tony broke off on a discord prompted by the reflection that he wasn't paying Julie anything at all. "Um! That is— Nothing to worry your head about. I have everything in hand."

Georgiana took leave to doubt it. When Tony's papa had told her she shouldn't worry it meant the exact opposite. She feared her son took after him in that regard. "Never tell me you're under the hatches again." She reached for her smelling salts.

For a brief instant, Tony considered presenting his mama with the truth. The impulse did not stay with him long. If Georgiana learned the sequence of events that had led to Julie's presence in the Ashcroft household, to wit his gaming debts, she'd banish him to the country for a year.

And if the word got out that his mama held the purse strings, he'd never be able to show his face in his clubs again.

"Not a bit of it!" he said. "Don't know where you took such a queer notion. Must have been all that tea you drunk. You should apologize."

Georgiana should give him a good shake, like she had when he was younger. "Tell me again how you found Miss Wynne."

He hadn't found her. She'd found him. Or Cap'n Jack had found them both. Tony wished he could recall what he had previously said.

"It was Rutledge," he ventured. "Told him you needed someone because old Milly had run off, and he mentioned Miss Wynne. Fate, that's what it was."

Georgiana wondered if she'd given her son one too many shakes already, and thus disordered the proper working of his brain. "You said she was connected to Babbington."

Had he? Tony couldn't remember. Not that it much mattered, because he'd pulled both names out of his hat. "She is! Related to them both."

Definitely, she was going to have a spasm. "I was not," sighed Georgiana, "born yesterday."

Tony's understanding might not be powerful, but he was not so lacking in intelligence as to comment on his mama's age. "Don't know why you should be in a pucker. Julie's a good sort of girl."

"Good sorts of girls don't traipse about the city unescorted."

"You don't know that she *is* traipsing about the city. She might have simply felt the need to take some air." Tony glanced at the door.

"Sit," said his mama sternly. "Stay. I should turn her off."

At thought of the consequences of such an action, Tony blanched. "You can't."

"What nonsense is this? I run the household as I please."

Tony contemplated a certain individual's displeasure were Julie to be turned off, and the unhappy outlets that displeasure might take. "Not in this instance, you don't. And that's an end to it."

So shocked was Lady Georgiana by this unprecedented display of defiance that she stared open-mouthed. Tony didn't notice, for the tea tray had arrived, complete with pot and sugar box, cups and saucers and a cake plate piled high with an assortment of biscuits and macaroons. The maidservant carefully set her burden on the card table and backed out of the room.

Georgiana picked up the teapot and took advantage of the familiar ritual to marshal her thoughts. In the normal course of events, Tony couldn't say boo to a mouse. Yet moments ago he had said 'no' to her face. It was clear as the nose on *his* face—an unimpressive article also reminiscent of his wretched sire—at whose doorstep this outrageous conduct might be laid. Tony at last showed preference for a female, an event so long in coming Georgiana had begun to wonder if his preferences lay in another direction and now found she regretted that they did not. He had formed an attachment to the girl he'd brought home as a companion for his mama, which was the sort of thing his papa would have done, so she supposed she shouldn't be surprised.

She watched her son consume a ginger biscuit, in the process strewing crumbs down his canary yellow waistcoat. "Whatever is going on between you, I'll not have it beneath my roof," Georgiana said.

Tony had no notion his mama had decided he resembled his papa in more ways than she had hitherto realized. Thinking of the reasons for Julie's presence in the household, most specifically the Cap'n—at least Tony could claim he'd never cheated at play, for whatever good it did him—he retorted, "It ain't your roof. And you have no more say about what goes on beneath it than I do."

Worse and worse! Georgiana took a great gulp of her tea, and then replaced the cup in its saucer with an audible clunk.

Confronted by the unmistakable signs of an outraged mama—flared nostrils, compressed lips, knitted brow and the abuse of china—Tony lost his appetite. He feared for a dreadful moment that he had been found out. Further reflection led him to conclude Georgiana couldn't know about Cap'n Jack, not unless she could tell by looking at a fellow what he was thinking, which he fervently hoped she could not.

Tony was caught between Sicily and Charbydis, or whoever those two sea monsters were that ate any sailor who came too close. In this case, the lesser of the two evils was clearly his mama, and the best that he could do was try to get over heavy ground as light as he might. "You ain't going to have one of your fits, are you?" he said bracingly. "Because I have to tell you it won't do any good. And don't go plaguing me with questions, because there's some things a fellow don't want his mama to know about."

There were any number of things a fellow's mama didn't *want* to know about. "The chit has neither breeding nor wealth nor countenance to recommend her," Georgiana pointed out.

Tony didn't immediately grasp the thrust of his mama's conversation, a not unusual occurrence, for he had long ago developed the habit of listening to one word in three. They had been discussing Julie, had they not? He'd told his mama she must withdraw her threat to turn Julie off.

"Can you imagine what people will say if word of this gets round?" Georgiana continued, for she hadn't ceased speaking while her son cudgeled his brain. "Lord Ashcroft smitten with a wretched little nobody—all Society will titter behind their gloves. A parson's daughter. A hired companion! I warn you, I won't be made a laughing stock."

Smitten? Him? With a female? "But—"

"Not another word!" snarled Georgiana. "She has compromised you, I suppose, and is resorting to blackmail. It is no more than you deserve for making sheep's eyes at someone of that sort."

Tony had not previously realized that his mama possessed so vivid an imagination. He couldn't decide which misconception to address first. "Er—"

"Silence! I am thinking." Georgiana plucked a macaroon from the plate. The disobliging Miss Wynne—hadn't Georgiana told her on their first meeting that she wasn't to think she might catch Tony's eye?—must be gotten rid of, but how?

Chapter Fifteen

Who will watch the watchmen?
— Juvenal

The chandeliers blazed brightly. The orchestra strove valiantly to be heard above the chatter of the crowd. Everybody of importance was in attendance at Lady Jersey's midsummer ball, including the Royal Visitors—save the Grand Duchess, due to her dislike of music— for Lady Jersey was the Czar's current flirt, or one of them at any rate.

Alexander made a romantic figure as he swept around the dance floor. "Marvelous," remarked Ned, "how deficiencies of figure can be disguised by a nipped-in waist and extravagantly padded shoulders under large epaulettes. One hopes that Prinny won't take it in his head to try something of the sort."

"Prinny already has. It didn't serve. He has graduated to a corset." Kane had today been privileged to accompany the Czar and his sister to Whitbread's Brewery, where they'd been shown about by no less than Samuel Whitbread, one of the most radical of the Whig MP's. This circumstance had displeased the Prince Regent, who was seldom reluctant to make his feelings known. Kane was feeling immensely put-upon.

Sabine looked romantic herself in an evening gown of celestial blue satin and gauze. "That would explain the creaking," she said.

Kane glanced at her. "Creaking?"

"When Prinny bends. It is disconcerting. Someone should oil him, like one might a rusty hinge."

Kane looked startled at this irreverence. Then he gifted Sabine with not the heartbreaking smile that served him so well in both ballroom and boudoir, but a spontaneous grin that rendered him less lover-like and infinitely more likable.

Sabine studied him. "When you smile like that, you're almost as pretty as Ned."

Ned had been paying little attention to the byplay. Now he felt compelled to defend himself. "I'm not pretty," he protested.

Sabine raised one gloved hand to pat his cheek. "Of course you are. You have about you a tantalizing air of illicit adventure as well. Perhaps— Didn't Vikings have red hair? I can see you at the prow of a long ship. Pillaging and plundering and breaking hearts by the score."

"Yours among them?" Kane inquired.

Sabine turned back to the dancers. "I gave my heart away long ago. The set is ending. Shall we put me in the way of the Czar?"

The three of them attracted a great deal of attention as they strolled through the crowd. Sabine was generally believed to be Ned's latest paramour, or Kane's, or both. How the gossips would have stared to see her fitted out to accompany Wellington's staff on the line of march, perched atop a donkey with her small dog on her knee, followed by a second donkey laden with luggage topped by a cage of canaries, with a parasol in her hand and a straw hat on her head.

Neither the dog nor the canaries had accompanied her to London. Ned supposed they must be dead.

The Czar greeted Sabine with a pretty condescension. Kane and Ned, he brushed effortlessly aside.

The orchestra struck up a waltz. Alexander led Sabine onto the dance floor. "England, for all her wealth, is to Alexander no more than another Poland," remarked Kane. "With France out of the way, he believes nothing can stay Russia's predestined advance. Speaking of advances, here comes your cousin. I believe I shall retreat."

Hannah wore her customary black. Her hair was arranged in the Grecian mode with a curled fringe on her brow, and a mass of pendant curls at the back. "That woman is too old for you," she said.

Try as he might—and he *had* tried, for Clea's sake—Ned could not like his cousin. "Mrs. Viccars is seven-and-thirty, while I am thirty-two. That is not so great a difference."

"Gad. She admits her age?"

"Sabine and I are friends."

"Men and women may be many things, but friends are not among them. I remember Mrs. Viccars as a girl. She was spoiled and headstrong and refused any number of flattering offers, only to turn around and run off with a penniless younger son."

His cousin was a font of information. Ned wondered if she forgot anything she'd heard. "What do you remember about Julian Faulkner?" he asked.

"Carlyle's eldest? He died young. Carlyle was devastated about losing his heir, though he had a spare from his second wife." Hannah's attention was on the dancers. "The Czar appears quite taken with your 'friend'. Lady Jersey's nose will be put out of joint."

"Lady Georgiana's nose as well, since she and Sally are bosom bows."

So they were. Hannah brightened. Anyone with half a brain might have anticipated that Lady Jersey would soon fall from grace, said she, for Silence was a silly frivolous creature prone to constant chatter and the airs of a tragedy queen. Hannah set off in search of her old friend, keeping Ned in tow.

Lady Georgiana was easily tracked down. Atop her head she wore a cap of white satin edged with pearls and finished off with a plume of white feathers. The rest of her was decked out in mulberry crepe ornamented above the hem with silver cord. One and another portion of her person fluttered every time she moved. Laden down with indispensable items, her companion hovered in the background.

"All that hair, dear Hannah!" Georgiana said, before her rival could get off a shot. "I did not realize you had so much. Dorset, you will want to speak to Miss Wynne about Yorkshire. Be off with you, while your cousin and I have a comfortable coze." Hannah, who in point of fact did *not* have so much hair, but had appropriated it from a number of sources, looked annoyed. Julie deposited her burdens on an empty chair. She was unusually fashionable tonight,

Ned noted, in a lace gown worn over a chartreuse-colored silk slip.

A startlingly low-cut gown. As Ned watched, she tried to tug up the neckline.

Julie's resemblance to Sabine's miniature was startling. "Miss Wynne, I am yours to command."

She raised her chin and glowered. Ignoring her reluctance, Ned shepherded her toward the tall French doors that opened out onto the terrace. "Young ladies are expected to simper and bat their eyelashes at eligible gentlemen, not grimace as if they've bitten into a sour fruit. Bates thought you had recognized him. I see he was correct."

"What you are eligible for is Bedlam, my lord."

She was flushed and furious. Ned grasped her elbow and propelled her out onto the terrace, down the steps and along one of the lesser-traveled paths. "You and I, buttercup, are going to have a coze of our own."

"I don't wish to talk to you!" snapped Julie. "Not that it signifies. You're a lordship, after all, while I'm merely an ill-mannered baggage who has no notion of my place."

"Ah. Lady Georgiana, I presume."

"You set a spy on me, damn you. How long was he following me about?"

"Long enough. I know you went to Drury Lane. Are you an actress?"

"Are you cockle-brained?" She huffed out a breath. "You needn't bother answering that, my lord."

"I understand that you are angry with me. Were I in your shoes, I would be angry, too." And pretty shoes they were, dainty kid confections tied with ribbons round her neat ankles. "You are very fine tonight, sunshine."

"You needn't throw the hatchet at me. I know how I look." As if she couldn't help herself, Julie fingered the fabric of her gown. "Lady Georgiana had her abigail alter this to fit me. It's the nicest dress I have ever owned."

That, too, was a telling statement, to be saved alongside references to Newgate and St Giles. The dress was far from remarkable.

Save for the neckline, which made a man long to slide his fingers beneath the flimsy lace and silk.

Even as he told himself he shouldn't, Ned brushed his knuckles against Julie's soft cheek. "I'll make you a promise, *canaria*. I'll never tell you something that isn't true."

Her eyes lifted warily to his. "'*Canaria*'?"

"Portuguese for canary." Ned smiled at her expression. "'*Frag*' means frog, if you want to know. And '*feijão verde*' is green bean."

She stood still beneath his hand, yet at the same time seemed poised on the verge of flight. "Lady Georgiana warned me that you might try to trifle with my virtue."

Ned's fingers trailed from her cheek down the smooth column of her throat. "Did she, indeed?"

"I told her I thought I'd know if I was being trifled with. Is that what you're doing, my lord?"

Ned supposed he was. He almost felt ashamed. "I've told you already that I'm yours to command."

She snorted. "You also said you wouldn't lie to me. The truth is that you're nothing of the sort."

Ned wasn't so certain. "Would you like me to be?"

"You can't gull a gammoner, my lord." Julie set her hand against his waistcoat. "It's Rose who is the parson's daughter. My friend at Drury Lane. Why aren't you a soldier anymore?"

Ned wondered if she realized how intimately she was touching him. "Most young ladies would prefer not to know about such things."

"I'm not most young ladies, am I?"

So much was she not most young ladies that Ned experienced an almost unbearable desire to kiss her. "I'm no longer a soldier because I became a bloody earl."

Julie smoothed the lapels of his coat. "Betwixt and between, aren't you? No longer a soldier, and not wishing to be an earl. But you *are* a lordship, whether you wish it or no. Sometimes there's naught one can do but play out the hand that's been dealt."

"Is that what you're doing? Playing out the cards you were dealt?" Her hand rested against his ribs. Ned wondered if his watch was still in place.

Julie studied his cravat. "I'll return your statue. And then we'll be done."

She'd driven him daft, Ned decided; otherwise he wouldn't have been so inept as to remind her of who and what they were. "What did you do with the glove?"

"I can't tell you that."

"Things would be much simpler if you could bring yourself to trust me." Not that Ned had expected she would.

Julie looked up at him, lips parted to speak. Ned succumbed to impulse, cradled her face between his hands and gently brushed his mouth against hers.

The kiss did not stay gentle long. Julie's hands clutched at his shoulders as if to keep her balance. Ned traced the outline of her lips with his tongue. She tasted like temptation, and honey, and lemonade.

She made a funny little noise deep in her throat. Wrapped her arms around his neck. Ned ran his hands over her slender body, her back and waist; drew her more tightly to him, her belly soft against the hardness of his groin.

Had he shocked her? It seemed not. Her hands burrowed in his hair and she kissed him back with considerable enthusiasm and an enchanting lack of skill.

If only— Reason reasserted itself, and along with it came the questions Sabine and Kane had raised. Much as he might want Julie, Ned couldn't stand back while she committed another crime. He recalled the numerous crimes he had committed during his chequered career and amended the thought: he couldn't stand back while she committed a major misdeed. "I don't want to let you go," he murmured, against one delicate earlobe.

Julie gave no indication of wishing to be let go. "No one has ever kissed me before," she whispered. "I wish you'd do it some more."

How could he refuse? Ned swept her up in his arms. "Are you daft?" Julie demanded. Ned thought he surely must be. There was nothing for it but that he must kiss Julie again and again.

The night was overcast, and the gardens only dimly lit. In the intimacy of the shadows, Lady Jersey's ballroom might have been a world away. Ned pulled Julie down with him on a marble bench.

The stone was cold. She was not. In a trice he had her sprawled across his lap and was exploring the confines of her low-cut bodice. One sweet breast fit perfectly in his palm.

Viking forebears or no, Ned could hardly ravish a damsel in the middle of Lady Jersey's garden. He drew back and leaned his forehead against hers, both of them breathing hard.

Julie murmured in disappointment. If Ned didn't have her off his lap he wouldn't be held accountable for what happened next, and so set her on her feet and put her clothing to rights. "There's no room in this gown to conceal anything," he remarked.

She stiffened. "You think I mean to snaffle something tonight."

Ned ran his thumb over her lower lip. "I think you already have." He might have gone on to mention that said snaffled item was his good common sense, but Julie drew back her fist and thumped him with it, hard. Ned yelped and clutched his ear. Julie gathered up her skirts and fled back along the pathway to the house.

Chapter Sixteen

Our advantages fly away without aid. Pluck the flower.
— Ovid

The hour had grown quite late by the time the occupants of Ashcroft House at last retired to their beds, Lady Georgiana to mutter unkind things about Hannah in her sleep, and Tony inexplicably home early from one or another gaming hell.

Julie glanced one last time around her room. Were someone to check her room, they would think that she was sleeping, due to the pillows she had arranged beneath the coverlet on the bed.

Were Lady Georgiana to see her in these breeches and boots and old furze jacket, she would expire of an apoplexy on the spot. Julie stuffed her hair under a boy's cap, opened the window, and slipped out. She crept carefully along the ledge, down the tall oak tree, through the garden, past the stable-block, and out into the dark streets.

Ned did not return to Lady Jersey's ballroom. Julie had spent the rest of the evening alternately scolding herself for her ill-temper and expecting that he would denounce her for boxing his ear. Lady Georgiana had been curious about their conversation and skeptical of Julie's explanation that Lord Dorset had informed her 'York' derived from the Latin name for the city, *Eboracum*, which in turn derived from the Brythonic *Ebon-acor* meaning 'Place of yew trees'; but she did not scold. On the contrary, so amiable was her ladyship that Julie's suspicions were aroused.

No one was following her tonight. Julie was almost certain. She hadn't forgotten Pritchett's warning that she should watch her back.

Temple Bar archway lay before her, the boundary between the City and Westminster, where the Strand became Fleet Street. A few yards further lay old St. Dunstan's Church, its two giants striking the hours. Fleet Street was home to the London press as well as coffee shops and taverns; a favorite haunt of showmen, popular exhibitions, and freaks. Many Londoners still mourned the recent closing of Mrs. Salmon's Wax Works, most specifically tableaux that depicted shepherds and shepherdesses making violent love.

Salisbury Court then, and finally her destination. Julie gazed up at the old building as she paused to catch her breath. The fanciful structure suited its current owner. No more than Ned did Wakely Court care about taking on the trappings of an earl.

She rounded a corner. The library windows loomed high above her head. Fortunately, the drainpipes were of newer construction than the house itself.

The library window opened easily, as it had before. The room was no less cluttered than on her last visit. Julie didn't see how a person could read so many books in ten lifetimes.

She eased over the sill. An ancient carved chair was pulled up before the fire burning low in the hearth. In the chair sprawled the current earl. He wore boots and breeches and a loose linen shirt. In one hand he held a brandy glass.

He was watching her. "Why are you in my house and dressed like that?"

Julie winched at the chill in his voice. She was the one with a right to temper, wasn't she, so why should his annoyance make her belly churn? "I didn't expect that you'd be awake."

"I was remembering Badajoz." He lowered his gaze to his glass. "There was a complete breakdown of discipline when the town finally fell. Drinking, raping, looting. Several officers were injured trying to restrain their men. Before it was over, a number of soldiers had been hanged in the town's main square."

Since he didn't seem inclined to toss her out, Julie wandered around the room. Her last trip had not allowed for a leisurely inspection. "I have bad dreams too, sometimes."

Ned glanced at her. "What are your bad dreams about?"

"This and that." Mostly Cap'n Jack. A book lay open on the table at his elbow. Julie craned her neck to see the title.

"John Debrett's *Peerage of England, Scotland and Ireland*. Have you brought back my stolen property?"

Julie pulled the statue out of her jacket and held it out to him. Ned said, "And so, Taweret returns. You're done with me, then."

What she was, was moon-mad. Julie dropped down on the floor in front of his chair and wrapped her arms around her knees. Rose's words echoed in her mind. *'Does he take your fancy, Jules?'*

Ned turned the statue over, inspected the strange hieroglyphic markings on the base. "Do you know what a cipher is, Miss Wynne?"

What Julie knew was that his lordship's shirt was open at the throat, revealing a tantalizing glimpse of sun-bronzed chest. There was a dark edge to him tonight, as if he hovered much closer to the adventurer than the earl. "I had four years to learn my way about your world. Some things got left out."

"Four years?" Ned set the statue on the table beside his book and brandy glass.

"After I was taken out of Newgate. Rose taught me to act the lady then."

"And why did she do that?"

"Neither of us had a choice." Thought of what Cap'n Jack would do if he knew of this conversation sent a shiver along Julie's spine.

"Since you fear being clapped back in Newgate, I assume your friend is also being blackmailed. As well as Niddicock, which would explain your presence in Ashcroft House." Ned leaned forward and pulled off her cap. "I don't expect you'll tell me who your master is. What is it you're to snaffle next?"

He smoothed his fingers through her curls. Julie wished she were Ophelia, so that she might purr. "I don't know who he is, or what. Ask me no more questions, for I have already said more than I should. I'm sorry I hit you so hard."

"It's I who should apologize." Ned put his hand beneath her chin and tipped up her face. "For kissing you."

He'd lit a fire in her was what he'd done, and only he could put it out. Julie was acutely aware that she was alone with him in his library, the rest of the world fast asleep, including his sister and their dog.

Ned would have kissed a lot of ladies. Both Georgiana and Rose had told her so, not that Julie couldn't have figured that out for herself.

No doubt those other women were much more skilled at such things than she. "You didn't enjoy it," she said.

"I meant that it wasn't well done of me." Ned grasped her wrists and drew her closer, until she knelt on her knees between his spread thighs. "As for kissing you, I enjoyed it very much. It occurs to me that I've never kissed someone wearing breeches. I think I must discover what it's like."

He pulled her up to him. Julie went willingly. She smelled the brandy on his breath. Then he drew her closer and his mouth brushed against hers. It felt so lovely that Julie parted her lips and tried to kiss him back. She must have done it halfway right, because he groaned.

Julie rested her hands gingerly on Ned's strong shoulders. His lips stroked down her throat. "You brought me my statue," he murmured. "What shall I give you in return?"

Heaven, Julie thought, and wondered if she dared ask.

In Lady Jersey's garden, he had touched her breast. He'd bent his head and put his mouth against her flesh. "You touched my, um, chest."

"I did."

"I would like to touch yours."

Ned drew back to study her, then set her away from him and stood. Julie watched, bemused, as he crossed the room. The earl had a nice bottom. She could not recall having ever paid attention to a gentleman's bottom before.

He locked the library door. Eyes fixed on hers, Ned pulled his shirt over his head, and let it fall to the floor.

Fine auburn hair dusted his broad chest, snaked down his flat belly to disappear beneath the waistband of his breeches. Julie was put in mind of the statues of ancient Greeks Rose had once taken her to see. But Ned's was a soldier's body: lean, strongly defined with muscle, made imperfect by numerous scars. As he moved to stand in front of her, Julie rose shakily to her feet.

She placed her hands against his chest. The warmth of him swept up her arms and through her body and down to her toes.

Along the left side of his torso ran a jagged blemish. Julie traced it with her fingers. His muscles quivered under her touch. "Badajoz," he said.

He was like some great jungle creature holding still so that she might pet him. Such beasts were dangerous, Julie reminded herself: they clawed and bit and maimed. She shrugged off her jacket, took hold of her own shirt.

"Let me." Ned tugged the garment loose. His hands slid under the rough fabric. She shivered as his fingers brushed her bare skin. He kissed her again as he scooped her up in his arms, sank back down in the chair by the fire with her on his lap.

His hands stroked down the length of her, learning the curve of hip and thigh. He plucked out the knife she carried in her boot and raised an eyebrow.

"A person has to look out for herself."

"You are the least defenseless female I have ever met." Ned set the knife aside and bent his head to her throat. "The last time you were here, you modeled my drapery. I have wanted to see you that way again ever since. Does this feel good to you?" His tongue licked against her neck, across her collarbone, and lower. "And this?"

'Good' was far too bland a word. "I think, my lord, that you may be trifling with me now."

Against her breast, she felt him smile. "You are most astute, Miss Wynne."

His lips closed around her nipple, gently tugged. Sweet sensation swept over Julie. She squirmed around to sit facing him, straddling his lap, her most intimate parts pressed against his. "You must allow me to do some trifling of my own. It's only fair."

"Well, then." Ned leaned back in his chair.

He was a feast set out before her. Julie couldn't decide whether to begin at the top, or the bottom, or in between.

At the beginning, then. His eyes closed as she traced the contours of his face, his aristocratic cheekbones and wicked mouth and piratical chin. Further exploration revealed that Ned's flat male nipples were as sensitive as her own. When she nibbled at his earlobe the bulge in his breeches grew larger, and hard as a stone.

Fascinating, the functioning of the male organ. Julie was impressed. Though she had scant practical experience of such matters, the earl's dimensions seemed to her nothing short of remarkable.

He was hot. Very, very hot. Julie felt prodigious warm herself.

She wriggled. The bulge responded. Ned caught her hips, and held her motionless. "Stop now or I won't be accountable for what happens. I'm not sober, as you may have guessed."

He *was* a gentry cove. Whether he wished to be or no. Sober or cast-away. He rubbed shoulders with emperors and princes, wickedly dark gentlemen and ladies so lovely as to have stepped out of a fairy tale.

While Julie was a criminal, who would someday have her neck stretched. Life was precious to her, and entirely too short. "I don't want to stop. If you take my virtue, I won't mind."

Ned didn't immediately answer. Julie bit her lip, wishing she might take back her words. Had Rose been present to hear such stuff come out of her mouth, she would have brought out a bar of soap.

But Rose wasn't present, and Julie couldn't unsay her rash invitation, could only wait and see what the earl would do. He didn't seem flattered by her offer. Which wasn't surprising. The man would have received countless prettier invitations than hers.

All the same, he might sham some appreciation. Instead he said, "I'd advise you not to try and run a rig on me, my girl." Before he could say more, there came a discreet tap on the door.

Julie scrambled to her feet. Ned pulled on his shirt. "That will be Bates." He crossed the room and released the lock. Julie retrieved her jacket and tugged her clothing back into place.

The bellows-mender stood in the hallway. He had exchanged his costume for nondescript dark attire. "All's quiet at Ashcroft

House, sir. Everyone is safely abed."

Julie cleared her throat. Bates looked around and scowled. "Miss Wynne is ready to go home," said Ned. "You will see her safely there."

Julie picked up her cap and jammed it on her curls. "No need. I know the way." Spine stiff as a poker, she walked past Milord Aggravation and snatched Taweret up off his desk.

He swore and grabbed for her, but missed. Quick as lightning, Julie was out the open window and down the drainpipe and lost in the night.

Chapter Seventeen

What a pleasant stain comes from an enemy's blood.
— Pubilius Syrus

London showed its true nature after dark, when the fog was thick, and the lamplight dim. The worst house burglaries took place then, the most violent crimes, as the denizens of the underworld ventured in search of prey. Resurrection men sought out corpses for resale to surgeons. Whores whispered obscene invitations from darkened doorways. Reckless young lordlings wagered entire fortunes in establishments where wiser men never set foot, thereby leaving themselves open to assault and theft and blackmail. It was Cap'n Jack's favorite time of day.

His coach rattled slowly through the gloom, past a ramshackle collection of stalls and sheds where a fruit and vegetable and flower market squatted smack in the middle of the square. Public houses stayed open late near Covent Garden due to the market, the public theaters, the coachmen's watering-houses located nearby. Women could be found any way one fancied here: dressed or no, tight-laced or loose, painted or fresh-faced. Bound up. Done up. Raw. An annual list of prostitutes was hawked under the Piazza, stating details of age and appearance, the specialties for which each harlot was remarkable, along with places of residence.

The hackney rolled to a stop. Cap'n Jack paid off the driver and sent him away.

Inigo Jones's Piazza had arcaded houses to the north and east. To the west was the church of St Paul. A soldier had once been hanged in the market for running from his colours, and the poet Dryden assaulted as result of some unwise verse. Today a man could scarce walk down the street at midday without risking his handkerchief, pocket book or watch.

A hand tugged at the Cap'n's sleeve. The hand was attached to a street doxy with soiled fingers and dirty hair. A virgin might have ten guineas for parting with her maidenhead, several times over. What was lost could be surgically restored.

This one's maidenhead would be long past replacing. She was no longer young. Cap'n Jack raised his walking stick, brought it down hard on her grasping fingers. The doxy whimpered and melted back into the night.

A large wooden sign hung outside the tavern, on it a faded painting of the three pigeons after which the place was named. Beyond the narrow doorway lay a long covered passage that opened into a well-lighted quadrangle, around which stood the tavern rooms. The Three Pigeons was popular with actors and managers from the nearby theaters. It was the resort of men of fashion and loose character, and women of no character at all; the scene of midnight orgies and drunken brawls where murders and assaults frequently occurred.

Cap'n Jack followed rowdy voices and laughter deeper into the house. The taproom was long and low-ceilinged, the air thick with tobacco smoke. Small lamps glowed in the corners. Sawdust was strewn on the floor. The Cap'n paused to let his eyes adjust to the shadows, ordered an egg-hot, then continued on his way.

The next chamber was in an uproar. Spectators mounted upon chairs, tables and benches were cheering on two half-naked wenches engaged in a shrieking, scratching, hair-pulling wrestling match on the floor. In the third room a posture woman was going through her paces, which involved a paucity of clothing, a massive silver platter, and an ingenious use of vegetables and fruit, Covent Garden market being just outside the door. Pritchett stood apart from the business, looking as if he wished he might arrest everybody present on charges of obscenity.

The Cap'n strolled toward him. "And?" he said.

"The woman is upstairs, as you ordered. As of a half hour ago."

She would be growing more desperate by the moment, which

served the Cap'n's purpose. "You disapprove?"

Pritchett eyed the Cap'n's walking stick. "'Tis not my place."

"See that you remember it. Have you discovered why it took so long for me to receive the glove?"

"Jules said she couldn't get away sooner."

"Jules gets away as often as she pleases." The Cap'n gazed at the naked posture woman, who now lay flat on her back, knees drawn up under her chin, hands clasped under her thighs, much like a trussed chicken save for the lighted candle inserted in a place not intended by nature for such. "She might prove more biddable after passing some time here."

The Runner looked at the posture woman, and quickly away. Satisfied that he'd made his point, the Cap'n added: "I assume you are unaware that she went to Wakely Court tonight."

Pritchett's startlement was plain to read. The Cap'n raised his walking stick and tapped the Runner's shoulder with its ornate silver head. "Never think you are my sole source of information. Or that you cannot be replaced. Since Jules is so fond of Wakely Court, she may fetch me a small notebook containing a handwritten copy of a most unusual text: *Cryptographia, or the Art of Decyphering* by David Arnold Conradus."

Jules had gone again to Wakely Court? Rose suspected that she fancied the earl. Deeper and deeper into the quagmire they sank, and if there was to be a rescue, Pritchett didn't know by whom. He applied his handkerchief to his spectacles, and hoped his thoughts didn't show on his face. "Do we have any notion where the notebook might be?"

"No, but 'we' will find it, or I will know why not." Cap'n Jack went on in considerable detail about what would happen if 'we' failed. Parliamentary Select Committees were mentioned, as well as the tendency of police officers to be influenced by monetary considerations, for example allowing certain criminals to get away with minor crimes for which the rewards were slight until they went on to commit major crimes for which considerable blood money would be paid. Pritchett intensely disliked the conversation, for he was guilty of all this and more, and not solely on Captain Jack's behalf.

After scolding Pritchett as if he were an unsatisfactory servant on the verge of being turned off without a reference, the Cap'n offered him the freedom of the house. The Runner refused.

Ciphers, mused Cap'n Jack, as he left the room, for he had made inquiries and thereby discovered that the current Lord Dorset had survived considerable time spying behind enemy lines during his service in the Peninsula. In addition to possessing the devil's own luck, Ned Fairchild had a talent for investments. He'd no need of the Dorset properties, or his prize money, or the occasional bank draft from the War Office. Thanks to their grandmother, his sister was wealthy in her own right.

A plump whore hovered at the top of the stairway. On sight of Cap'n Jack, or Cap'n Jack in his current incarnation, because the face he presented here was not the face he showed the greater world, she stared at the carpet. "I've been keeping an eye out, like you said."

The wench was terrified, and trying not to show it. Cap'n Jack had bought her from her brother, who ran a low tavern; had taken her maidenhead himself. She'd not forgot it yet.

He caught her by the throat and squeezed; admired how the red prints of his fingers stood out against her fair skin like bright paint on a canvas. "The woman is in your room?"

"Just like you said."

"No one has seen or spoken to her?"

She tried to shake her head. "There's not been so much as a peep out of her. I think she's afraid."

Only a fool would not be frightened. Cap'n Jack released the whore's throat and caught her arm instead. "You weren't to talk to her."

"I didn't! I swear I didn't!" she wailed.

Cap'n Jack twisted her arm behind her back. "Talk to anyone about her and you won't talk to anyone again. Do you understand?"

The girl nodded, mutely. Cap'n Jack let her go. She scurried down the hall. He unlocked the door and entered her room; locked the door again behind him and pocketed the key.

The walls were thick, as was the carpet that muffled the floor.

The window was doubly secured, first with shutters and then with heavy drapes. A looking glass was positioned so that those who were so inclined could observe what they did.

At the window waited a cloaked woman. "Greetings, Madame Morel. Ah, but under the circumstances we need not be so formal. I shall call you Amélie."

She parted her lips, but said nothing, as if finding herself in such surroundings had temporarily deprived her of speech. Cap'n Jack didn't know the woman personally, but he knew her kind.

He moved closer. She shrank back. In her mid-twenties, he estimated; black hair and dark eyes, very *ravissante*, very French.

From his coat pocket, he drew out the stained glove. "You've nothing to say? Then I shall continue. You're misplaced something, I believe."

Her eyes fixed on it. "*Nom de Dieu,*" she breathed.

"*Le bon Dieu* will not assist you." The Cap'n stopped in front of her, so close she could have reached out and caressed him had she wished to, which she clearly did not. "You were foolish to retain such a memento, *n'est ce pas?* Because now it has come into my possession, and I may decide whether the world finds out that you have been indiscreet. Do you understand? You are in my power, *mignonne.* I may do with you as I will."

He spoke no more than the truth. He could keep her locked up in this place indefinitely. Could make her into the centerpiece of a tableau like the one downstairs. Would do so in an instant, if she did not obey.

She would obey. This one had no spirit. She was quivering like a frightened rabbit, and he hadn't touched her yet.

Her terrified eyes fixed on his face, as if seeking to find some shred of humanity there. "Who are you?" she whispered.

Unfortunately for Mme Morel, he had no humanity left in him. "You may call me *Mon Capitaine.*"

Chapter Eighteen

Woman is always a slippery, changeable thing.
— Virgil

Ned sprawled on the sofa in the library, a cool cloth laid upon his brow. The sofa was uncomfortable, but it was unlikely he would be comfortable anywhere, having sought solace for the debacle of the previous evening in his brandy decanter, and as a result suffering an extremely sore head.

He was additionally suffering the company of his closest friend. "She returned the statue?" Kane inquired.

"She did."

"I hesitate to ask, but in that case why don't I see it now?"

"Because she stole it back again." Ned wadded up the cloth and tossed it on the floor.

"And why did she do that?"

"I insulted her."

"Ah."

Ned gazed at the old ceiling, with its massive beams and plastered lath, and debated which among the things Julie had told him that he cared to share. "At which point she snatched the statue and went out through the window. She has an aversion to doors."

"You are leaving out a great deal, I think."

So Ned was, such as the sickness he'd felt in his belly when he thought Julie had meant to be done with him. And then she'd sat down on the floor in front of him, and looked at him with those amazing blue eyes, and he would have given her the statue and everything else in the house if only she would stay.

She *had* stayed. Ned could have had her in this very library if only he hadn't opened his stupid mouth. Instead, he'd driven her away. He might have shot himself if it didn't involve the effort of getting up off the couch.

He'd been the first to kiss her, to caress her as he had. He meant to be the first to do far more. Providing she stopped abusing his person long enough to permit matters to proceed.

Not that he could blame her. She offered him her virtue and he insulted her. Ned wondered when he'd become such a clod.

"I dislike pointing out the obvious," said Kane, when the silence had stretched out so long it became clear Ned wasn't going to tender further confidences, "but she is a thief."

Ned wished Kane would stop dwelling on that detail. "So am I," he said. "For that matter, so are you. We're forgiven because our crimes benefit our country. Hers are committed in order to survive."

Kane inspected the astrolabe that Clea had recently retrieved from the attic, an elaborate instrument bearing a star map, and a zodiacal circle, and other devices useful in measuring the positions and movements of heavenly bodies. "I see."

Ned doubted that Kane did. When Julie climbed out the window Ned had wanted nothing more than to go after her. To storm into Ashcroft House and demand the return of what was rightfully his. He would have done exactly that, if other matters hadn't been at stake.

No female before had affected him like this, not even Bianca, whose face he could scarce recall. Ned wouldn't forget Julie's face, even if he never saw it again. He'd never forget the feel of her beneath his hands, the taste of her mouth.

Bates was watching Ashcroft House. Should Julie flee, Ned would follow and fetch her back. "She knows she can't pawn the statue. When she's done being angry, she'll return the blasted thing."

Maybe she would, but for what purpose? Kane touched a finger to the movable pointer in the middle of the astrolabe. "Alexander is fascinated with Sabine."

"Most men are."

Kane shot the earl a glance. Ned's features revealed nothing, and his eyes were closed. "Do you trust her?"

Ned half-opened one eyelid. "Sabine? Of course. You sound like you do not."

"I'm suspicious of her timing. Why return now, after so many years away?"

"Perhaps she has an interest in seeing the peace negotiations play out."

"If they ever do," Kane muttered. The Czar was less interested in redrawing the map of Europe than in annoying the Regent, whom he dismissed as 'a poor sort of prince', and impressing the ladies with his mastery of the waltz. "She's keeping secrets, all the same."

"Of course she's keeping secrets," Ned retorted. "So are you. Must I point it out again?"

"That's a different matter." Kane began to pace. "I dislike this resemblance between Sabine's miniature and your Miss Wynne. As well as the similarity of names. One might inquire of Carlyle, I suppose, but the old man seldom comes to town. He has been ill for years."

'His' Miss Wynne? Julie didn't belong to Ned. Although she surely would have if not for the interruption provided by Bates. Had Ned not been drinking, would matters have gone so far? He liked to think he might have had more sense.

Julie hadn't a shy bone in her body. If he didn't stop thinking of her, he'd not have a soft bone in his. Ned wondered how long it would take Julie to forgive him this time. How absurdly tempting she had been in her cap and breeches. He wanted to dress her in fabrics and colors that suited her vivid personality. After which he wanted to undress her again.

What had they been talking about? Ah, Sabine's miniature. "The resemblance may be a coincidence. Hardly an unusual combination, blonde hair and blue eyes."

Kane shrugged off the suggestion. In his line of work, only a fool believed in coincidence. "You know nothing about this girl."

Ned knew she was curious. How far did Julie's curiosity go? If it *was* curiosity, and not part of some elaborate plot. Kane saw connections everywhere. Frequently Kane was correct.

But not in this case. Not unless Julie's inexpert kisses and innocently erotic explorations had misled Ned in a manner that the most skillful female agent had not been able to achieve. He watched Kane take another turn around the room. "The Grand Duchess was involved in a plot to assassinate her brother, was she not?"

Kane gestured impatiently. "Catherine knew nothing of the conspiracy to depose the Czar and put her on the throne."

"Yet it appeared at the time that she might have. The point being that things aren't necessarily what they seem."

Silence descended on the library, while Kane considered Campbell's latest report that Napoleon was planting mulberry and olive and chestnut trees on Elba, establishing a body of refuse collectors to clean the streets of Portoferraio as well as setting up a market for bottled mineral water from a spring at Poggio, and at the same time inspecting the salt ponds and water supply and recording the amount of lettuce and grapes eaten in his own household; and Ned nursed his sore head.

Ned was made dizzy by Kane's incessant pacing. "The name of this particular game," he offered, as an olive branch, "appears to be blackmail. Niddicock is being blackmailed. One hesitates to guess why."

Kane swung round. "Blackmail?"

"Julie has an actress friend named Rose, at Drury Lane. Rose taught Julie to act the lady—or tried to do so. She has been in Newgate. Julie, that is, not Rose. So far as I know. Who is behind these things, she can't be brought to say."

"If someone else *is* behind it." Kane moved closer to the sofa. "Which brings us back to the recent spate of thefts."

"I realize you're required to be of a suspicious nature, but it grows annoying after a time." Ned met Kane's gaze, and held it. "Lady Georgiana warned Julie that I might make an attempt on her virtue. She brought back the statue all the same."

It wasn't enough that Kane couldn't turn around without tripping over one or another of the Eminent Annoyances and must attempt to prevent diplomatic negotiations—such as they were—from further breaking down. Now he must also try to circumvent catastrophe on this additional front. "I'm not sure you should tell me more," he said.

Ned wasn't sure either, but he continued nonetheless. "I kissed her. Julie, that is, not Lady Georgiana. I'll swear she hadn't been kissed before. Then I said there was no room in her gown to hide anything, and she thought I thought she was bent on larceny, and boxed my ear."

"You have an interesting investigative technique."

"When Julie brought the statue back, she was clad in breeches. I kissed her again. Matters progressed."

Clearly, matters had. "Plundering, were you?" said Kane.

"She had a knife in her boot."

"Did she threaten to use it on you?"

"I'd like to think we live in a world where men don't prey on those with lesser strength, but we both know that isn't true." Ned dared try sitting up. The room rocked in a nauseating manner. "She's in over her head, Kane."

"I'll agree that someone is."

"If anyone were to harm Julie in any manner," Ned said flatly, "I'd flay off the bastard's hide and make a mat of it to place in front of my hearth. Appalling to find oneself so primitive, but there it is."

So it was. "You want to rescue her."

The door swung open. Clea sailed into the library. "Naturally he wants to rescue her. Ned can't resist a damsel in distress." She was dressed for the out-of-doors. In one hand she held a roll of papers. Cerberus was tucked under her other arm.

The dog spied Kane, and snarled. Clea tsk'd and tapped his nose. Cerberus snapped at the rolled-up papers. Clea deposited the dog in the hallway and closed the door. "I am to have no more singing lessons. Even Hannah has come to realize it's not a good idea. I have decided I will study the pianoforte." She flexed her fingers. "Have you seen my astrolabe?"

"You were eavesdropping," said Kane.

Clea pulled off her bonnet. "No one tells me anything, so what do you expect?"

Had his head been less painful, Ned might have been sympathetic. As it was, he felt annoyed. "I expect that you will conduct yourself like the young lady you say you aspire to be. Which does not involve listening at keyholes."

Clea folded her arms beneath her bosom. "I am not a child."

Kane looked bored. "Stop acting like one, then."

Clea's lower lip trembled. For an instant she seemed very much the child she claimed she no longer was. "How long were you listening, puss?" Ned asked.

"Long enough." Clea walked to the desk. "I heard you talking about our thief. Miss Julie Wynne from York."

Both men stared at her. Clea shrugged. "I recognized her straightaway, but you seemed to want her identity kept secret, so I didn't say anything. I would like to speak further with her. She was interesting."

Ned sat up straighter, despite his spinning head. "Until we decide what she's up to, you'll do no such thing."

Clea glared at him. "You're treating me like a child again."

"You *are* a child." Kane was stern. "Keep your distance from Miss Wynne."

"I see how it is. I'm to stay home and practice my manners while you have all the fun." Clea stalked across the library and threw open the door.

Cerberus had been waiting in the hallway. He raced into the room, slavering, all his numerous teeth on ferocious display. Kane snatched up the fireplace poker. Ned fell back on the couch.

Clea closed the door on them. In the ensuing mayhem, neither paused to realize she'd not given them her word.

Chapter Nineteen

Woman outshine men in scheming.
— Pubilius Syrus

It was a lovely afternoon for shopping, if one enjoyed that sort of outing, which Julie did not, although she liked looking at the pretty windows well enough. Milliners and stationers, silversmiths and booksellers, wine merchants and pastry-cooks—Lady Georgiana must inspect them all, with Julie and the sturdy footman trailing along behind. The footman wore Ashcroft livery; Julie, a high-waisted muslin gown and flower-trimmed straw bonnet. Lady Georgiana was decked out in aubergine, topped by a hat *à la* Uhlan, the crown in the form of a lozenge and the front pointed like a helmet, striped with broad swaths of aubergine and rose, with flat feathers to match.

They bypassed the barber's pole, and the pawnbroker's three glass balls. Lady Georgiana spent an exhausting interval inside a shop that had a yellow-fringed crimson umbrella hung over the door, and emerged with a pretty lace parasol. Her enthusiasm for shopping no whit diminished, she then directed her footsteps, as well as those of her less enthusiastic companions, to a Ladies Bazaar for the Sale of Miscellaneous Articles. Julie was grateful that the bazaar was indoors. Her shoes had not been made for prolonged tramping over cobblestones. She gazed about with interest, having never visited this particular bazaar before.

It was a sort of street under cover, a large long room with a row of shops on either hand, and a thoroughfare between. At the far end, a splendidly costumed man stood talking softly to an irritable macaw perched on a wooden pole. According to Lady Georgiana, the man and the macaw belonged to the menagerie located above stairs alongside a picture gallery.

The menagerie would not be so fine, Julie thought loyally, as the Exeter 'Change. From force of habit, she considered how a clever thief might filch merchandise from the stalls. Shopkeepers in general didn't protect their goods properly, put them on open display near open doors. Many were the times she'd snuck in on hands and knees and slid merchandise from counters without the shopkeeper being any the wiser until after she made her escape. Small items were good for stealing, such as handkerchiefs. Her fingers itched.

Lady Georgiana concluded her purchase of purl-edged ribbon and handed the package to her stoic footman. "You are very quiet, miss. How is it again that you know my son?"

"From Yorkshire, my lady," Julie said.

"Yorkshire," repeated Lady Georgiana. "I cannot think when Tony might have been there."

"I didn't mean the viscount was in Yorkshire," Julie countered quickly. "Did you know that the churches in York are mostly from the medieval period? At the city's center stands York Minster, the largest Gothic cathedral in Northern Europe."

Lady Georgiana knew that she wasn't going to be out-jockeyed by a dab of a girl. "I daresay there is a great deal of glass."

Julie blinked at her. "Glass?"

"Stained glass, you little goose. York as a whole and particularly the Minster have a long tradition of creating beautiful stained glass. Some dates back to the twelfth century. As you should well know."

What had Rose told her? Julie tried to recall. "Oh! I mistook your meaning. The Great East Window is the largest example of medieval stained glass in the world. It stands seventy-six feet tall."

A clever recover, allowed Georgiana. But of course the chit was clever or they wouldn't be in this fix. "And the stone is such a lovely weathered gray. How many altars are there, do you think?"

Julie thought that if Lady Georgiana grew wise to her, Cap'n Jack would not be pleased. "I've never counted them."

"There are thirty altars. The stone is not gray but creamy white, limestone quarried in nearby Tadcastle. How *do* you know Tony? I'll have the truth, if you please."

If Julie pleased? In a pig's eye. "Like I said, my lady, I don't know the viscount. Or I didn't before. We have mutual acquaintances. And as for the stone, it depends on the light."

Another nice save, conceded Georgiana. It might even be true.

The baggage had caught Tony's eye when he wasn't looking. Perhaps, with the proper encouragement, some other gentleman might be persuaded to take her off their hands. "You have been going out in society a great deal. My cast-offs look well enough on you, but I believe we might have a new gown or two made up. Or even more, if you play your cards well."

Warily, Julie inquired, "How might I do that?"

"Don't play the innocent with me!" snapped Georgiana. "You may leave, that's how."

The chit gaped at her as if she'd grown a second head. "I can't do that."

"Think about it," said Georgiana, though it went against the grain to try and buy the creature off. "Tony will stand the reckoning. Or rather, *I* will. The dear boy hasn't a powerful understanding of financial matters. One doesn't wish to admit one's own child is a sad shatterbrain, but there it is." If Miss Julie Wynne from York anticipated she might plunge greedy fingers into the family coffers, that would surely put her off.

Georgiana had misjudged her opponent; her words had the opposite effect. Tony may have been on the wrong side of the hedge when brains were given out, admitted Julie, and perhaps he was the most luckless gamester in all the town; but he didn't deserve to be bullied by both his mamma and Cap'n Jack. "He is not so bad as all that," she protested.

Not? Tony was a perfect block. Who, Georgiana recollected, had said this little sneaksby was a good sort of girl. If Julie dared defy her to take up the cudgels on Tony's behalf, things had progressed further than she had realized.

What was needed here was a plumper goose to pluck. Considering where she might best find one, Georgiana grasped Julie's arm with one hand and her parasol with the other and set out through the busy streets.

Julie glanced over her shoulder. There was Bates, paused by a barrow to buy a penny pie. Today he was pretending to be a porter. What would he do next? Hawk doormats, or display rabbits on a pole?

Bates looked up, caught her watching him. Julie winked. Lady Georgiana tugged her arm. "What are you gawking at, girl?"

Julie turned hastily away. "Nothing, my lady."

"If you call me 'my lady' once more this morning," Georgiana snapped, "I shall wrap this parasol around your neck."

Her ladyship was in another of her snits. Julie hoped the porter's shoes were more comfortable than her own. Bates had been trailing after them since they left Ashcroft House.

Ned wanted his statue. He would *not* want to speak to her again. Julie could hardly blame him. She'd hit him over the head, kicked him, boxed his ear.

She hadn't bit him. At least, not *very* hard.

And in the midst of all that madness, he'd taken her knife from her, and she hadn't thought to snatch it back. Pritchett had given her that blade, on the occasion of her graduating from boy's breeches to a proper dress. He'd said a runt like her should have some way to defend herself other than her mouth. The knife had come in useful more than once. It wasn't likely Lady Georgiana would look the other way while Julie ducked into a shop and filched another to take its place.

Ahead lay Lady Georgiana's next stated destination, a linen-draper's shop of such exalted nature that in the normal way of things Julie would never have dared poke her larcenous nose through the front door. Yet here she stood on the threshold. Life was prodigious strange.

In the fine high windows of the shop, a cunning device displayed fabrics so that they hung down like the folds of women's dresses. Inside were two large rooms fitted up from floor to ceiling with shelves and oak counters and merchandise displays. Georgiana was surrounded by shop assistants the instant she appeared.

A discussion of fabrics was soon underway—India muslin, an-glo-merino, gros de Naples; percale and jaconet and silk. Colors were considered next. Jonquil was inappropriate for a young lady with Miss Wynne's coloring, and daffodil as well. Pomona green might serve as a trimming, and coquelicot, but both were much too bold for someone so young—No? Lady Georgiana must know best. Miss Wynne would have one gown made up in the color of field poppies, and another in apple green.

Miss Wynne was overwhelmed by the idea of buying a gown new-made instead of from a used clothing dealer. She watched as Lady Georgiana held a bolt of fabric to the light and inspected it for flaws. Would Ned think her pretty when he saw her in dresses that had been made for her, and not cut down from someone else? Julie couldn't stop thinking about their last meeting. Each time she tried to send her thoughts in a different direction, they swung around and crept right back.

Rose had told her how matters progressed between a man and a maid. What Rose had neglected to mention was how pleasant that progression felt. Julie wanted to be trifled with some more. She wanted to trifle with Ned.

Alas, the feeling wasn't mutual. She'd tried to toss her bonnet over the windmill, only to have it handed politely back to her, and sent on home.

Now she was ordered to break into Wakely Court and steal a book. She might as well take up residence there.

"Perdition," muttered Lady Georgiana, under her breath, and Julie returned to her surroundings with a thump. Sailing toward them like the skeleton of a once-proud schooner was Lady Dorset. On her head was perched a large-brimmed straw bonnet trimmed with ribbons and a veil.

The ladies settled in to gossip. Georgiana fired the opening salvo, for she had intimate knowledge of a recent barge trip un-dertaken by the Royal Sovereigns down the river to Woolwich. The Czar, she explained, had been most interested in the rocket displays. His sister, always curious about the wonders of science, had enjoyed the explosions more than the music that accompanied them wherever they went. The following day they traveled to Oxford, where the Duchess offended everyone by having the organ stopped the moment it was struck up.

"Pish tush!" interrupted Hannah. "That is all old news. Sabine Viccars was one of the party. Alexander paid her very particular attentions. Even the Grand Duchess favors her, and Catherine is hard to please. What of it? Some of us have more important fish to fry."

Hannah had lost interest in the Distinguished Visitors? Lady Georgiana ventured, "You are in high spirits today."

"And so I should be." Hannah settled her bony hindquarters on a chair. "I have found Dorset his bride."

Lady Georgiana raised her eyebrows. "I didn't realize he was in the market for a bride."

"He'll have one, want her or no," retorted Hannah. "It is Ned's duty to the title, and so I have told him more than once. Since chits straight out of the schoolroom don't suit him, I have settled on Madalyn Tate. She is seven-and-twenty, widowed, and has already produced a set of twins. Moreover, she and Ned are acquainted, and rub on well enough."

Georgiana could find nothing with which to quibble in this way of thinking. "It would be an unexceptionable match."

"The gel has good bloodlines," continued Hannah. "She is connected to both a duke and a marquess. She is intelligent but not too intelligent, pretty but not too pretty, and her conduct leaves naught to be desired. Since she has been married, she'll know what to expect, and won't be hanging on Ned's lips or enacting romantical high flights."

Lady Georgiana glanced at Julie, who had developed a sudden interest in the seam of her glove. "What has Dorset to say to this?"

"It doesn't matter what he says. He will marry her."

Rose had explained the callous nature of matrimony among the upper classes, who were more inclined to wed for fortune or property or social position than for love. Julie thought, poor Ned. The shopkeeper with his wife might well be happier, not withstanding having less to eat.

On the other hand, the earl had been making sheep's eyes at another woman while Julie was sitting on his lap.

"I'll be glad to have the business settled, my position being most unlike your own, dear Georgiana." Hannah bared her teeth. "Once your Tony marries, you will be pensioned off. No bride wants her mama-in-law living under the same roof."

Tony wouldn't be taking a bride in the near future, resolved Georgiana. "You are so confident that Dorset will fall in with your plans?"

"Dorset will do as I tell him." Hannah fluttered her fingers at an approaching acquaintance, and rose. "Should he prove difficult, he will discover that I have more than one string to my bow."

Georgiana watched Lady Dorset greet the newcomer. The two women huddled together like washerwomen gossiping over a fence. "By the time Hannah informs all her acquaintance of her plans for Dorset, she might as well have placed an announcement in the press. You like him, I think."

Color rose in Julie's cheeks. "We talk about Yorkshire."

"Ah, yes. How could I have forgotten Yorkshire?" In Georgiana's experience, which was not inconsiderable despite her enfeebled state of health, rascally earls where not prone to do as they were told; were, indeed, much more like to do the opposite, which might march well with her plans. Did Julie disgrace herself with Dorset, Tony would not only be freed of his infatuation but Hannah's nose would also be put out of joint. "I believe you shall have an evening gown. Silk would be appropriate, with an interesting décolletage. You aren't ample in that area, but a good modiste can compensate."

Ned hadn't found her bosom lacking, Julie thought resentfully. Unless he'd been being polite?

She wouldn't be able to look him in the face again after what she'd done. What she'd let him do. What she'd *invited* him to do. She'd made a cake of herself and now Ned was to marry someone named Madalyn and Julie wished to howl.

Hannah hurried back toward them, crimson with excitement. "The French ambassador's wife has hanged herself. Is it not the most shocking thing?"

Chapter Twenty

Tears are sometimes as weighty as words.
— Ovid

News of Amélie Morel's suicide raced through London, speculation nipping close on its heels, for there was nothing the *ton* liked better than tearing to shreds one of its number who'd been careless enough to get caught out doing something he or she should not. What Mme Morel had done to warrant a resolution so extreme as hanging had not yet been ascertained, but rumor had her embarked upon everything from engaging in liaisons with inappropriate paramours to selling secrets of state, for her husband was after all a diplomat. M'sieur Morel was so devastated by this furor—or so gossip had it—that he was closing up his house and packing up his mistress and setting sail for France.

Wakely Court was quiet tonight. Clea had been appropriated by Hannah for the evening. Cerberus sprawled on the hearth gnawing a bone. Ned stood at the library window, looking out into the darkness, thinking that if he hadn't given that stained glove to Julie, the French ambassador's wife might still be alive.

Came a tap at the door. "Come," called Ned. He didn't turn around.

Tidcombe managed to convey disapproval through the mere clearing of his throat. "A young person to see you, my lord. She won't give her name."

Not Kane, then, which was a relief. Ned wasn't eager to hear what his friend had to say about this latest development. "Send her in." He had little doubt of the young person's identity. Unusual of her to enter by way of the door.

"Yes, my lord," Tidcombe withdrew.

Cerberus sprang to attention, lips curled back in a snarl. "Shut up," snapped Ned. "Or I shall give you to the cat's meat man."

"Would you?" said Julie, as she stepped into the room.

"No, because Clea would dislike it. She's unaccountably tolerant of the beast." Ned picked up the mangled bone and tossed it out into the hall. Cerberus raced after it. Ned closed the door. Under her dark cloak, Julie wore a pretty, if outdated, printed muslin dress. Her face was pale and drawn.

Ned had seen that expression before, on the battlefield. He opened his arms. She flung herself against his chest and burrowed into him.

Her grief was silent, and all the more poignant for it. She wept as if she'd never wept before. Quite possibly she had not. Before lowering one's defenses sufficiently to indulge in a good cry, one needed to first feel safe. Ned held her close and whispered soothing nonsense. The hood of her cloak had fallen back and her curls tickled his chin.

He dropped a kiss on the top of her head. She jerked back. "Why did you do that?"

With his thumb, he brushed tears from her cheek. "I was comforting you," he said.

She stepped out of his embrace. "That poor woman's dead, and it's my fault."

To some extent, Ned agreed. They were both to blame. "Someone wanted that glove badly. But you are hardly responsible for its significance to Amélie Morel."

Julie shook her head. "I'm the one who took it away."

So she had, and the memory would haunt her. Ned said, "If you hadn't taken it, what would have been your punishment?"

Julie bit her lip. He added, "If someone strikes you again, you must tell me, and I'll cut out his heart. Who is behind all this, Jules?"

She stared. "What did you call me?"

"Jules is an obvious nickname. Why do you look at me like that?"

"Rose calls me Jules, and— My friends."

"Am I not one of your friends?"

"You," Julie retorted, with a trace of her usual spirit, "are a bloody earl, and you're going to marry a girl named Madalyn, so you shouldn't be playing your games with me, even if I asked you to, which I know I shouldn't have, so we will forget all that if you please."

She'd managed to startle him. "I'm going to *what?*"

"Your cousin told Lady Georgiana that you're going to marry Madalyn Tate. Who is of good birth, widowed, and already has a set of twins so it's a fair bet you can get an heir on her." Julie gave the old globe a ferocious spin. "Lady Georgiana says that the way your cousin is spreading that news around the town, you won't have much choice but to do as she wants."

Ned wouldn't strangle Hannah, but only for Clea's sake. "In spite of what my cousin might intend, I'm not going to marry Madalyn Tate."

"Unless Lady Dorset manages to trick you. She seemed to think she might."

Hannah could try. She'd have no more success than Joham Sandoval. "Would you mind?"

"If you married?" Julie shrugged. "Why should I?"

"You might have reason to think that I'm partial to you, since we kissed and all."

"I expect you've kissed a lot of girls, my lord." She picked up Clea's astrolabe. "You've said yourself that you're an eligible gentleman."

"My cousin seems to think so. However, I frighten most of her candidates witless, which doesn't bode well for a felicitous married life. I almost did marry once. Her name was Bianca. We met while I was living in Lisbon."

"What happened?"

Any number of things, including his discovery that the lovely Bianca couldn't be trusted out of his sight. "Her family could not approve."

Julie frowned. "How can that be?"

"I wasn't an earl then," Ned said wryly. "Nor had any notion that I someday might be."

"Then won't her nose be out of joint when she learns you are."

Ned imagined Bianca had heard the news by now. He found himself grateful for the distance between England and Portugal. Julie moved from the astrolabe to the perpetual calendar. "*Are* you partial to me?" she said.

Ned realized she was nervous. "What do you think?"

Julie abandoned the astrolabe for the counting board. "You did kiss me, my lord."

"So I did." And he'd do it again in an instant, if she would stop flittering about. "Do you mind?"

"Didn't act like I minded, did I?" The pewter inkwell next engaged her attention. "I told Lady Georgiana I didn't feel well and wanted to stay home tonight. She wasn't pleased." Julie turned back to him, and took in a great breath. "I'm supposed to steal a book."

"What book is that?"

She pulled a piece of paper from her pocket. "Crypto-something. I wrote it down."

And wasn't this interesting? Ned retrieved the notebook from a shelf; carried it to the chair drawn up before the fireplace.

Julie peered over his shoulder. "Is that it? It doesn't look like much."

He flipped through the pages. "The origins of the *Cryptographia* are obscure. It is generally held to have been written by a monk. Men of the cloth were pre-eminent among the servants who secretly made codes and deciphered them for the princes and great captains of Europe during the seventeenth and eighteenth centuries."

"Why would anyone want something like this?"

"The author explains the peculiarities of the main European languages utilized in ciphers. The most common codes used in passing secret messages can be broken by anyone in possession of this notebook, a detailed knowledge of French, and a minimally functioning brain."

"Oh." Julie remained doubtful. "I didn't bring your statue back. But it's hidden away safe."

Ned could have cared less about the blasted statue. He was concerned about Julie being sent for the notebook. There was nothing in it of particular importance—unlike the copy in Kane's possession, which had some interesting notations added—but Kane would never be convinced of Julie's innocence if he learned of her current errand.

Was Ned a fool to believe her innocent? A wise man would surely keep his distance until he determined just who and what she was. But then Julie caught her plump bottom lip between her teeth and desire shot straight to his groin and there was nothing for it but that he must bite that pretty lip himself.

Ned tugged on Julie's arm. She squeaked and clutched at his shoulders and ended up sprawled in his lap.

He smoothed one hand over her bright curls. Julie clutched his wrist. "I thought maybe you trifled with me because you are a gentleman and you knew that was what I wanted you to do."

She thought he didn't desire her? He should leave it at that, and move her off his lap, and take himself safely to the far side of the room. Instead, Ned caught her hand, and kissed it. "What made you take such a cork-brained notion?" he inquired.

"I can't remember," she whispered. "I'm not able to think clearly around you. You make me crave things I can't have."

He drew her closer to him, saluted her earlobe, nibbled his way along the sweet line of her jaw. "Such as?"

"An ordinary life." Julie slid her arm around his shoulder. "I'd never thought of such a thing before you."

Her throat was smoother than the finest satin. Ned pushed aside her cloak. "What *is* an ordinary life?"

"Being able to go places and do things without forever looking over one's shoulder," Julie whispered. "And forever worrying about being found out."

His fingers stroked across her chest, dipped inside her low-cut bodice. Julie moved restlessly against him. Her scent filled his nostrils, and Ned was achingly aware of her body pressed against his own. He should slow down, he thought dimly, before they passed the point of no return; but his hand had slipped under Julie's skirt, and slid up her slender leg, over coarse stockings that were infinitely more erotic than silk, to the bare warm flesh above her garter, and he was not altogether in possession of his wits. "I'm glad you came to me," Ned murmured. Speech required immense effort. Julie lay draped in delightful disarray across his thighs.

She blinked at him, distracted, dazed. "I hope I wasn't followed. I don't want you involved."

"I already am involved," Ned retorted, without thinking. "I gave you back that damned glove."

This utterance restored them both to sanity. Ned jerked his hand out from beneath Julie's skirt. She scrambled off his lap and snatched up the notebook. "I have to go."

So she did, before Ned forgot he was a gentleman and pulled her back down on his lap. "Wait." He moved stiffly to the desk. From a drawer, he withdrew her knife.

She took it from him, eyes downcast. Ned rearranged her cloak around her shoulders, walked with her to the library door.

Julie looked up at him. "I know you don't trust me, but I promise that as soon as I can, I'll get your statue back to you."

"It's not that I don't trust you." Ned broke off as this clanker earned him a snort. "You have Bates following me," Julie pointed out.

At least she hadn't hit him. Ned walked with her down the quiet hallway. "You're caught up in a dangerous game. I don't want you to end up like Amélie Morel."

Julie tried to pull out of his grasp. "I won't hang myself."

Could she be so unaware of her own danger? "Are you sure Amélie Morel did so? It's not difficult to stage something like that."

Julie stared at him. "You think—"

Ned released her. "I think I can't keep you safe if you won't tell me who your master is."

"And I know I can't keep you safe if I do tell you." Julie pulled the hood of her cloak up over her bright curls and slipped out into the night.

Chapter Twenty-One

Lust wants whatever it can't have.
— Pubilius Syrus

Almack's Assembly Rooms were abuzz. Not only was Lord Saxe on the premises this Wednesday eve, he had brought with him Sabine Viccars, his rumored *inamorata* and the current object of the Czar's erratic interest; and while Sally Jersey might have liked to refuse her admittance, the other Lady Patronesses were curious as to what had prompted their favorite flirt to grace these august premises. Not one among them imagined for an instant that he had come to survey the most recent entries in the matrimonial sweepstakes. Frankly, no one cared. The sight of the baron in knee breeches was enough to make even the haughty Mme de Lieven think she might swoon.

Lord Saxe was himself curious about his presence here. Freed of his official duties for the evening—the Allied Aggravations were dining with Lord Liverpool and he had begged off—Kane had anticipated a leisurely opportunity to puzzle out the mystery that was Sabine. Instead here they were at Almack's, which was hardly to his taste. Or, he would have thought, to hers. In response to his inquiry about what game she was playing, Sabine responded that she was embarked on counterintelligence, and he should watch to see how the thing was done; and then set about scotching certain rumors by means of a few well-placed utterances, chief among them 'how very tiresome' and 'doubted the fidelity of my own ears', casual references to her 'dear Ned' and the foolishness of those who believed every *on-dit* that they heard.

"And we are interfering why?" Kane asked, as they ascended

the grand staircase.

"Because we can." Sabine appeared oblivious to the curious glances being cast their way. "If the gossip is permitted to go on, Ned won't be able to deny the rumors without embarrassing the girl. Which his cousin is counting on, no doubt."

In that case, Hannah would be annoyed that Amélie Morel had gone and hanged herself just as speculation was starting to gain momentum, thereby stealing the spotlight from Ned. Kane wondered if Mme Morel was in a place to know that some good had come from her demise. Sabine had a certain momentum of her own, and an admirable way of making her way through a crowd. She was elegant in sea green gauze tonight, and a white satin cap graced with ostrich plumes. Ladies and their feathers. Kane wondered idly how many he had crushed.

Feathers, that was, not ladies. Lord Saxe didn't dally where hearts might be involved.

The large ballroom was profusely lit by wax-lights; decorated with gilt columns and pilasters, classic medallions and mirrors. Around the perimeters ranged sofas, the lady patronesses having their own throne at the upper end. The space reserved for dancing was marked off by silken ropes.

A country dance was ending. With a skill that might have been envied by the great Wellington, Sabine determined that Madalyn Tate was present, arranged an introduction, and left Kane to enjoy a conversation with Lady Jersey while she bore off her startled quarry—a young woman with a plumpish sort of figure, an abundance of dark curls, and a roundish sort of face; neither pretty nor an antidote, just an ordinary sort of female wearing a pink and white striped confection that gave her an unfortunate resemblance to a peppermint stick—to the adjacent tea-room for a private conversation over sour lemonade.

"Maddie Tate isn't what I would have chosen for Dorset." Lady Jersey had noted the direction of Kane's gaze. "Although since he was in the military, he might be capable of keeping her hellions in line. The twins look like angels, which proves that appearances can be deceiving. I can't imagine where they get their wayward natures, for both Maddie and their father were unfailingly well behaved. Although that may be the answer. All those repressed high spirits have come out in their offspring."

"Ah," commented Kane.

Lady Jersey was perfectly content conversing with herself, so long as one of the most handsome gentlemen in the room strolled by her side. "Maddie's papa arranged her first marriage and is on the look-out to make her another. She will marry not to her own advantage, but to his."

"And so he is conniving with Lady Dorset." Since Kane was here, he might as well shove in his own oar. "However, it won't serve."

Lovely, lovely gossip. Lady Jersey was in bliss. "Nonsense! I had it from Hannah herself. By way of Barbara Watson and Ada South, admittedly, but they swear every word is true."

"I don't doubt your sources. However, the truth is …" Over her shoulder, Kane saw Sabine return to the ballroom. Madalyn Tate trailed behind, hectic color in her cheeks. "To use the word with no bark on it, Lady Dorset has not recovered from the shock of her son's death. One dislikes to suggest the dowager might be in her dotage, but the fact remains that she's got hold of the wrong end of the stick. Her desire to see Ned leg-shackled has clouded her perceptions. These things happen, alas, when women approach a certain age."

Lady Jersey twinkled at him. "And no one knows more about women than you."

Kane accorded this coquettish salvo the attention it deserved, which was none, but managed to convey to his companion that he held her in the utmost admiration. Sabine paused behind them, raised an eyebrow. Ever so slightly, Kane shook his head. "We must pity Lady Dorset rather than condemn her for misguided notions," he said. "Of course the knowledge of her failing faculties will remain among ourselves."

Of course it would do no such thing. "My lips are sealed," Lady Jersey breathed, and then went off to share these delicious developments with a hundred of her closest friends.

"I told Mrs. Tate that Ned had his heart broken in the Peninsula," remarked Sabine. "And that I would be surprised if he ever got over it. What a pair of liars we are."

"I prefer to think of myself as a diplomat." Kane offered her his arm.

"Which is to say the same thing."

Sabine tucked her hand through his elbow. They strolled around the perimeter of the ballroom. Kane said, "So Ned had his heart broke?"

"I deemed it sufficiently melodramatic to appeal. Mrs. Tate is now aware that I will go to any lengths to prevent this entrapment taking place. Of course she thinks I want Ned for myself. How generous we are to furnish the biddies so much to cluck about."

Kane made no comment. She surveyed the dance floor. "The grandest ball of the war was held at Cuidad Rodrigo. The largest house in the city was appropriated for the occasion. Damask satin hangings hid the damaged walls, and a sentry was stationed to stand guard over the carpet that covered the hole in the ballroom floor."

Sabine was almost as skilled at misdirection as Kane was himself. "Would you care to dance? I daresay you remember how. Even though it's been some time since you were so green a girl as to consider dancing at Almack's the pinnacle of social success."

Her glance was ironic. "Don't you know it's considered bad manners to refer to a lady's age? Let us leave this place before I fall into lamenting my lost youth."

The street outside was crowded. Kane waited in silence until his carriage made its way through the crush. He instructed the coachman to drive around until told otherwise, handed Sabine inside and settled on the opposite seat.

Kane watched as she pulled off her cap and gloves, pressed her fingers to her temples. Had Alexander bedded her? If not the Czar was truly a madman, for only a madman wouldn't desire a physical relationship with Sabine. As if privy to his thoughts, she said, "The Czar wants to move Russia's borders several hundred miles west, thus reviving Poland but making it subordinate to St. Petersburg.

This is not to be viewed with alarm by the other European powers, you understand."

She didn't want to discuss their expedition to Almack's? Kane promptly decided that they must. "Lady Dorset may be a harridan, but she has the right of it. Now that Ned has come into the title, he must wed."

"For the sake of the succession." Sabine responded. "As must you."

At least she was sufficiently aware of Kane to realize he *had* a title. "I have several younger brothers who are capable of stepping into my shoes should the need arise."

Sabine smiled. "Piffle. You are waiting for Clea to grow up."

What did one say in response to so outrageous a suggestion? Silence seemed the most prudent course. Too, Sabine's smile had temporarily robbed Kane of his breath.

She drew her cloak more closely around her, as if it were insufficient to ward off chill. He retrieved the carriage rug and draped it across her lap. "Your teeth are chattering. I would never forgive myself if you took ill on my watch."

She buried her hands in the rug's warmth. "Blame it on this wretchedly damp English weather. You are the consummate diplomat, are you not?"

"The consummate liar, you mean. Oddly enough, this time I spoke the truth."

Sabine tilted her head and studied him. "How appalled you look. Don't take it so to heart. Sometimes as one ages one becomes less adept."

Kane disliked the amusement he heard in her voice. "I promise you, my abilities are not in question. Should you have an interest, I would be pleased to demonstrate."

"Of course you would," she responded. "You are extremely unfaithful and wholly unrepentant and a marvel of discretion at the same time: that most unusual paradox, an honorable roué. Many a woman will try to attract your interest, despite knowing she cannot hold your heart. The challenge for you, I think, will be when one does not."

She'd noticed that he'd noticed her lack of reaction to him. "I'm surely not so shallow," Kane responded, his pride stung.

Sabine let her head rest against the back of the seat. "No, you are not. I am weary and consequently being cruel."

An odd notion, that a woman should be cruel to him. "You don't speak often of your husband," Kane remarked.

She didn't react to the change of subject. "Frances was all that is kind and good."

"Was Julian Faulkner also kind and good?"

"Julian was a golden lad." Sabine closed her eyes. "He was all high spirits and longing for adventure and the devil take the hindmost. It wasn't in his nature to think of the future, or worry about responsibilities, or consider his eventual position and his wealth; he lived for the present and trusted tomorrow would take care of itself. He had a tremendous thirst for *knowing*—always wanting to see what was over the next hill and to understand how it came to be there. And he possessed a profound loyalty to his friends."

"Of which you were one."

"I was. Francis was another. We grew up together, we three. I alone am left. If Miss Wynne is kin to Julian, I must make sure that things are well with her."

Julian Faulkner had no monopoly on loyalty. "Might she be a by-blow?" inquired Kane.

Thoughtfully, Sabine regarded him. "It's possible, I suppose. But had he known about her, Julian would have made arrangements for her care. From what you've told me, the girl grew up on the streets."

"So it would seem." The girl was a thief. Who had spent time in Newgate. And who Ned had been kissing, if not worse.

Ned wanted to rescue her. Sabine wanted to know more about her. Clea wanted to become her bosom-bow. Julie Wynne was having a profound effect on a great many people, and her timing so inconvenient it must surely have been planned.

Beneath Sabine's fine eyes lurked faint shadows. Kane leaned forward and withdrew her hands from beneath the rug.

She did not pull away from him. The pulse beneath his fingers was sure and steady and perhaps a little faster than it had been a moment past. "What monsters do you see, I wonder," Kane murmured, "when you close your eyes at night?"

Sabine raised an ironic eyebrow. "Are you offering to help me sleep? Despite believing that passion is ephemeral, and one night's feast the next morning's stale crumbs? You will have seen the inside of more boudoirs than you can count."

Kane raised her hands to his lips. "Perhaps. The question is, I think, whether I will see the inside of yours."

Chapter Twenty-Two

It is less to suffer punishment than to deserve it.
— Ovid

Drury Lane was crowded to the rafters (or if not the rafters, since none were in evidence, its arched ornamented ceiling); from galley and pit to luxurious private box. The audience was less interested in the entertainment than in each other, and anxiously awaited the arrival of the Distinguished Visitors, who were engaged with Lord Castlereagh and expected afterward to honor Mr. Kean by observing his Othello. Lady Georgiana was in alt tonight, the current rumor that Lady Dorset had gone out of her head proving a more effective restorative than any nostrum; and took great pleasure in informing anyone who would listen that dear Hannah had always been *strange*. A few of those present observed that Mr. Kean was in especially fine fettle—if his face and person were not consistent with the character, he nonetheless delivered bursts of energy and emotion hitherto unsurpassed, or so said Mr. William Hazlitt, whose opinion could be trusted on such things—but the rest might as well have been at the Olympic Theater, watching a performance of trained dogs.

Since her new dresses weren't yet ready, Julie wore another of Lady Georgiana's gowns, this one fashioned with a closely fitted bodice and a deep square neckline in a shade of blue that her ladyship explained was called 'Marie Louise' after Napoleon's empress, and made of a fabric called Caledonian silk for reasons left obscure. The garment was lovely, even if Julie felt it put too much of her person on display. In addition she was fitted out with white kid gloves that reached to just below her elbows, a long rectangular silk shawl, and satin slippers with roses on the toes.

She was fixed up awful nice. Julie smelled a rat. However, she had learned at an early age that one shouldn't look a gift horse in the mouth unless one wished to become acquainted with its teeth. If Georgiana had taken a sudden inexplicable interest in Julie, Tony was acting just the opposite, shying away whenever she came near him as if afraid she might carry the plague, and leaving her feeling unexpectedly as if she'd lost one of her few friends.

Julie wished she'd never met the Ashcrofts, mother and son. Georgiana left off crowing about Lady Dorset's comeuppance to marvel at the intelligence that Princess Charlotte had finally refused the Prince of Orange, which came as no particular surprise, for were there not an embarrassment of considerably more handsome foreign princes in the city, and hadn't the princess been meeting clandestinely with the King of Prussia's nineteen-year-old nephew? Her ladyship was distracted by another of her cronies then, and Julie took the opportunity to slip away. All in all, now that she had the privilege of observing performances from the luxury of a private box, Julie preferred backstage.

Rose was waiting in the dressing room. She wore Desdemona's long flowing robe.

Julie pulled out the notebook she'd hidden beneath her shawl. Rose eyed it doubtfully. "That can't be worth much."

"Neither was the glove," retorted Julie. "And a woman hanged herself for that."

Rose hadn't known about the hanging. She'd heard gossip; it would have been difficult not to; but hadn't equated that gossip with Julie's pilfered glove. She grimaced. "Where did you find this?"

Julie glanced over her shoulder, assured herself that they were alone. "At Wakely Court. I told Ned I needed it and he gave it to me. It's used for making and breaking government codes."

Rose opened the notebook, rifled through the pages before locking it away in a drawer. "*Why* did he give it to you?"

Because Julie's brain had turned to noodles and she'd told more than she should. "He knows about the blackmail."

"How?"

Julie toyed with the makeup pots. "There's no flies on Ned."

There were no flies on Rose, and furthermore she'd asked to have inquiries made. Belatedly, she wondered if it had been the best idea to make Pritchett aware of Julie's relationship with the earl.

Too late, now, for sniffling over spilt milk. Pritchett had confirmed her suspicions that Lord Dorset was a rogue.

Rose knew how it was with rogues. "You are drawn to him," she sighed, "like a moth to the flame."

"Ballocks." Julie set the makeup pot aside.

Rose knew what she knew, and from experience; and if her amours ended sadly, she had enjoyed herself along the way. Nor had she outgrown the pleasures of the flesh, for she had acquired a handsome new admirer and an assignation after the play. "You must try and fix Dorset's interest, if you can't turn away. Cast out lures but withhold the ultimate favor and you'll have him eating out of your hand. An earl dangling at your slipper-strings can't do you any harm."

Julie didn't tell Rose that matters had already progressed in a manner that strongly indicated withholding wasn't in her nature. "Mayhap I should lay down on the floor in front of him so that he may trip over me."

Rose winked. "Arse over teakettle. You can do it, my girl. Keep in mind that gentlemen always want what they think they can't have. Don't give me that look! This is a case of do not as I do, but as I say." There was no time for further good advice. Rose was due to die onstage.

Julie made her way slowly back to the public area. She was in no hurry to return to Lady Georgiana's box. Was Cap'n Jack in the audience tonight? If so, he was unlikely to be dressed in a high-waisted white muslin gown like the young lady blocking her path.

A familiar young lady with mahogany curls and dimples and eyes of a bright green. Said Clea, "Am I not demure? I have been persuaded that I must learn to walk before I run." She gazed enviously upon Julie's gown. "That is an astonishing neckline. I wish I had a bosom. Kane says it doesn't matter, but I don't know that I believe him, even if he has had a thousand lovers and should know about such things."

Ned's sister was relentless. "I don't think it's proper for you to be wandering around by yourself," Julie said.

Clea showed not the least repentance. "*You* are," she pointed out. "I've been following you."

"Yes, but I'm not …" Overwhelmed by all the things she wasn't, Julie fell silent.

"I'm not alone, exactly. Just momentarily misplaced." Clea linked arms with Julie. "Now tell me, what are gingambobs?"

Julie recalled their first meeting, and the way she had behaved. It was a wonder Ned spoke to her. He might *not* speak to her again if she continued this conversation. "Don't tell me I'm too young," added Clea. "You're not much older than I am."

"I was never as young as you are."

"Have I annoyed you? I didn't mean to. It is very frustrating when people refuse to explain things and claim it's for your own good when what they're really doing is trying to keep you well wrapped in lamb's wool. I sometimes feel like I'm locked up in a cage."

Julie knew what it was like to be imprisoned. "Stones. Gingambobs are stones."

"Stones?"

"Nutmegs. Twiddle-diddles." Julie gestured. "A gentleman's—"

"Testicles." Clea had been in the Peninsula with her brother and therefore was not half so well wrapped as her cousin Hannah might have liked. "There are many other things that I'd like to know. For instance, how does one go about breaking into a house?"

Ned might overlook Julie battering his person, but damage to his sister would be an unforgivable trespass. As would further harm to his sister's sensibilities. "Drury Lane is the most haunted theater in the world," Julie countered. "If you see someone dressed like a nobleman of the last century, with powdered hair and a tricorn hat, a cloak and riding boots and sword, that is the Man is Grey."

"I'd hoped Wakely Court might have a ghost, but instead we have Cerberus." Clea glanced over Julie's shoulder. "Oh, dear. Now the fat is in the fire."

Julie turned to see Clea's brother walking toward them. He was wearing a long-tailed evening coat of bottle green with covered buttons and a pale buff waistcoat. The starched points of his shirt collar framed an intricately tied cravat. His boots were mirror-bright from shining, and his kerseymere pantaloons so well-fitting that Julie felt like fanning herself.

He inspected her in turn. His gaze lingered at her neckline. His eyes burned a brilliant shade of green.

Julie felt embarrassed; she'd wept all over him. And seen him without his shirt. Had felt the evidence of his wanting her. His warm look suggested his thoughts might be following a similar path.

Clea cleared her throat. "Here comes my friend Elizabeth, and her parents. They probably think I've gotten lost. Ned is taking me to see a display of equestrian acrobatics at Astley's Amphitheater, Miss Wynne. Do say you'll come along." Before either of her companions could comment, she darted away.

"My sister has a talent for making exits." Ned watched Clea until he saw that she did indeed rejoin her friends. "What did she want?"

"She may have taken the notion that I know how to pick a lock."

"I shudder to think what locks Clea may aspire to pick. Since she is determined to make your acquaintance, we may as well bow to the inevitable. I will ask Lady Georgiana if you may accompany us to Astley's Amphitheater. Would you care for that?"

Would she care to enjoy amazing feats of horsemanship and acrobats, rope dancers and juggling clowns? Had everyone around Julie gone mad? "You don't want your sister rubbing shoulders with me. What if—"

"Gammon." Ned took her hand and placed it on his arm. "You said you wanted to be able to do things and go places without fear. Here's an opportunity. No harm will come to you in my company."

On the contrary. A great deal of harm could come to her, as well as to him. Still, Julie was touched by the earl remembering that she'd said she wanted an ordinary life.

In an attempt to hide her feelings, she changed the subject. "Lady Georgiana is crowing over the gossip about your cousin. I suppose Lady Dorset is cross."

"Lady Dorset has taken to her bed," Ned said with satisfaction. "I doubt she'll stay there long, alas. One never knows how these rumors get their start, although Hannah has a notion, and is furious with Kane. I have compounded her chagrin by publicly apologizing to Mrs. Tate for any embarrassment this nonsense—and I did call it nonsense—has caused her. I'm cross myself about the *on-dit* that I left my heart behind in the Peninsula. That was Sabine's contribution, I think." Instead of returning Julie to Lady Georgiana's box, he was leading her deeper backstage. "I know so few things about you. Do you wish to marry? Most young ladies your age do."

Julie was tired of pointing out she wasn't a young lady. "What would I do with a husband? It's hard enough to look after myself."

"Your family should be looking after you."

"Like you look after your sister? You should keep her miles away from me."

"I have yet to prevent Clea doing anything she wishes. You will have delivered the notebook. How did you manage that?"

"I told Lady Georgiana it was a spiritual lesson-book and I thought I should have it with me if I was going somewhere so wicked as the theater. She told me I must make sure to keep it out of sight." Julie grinned. Ned laughed.

They were deep in the bowels of the theater, in a storage area containing flats not in use for the current production—temples and tombs, palace interiors and exteriors, city walls and rural prospects—alongside a pair of wave-rollers, complete with handles for turning them, and a cloud apparatus machine. Ned backed Julie into the shadows and took her face between his hands and brushed a kiss against her lips.

An entirely too chaste kiss. He'd had his hand up her skirt. Julie wanted it there again.

"Keep looking at me like that," Ned murmured, "and I won't be held responsible."

Was he going to offer her that slip on the shoulder now? Julie wondered what she would say. Rather, she knew what she wanted to say, but wondered how to properly phrase it. 'Tumble me now' sounded a trifle too direct.

"Ned," came a voice from behind them. "I've had the devil of a time finding you. I am sorry to interrupt."

"It's I who am sorry," Ned said, but to Julie. "Kane, I don't believe you've been properly introduced to Miss Wynne."

"So I have not. My pleasure, Miss Wynne." The baron's tone suggested it wasn't pleasure that he felt. "Much as I dislike to interrupt your conversation, Ned's presence is required elsewhere."

Julie flushed at the emphasis he put on 'conversation'. Ned took her hand. "Indeed my presence *is* required. By Miss Wynne. If that is all …"

"The Royals have arrived. Platoff is growing bored of all these tedious long dinners and requires intelligent discourse for a change. Which, oddly, he expects you may provide."

The men were angry with each other. Julie suspected it was her fault. She said, "I'll make my own way back."

"You will not. Platoff can wait." Ned kept firm hold of Julie. The baron turned on his heel and strode away.

He knew, thought Julie. Lord Saxe knew who and what she was. "I can't go with you to Astley's," she said.

"Have you ever been to Astley's? Do you think you wouldn't enjoy it?" She shook her head. "Then I'll hear no more arguments," said Ned.

Lady Georgiana was pleased to see the earl, and delighted to utter civil whiskers about his poor cousin, and surprisingly gracious about the proposed excursion to Astley's. Ned left the box accompanied by the audience singing "God Save the King". The Czar cordially joined in. A pity Their Majesties had missed *Othello* altogether, murmured the spectators, but at least the afterpiece remained to be enjoyed.

"Slyboots," said Georgiana to Julie, after the singing had ceased.

Julie protested, "I felt the need for some air."

"Proper young women don't need air." Lady Georgiana raised her quizzing glass and inspected Julie through the lens. "You have gotten rumpled. Where is your notebook?"

"I encountered someone more in need of it than I."

Lady Georgiana harrumphed, then settled back to enjoy *The Woodman's Hut*, a somewhat tedious undertaking that was enlightened by frequent demonstrations from the audience. Julie was left to her own thoughts.

On the one hand, she wanted more than anything to go to Astley's with Ned and his sister and pretend for a short time that she was an ordinary person with an ordinary life. On the other, while Ned might be trusted not to betray her, she hoped, his friend the baron would no doubt be pleased to see her hang.

Chapter Twenty-Three

Every day should be passed as if it were to be our last.
— Pubilius Syrus

Tony might have thought—*if* he thought, which he took great pains
to do as seldom as possible, because the inevitable conclusion he
arrived at on those rare occasions when he chose to exercise his
brain was that he was in a sorry plight—he would be safe in Bond
Street from interruption by scolding mamas and Bow Street Runners
who were no better than they should be. And in fact he had executed
many errands without the sort of interruptions that plagued him of
late. He had visited Schweitzer and Davidson of Cork St, Meyer and
then Guthrie, establishments that enjoyed his patronage and were
hopeful that at some time in the near future he might settle his
accounts; had ordered trousers from Stultz and Hessian boots
from Hoby in St James St; had visited a hatter and hosier and per-
fumer and paused by a confectioners shop for a cherry tart, even
though his mama, who said he should keep an eye out for his
manly figure, would have disapproved. But Tony's mama disapproved of so many things that it was difficult to keep track of them,
and he was forever setting his foot wrong, at which point she would
either fly off the hooks or look at him in that pitying manner as if
she was lamenting his lack of wit.

Tony didn't believe he was as totty-headed as his mama
thought, and moreover she had several maggots in her own brain,
as shown by her belief that Julie was blackmailing him, and therefore shouldn't be one to talk. Tony conceded that Georgiana had
got the blackmail business partly right, though he suspected Julie
was as much a cat's-paw as he. For his mama to take it into her

noggin that he had compromised someone, however...

It just went to show that despite her high opinion of herself, Maman wasn't up to snuff. If anyone had been compromised, it was Tony himself. Yes, and misled also, because Julie had said she would set things right, and Tony hadn't seen any sign of her doing so yet. He was disappointed in the girl. And *now*, despite all his mama had said to him about scheming hussies and rascally earls, she'd started being nice to Julie, giving her dresses and taking her shopping. Tony despaired of understanding females.

He *did* understand shopping. It was an excellent distraction for shattered nerves. Therefore, Tony took himself off to Weston's establishment, and ordered made (against the tailor's recommendation) a waistcoat in alternating shades of Evening Primrose and Periwinkle Green.

What did Weston know? huffed Tony, as he left the shop. He could see the waistcoat in his imagination, and splendid it was. The viscount flattered himself that he had a nice notion of such things, even if he might not go so far as Brummell, and have one craftsman fashion the fingers of his glove and another the thumbs, or have his boots polished with champagne. He knew he made a fine appearance in his nankeen breeches and brown jacket, the waistcoat with the orange stripes that nicely complimented his bright red watch fob; his gloves of fine leather and tall beaver hat. His cravat was tied in the intricate Waterfall; his boots gleamed like polished glass, for all his valet eschewed champagne; his hair was styled in the fashionable Titus, cropped short everywhere but at the front with curls combed forward to resemble a Roman emperor...

He was, Tony assured himself, complete to a shade. He felt, in that particular moment, on top of the world. Then a hackney coach drew up beside him and Pritchett popped his head out the window and said, "Get in."

Just like that, between one moment and the next, Tony's spirits deflated like a burst balloon. It was damned unfair. He gazed in an opposite direction. If he ignored Pritchett, the Runner might go away.

The Runner did not. "Get in," said Pritchett. "Or I will get out."

Stroll down Bond Street arm-in-arm with a Bow Street Runner? Tony thought not. He climbed into the cab, trying not to think who might have ridden in it before him, and what they might have left behind.

Pritchett was holding a sprig of lavender to his nose. "You've been avoiding me," the Runner remarked.

Tony wished he'd thought to bring a scented handkerchief. Not that he'd anticipated riding in a hackney-coach. He *might* have anticipated it, had he been thinking properly, for this was all of a piece with everything else that was besetting him these days. Foresight, that was the ticket. A fellow needed to anticipate what nasty turn his ill-luck might next take.

Pritchett jabbed Tony with his gilt-headed baton. "Cat got your tongue?"

Cat? Tony looked around the cab. If there was a cat in here somewhere, it might account for the smell.

And if Pritchett didn't stop poking him with that baton, Tony was going to poke him back. "I don't see a cat. There isn't one, is there? You were being clever. I don't know why people can't say what they mean."

Of course there wasn't a cat. Pritchett closed his eyes, counted to five hundred, and opened them again. "You're not doing yourself any favors by playing least in sight."

On the contrary. Tony was doing himself an immense favor by avoiding unpleasant encounters such as this. But he hadn't avoided this one, had he? Which went back to his previous reflections on foresight. "Can't blame a fellow for trying," he muttered.

Pritchett could blame him, and did. The Runner had better things to do than follow foolish lordlings around town. Such as determining how to save his own skin.

Pritchett didn't like this business of a stolen codebook. The penalties for treason were severe. And if anyone was caught doing anything he shouldn't, it wasn't likely to be Cap'n Jack.

"You might outrun the constable," said Pritchett, "but you'll not outrun the Cap'n. Was you to try, he'd take out his displeasure on your mama."

"Don't *you* prose and preach at me!" snapped Tony. "I have enough of that at home. If your Cap'n dares try and cross swords with Maman, she'll make short work of him. I'll wager a monkey—"

"You don't have a monkey!" Pritchett interrupted. "And you don't want your mama tangling with the Cap'n. Trust me on that, Ashcroft."

Tony wasn't so sure. What kind of unnatural parent called her sole offspring a numbskull? It might serve Maman right if she was to have a scare. But then she'd blame that on him, like she did all else. If Tony had known what was to come of it, he wouldn't have picked up that first deck of cards. Now the sole relief to be had for the troubles pressing down on him was to spend the ready as easily as if he was flush in the pocket, which he wasn't, on things he didn't want or need; and Pritchett needn't pull a long face over him and point out there would come a day of reckoning, at which point he would be in an even worse case than he was now, hard as that was to imagine, thank you very much.

The viscount was a pigeon for the plucking, thought Pritchett, just as Jules had said; a lamb ripe for fleecing, a chicken waddling straight toward the stewing pot.

The Runner was astonished to find himself experiencing equal parts exasperation and regret. Perhaps he *was* developing scruples. Inconvenient, if true. A sympathetic nature was no asset in a villain. Villain, Pritchett was. And he didn't care to know what the hen-wit was now nattering on about.

Neither did Pritchett care to know about Jules getting close to Dorset, but know it he did. Rose had reservations. Any right-thinking person would. She also had some fanciful notion that the earl might ride to Julie's rescue like some knight of old.

The actress's years upon the stage had left her with a taste for melodrama. If rescues were to be ridden to, Pritchett wished someone might ride to his.

He didn't dwell wholly in his employer's pocket. Pritchett knew things he'd not tell Cap'n Jack. Such as that Jules had retrieved the notebook by way of Wakely Court's front door, and from the earl's own hand.

That Pritchett hadn't told the Cap'n, however, didn't mean the Cap'n didn't know. Impossible to be sure who was and wasn't under the Cap'n's thumb.

Dorset wasn't. Yet. He thought.

M'sieur Morel wasn't, because his wife had chose instead to hang herself. Cap'n Jack was furious as a result. Pritchett suspected the Cap'n had sought access to M'sieur's diplomatic dispatch box.

Dorset should look to his sister. The Cap'n knew to attack a man's weakest spot.

Tony disliked the Runner's silence. Truth be told, he didn't like the Runner, but he was not sufficiently deficient in the nous-box (no matter what his mama thought) as to say so out loud. "Maybe I should ask if the cat has got *your* tongue. Unless you only meant to scold, in which case I wish you'd let me be about my business, because the smell of this carriage is enough to put a man right off his feed. My valet will raise the devil of a dust about getting the stink out of my clothes."

The viscount was surrounded by people prone to excesses of emotion. "You are to fetch something for the Cap'n," Pritchett said.

Tony didn't like the sound of this. "Fetch what? From where?"

"A statue with the head of a hippopotamus, legs of a lion, tail of a crocodile, human breasts and swollen belly." Pritchett gestured with his hands. "About this size. He expects you'll find it in Miss Wynne's bedroom. Where in her bedroom, I don't know exactly. You'll have to search."

If that wasn't the outside of enough. It went against Tony's principles to go snooping through a female's bedroom. And yes, he did have principles, though the Runner might not think it; just because a man made mistakes didn't mean he lacked integrity.

Tony's protests fell upon deaf ears. Or if not deaf, because Pritchett could not fail to hear him, on ears that could have cared less about his horrified dismay.

"I'm no thief," insisted Tony. "And I won't be made into one, so there!"

"No?" inquired Pritchett. "What else do you call it when you order things from merchants knowing your pockets are to let? Your creditors won't be so obliging if they realize you can't pay the shot. Fetch the statue like you're told."

Tony sputtered with indignation. Pritchett was threatening him. Which went to show that one should never trust a man in spectacles. Not that Tony *had* trusted Pritchett, not for an instant, but still he felt as if he'd taken a sharp blow to his breadbasket.

The cab drew to a halt in front of Ashcroft House. Tony grasped the door-handle. Pritchett said, "Remember the French-woman who hanged herself?"

"Remember her? Why should I? I didn't know the wench." Since this sounded cold, Tony added, "Poor thing. But what does some dead Frenchwoman have to do with the price of peas?"

"Cap'n Jack."

What Cap'n Jack had to do with peas, Tony could not imagine. Thought of what the Cap'n might have had to do with a dead Frenchwoman, however, caused him to tumble headfirst out of the cab. Pritchett pulled the door shut behind him and repeated, for good measure, "Dare the Cap'n and be damned."

Be damned, decided Tony. That was Pritchett in a word. The bedamned Runner had ruined his shopping expedition and now the anticipation of his lovely new waistcoat had been spoiled.

Tony brushed himself off, stomped up his front steps and past the footman waiting in the hall, who wondered why his master chose to travel around town in a hired hack when he owned several fashionable carriages himself. Tony belatedly recalled that he had set out in one of those spanking rigs earlier today. Ah well, his groom would eventually grow tired of waiting and come home.

Or maybe he wouldn't. Maybe the groom would turn out to be like Mildred, who went to Oxford Street to match a length of ribbon and never returned home. Tony might have liked to not return home himself, if not for his harp.

"Miss Wynne has gone out and Lady Georgiana is lying down," the footman said, in response to Tony's query. The viscount withdrew to his study, leaving orders that he was not to be disturbed. He fortified himself with brandy before again poking his head out into the hall. Several moments later he had achieved an elevated heartbeat and a heightened awareness of the staggering number of servants he employed, a matter he hadn't considered before he attempted to avoid the lot of them. Tony closed Julie's bedroom door behind him, and wiped the perspiration from his brow.

The room looked no different from when Mildred had slept in it, a fact Tony knew because his mama had demanded he inspect the items that poor Millie left behind. Everything was tidy. Not a pin was out of place. No ugly statue sat out in plain sight. Feeling uncomfortably as if he was trespassing in his own house, Tony opened the wardrobe.

There was little enough to see inside. Astonishing, that a person could get by with so few items of attire. Tony moved on to the tallboy.

What if he didn't find the statue? What would the Cap'n do? Tony's belly churned. Perhaps an attack of indigestion was coming on, result of the tart he'd ate. Or his interview with Pritchett. Or the brandy that he'd drunk. Maybe he was developing nervous agitations like his mama.

Yes, and why should he not? He could hardly be expected to steal things if he was sick in bed. As he pondered the benefits of a prolonged convalescence, Tony rifled through the mysterious garments in the tallboy drawers. A corset caught his interest, and he inspected the device more closely, turning it this way and that. Certain areas were reinforced with cotton cording, others stiffened with quilting, so that parts of the body could be prevented from expanding as they wished. Tony contemplated his own tart-filled breadbasket and the application of similar principles to a gentleman's waistcoat.

Came a shriek behind him. Tony spun around, the corset clutched to his chest. In the doorway stood his mama, horror writ large on her face.

Chapter Twenty-Four

He who is bent on doing evil can never want occasion.
— Pubilius Syrus

Astley's Royal Amphitheater was located in Lambeth, near the Westminster Bridge. While the structure's exterior was generally considered unimposing, the interior was accorded one of the most splendid in London, done up as it was in white, lemon gold and yellow, and lit by a huge chandelier containing fifty patent lamps plus sixteen smaller chandeliers with six wax lights each. The amphitheater boasted one full tier of boxes, with two half tiers at the side; and above the half tiers, the galley slips. The sawdust-covered equestrian circle was bounded by a four-foot-high enclosure painted as stonework, the curve of the circle next to the stage forming the outline of the orchestra, and the remainder that of the pit, which contained fourteen rows of seats and had a spacious lobby as well as a bar for refreshment. Rich crimson draperies adorned the private boxes. A faint smell of horses hung in the air.

From one of those private boxes, Lord Dorset and his guests had thus far observed a Grand Oriental Dramatic Spectacle and an elaborate equestrian pantomime; rope dancers and jugglers and acrobats. Clea was most impressed by the gentleman who balanced with his knees on the saddle, his horse running ahead at full speed; and from that position leaped over a ribbon extended ten feet. For her part, Mrs. Viccars admired the lady who juggled four oranges in the air while she rode around the ring. Miss Wynne was more impressed with the stage itself, which was larger than that at Drury Lane, and very well adapted to the introduction of grand spectacles and pantomimes. Platforms rose one above another and extended straight across, strong enough that riders could gallop across them, yet so constructed that they could be masked by scenery, and set up and removed in a short period of time.

Lady Dorset hadn't been invited to join the party. Hannah was not yet showing her face in public, which was a good thing, because Ned hadn't got over his wish to do her violence. Nor did Lord Saxe accompany them, though he might have preferred Astley's over an inspection of the Military Asylum and Chelsea Hospital in company with the Eminent Nuisances, to be followed by a splendid dinner at the Merchant Tailors' Hall.

Kane didn't approve of this expedition, and so he had told Ned. He didn't think Clea should be hobnobbing with a thief. The baron might have felt differently had he been with them in Portugal, where Clea had hobnobbed with worse than thieves.

Ned shifted position in his seat. He had placed Julie next to him, not the wisest arrangement considering how badly he wanted her in his lap again, but he was not sufficiently a saint to deprive himself of the warmth of her arm pressing against his, and the smell of her perfume.

Clea leaned forward, intent on the gentleman singing about a mock courtship between a frog and a mouse. Julie stole a sideways glance at Sabine, who might have performed onstage herself, so well costumed was she for this event. The older woman's pale hair was drawn up in a Grecian knot, with a profusion of tiny ringlets escaping to frame her face. Her gown was of the high-waisted diaphanous style made popular in France by Leroy; her shawl woven from the fleece of wild Kashmir goats, expensive but light and warm. She wore a necklace and matching earrings fashioned of sapphires set in gold filigree. Julie's eyes lingered on the stones.

"Tradition holds that Moses was given the Ten Commandments on tablets of sapphire, making it the gemstone most often chosen by kings and high priests," murmured Ned. "It's said that a necklace of sapphires will cure a sore throat."

Julie rolled her eyes at him. "I wasn't going to pinch the things. I just thought they were nice."

So they were. Ned wondered what kind of jewelry Julie might like. She appeared the unexceptionable young lady in white muslin with pansy-pink flowers, which Ned assumed was another of Lady Georgiana's cast-offs. Clea was demure in long-sleeved yellow cambric with a sash brought round her waist and tied on the left. For all the play-acting in this box, they might have formed their own theatrical troupe.

"The old black cat jumped over the wall
And ate the rat, the mouse and all. . ."

Clea sang along with the performer, and joined in the applause.

Sabine's expression was pensive. "Do you remember the Grotto in the Largo de São Paolo? Lisbon seems long ago and an immense distance away."

A brief time passed in reminiscences. Ned described for Julie the city's cathedrals and white houses, flowers and orange groves; the narrow streets of the Bairro Alta and the riot of color in the Chiado fruit market. Clea chimed in to explain that in the Peninsula she had carried her own brightly striped umbrella, for the sun was fierce, the roads were dusty, and there was little shade. Sabine contributed an account of large green lizards and other vermin such as spiders, mosquitoes, scorpions, snakes and ants and flies which insinuated themselves everywhere. The conversation moved on to the liberation of Spain and the battle of Vitoria; the storming of San Sebastian, the horrors of Badajoz. "'All the business of war, and indeed all the business of life, is to endeavor to find out what you don't know by what you do'," concluded Sabine.

Clea sat up a little straighter. "Are we playing quotes? That was Wellington. 'You should go to a pear tree for pears, not an elm.' Syrus." She nudged Julie. "Your turn."

Sabine also turned to Julie. "You are from Yorkshire, Miss Wynne? A parson's daughter, I believe?"

"I am."

"Your parents are deceased, I'm told. Have you other family? Frequently it is the younger son who is destined for the church."

"There is no one. That I know of, at any rate." Before Sabine could ask further questions, Julie launched into a discussion of tithe dinners and bell ringers, Bible study and the Penny Bank.

"We should suggest to Hannah that she become involved with charitable affairs," commented Clea. "It would give her something to do with her time. I am abandoning my attempts to learn the pianoforte; too much practicing is required. I found a lute in one of the attics earlier today, and have decided I will learn to play that. Oh, look!" She pointed at the ring, where an equestrian was dancing a hornpipe on the back of a galloping horse. He somersaulted backwards, leapt from the animal and remounted in the same sprint to face the horse's tail. Clea leaned forward, the better to see. Sabine watched Julie, her expression unreadable.

Ned, in his turn, was watching his friend. Kane claimed he didn't trust Sabine.

She glanced again at Julie. "Your papa the parson approved of attending such spectacles as these?"

"My papa the parson believed people were entitled to amusements, so long as duty wasn't shirked," Julie replied. "He was a keen follower of all field sports, and had a particular fondness for birds, which he shot and had stuffed for his collection. We had dead things perched all about the house."

"'*Acta deos nunquam mortalia fallunt*'," Clea said cheerfully. "The deeds of men never escape the gods. Hush, or you will miss The Flemish Hercules. According to the playbill, he is to somersault through a hoop of fire, sail over seven horses, and leap over a banner twelve feet high."

At the present moment, Hercules was supporting a seesaw platform and a trained horse. The horse walked to the middle then tilted the apparatus one way and the other with a step forward and then back. Julie was put in mind of the freaks she'd seen in Fleet Street, the posture-master who could extend his body in countless deformed shapes, the man who ate live coals and sucked on a red-hot poker five times a day. Clea in her turn was reminded of the *Art of Love*; and confessed to disappointment that Ovid, despite all his technical advice, barely mentioned the act itself. Ned thought of the touch of Julie's fingers as she traced his scars.

He caught Clea's eye. "Oh!" she said. "It is almost intermission. Will you accompany me, Sabine?"

"Of course."

Ned thought Sabine seemed eager to remove herself from the box. Maybe Julie's resemblance to Julian Faulkner was too painful, or maybe it wasn't painful enough. Ned surveyed the other private boxes, was surprised to find Lilah gazing back at him. He wouldn't have thought a brothel's madam would have a taste for amusements such as this.

Lilah inclined her head. Ned nodded in return.

"I'm sorry you aren't enjoying yourself," he said to Julie, who was still watching the stage. "Sabine and Clea are old friends. I thought they might entertain one another and leave me to entertain you."

Instead of showing interest in being entertained by Ned, as he had half-hoped she might, Julie toyed with her reticule. "Have you known Mrs. Viccars long?"

"Several years. She and her husband were a second family to Clea when we were all in the Peninsula. Francis was slain at Badajoz."

"Are you going to marry her?"

Ned blinked. "I most definitely am not. What tittle-tattle have you been listening to now?"

Julie scowled. "When you do decide to marry someone, you must tell me. Because. You know."

"Because?"

"Because then there'll be no more trifling. It wouldn't be right."

Not surprisingly, this comment put Ned in mind of the trifling he had already done. When he'd taken off his shirt and had Julie sprawled on his lap; had caressed her bare breast and had her pretty nipple in his mouth. After which she'd had his nipple in *her* mouth, along with his earlobe, though hardly at the same time.

He thought of her sharp knife, and wondered where she'd hid it. Perhaps it was strapped to her thigh. Perhaps he might disarm her with his hands and lips and teeth…

And perhaps he should distract himself before an embarrassing event occurred. "Speaking of touching—"

"We shouldn't be speaking of it," retorted Julie. "We wouldn't be if you weren't sitting so close."

"We've sat closer," Ned said wickedly. "I enjoyed it well. I thought you did too. Have I offended you, sweetheart? I admit that during our last meeting things got out of hand."

"It isn't that."

"What then?"

"He's here tonight."

There was another man in Julie's life? Ned said, "Who, pray, is 'he'?"

Julie cast him a reproachful glance. "It's *your* lap I sat on. As well as the rest. There'll definitely be no more touching if you think I'm the sort of girl who sits on more than one lap at a time."

Ned didn't think it. He would have been surprised if Julie had ever sat on any lap other than his own.

"I'm a dolt," he admitted. "If you need to box my ears again, I'll make no effort to defend myself."

Julie almost smiled. "I'll think on it. Him you call the puppet-master, that's who's here tonight."

Only years of experience enabled Ned to remain sitting calmly in his seat. "Point him out to me."

"I don't know what he looks like."

If Julie clenched her fists any tighter, she'd split her gloves. Ned pried her fingers open and took one hand in his. "If you don't know what he looks like how can you know he's here?"

"He's got someone watching me. By now he's probably watching you too. If you're not careful, you'll find yourself doing things you'd rather not."

"No," said Ned, "I won't. I can take care of myself. If you'd let me, I might take care of you. And no, I'm not offering you carte blanche. Although if you would like me to, I might."

She shook her head at him; after a moment's indecision, withdrew a folded square of paper from her reticule. "Don't let anyone see."

Ned took the note from her, read through it twice. *Rat's Castle. Tonight.*

"When did you receive this?"

"It was put into my hand when we first arrived. That's how I know he's here. You look cross."

Damned right Ned was cross. "The bastard could have waited until the entertainment ended to give you his note. He took his pleasure from ruining yours. Bates is in the audience, keeping an eye out. With luck, he may have seen the note being passed."

"He won't have seen anything. No one does."

"Julie." Ned waited until her eyes met his. "You must realize that this business has gone too far."

"You're like a terrier that's got a rat between its teeth. Thinking you may shake it to death."

"I may shake *you*. If you don't tell me the rest."

"Very well, if you must have it," muttered Julie. "He's known as Cap'n Jack."

Chapter Twenty-Five

It's too late to ask advice when the danger comes.
— Pubilius Syrus

She'd told what she should not. She'd peached on Cap'n Jack. For all Ned claimed he could protect her, the Cap'n would have her head as soon as he found out. Whatever had possessed her? Some daft notion that she wished to see the earl without his shirt again before she died? Julie returned to Ashcroft House to change her clothes before sneaking out again, and discovered that her things had been disturbed.

Maybe a servant had been curious. And maybe not. Julie made sure Ned's statue was safe in its hiding place. She tucked her knife securely in her sleeve and then set out.

Swells and beggars. Haves and have nots. Unless a girl wore blinders, the gulf between rich and poor was evident everywhere in London she looked. One street was lined with noble colonnades, bow windows and gleaming doorknockers; the next with gin-shops, pawnbrokers and broken-down dwellings so squalid they literally oozed filth. A mere few steps from the Strand to Fleet Street; another hop and she was in the Holy Land, made up of the adjacent slums of St Giles, named after the beggars' patron saint, and Seven Dials, where as many streets converged. Stinking alleyways wound between rotting tenements and taverns left over from an earlier century, in some places so narrow she had to turn sideways to pass. Julie rounded a corner, taking care not to stumble into a refuse heap composed of slops and ashes, rotting vegetables, offal from the butcher's stall. Where once she had been used to it, the stench now stung her nose. When the cesspits beneath the houses overflowed, they drained by means of a crudely built culvert into a partly open sewer trench in the middle of the street.

Overflow, the cesspits frequently did. As the ancient buildings overflowed with people seeking shelter from the night. It wasn't long past that Julie had no regular place to sleep. When her idea of riches had been to have enough pennies in her pocket to buy a spot in a lodging house crammed cellar to garret until there wasn't room for another louse. Six to a bed or more; six strangers, sick or healthy, drunk or sober, young or old. Julie had never slept alone in a bed before Pritchett bought her way out of Newgate.

Pritchett, on behalf of Cap'n Jack. Who was sending her back to the last place she wished to go. Julie pulled her shabby jacket closer around her and her cap down further on her brow. She passed haggard men with uncombed hair, women with gin-bloated faces and short pipes in their mouths, children in tattered jackets and broken-out shoes and breeches tied at the waist with bits of string.

Some remained upright. Others sprawled senseless in the street. Drunk for a penny, dead drunk for two, and no straw on which to sleep.

The steeple of St. Giles rose stark against the sky. Orator Jones was at his usual post near the churchyard's entrance, close by the gate adorned with a bas-relief of Judgment Day. He had on several hats tonight, along with numerous waistcoats and again as many jackets; was additionally girdled about with rag-wrapped parcels and canisters, matches and a tinderbox, a battered Bible and several tattered issues of *The Gentleman's Magazine*. His long beard was dirty yellow. On his fingers were numerous brass rings.

Julie handed him a scone liberated from the Ashcroft kitchens. "How blows the wind tonight?"

The scone disappeared into one of his waistcoats. "North-northwest. It is not, nor it cannot come to good. Take yourself along home, young Jules. The mouses are astir."

Orator was as quick to quote the Bible as Shakespeare and whatever else might take his fancy. Still, his current preference for Hamlet caused Julie's unease to ratchet up a notch. She wished she could indeed take herself along home—wherever 'home' might be —instead of prowling through the night like a cat in the gutters, looking for intrigue.

Through a gateway into Ivy Lane, then along a path that led to the center of St Giles's. Rat's Castle stood on the foundations of a leper hospital built by Queen Matilda in the eleventh century. More recently, the large dirty building had been the spot where condemned felons, on their way from Newgate Gaol to be hanged at Tyburn, had stopped for a bowl of ale. Now it was occupied by pickpockets and prostitutes and other members of the thieving fraternity. In the taproom, Tweaguey Tom would be playing his fiddle, while ten or a dozen lads and lasses enjoyed the dance, and smoked and snickered over glasses of gin and water, more or less plentiful according to the proceeds of a night passed in the pilfering of watches and money from drink-addled swells foolish enough to frequent cockfights and low gaming halls.

Julie's footsteps slowed. Once she would have joined the revelry without a second thought, a thumb to her nose for jingle-brains like Tony, who spent more on wine each year than his lowliest servant would earn in a lifetime, and gambled away his own future in a single night of play. Now instead of black-and-white, she was seeing shades of gray.

It was her that was betwixt and between. Julie was no lady, even if she'd gotten used to going about in petticoats and stays and walking like a girl. But neither was she the street urchin who had dropped by the Castle for gossip and a pint. It was all the fault of a certain earl, who didn't act like he should. Who'd sat her on his lap and had his hand up her skirts and taken her to Astley's where more than all the spectacle she'd enjoyed sitting close to him.

After all his soldiering, Ned found it dull to be an earl. Julie would have given all she owned to be dull for a while. Especially in this moment, because she'd stopping paying attention to her surroundings and now stood smack in the middle of a bleak alley with a hulking brute looming up in front of her.

He smiled, revealing missing teeth. "Here's our little pullet, come home to roost."

Julie twisted her wrist and her knife slid into her hand. So much for pretending she was an ordinary person with an ordinary life.

This was what Orator had meant. Carbuncle-faced Mick with his malmsey nose had been expecting her. And Mick had found out that 'Jules' was a girl.

She'd pretend it didn't matter. That she wasn't afraid. When he came close enough, she'd ram her blade into his belly. "Move out of my way."

Mick didn't budge an inch. "Word is, chick-a-biddy, you've got above yourself."

Came a snicker from behind her. Julie spun round to see another of the persons she would most rather have not. "I'll get above you, missy," Pego leered. "Like it bread-and-butter style me-self."

One knife. Two thugs. Her odds were worse than Tony's. "Mother Yarwood sent for me," Julie said, in the tone Georgiana used to scold her servants. "Let me pass."

"It's us as have come to fetch you. Make sure you arrived all in one—" Mick snickered. "Piece."

He advanced. Julie retreated. Pego followed as if they were doing some intricate ballroom dance.

"And it's us that'll be kept waiting, 'cause someone else is to have you first." Pego grabbed his genitals and provided additional, graphic detail. If Julie wasn't certain of all the things he mentioned, 'wearing your muff' and 'suck my sugar stick' were clear.

"You may kiss my arse, lobcock." She gripped her blade.

"Uppish, ain't she?" marveled Pego.

"Rightly needs a lesson." Julie glanced in Mick's direction, and he threw a handful of dirt in her eyes. Blinded, she struck out, felt the knife wrenched from her hand.

She was heaved over someone's shoulder. Cruel fingers pinched and pawed. Julie shrieked; kicked and twisted; jabbed her elbow into her captor's throat and her teeth into his arm.

He cursed. A fist slammed into her jaw. Julie's head snapped back so hard rockets burst before her eyes.

A shot rang out. Mick jerked and cursed. His grip on Julie eaed and she flung herself aside, landing in an awkward tangle, her left arm twisted beneath her, the air knocked out of her lungs. She scooted backwards through foul-smelling rubbish until her back rested against what felt like a wall. Her entire body throbbed like a bruise. She'd had worse, Julie told herself, as she struggled to catch her breath. Her eyes were watering furiously.

All around were sounds of struggle. When her vision cleared, Julie saw Mick sprawled senseless on the pavement, blood streaming from a bullet wound to his thigh. Pego was putting up a good fight. Bates planted a muzzler that sent him to the ground.

Ned knelt in front of her. He looked much less an earl than one of the more successful sort of criminals, a gentleman of the road or a master thief, decked out in a long many-caped coat and jaunty beaver hat. "Are you all right?"

"Just dandy," growled Julie, because she was frightened and her arm hurt and it was her who wanted what she couldn't have. "What took you so long? I thought for certain you'd got lost."

"I'm sorry, buttercup." Ned inspected her cheek, felt her tender jaw. "The night is so dark, and you're so quick, and we had to lag behind so no one realized we were there. I lost several years off my life when I heard you scream."

Julie *had* screamed, hadn't she? Like a simpering debutante at sight of a mouse. She was growing soft.

Mick groaned and began to stir. Bates silenced him with a well-aimed blow. Disaster had been averted, for the moment. Julie turned her head and vomited.

Ned handed her his handkerchief. Bates cleared his throat. "Begging your pardon, sir. Street fights are common enough hereabouts that no one's likely to come looking, but it might be a good idea to make ourselves scarce."

"Right you are." Ned tucked away his pistol, took Julie's hand and pulled her to her feet.

It hurt like blazes. She yelped. Ned let loose a string of oaths more colorful than any Julie had heard in all her time in the streets.

"You should have said that you were hurt." His hands moved

over her. "I don't think anything is broken. Take a deep breath." As she did so, he lifted her into his arms. Bates paced alertly alongside his master as they headed back toward the more civilized part of town.

Every footstep hurt. Julie didn't mind. The earl had proved himself a good man to have at one's back. Or front. Or anywhere in between. "I'm ruining your coat. You'll never get it clean."

"The devil with my coat. Who were those men?"

"Mick and Pego. They're Mother Yarwood's bully-backs." Who provided whatever services might be needed regarding unruly whores and customers alike.

Ned swore again, this time in a foreign language. She wondered if it was Portuguese.

Why had Mother Yarwood turned against her? Julie had done nothing to rouse the woman's wrath. Unless Cap'n Jack knew she'd blabbed.

One thing was certain: Julie wouldn't soon be visiting the Holy Land again any time soon. "Where are you taking me?"

"To Wakely Court. You can hardly return to Lady Georgiana smelling like a sewer rat. And I want to have a closer look at that arm."

She *was* a trifle fragrant. Ned didn't seem to mind. Julie thought of Rose. Dangling at her slipper-strings, indeed.

Chapter Twenty-Six

*Show me a lover with self-control, and
I'll give you his weight in gold.* — Plautus

James the footman sleepily opened the front door, gaped at sight of his master carrying a ragamuffin. "Hot water, and lots of it," said Ned. "Liniment and bandages. Bring them to my room."

Tidcombe hurried into the hallway, a robe thrown on over his nightshirt, a voluminous nightcap perched on his head. Unlike the footman, he was not deceived as to the ragamuffin's sex. "The young person will need other clothing. Perhaps Mistress Clea …"

"No." Ned was already halfway up the stair.

"Mayhap the stable boy has a spare rig," suggested Bates.

And mayhap the cook wouldn't burn the porridge, so that Tidcombe might enjoy his breakfast for a change. Tidcombe sent the footman to inquire of the stable boy if he had an extra set of clothes. Meanwhile Bates set out for the kitchen to oversee boiling water and bandages, behind Tidcombe's back as it were, thereby putting the butler's nose further out of joint.

Julie was very quiet. Ned recognized excitement's aftermath. He'd witnessed the phenomenon before, had felt it himself. One braced to face danger, and when the danger passed, experienced a letdown of the nerves.

What might have happened had she not shown him that note, had she not been persuaded that they should follow her? Julie hadn't thought it fitting for an earl to traipse through the Holy Land in the wake of someone like herself. Didn't understand that Ned would happily traipse after her anywhere. "Trust me," he said.

"Don't have much choice, do I?" Julie buried her face against his chest. Only when Ned kicked open the door to his bedroom did she raise her head.

He tried to see the chamber through her eyes. It was luxurious, as befit the master of this venerable pile, with Turkey carpets on the floor, and ancient tapestries on the walls. The stone fireplace's arched opening was spanned by a simple mantle with two elegant rosettes on either side. The formidable four-post bedstead was carved within an inch of its existence, headboard and footboard alike. The room was additionally furnished with chairs upholstered in silks and velvet, a number of chests used for various purposes, a writing desk with two pedestal cabinets of exquisite silversmith's work.

Julie leaned back against him. "The Cap'n must know I told you."

"That's not likely," Ned replied, thinking she must be frightened indeed if she wasn't inspecting the room and noting what items might be easiest to filch. "Maybe he's angry with you for some other reason. The codebook might not be what he expected."

Julie stiffened. "What do you know that I don't?"

"There's another codebook, sunshine. Though not in this house."

"You might've told me sooner," she muttered.

He might, had Ned been sure of her. Bates came through the doorway, trailed by the Marys with buckets of hot water and James with a huge copper tub; followed in turn by Mrs. Scroggs with an armful of clothing and an air of curiosity. Tidcombe oversaw the preparation of the bath, his expression long-suffering, his nightcap tipsily askew. When the lot of them at last departed, Ned set Julie on her feet.

Her face was pale beneath its dirt. She attempted to remove her jacket, and winced. Ned took hold of the shabby garment and ripped it from neck to hem. The shirt followed. Julie clutched her damaged arm protectively to her chest. Ned set her on a carved chair, pulled off her shoes and stockings. When he unfastened her breeches, she blushed bright pink.

This wasn't the way he'd imagined disrobing her. Ned wanted

her flushed not with embarrassment, but lust. "I will leave the rest to you." He walked to the far side of the room and stood staring at a tapestry that depicted the hunt of the wild boar, listening to clothing rustle and water splash as Julie stepped—slipped, it sounded like—into the tub.

She cleared her throat. "It's all right to turn around."

Ned did so, and immediately wished he might climb into the bath with her. To distract himself, he gathered up her cast-off clothing, and his greatcoat, and dumped the lot out into the hall.

He shouldn't watch her, Ned told himself; but couldn't look away. Not much of Julie was visible above the edge of the deep tub. A glimpse of her bare arms and shoulders made him desperate to see the rest.

Ned leaned against the wall. He must think of something less provocative than the naked young female in his bath. Such as what use 'Cap'n Jack' meant to make of his codebook. Had meant to make, unless Ned missed his guess, of a certain French diplomat.

Codebooks. Diplomats. Matters of national importance. Ned decided reluctantly that he must mention Cap'n Jack to Kane.

Julie stole a glance at him. "This is very strange."

Strange wasn't the half of it. "Would you prefer I leave the room?"

She shook her head, to his relief. "I meant it's strange that you're an earl. You didn't act like one tonight."

"I was never meant to be one. There's been a lot to learn. Fortunately, the estates rub on well enough without me doing much more than keeping a watchful eye out for neglect or waste."

Awkwardly, Julie tried to apply a soapy cloth to her damaged arm. "I can't imagine what it's like."

Definitely Ned was a nodcock, so set on doing nothing to alarm her that he'd forgotten she was hurt. He threw off his jacket and knelt by the tub.

Julie blinked as he rolled up his shirtsleeves. "I need to see for myself that you're not badly damaged," he said.

She didn't argue with him, or protest as he searched for strained muscles, joints that might have been pushed out of place.

He wasn't caressing her, not really, Ned told himself, as the back of his hand brushed the underside of one soft breast.

Julie's breath caught. Ned clenched his teeth. He could see her body clearly through the soapy water. If he didn't move away from her soon he was like to spontaneously combust.

"You're going to have a nasty bruise," he said, finding this an excellent excuse to trail his fingers along her jaw. "And you'll need to be careful of that arm."

Julie rubbed her cheek against his hand. "You meant me to have pleasure, didn't you? Earlier tonight?"

"I mean to give you a great deal of pleasure, but this is neither the time or place. Here, let me wash that muck from your hair."

She bent her head. Ned lathered soap through her matted curls, rinsed, repeated the process. Mick and Pego should be shot for hurting her. Dismembered. Eviscerated. Their heads stuck on pikes adorning London Bridge. Ned had been sorely tempted, but brutes like those merely did what they were told. He had let them go as warning that Julie no longer lacked protection. "You mentioned Mother Yarwood. Who is she?"

Mother Yarwood, explained Julie—as Ned lifted her and toweled her dry, rubbed her arm with liniment and helped her don the stable boy's clothing, a temptation-laden task: she had decided it was all right for him to see her naked though she didn't know how she should act, and her self-consciousness proved more erotic than the posturings of the most skilled courtesan—was a woman of considerable enterprise, one of her undertakings being to snatch children off the street and train them up in crime. Julie supposed she should be grateful to have been given a place of sorts, but if Mother Yarwood hadn't taken her, some other would. Like everybody else in the Holy Land, Mother Yarwood answered to Cap'n Jack.

By the time Julie had finished talking, Ned had her set before him on a stool in front of the hearth, a hairbrush in his hand. The stable boy's shoes having proven too big, her feet were bare.

She shifted around to face him. "About the other—you think I'm too young."

"You *are* too young. But I don't think of you that way." Ned crooked a finger under her chin and tipped up her face. "Those eyes of yours have seen enough for someone twice your age. While I am twice your age, or almost."

"I don't think of you that way. It's because of how you act." Her smile faded. "Your friend, Lord Saxe. He knows who I am."

"Buttercup," said Ned, with feeling, "*I* don't know who you are."

This declaration, for some odd reason that only another female might have understood, had Julie scrambling into Ned's lap. "How much *does* the baron know?"

Since she was in his lap, he might as well enjoy it. Careful not to disturb her damaged arm, Ned cradled her against his chest. "I've no idea, and it doesn't matter. If you're a trap, as Kane suspects, I am firmly caught. Now that you have me, what do you mean to do with me, sweetheart?"

Her breath, as she laughed, was warm against his neck. "If you were a fish, I would toss you back."

"No you wouldn't." He smoothed his hand over her hair.

"No I wouldn't. But I should." And then, gruffly, she allowed as she wouldn't mind it if he trifled with her more. "Yes, I know I'm damaged, and you think you shouldn't, but hear me out. I'd made up my mind before, but now I'm doubly sure. If you was to tumble me, I wouldn't be worth so much to a buttock broker then."

Never had he had a more blunt, or appalling invitation. "This is not a good idea," said Ned, in defiance of those portions of his person that thought it an excellent notion indeed. "You've been set upon, and threatened, and aren't thinking straight."

Julie plucked at a loose thread on her trousers. "You don't want me any more. Is it because of what happened tonight?"

Ned was used to females. One way and another, he'd dealt well with females all his life. Why, with this particular female, was he forever setting his foot wrong?

Julie didn't understand that everyone she'd known had used her for one purpose or another. Nor would Ned wish her to realize. But he couldn't also use her and then set her aside.

He didn't think he could set her aside at all, as witnessed by her comfortable perch on his lap.

Ned brushed damp curls back off her forehead, tipped up her face so he could look into her eyes. "What happened tonight only makes me want you more." She looked skeptical. "Truly. On my honor as a gentleman."

"I'd rather have the word of a gamester." Julie caught his hand and placed it against her breast. "A gamester plays out the cards he's dealt."

Lord, but Ned was tempted. Before he could give in to his baser nature, his sister emerged from the dressing room, a bundle tucked under one arm, and Cerberus beneath the other. The dog snarled. Ned snatched back his hand.

"'*Da mihi castitatem et continentiam, sed noli modo*'. St. Augustine," said Clea. "Make me chaste and pure but not yet. The two of you are setting me a dreadful example. What is a buttock broker, pray?"

Julie tried to scoot off Ned's lap. He held her fast. "Speaking of dreadful examples. Have we not had numerous conversations about eavesdropping?"

"There is a passage in my dressing room. It leads out into the garden through the old Tudor drains." Clea settled in one of the upholstered chairs, Cerberus and her bundle both clutched on her lap. "I suspected some mischief was afoot the instant Bates started hovering in the hall. Now tell me everything."

Muttered Ned, with feeling, "Heaven forbid." Julie said, "A buttock-broker is a bawd. A dimber cove is a pretty fellow—"

"—Like Ned," offered Clea.

"—and a bumfiddle is a backside. A purveyor of pronouns is a schoolmaster, a tickle-text is a parson, and to dance is to shake a toe." Julie glanced up at Ned. "I must return to Ashcroft House, and have lost my knife."

"Ned will loan you one of his," said Clea. "An excellent knife, souvenir of the Peninsular Campaign. Why must you return to Ashcroft House? You could stay here with us. Oh, I see. We must act as if nothing unusual has happened. So as not to sound the alarm."

Ned wished he might keep Julie. He wanted her, fairly desperately; even more, he wanted her kept safe. "You won't be climbing for some time, sunshine. Will you be able to get back into the house?"

"I came out through a side door and left it unlocked."

Cerberus grew bored with his ill-temper and curled up for a nap. Clea patted the dog. "I would like to climb a drainpipe. Will you show me how?"

"She will not," said Ned. "Unless it's your intention to send me into a brain fever thinking about what drainpipes you might wish to climb." To Julie, he added, "You'll go nowhere without an escort."

"After tonight, I wouldn't mind if an entire regiment tramped around in my wake." Julie bent to pick up the stable boy's too-large boots.

Clea held out her bundle. "Good stout walking shoes from the Peninsula. See how helpful I can be?"

Chapter Twenty-Seven

Don't wish ill for your enemy, plan it.
— Pubilius Syrus

An accident at Astley's? Lady Georgiana had never heard of such a thing. Not surprising that the performers might occasionally be battered and bruised; it was hardly natural to ride a horse whilst standing on one's head; but for a member of the audience to be similarly afflicted was the outside of enough.

"I should have never given my permission. I don't know what I was thinking," she said aloud. In point of fact, Georgiana knew exactly what had been going through her mind; to wit, that Lord Dorset was the perfect person to distract Julie from her son. The earl could have distracted even Georgiana, had he cared to, which naturally he did not because she was too old, a circumstance that put her further out of charity with everyone in her vicinity.

"Let us lay our cards on the table! While this horrid business cannot be what I like, I may at least make sure it doesn't become known all around the town. I will insure that you have a generous amount of pin money, Miss Wynne, in return for which you will insure that Tony does not . . ." Georgiana fumbled for her vinaigrette. "That Tony does not! And so *you* do not, he will stick close to you as a court plaster from now on." She sailed ahead of them through the shop door, a vision of exacerbated elegance in jaconet muslin with a deep flounce and ruff and a lilac cloth pelisse, a bonnet of yellow twilled sarcenet tied with a long bow of lilac ribbon and adorned with a bunch of violets in front.

Before Tony could shepherd her into the shop, Julie caught his arm. "So I do not *what*?" she said.

"Deuced if I know." Bad enough, thought Tony, that his mama regarded him as if he were a caperwit. Now Julie was frowning at him in the same way.

He supposed it was his duty to clarify matters. "I have been avoiding you."

"So I noticed. Why?"

"Maman took the notion I'd been compromised." Julie looked blank. "By you," Tony added, in case he hadn't made that clear.

Now Julie looked astonished. "I compromised you?"

"Of course you didn't compromise me! I'd have known it if you did, wouldn't I?"

Julie wasted a brief moment considering the numerous things Tony didn't know. "Lady Georgiana thinks I compromised you?"

"*Thought* you'd compromised me, and was blackmailing me as a consequence, and that's why I brought you into the house." Tony was glum. "She knows better now."

"Knows better?" Julie gave him a shake. "You didn't tell her—"

"Hsst! I meant Maman took another notion. Because of your corset. I was looking at it when she came into the bedroom."

"*You* went through my things?"

Tony had the grace to blush. "It isn't like I wished to! I was told to find a statue. Sounds like a deuced ugly thing."

"Ahem!" Lady Georgiana loomed in the shop's doorway. "I do not believe Julie would care to have her fitting in the street."

Julie didn't give a fig about her fitting. She was mulling over Tony's admission that he had been told to search her room.

The girl had questions, Tony decided. Stood to reason that she would. She'd want those questions answered. Avoiding her had been the right thing. It occurred to Tony that he had tried to avoid Pritchett, and look how *that* had turned out.

Down on his luck as Tony had been lately, he wouldn't have been surprised to see the Runner pop up again at any moment. A swift glance around the dressmaker's shop revealed no bespectacled little man with thinning hair. Tony was perfectly at ease in these surroundings, though he suspected Julie was not, a circumstance that might have exercised his imagination had he given it more than a moment's consideration. He had dressed in accordance with his dejected spirits—jacket of Devonshire brown with extremely large buttons of his own design, waistcoat of parma violet, cravat tied in the Mail Coach because it required very little starch, appropriate because if Tony had any starch in his backbone he wouldn't be in this fix—but the shopkeeper's wares soon distracted him sufficiently that he was able to engage in a discussion of the relative merits of alliballi and pullcat, chine silk and shagreen; put forth his opinion of the colors Morone and Aurora, Cossack green and Russian flame. His spirits revived further when his mama withdrew with Julie into one of the smaller fitting rooms.

Julie was as uncomfortable as Tony had suspected. For one thing, her long-sleeved chintz dress and chip straw hat had been provided not by a fashionable modiste but a used clothing store in Monmouth Street, Seven Dials; and if Julie had once believed they belonged to a nobleman's disgraced daughter, she knew better now. For another, trying on clothes was made awkward by her damaged arm. She stood silently on the stool while a seamstress twitched and adjusted and stuck pins in the fabric draped around her, all under Lady Georgiana's watchful eye.

The new dresses were breathtakingly pretty. Under other circumstances Julie might have enjoyed herself very well. Instead, she puzzled over Lady Georgiana's statements. As best she could make out, Tony was to dog her heels while she was to prevent him from doing some unknown thing.

Ned's knife was strapped to her thigh beneath her petticoats. If the seamstress was aware of its existence, she gave no sign. The poor woman was being driven distracted by Lady Georgiana, who had decided that where she once wanted Julie's bosom placed on display, now she wanted her neckline drawn up to her throat.

She was also having second thoughts about bright colors. Julie envisioned her pretty dresses being snatched away. "I like them as they are," she interjected. "If you do not, I'll pay for them myself, out of the pin money you promised to provide." Georgiana's jaws snapped shut. She looked as if she had bit into a sour plum.

The fittings went smoothly after that, Georgiana's complaints being confined to a tight-lipped minimum. Julie was buttoned back into her plain chintz dress and the gowns promised for delivery within the next few days. She returned with Lady Georgiana to the shop's main room, where Tony had been amusing himself, first with fashion dolls and patterns, then with the various trimmings stored in the drawers behind the counter, lace and braid and ribbons, buttons and beads. The viscount couldn't sit long in one place, and had a passion for pretty things.

His mama glowered at him. Tony set aside the fan he'd been inspecting, which featured a bucolic rural scene painted on the silk. Lady Georgiana was in her own turn distracted by the arrival of an acquaintance and the intelligence that the ladies of Britain, headed by the Duchess of York, were getting up a subscription to erect a monument to Lord Wellington, now Marquis of Douro and Duke of Wellington, who was due to soon arrive in London and make his first appearance in the House of Lords, which would be the signal for another round of celebrations to begin. The monument was to be formed of cannon taken by him in numerous engagements, and would occupy a prominent site in Hyde Park. Opinion at present inclined toward a group of classical steeds, but a certain contingent favored a colossal bronze nude. Upon learning Lady Dorset was among those who championed the horses, Lady Georgiana cast her vote for the nude.

"Maman's crowing on account of Lady Dorset being in her dotage," Tony muttered. "I don't know why Maman should be, because she ain't far behind."

Julie's thoughts returned to their previous conversation. "Why not tell Lady Georgiana it was a mistake?"

Tony was confused. "Hannah ain't in her dotage?"

"No— Yes— I don't know! Nor do I care. I meant that your, ah, acquaintance with my corset was a mistake."

"It wasn't a mistake. I was curious about the construction of the thing. It don't signify. Or shouldn't! Just because a fellow ain't addicted to wenching don't mean he's a Miss Molly."

Julie recalled from her time on the streets that there were men who preferred the company of their own kind. "Ah," she said.

"There ain't no 'Ah' about it!" Tony snarled. "If I'd rather study the harp than pugilism, so what?"

There were, Julie reflected, some advantages to not having had a parent. "You know your own business best."

"Tell that to Maman. She thinks she knows more than I do. Said that she would *fix* me. I don't want to be fixed. Perfectly happy the way I am." Tony reconsidered. "Or I was! About that statue. I don't suppose you'd care to give it to me? Or tell me where it's hid?"

"I would not." Someone knew she had Ned's statue. How?

"I thought you'd say that." Gloomily, Tony studied her. "That's a dandy bruise you have on your chin."

So it was, and a thick application of rice powder hadn't hid it. "I walked into a door."

Tony snorted. "I ain't enough of a corkbrain to believe *that* clanker. What really happened?"

"The Cap'n, that's what happened," Julie hissed.

"Heigh ho!" said Lady Georgiana, behind them, causing both to jump. "What are the two of you whispering about? I'll tolerate no more secrets, do you hear me? Come along. We have other errands to run."

Tony awarded his mama an unappreciative glance. "It ain't polite to interrupt."

"Fiddle faddle!" Georgiana swept them before her through the shop like they were dirt and she a broom. "It is time, son, that you choose a companion for life. Madalyn Tate is from all accounts a biddable enough female. Dorset has thrown her over, and she will be grateful for any crumb. Furthermore, she has already proven she can produce a son. Understand me, Tony. There *will* be a son."

Son? Wife? Had he just been called a 'crumb'? "You don't like children. Said so yourself," protested Tony, appalled.

"Try not to be more of a sapskull than you can help." Georgiana pinched his ear. "You are a viscount. Viscounts require heirs. This predicament is entirely your fault."

His fault? *His* fault? It was not his fault but Georgiana's that they were in this pickle. Were she not so clutch-fisted, Tony would have had the wherewithal to pay off his vowels.

If only, when his papa unexpectedly expired, Tony hadn't permitted his mama to meddle with matters of finance. At the time he had been too overwhelmed to protest. Now he didn't know how to wrest away the purse-strings without her raising a rumpus, and turning blue in the face, and drumming her heels on the floor, which was a sight no man wished to see, especially if the rumpus-raiser was his own flesh and blood. However, if she *was* discovered to be in her dotage— Tony was a grown man, and should be able to manage his own affairs.

Should be able to. He hadn't done an impressive job of it so far. Georgiana was still going on about scandals, sick-making prospects, and prospective brides. "Maman," he interrupted, "cut line."

"You raise your voice to me, you ungrateful child?" Georgiana pressed a hand to her breast. "You might spare a thought for my indifferent health."

"Why should I?" inquired Tony. "If you was half as sick as you wish the world to think you are, you wouldn't have the energy to be always cutting up stiff."

"I never!"

"Yes, you are. Doing it right now."

Julie was stiff from standing. Her jaw hurt. Wanting no part of another Ashcroft family squabble, she was first out the shop door. Behind her, mother and son continued to batter one another with uncomplimentary terms. Georgiana got in two good thrusts with "rattle-pate" and "cabbagehead". Tony retaliated with "nasty, twitty old flap-dragon." Georgiana fumbled for her vinaigrette.

Pedestrians thronged the busy street. Coachmen shouted and cracked their whips. Hooves clattered against cobblestones. Street sellers shouted out their wares. The sun shone brightly for a change, and people had ventured out of doors to enjoy the treat.

Julie was suddenly hungry for sheep's trotters, or a Chelsea bun. She watched as a pickpocket walked boldly toward his prey, took an expensive handkerchief from his pocket as if to wipe his nose. This was done with a horizontal flourish in front of his quarry's chest. Under cover of the flourish, the thief's other hand moved up unobserved to draw the pin clear of his victim's scarf.

Julie wistfully recalled the days when she'd had no more to worry about than her next meal. Life had been simpler then. Before she wound up in Newgate, and met Pritchett, and Ned.

She was nobody. Ned was an earl. Yet he'd taken her to Astley's, just as if she was a lady, and she could have thought herself in heaven if not for Cap'n Jack.

And then Ned had rescued her, taken her to his home and found her clothes and given her a bath. He didn't take advantage, much as she had wished he would, and so she had boldly placed his hand on her breast. Had felt him against her bottom, growing hot and hard. If not for Clea interrupting, Julie might have said goodbye to her girlhood in that great carved bed.

She'd resented the interruption greatly in the moment. Now she didn't mind so much. There was nothing romantic about her being battered and bruised and dressed in a boy's clothes.

'Romantic?' Now she sounded as sappy as Rose. Julie had sent off a note this morning warning her friend to be on guard. She watched a chariot rattle by, drawn by cream horses and heralded by trumpets and drums, advertising the Pleasure Gardens at Vauxhall.

Behind her, Lady Georgiana's arguments trailed off. Julie half-turned—

And felt a sharp blow between her shoulder blades. She stumbled out into the street, smack in the path of an iron-wheeled carriage traveling at considerable speed. The driver's horrified face loomed terrifyingly close as he hauled back on his reins.

A strong arm scooped around her waist and hauled her out of danger's path. "You must be more careful where you step, Miss Wynne," said Lord Saxe.

Chapter Twenty-Eight

You cannot put the same shoe on every foot.
— Pubilius Syrus

"She was pushed," said Kane. "I have no idea by whom. Niddicock would like to think it was an accident."

"Niddicock," retorted Ned, "is caught fast under a blackmailer's thumb. He might have pushed Julie himself." He brought his companion current with recent events, not the amazing equestrian feats at Astley's, but the aftermath. "The puppet-master's name is Cap'n Jack. No sooner did Julie tell me than she was almost snatched up. Since she received the note *before* she told me, the thing must have already been planned. If this is an example of how the Cap'n reacts when thwarted, Julie is right to be afraid." The only thing preventing Ned from going immediately to reassure himself that she was unharmed was a reluctance to tip his hand. If the Cap'n didn't know yet that Julie had betrayed him—and how could he know? Ned disregarded Kane's speculation that Julie might be playing a deep game—then Ned must do nothing to suggest that he knew more than he should. Which meant he must pretend it was a normal occurrence for a girl dressed like a boy to be set upon for purposes of being imprisoned in a brothel, and the next day came perilously close to falling in front of a speeding carriage. Why Kane had been present to affect so miraculous a rescue, Ned didn't need to ask. Kane was sufficiently suspicious of Julie to be keeping an eye on her himself.

Kane's suspicious eye was currently fixed on Ned. "Niddicock wouldn't have had the brass to push her," the baron pointed out.

Ned was not so certain. Impossible to predict what a man

might do if driven to take desperate steps. He felt like resorting to dramatic measures himself.

"This might be about the codebook," he said aloud. "The one that Julie filched not being the one the Cap'n wants."

"Ah." The codebook in Kane's own possession, with notations of payments made for clandestine intelligence services rendered, would greatly broaden a blackmailer's scope. "A spy, perhaps?"

"Or in the employ of one." Ned gazed at the glittering throng massed in Lady Escue's reception rooms. "That might explain how he knew about the notebook in the first place."

As if matters were not already complicated enough, reflected Kane. "M'sieur Morel claims to have no idea why his wife hanged herself. If he has a mistress, he informs us, what Frenchman does not? His wife never showed the slightest interest in the details of his work, and why should she have, pray? Everyone knows that political matters are beyond the grasp of the female brain. There will naturally be an inquest."

"And the foregone conclusion, that Amélie Morel died by her own hand," remarked Ned. "I, for one, am not convinced."

"Nor am I. You look like you are bent on mayhem. A more amiable expression would not be out of place."

Ned bared his teeth. It was the closest he could come to a smile. Julie was tucked away at Ashcroft House, Lady Georgiana's nerves having been so over-taxed by the near-accident that she took to her bed. Tony too was spending the evening at home, upset that something had happened, or almost happened, to a young woman residing under his roof, and if she hadn't been under his roof at the fateful moment, he was still responsible for her, so she should remain indoors where she'd be safe.

Safe, thought Ned. Safe, that was, unless either Lady Georgiana or her muttonheaded son were responsible for Julie's stumble out into the street, which might be assumed to be the case if she next took a sudden tumble down the stair. In that case, Ned would deal with the Ashcrofts himself, and be damned to behavior fitting an earl, a subject about which he had heard a great deal tonight, having been badgered into serving as his cousin's escort during her reemergence into the Polite World. Ned had been fit to throttle her until Kane and Sabine arrived, an event which made Hannah gnash her teeth, because she had no sooner set out to squelch the rumor that Ned was meant for Sabine Viccars than Mrs. Viccars contrived to neatly cut him out of the flock of marriage-minded females, remarking at the same time that Maddie Tate was a good sort of girl and wasn't it a pity that there were those who had nothing better to do than make up unkind tales out of whole cloth.

Three ostrich feathers swayed in their direction, attached to a small satin hat perched precariously atop Hannah's head. "I suggest the library," said Kane. "Lady Dorset does not strike me as a female with an affinity for books."

Kane was not in the most amiable of moods himself. He had earlier spent several hours at the Guildhall, where the City of London was entertaining the Allied Annoyances and seven hundred assorted guests at a cost of £20,000, approximately a quarter of Napoleon's entire budget for a year on Elba. Sabine had also been privileged to attend, along with Countess Lieven and the Duchess of York, result of the Grand Duchess having decided at the last minute, despite the fact that females were not invited to civic occasions, to accompany the gentlemen.

Matters had deteriorated rapidly from that point. Prinny, who had planned to share a carriage with the Czar, thereby avoiding being boo'd by the crowds, was not pleased. He had been even less pleased when, after being forced to await the arrival of Alexander and his sister for an hour, he was kept waiting longer while they stopped to talk with two of his most bitter enemies. The Grand Duchess then took exception to the music. Prinny had been forced to beg that she allow the National Anthem to be sung. At last, reluctantly, she conceded, causing Lord Liverpool to remark that if people didn't know how to properly behave, they should stay at home.

Kane wished he might have done so. When Prinny left the Hall at half past eleven, he and Sabine escaped. Now here they were at another tedious entertainment, result of Sabine being again set on rescuing Ned. Her efforts to discourage the matchmaking mamas by claiming a romantic disappointment had backfired: any number of young ladies now wished to try to help mend the earl's broken heart; would probably still have wished to do so—so great was the lure of becoming a Countess—if he wasn't pretty as a picture (as one admiring young lady put it), but had a limp, or a squint, or stank like a goat.

Kane knew how it felt be hunted. As an astonishingly wealthy baron, he was only marginally less eligible than his friend. However, his reputation as a dangerous flirt stood him in good stead. Ambitious parents tended to eye Lord Saxe askance, aware he'd not easily be brought up to scratch.

Sabine's arrival caused a stir. She wore a long-sleeved gown of claret-colored velvet, cut low in front and behind. Ruby drops gleamed at her ears and throat. Her fair hair was gathered into curls on the back of her head. She wove her way toward them through the crowd.

Sabine Viccars was the most beautiful woman Kane had ever seen. As well as the most calculating. He imagined she'd been busy spreading rumors that would put Hannah further out of charity with them both. Kane waited until they reached the solitude of the library, the door firmly closed behind them, to relate the latest news. Sabine had already been told about Julie's close escape from being crushed under horses' hooves and carriage wheels.

As Kane spoke, Ned strolled around the tidy library, which was much unlike his own; it contained a great deal of gleaming dark wood and leather-bound volumes lined up neatly on the shelves. He thought the chamber would have benefited from Cerberus sprawled on the hearth and Clea snuggled in one of the deep chairs, reading Ovid and/or a fashion magazine.

Sabine frowned. "Are we certain there is a connection between these things?"

"Nothing has been stolen since the codebook." Ned picked up the fireplace poker and applied it to the embers burning on the hearth. "The item the Cap'n now seems most anxious to retrieve is Julie herself."

Sabine wanted to know more about this Cap'n. Ned told her

what little he had gleaned from Julie, and about Mother Yarwood, who trained up young thieves. "There is a place in the Holy Land known as Rat's Castle. Julie was bidden to meet Mother Yarwood there. Someone meant for her not to arrive."

"You may be making mountains out of molehills," remarked Kane. "London has long done a brisk trade in virgins. Are we sure the chit *is* a virgin, Ned?"

Ned threw down the poker. "We're sure you wouldn't disapprove so greatly if I hadn't become a bloody earl."

Kane knew he was behaving badly. He couldn't stop himself. "You inherited a title, and with it responsibilities. Instead of tending to them, you spend your time dangling after a sticky-fingered stray."

"You're starting to sound like Hannah," Ned retorted. "It must come from being born with a silver teaspoon shoved up your arse."

Kane wavered between apologizing and bidding Ned to blazes. Before he could do either, Sabine touched his arm. "You *are* being a bit of a prig. If Miss Wynne is an innocent, as Ned believes she is— and I think you must agree that at this point he probably has a good notion of the truth of that—we can hardly let her fall into a villain's hands, whatever her background may be."

Kane thought that Sabine was being overly influenced by Julie Wynne's resemblance to someone she'd once known. "You have had an opportunity to the girl."

Sabine removed her hand from his arm. "Sometimes I saw a similarity to Julian, sometimes not. Perhaps it is merely as they say, that each of us has a twin."

Was she being truthful? Kane couldn't tell. His usual ability to read people didn't apply to Sabine.

She and Ned were speaking low together. Kane turned away. He was used to females feeling possessive of him, not the other way around. The shoe was on the wrong foot now, and he didn't like it much.

He did like Sabine, however, though he didn't understand her. Even when a man held her in his arms and listened to her sigh with pleasure, there was a part of her that remained beyond his reach.

Was this how Kane's lovers felt about him? That he satisfied a momentary craving, fulfilled a fleeting passion, but was ultimately of no more lasting substance than a morsel of fine chocolate, briefly sweet on the lips and tongue, leaving behind a slight bitter memory along with the sweet?

And when had he started wanting to be remembered? He was a rakehell, was he not? Rakehells didn't go around hoping their memory would be fondly tucked away in some corner of a lady's heart.

The conversation faltered. Sabine drew her shawl closer around her shoulders. Kane asked, "Are you cold?"

"I'm always cold," she responded.

"Not always," he said.

Ned raised an eyebrow. Sabine ignored them both. "Our absence will have been remarked. We should return before I stand accused of engaging with the pair of you in a *ménage à trois*. Your cousin would enjoy that, I think. The speculation, not the act."

"Hannah wouldn't dare. We have had a conversation concerning repercussions." Ned opened the library door.

Kane couldn't stop himself from adjusting the shawl around Sabine's shoulders. His fingers brushed against the nape of her neck.

She glanced up at him. "Thank you. And yes, you may."

Kane's heart beat a little faster. He had an appalling suspicion that he'd blushed. "I shall be delighted to be of service to you, of course."

"I didn't expect that the delight would be all mine."

Ned pretended not to hear. He wished his friends enjoyment of their moment together, for it was unlikely to be more than that, and at any rate who was he—unlike Kane—to judge?

He should have kept Julie with him. If not for Clea, Ned would have done precisely that. He was already responsible for Clea knowing much more than she should about the world. Forget banning Ovid. He should forbid his sister to have anything more to do with *him.*

The crowd pressed close around them. Ned lost track of Sabine and Kane. Over the tops of the nearest heads, he saw three feathers progressing inexorably in his direction. Doubtless Hannah had another young lady in tow, with whom he must dance and carry on a polite conversation, while at the same time discouraging her from thinking she might be his bride.

He had no heart for it, yet couldn't take his leave. Ned owned Hannah an atonement. She had been embarrassed by his friends.

He glanced around. He'd had an itchy feeling between his shoulder blades all evening, as if a hunter had him in his sights.

Matchmaking mamas merely, Ned assured himself. Battlefield nerves.

Julie was safe at Ashcroft House. She couldn't step a foot out-doors without sounding the alarm.

Chapter Twenty-Nine

A woman is always better seen than heard.
— Plautus

Julie was having a lovely dream. She had returned to Wakely Court, and the earl was with her in his tub, giving her a bath the likes of which was causing her to thrash about and moan. His hands were all over her, touching, teasing, tempting. She wanted him closer. She wanted him lying alongside her in his ancient carved bed.

She reached out, to draw him to her. Her questing hand hit hard against what felt like an arm encased in a rough serge sleeve.

Julie wakened abruptly. There should be no arm in her bed but her own, and that wasn't wrapped in serge. It wasn't wrapped in anything, for she'd tumbled into bed wearing merely her shift, too exhausted by the events of the day to change into a nightdress.

Nor should there be about her the smell of unwashed flesh. She'd become particular about being clean.

Someone was in her room. A male someone, from the feel of that arm. And definitely not the male she'd been caressing in her dreams. Did he realize she was awake?

No question but that Julie was growing soft. Ned's blade lay on the dressing table, beyond her reach. Maybe if she was quick she could get to the knife while the intruder was off guard.

Julie edged away. The arm hauled her back. She kicked and punched and opened her mouth to scream. A wad of some foul-tasting fabric was shoved between her teeth. The man—men, she realized; there were two of them—were efficient and swift. In no more than a clock's tick she was bound and shoved into a sack.

She fought against them, made as much noise as she could

through the suffocating gag. Her efforts earned her another sharp blow to the jaw. Julie struggled to remain conscious as they carried her down the stairs and outside.

No one tried to stop them. Perhaps no one had seen. And perhaps Tony had let the men into the house, and that was why he had insisted she stay indoors tonight.

Julie was flung onto the hard floor of a carriage. From the stink of it, a hired hack. She heard a murmur of unfamiliar voices, and then the horses set out. Every bump and rattle jarred her bones. Pretending to be stunned, Julie pulled stealthily at her bonds. Stealthily, and futilely. She was trussed up like a bird for the cooking pot.

Whose cooking-pot wasn't in much doubt.

Ned had wished to keep her safe. Julie hoped he would carve out Tony's gizzard when he found out she was gone. Or maybe she'd take that pleasure for herself once she got out of this mess.

That she might not get out of it, Julie dared not think. She banished that cringing, crippling doubt to a far corner of her mind.

The carriage rattled through the streets, lurched to a halt. Rough hands grasped and tugged, tossed Julie over someone's shoulder as impersonally as if she'd been a sack of coal. Distant muffled voices came to her, and laughter, and music, and a growing suspicion of what sort of place this was. She was jostled up a flight of steps and flung onto a bed. Julie lay very still.

"Shouldna have hit her so hard," said the first unfamiliar voice.

"Makes no difference at the long run, does it?" retorted the second, as its owner yanked off the sack. "She's here as himself wanted her."

The first man allowed as he wouldna want to *be* her. Julie heard the door snick shut. She didn't much want to be herself, either. Cautiously, she opened her eyes.

The room was small but nicely furnished with rosewood and expensive Argand lamps and silk paper on the walls. Julie noted the heavily draped windows, glimpsed herself in the ornate looking glass that reflected the bed. The older of her bruises had turned brilliantly green and purple, and her shift was caught up under the ropes around her thighs. Her hair stuck out in all directions, like the quills of a startled hedgehog. Her eyes were huge in her pale face. She looked terrified.

She *was* terrified, but it wouldn't do to show it. With effort, Julie eased the expression from her face. She prayed no one would wish to tumble someone looking as hard-used as she did.

Tumbling was what men did in establishments like this. Julie knew a brothel when she saw one. She'd never before had the opportunity for so close an inspection, her fingers considered too nimble to be wasted on any but the pilfering trade.

It seemed someone had decided her fingers were not valuable anymore. She tried not to remember that deflowering a virgin was said to be a sure cure for the pox.

Julie had wanted her first time to be with Ned. Had dreamed she might have a few moments' happiness with the earl. And so it could have been, *should* have been, except that he was as contrary as any man ever born, saying he wasn't offering her a slip on the shoulder, though he might if she wished him to, but all the same undressing her, and caressing her, and kissing her in places she'd never realized were designed *to* be kissed—and then refusing to take advantage because the time wasn't right.

Concentrate, Julie told herself. She tried again to ease her wrists, managed only to tighten the knots. She wriggled closer to the edge of the bed. There was nothing in the room that might serve as a weapon, save the water pitcher and chamber pot, and she could hardly pick them up with her hands bound.

The door opened, and she froze. A man walked into the room, a tall man dressed in black, with dark hair and darker eyes, who carried a walking stick with an ornate knob.

He closed the door behind him, moved toward the bed. Julie scooted back as best she could; each movement made her arm ache worse. He placed the knob of his stick under her chin and tipped up her face so that she was forced to look at him. "You're not in prime twig, are you, Jules? It's beyond my comprehension how you caught Dorset's interest. Where's the statue, if you please?"

Cap'n Jack, she made no doubt. "I don't have the statue. I gave it back."

He slapped her. The Cap'n was skilled at slapping. Julie licked away the blood from her split lip.

"That was ill-advised of you," he said. Julie didn't know if he referred to her returning the statue, which she hadn't; or her lying to him, which she hoped he didn't realize. The Cap'n continued: "How did you know to steal the thing in the first place?"

'Know to' steal it? The statue must be worth more than Ned had said. Julie shrugged, or tried to. "Caught my eye, it did. As to why I filched it—it was there."

"It was there and so were you and therefore you took it? Forgive me, Jules, if I say I find that difficult to believe."

Julie found it difficult to hide how sick she felt. "I was looking for something to tide Rose over while I was away."

"And you just happened to choose Wakely Court to rob." The Cap'n turned away from her. "We'll come back to that. Tell me about Dorset's notebook."

Julie reminded herself that she wasn't supposed to know the Cap'n had the wrong codebook. "What about it? I found it in the library."

"What else is in the library?"

"A precious lot of dusty old books, that's what." Julie decided a change of subject might be wise. "Why did you almost have me run down by a carriage? I can't steal anything for you if I'm dead."

So much for distraction: the Cap'n moved closer to the bed, stroked the tip of his walking stick along her calf. "If I'd wanted you crushed to smithereens, my dear, crushed you would be."

His dear? The notion made her shudder. As did the cold metal tip snaking its way up to her knee. "Is it because of you that poor Frenchwoman hanged herself? After I snagged her glove?"

He didn't answer. She had not expected he would. The walking stick continued its upward journey. Julie was glad for the ropes that kept her legs clamped shut.

The Cap'n might have read her thoughts. "Dorset is intrigued by your inexperience. You should be grateful to me, because I let it be known that anyone who interfered with you in that manner would incur my wrath. But now… Dorset will hardly want another man's leavings. Careless Jules. You've lost your chance."

He was trying to frighten her, and succeeding very well. "I don't see much to thank you for," Julie muttered. "Since I'm being set upon and near run over by carriages and snatched right out of my bed."

His fingers dug painfully into her bruised chin. She couldn't turn away. "You were released from Newgate because I saw a use for you. However, you appear to be in need of convincing that you should do as you are told. Mick and Pego are angry about the events of the other evening. It seems to be a matter of damaged pride."

"Mick and Pego may go to hell and pump thunder," retorted Julie, proud that her voice didn't shake.

"No doubt they shall. In the meantime I've told them they may have you when I'm done. I've made a wager with myself as to how much of their attention you'll be able to tolerate." The Cap'n pulled a blade from his walking stick and slashed the ropes that bound her ankles. "Never fear, my dear, you *will* survive. Indeed, you'll be an old hand at it soon enough."

He did mean to break her. She wouldn't let him, no matter what he did. At least she hoped she wouldn't. Julie scrunched herself into the smallest ball possible at the far end of the bed.

The Cap'n took hold of her ankle. Julie got in a good kick to his jaw before he caught the other—and there came a knocking at the door.

He snarled.

The knocking persisted. The Cap'n released Julie and strode across the room, cracked open the door. Julie caught the words "constable" and "downstairs".

The Cap'n cursed. "I'll be back, and we'll finish this. Think about that while I'm gone, Jules."

The door closed. Julie heard the click of the lock.

Her legs were free. She struggled frantically to rid herself of the ropes that bound her arms so tight behind her back that her hands had gone numb.

If she broke the water pitcher, she might manage to saw herself loose. If she didn't saw a vein open in the process and bleed to death, which was preferable to lying under Cap'n Jack.

She wouldn't, absolutely couldn't, in this moment think of Ned. Julie scooted off the bed and was halfway to the door when the lock clicked again.

No! The Cap'n couldn't come back so soon. As the door swung open, Julie prepared to run straight at him, and catch him off guard, so as to attempt an escape, which would hopefully make him mad enough to hit her again. If she was going to be raped, Julie would much rather be knocked unconscious first.

Not Cap'n Jack, but a woman entered the room. An elegantly dressed woman with chestnut hair and lavender eyes. Julie's lips parted. The woman gestured for silence. She made short work of the remaining knots.

Julie rubbed her aching arms. The woman glanced out into the hall, beckoned, whispered: "Quickly, before he returns. Go down the back stair."

The hallway was deserted; the steps dark, narrow, and clearly reserved for servants' use. Julie snatched up a mop-stick mid-flight. More than ever, she wished she had her knife. No, not more than ever, because she would have dearly loved to part the Cap'n from his pizzle. She also wished she was wearing something more substantial than a shift.

If a constable had come calling, he wasn't being welcomed. Julie heard the crash of glass and wood, accompanied by angry shouts. The servants were either involved, or had prudently fled, because she met no one on the stair.

The back door lay before her. Julie burst through it—and almost bashed Bates with the mop-stick before she realized who he was.

He caught her by the shoulders. "Are you all right?"

Julie nodded.

Bates took off his coat and wrapped it around her. They fled.

Chapter Thirty

It is well to moor your bark with two anchors.
— Pubilius Syrus

The evening was far advanced when Ned arrived home, weary in both body and mind. Hannah had been a harsh taskmistress, exacting her pound of flesh by means of his attendance on each unwed female in the crowded rooms. Ned had gritted his teeth and done his duty by his cousin, and was left with no inclination to repeat the effort any time soon.

It wasn't Hannah but Julie who occupied Ned's thoughts as he mounted his front steps. Julie, with her unknown origins and unexplained mishaps. When Bates opened the door, Ned took one look at his batman's face and understood the uneasiness that plagued him all evening had not been without good cause.

Bates gestured for silence. Ned followed him into the library and closed the door, listened to an account of Julie's misadventures with growing anger and dismay.

"I couldn't stop them taking her, so I followed. And I didn't like leaving her there for an instant, but I had to get help." A look at Ned's face caused Bates to quickly add, "Sir, she's all right. I was going in to search when she ran out the back door. Almost knocked me unconscious with a mop-stick, she did. I brought her in through the tunnels, so no one but us knows she's here. I didn't know if you'd be wishful of Miss Clea being involved, but with all that happened—" He reddened. "Well, she's a female. Miss Clea has put her in the turret room."

"You did exactly as you should have, and I'm grateful to you for it. Now get some rest." Ned took the candle that Bates handed him and approached the bookshelves. A twist of the concealed lever and the hinged section swung aside. Ned climbed the steep stair. Behind him, the bookshelf swung shut.

Ned passed through the attics proper, a treasure trove of boxes, crates, ancient furniture and artifacts. The entrance to the turret room was camouflaged by a tattered wall hanging and a massive sideboard. Clea had discovered the hidden chamber during her explorations. None of the household servants, including Tidcombe and Mrs. Scroggs, knew the room was there.

The murmur of voices reached him as soon as he opened the door. "Magnificent, isn't he?" said Clea. "Notice the rings on all his fingers and the signet on his thumb. His ears are pierced so he can wear love tokens. That isn't a wig, he let his own hair grow long."

"Who is he?" Julie sounded less frightened than intrigued.

"His name is Francis Wakely, and he was a Restoration rake. This is his house. That was that cloak. I found the portrait wrapped in an old rug."

The upper door stood ajar. Ned paused in the shadows at the top of the stair. It would do Julie no good to see him foaming at the mouth like a rabid dog.

The turret room was small and semi-circular. One wall backed up against the chimney, which helped keep it warm. Ned hadn't seen the chamber since Clea made it her lair. He noticed that his sister had closed the ancient window curtains to block the candle light. Julie's mop-stick leaned against one wall.

Ned recognized the faded Chinese paper, the Oriental rugs on the floor, but as for the rest... Bates must have helped Clea with the daybed; she could never have dragged it up the stairs by herself. The thing must have been over seven feet long. It was piled high with pillows in faded reds and blues, yellows and greens.

A tasseled coverlet lay folded at one end of the daybed. At the other end perched Julie, wrapped in a satin-lined black velvet cloak adorned with tarnished gold lace and pearl embroidery.

Ned's eyes moved over her, noting the new bruises on her pale face, the swelling of her lower lip. She seemed bemused by her surroundings, and well she should have been. The chair in which his sister sat was carved with roses and daisies and strawberry blossoms, leaves and fruit and a caterpillar worked cunningly into the design.

Julie was staring at the chimney wall, from which a painted rakish gentleman—clad in a long coat with slashed sleeves and upturned cuffs; brocaded waistcoat, ruffled long-sleeved white shirt, and lace cravat; breeches with stockings gartered just below the knee; square toed shoes with red heels—gazed out with an expression of jaded unconcern. "He looks a right rogue."

"From all accounts, he was," Ned commented, as he entered the room. From his perch on Clea's lap, Cerberus growled.

"Hello, Ned," Clea said brightly. "We're glad you're home. I thought about sending Bates for you, but decided it was better you didn't act as if something urgent had occurred. No one will think to look for Julie here. It would hardly be proper for us to harbor a runaway. If someone *does* inquire, the servants won't know she's in the house."

Clea looked the merest schoolgirl in her simple cotton nightgown and wrapper, her mahogany curls in wild disorder. Her voice, however, sounded alarmingly adult. Ned knew his sister. Clea was feeling protective. There would be no keeping her out of this business now.

"You've done well," he told her. "Both you and Bates. Go to bed. I'll take care of Julie."

Clea took a firm grip on Cerberus and stood up, surveyed the small room one last time to make sure there was nothing she had overlooked. Large supply of candles. Corner stand with ewer and chamber pot tucked away discreetly inside. Brush and comb and clean linen; fruit and biscuits from the kitchen; a carafe of water and a chessboard.

Most important, Ned was here. Clea had done a good job of diverting Julie from what had happened to her tonight—Bates had been vague about the details, but Clea had no trouble figuring them out, or as many as she cared to, because she was after all a mere fifteen and there were things she didn't *want* to know—but the matter must be addressed. Ned was very good at addressing matters with females. Clea bid them good night, and descended the stairs.

Ned noticed that his sister had appropriated his brandy from the library. The level of the decanter's contents had decreased. He wondered if Clea had been drinking, or Julie, or both. He wondered also what he was to say to Julie; if he should even be present, recent events quite possibly leaving her in no mood to be at ease with any man. Ned poured some liquor into a glass.

While he pondered how to gently broach the subject—if he *should* broach the subject, or leave it for another day—Julie mumbled, "Thank you," not meeting his gaze.

"You owe me no thanks." Ned drained the glass and set it down. "With all that's been taking place, I should have increased your guard. I shouldn't —"

"— have let me go back to Ashcroft House?" Julie drew up her knees and hugged them. "I'm not yours to order around, my lord. And if we're going to play the 'shouldn't' game, I shouldn't have filched those teaspoons and wound up in Newgate in the first place."

"Teaspoons?" inquired Ned.

Julie rested her cheek on her bent knees. "I was hungry. They were there. Where they shouldn't have been, as I recall, and I shouldn't have been there either, and at the moment I can't say why I was. It was a long time ago."

If Ned was to make himself unthreatening, he couldn't continue looming over her. He had a choice of seating himself in either Clea's abandoned chair or beside Julie on the day bed. She had drawn herself up in a defensive ball under the velvet cloak. Ned dropped down beside her, prepared to immediately move away if she so much as flinched.

She didn't flinch, but neither did she relax. "They took me out of Ashcroft House. I don't know how they got in. I know I didn't leave the side door unlocked."

Ned leaned back against the pillows piled at the daybed's far end. "Tony, you think?"

"I did at first, but now I wonder. Lady Georgiana seems a more likely choice." Julie smoothed her fingers over the cloak's fine lace. Ned listened without comment to an explanation of Tony and the corset, and how Tony swore he wasn't a molly-mop even though he preferred to play the harp. Ned's own feeling was that while Niddicock's upper story might be sparsely furnished, he wasn't a bad sort. However, Ned could be wrong. They already knew that Tony could be coerced.

Ned was afraid to touch Julie. She was running on nerves. But if he didn't touch, he couldn't soothe her, or reassure himself. He reached out very slowly, removed her fingers from the lace, and twined them with his.

She gazed at their clasped hands. "I saw his face. Cap'n Jack. At that place. He's the one as had me brought there, and who sent Pego and Mick. He said he didn't have anything to do with the carriage. It might have been true."

Ned unclenched his jaw sufficiently to speak. "Did he touch you, buttercup?"

"Depends on what you mean by touch." Julie chewed her lower lip. "He hit me. And he poked me with his walking stick."

She was holding back, Ned realized. "Swear to me that he didn't damage you."

"He scared me. I thought I would never see you again. He said he'd ruin me for you, that once he'd had me you wouldn't want me any more." Julie's fingers tightened around his.

Ned didn't know what to say to her. His concern wasn't that Julie be untouched—*he* certainly wasn't—but that after the Cap'n was done with her, she wouldn't be Julie any more.

Ned had frequented his share of bawdy houses. The notion of Julie trapped in such a place made him ill.

Now that the Cap'n had let her see him, Julie was in further danger. The bastard hadn't expected she would escape.

She had fallen silent. "The Cap'n was trying to frighten you," Ned said. He hoped her reasoning hadn't followed his.

Julie relaxed enough to uncurl herself. "He asked about your statue. I didn't tell him it's hidden at Ashcroft House."

"Forget about the statue. Even if he found the thing, it would do him no good."

She tilted her head. "Why is it so important?"

"It shouldn't be, to him." Ned dared tug her closer. "How did Cap'n Jack know of my interest in you?"

"I told you he has eyes everywhere." Julie's cloak had slipped off one shoulder. Under it she wore a plain nightdress. It was too big for her, and the most fascinating garment Ned had ever seen.

Which was no way to be thinking about a young woman who had just escaped a brothel, and was consequently like as not to take her mop-stick to *him*. "Forget the Cap'n. He'll not touch you again."

Julie shook her head, tried to free her hand from his. "Thank you for rescuing me, but now I have to leave."

Ned had been expecting this reaction. He didn't release her. "And where will you go?"

"I'll disappear."

That was what he feared. "At least remain here until we decide what's best done."

Julie opened her mouth to argue. Ned raised his free hand to lightly touch her swollen lip. "Stay the night. What difference can it make?"

"You're putting yourself in danger. All of you."

"How so?" Ned kept his voice calm. "No one knows you're here. Bates is certain he wasn't followed. Since the pair of you came in through the tunnels, your arrival wouldn't have been noticed even if the house *is* under watch."

Julie hesitated; let out a deep breath. "Have it your way. But I don't want to be left alone."

Ned didn't want her to be alone. Until the Cap'n's claws were drawn, he didn't want her out of his sight.

He released her hand. Julie sat quietly watching as Ned stripped off his coat and waistcoat, pulled off his boots, unwound his cravat.

"You can't sleep in that." She didn't protest as he deftly unfastened her cloak. He added, "Scoot over." She scooted. Ned stretched out on the daybed.

Julie hesitated for a moment before she arranged herself stiffly at his side.

Ned slid one arm around her shoulders. Moments passed before she began to shake. When the tears came, he said nothing, but held her as she wept, his hand stroking gently up and down her back. Gradually, her body relaxed. Julie nestled as close to him as she could get, her cheek pressed against his heart.

Careful not to disturb her, Ned pulled the coverlet over both of them.

Though neither would have believed it possible, before dawn broke they slept.

Chapter Thirty-One

*He who holds the hook is aware in what waters
many fish are swimming.* — Ovid

It was quiet in the library, save for the sporadic clink of Clea's china chocolate cup, and the occasional canine snort and snuffle from Cerberus, who was dozing on the hearth. Ned sat silently behind his desk, studying a seventeenth century smallsword fashioned of Toledo steel. Julie explored the perimeters of the room, munching on a muffin taken from the plate sitting on the desk. She was rigged out in a pair of baggy breeches, yellow stockings and ribbon-tied leather shoes; a long-sleeved linen shirt; and, incongruously, a Spanish-looking shawl embroidered with bright flowers and trimmed with fringe. Clea, conversely, appeared remarkably grown up in a morning dress of pale green chintz that brought out the green of her eyes. Grown up, that was, save for the extravagantly plumed gentleman's hat she'd plopped upon her head. In her lap rested a bedraggled fur muff. The servants were off about their business. The library door was safely locked.

Lord Saxe picked up the smallsword, which along with Julie's clothes and the plumed hat numbered among Clea's latest finds. The weapon was complete with a small guard composed of two oval lobes fashioned in a figure eight, a single short quillion, two small arms and a knuckle-bow. "This is essentially a thrusting piece," he said, as he balanced it in his hand. "See how the relatively short blade tapers to a point."

That the baron would like to take the smallsword to her, Julie had no doubt. His eyes had almost crossed with anger when Clea announced she meant to be part of this council of war. Julie's own mood had been much improved by a few hours passed sleeping in Ned's arms. Or sleeping draped atop him, because that was how she woke. To her disappointment, sleeping was all they'd done. She ran her fingers over the copy of *Debrett's Peerage* that lay open on a shelf.

The scare she'd had at the brothel hadn't changed Julie's mind about dancing the feather-bed jig. At least, about dancing it with Ned. Unfortunately, he hadn't changed his mind either, about the proper time and place. She asked him, "Did you tell Milord High-in-the-Instep about Cap'n Jack? Because if you did, it could have been *him* as blew the gab." The baron scowled at Julie's choice of words, which was exactly why she'd spoken as she did.

Ned said, "Kane may be many things, sunshine, but a gab-blower isn't among them. Did the Cap'n say anything to you that would indicate he knew you'd told me about him? Because from what you've said, I suspect that if he *had* known, we wouldn't be sitting here now."

"Yes, well, I shouldn't be here."

"Amen," muttered Lord Saxe.

"'*Stultum facit fortuna quem vult perdere.*'" Clea stroked her muff. "If fortune wants to do you in, she makes you stupid. Syrus."

It wasn't fortune that wished to do her in. Julie met the baron's gaze. "All right then. What do you want to know?"

"You say you saw the Cap'n. Tell us what he looks like."

The baron sounded suspicious. Julie felt like thumbing her nose. She reminded herself that the man *had* saved her from being crushed to death under the wheels of an oncoming carriage, though he would doubtless have liked to push her there himself.

She described the Cap'n. "He dresses like a toff. Talks like a swell. Might have been any of the gentry coves I've been rubbing shoulders with these past weeks." She contemplated the man sitting behind the desk. He winked at her. "Excepting Ned."

A muscle twitched in the baron's jaw. "A tall dark-haired, dark-eyed gentleman. That hardly narrows the field. What more can you tell us? The smallest detail sometimes helps."

"What's the point? It was probably a disguise. There's ways for a person to seem taller or shorter, and he might have worn a wig." There'd be no changing those soulless eyes. Julie would know the Cap'n if they met again. "He'll be mad as fire that I escaped. Next thing, I'll be back in Newgate."

Clea could no longer restrain herself. "Why *were* you in Newgate?"

"I filched a set of silver teaspoons. When I was nabbed, I had on my person a diving hook and picklock, and a ginny to pull the grate."

"I thought you were a pickpocket."

"I was. I am. Which is why I got caught when I went on the day sneak."

Kane looked more disapproving. "What made you decide to broaden your theater of operations? If one may ask."

The baron was a handsome man. He knew it far too well. Julie skirted a tipsy pile of books and a stack of maps, came to a stop in front of him. "You have hair on your coat," she said, and brushed it off. "Probably from the dog."

How to explain her life to one who hadn't lived it? One, moreover, who had only contempt for such as she? Julie turned away. "There are class lines in the rookeries, no less than between rich and poor. A nipper goes from stealing apples to filching from stalls, and on to swiping stickpins and handkerchiefs. Natty lads aspire to be lifters and then knuckles, the better class of pickpocket who goes to public places and snaffles pocketbooks, watches, and that sort of thing."

Clea leaned forward in her chair. "Like you."

Julie touched the astrolabe, the use of which Clea had already demonstrated, along with her lack of ability on the lute. "I aimed above myself."

"How old were you?"

"When I was hobbled? Ten-and-four. I think."

"A year younger than I am now."

"That circumstance has escaped none of us," commented Kane. "You shouldn't be hearing this, Clea."

"I shouldn't be hearing you sound like Cousin Hannah," retorted that young lady. "I'll be glad when the Allied Sovereigns go home and you can return to being yourself."

Kane looked somber. "The peace is at last to be announced. Plans are underway for a victory celebration in Hyde Park."

Julie wondered why Lord Saxe should sound so unenthused about a celebration. Maybe he didn't like to see people enjoying themselves.

Ned tapped on the pewter inkstand. "We're getting off track. Julie was caught stealing teaspoons, and wound up in Newgate. Does that strike no one else as odd? Almost all prosecutions are initiated by private persons, at their discretion, and conducted in accordance with their wishes. In other words, a criminal can't be convicted unless a private citizen agrees to prosecute. Who would send a child to Newgate for stealing a teaspoon?"

Kane poured himself another cup of coffee. "Anyone who values his teaspoons, I should think."

Clearly the baron valued his. Julie gave the old globe a spin.

Lord Saxe resumed his interrogation. "What's the earliest thing you remember?"

"What does that have to do with anything?"

"Humor me, Miss Wynne."

She glanced at Ned. He nodded. Julie leaned a hip against the edge of the old desk, and thought back. She had a vague notion of being one of many, a roof above her head but not enough to eat, and overall the stink of gin; swarming the streets with other ragged bantlings in search of their daily bread.

Such children began to steal as soon as they were old enough to walk. By the time Julie came to the notice of Mother Yarwood, she was already making off with goods from places where adult thieves could not.

Clea was fascinated. "What sort of things?"

"Food. Small items of clothing, especially handkerchiefs. Brooches and bracelets, combs and looking glasses from the stalls. Rolls of fabric, tablecloths and individual fire-irons."

"What happens to them?"

"The goods are taken to an angling cove. A fencing ken.

Mother Yarwood has women in the streets who hide small things in their barrows until it's safe to pass them on." Julie moved away from the desk. "Most operators find themselves in the Old Bailey or Newgate long before I did. A shifting lad doesn't often live to an old age. His friends go with him to the gallows, giving him support so that he may die game, and have his last speech written down and sold, and be talked of for a week."

Ned, Clea, and the baron were all three watching her. Julie bent to give the dog's ears a scratch. He opened one eye, snapped his jaws, and went back to sleep.

Ned said, "You believe the Cap'n might be a member of the *ton*."

The Cap'n talked like a swell, Julie repeated. Not like someone putting on, as an actor did, nor even like Ned, who hadn't always been at home in aristocratic drawing rooms. The Cap'n spent enough time in those drawing rooms to know what was going on in the Polite World. She suspected he might be one of the elegant and expert criminals who promenaded in the West End, and attended fashionable assemblies, and were the true aristocrats of crime; who lived and dressed well, employed servants, acted every inch the proper gentlemen while meticulously planning out their robberies and swindles and frauds.

"But none of this," Julie concluded, "explains why he's had me doing the things he has."

"Why *did* you do them?" Kane inquired.

"Remove the wax from your ears!" snapped Julie. "Because he threatened me."

The baron contemplated her. "You don't like me much."

"It's not for my sort to like or dislike yours. You, on the other hand, are judging me as if I was a respectable female, which I'm not and never hope to be." Julie reached into her sleeve, withdrew the handkerchief that she'd palmed, and presented it to him.

"*Brava!*" Clea clapped her hands. Roused from slumber, Cerberus ambled over to her, pausing en route to snarl at Kane. A brief diversion then occurred, for Cerberus took exception to Clea having what he took to be a strange animal in her lap, and the muff had to be rescued, and the dog soothed.

The baron accepted his handkerchief without comment and tucked it away. "Inquiries thus far have unearthed little about your Cap'n. He is a shadow man, a chimera, a will o' the wisp."

Julie scowled. "He's real enough."

"The man you saw was real enough. But is he who—or what—you have been led to believe? Does this business stop with Cap'n Jack, or does he answer to a higher authority?"

"A head of the hydra?" Clea guessed. "Kane, you have a very complicated mind."

"Thank you. I think."

Ned grasped Julie's hand as she walked past the desk and pulled her down to perch on the arm of his chair. "You're wearing a path in my carpet, buttercup. Leave the pacing to Kane. The Hydra was a mythological creature with the body of a serpent and many heads, only one of which could be harmed by any weapon. If any of the others were severed, another would grow in its place."

"The stench of its breath was horrid enough to kill man and beast," contributed Clea. "Destroying the Hydra was the second labor of Hercules."

"Perhaps we may leave furthering Miss Wynne's classical education for another time," the baron interjected, thereby adding to Julie's annoyance, because he'd guessed she hadn't the slightest notion of who Hercules was. "We must discover the Cap'n's deeper purpose. What items have you stolen, and from whom?"

Julie had been dreading this. It went against the grain to own up to her misdeeds, especially in front of Ned.

But own up to them, she did. In truth, she had no choice. There was a brief silence before Clea said, "You must be very, *very* good. And very brave as well, to steal something right from under Prinny's nose."

"He wasn't in the room," Julie pointed out.

"Thank heaven for small favors," said Ned.

He didn't sound especially disillusioned. Julie risked a glance.

"Lady Jersey's ballroom?" Ned inquired.

"After you left."

The baron interrupted. "Lady Willoughby's amethyst necklace came to light in a pawn shop. Her husband, who redeemed the thing, is furious with her. This places the lady in an unfortunate position. He is the highest of sticklers and she hasn't yet produced an heir. Rumor has it that he now refuses to share her bed."

"None of these items is in itself of particular value," Ned pointed out. "However, they are all a source of embarrassment if they fall into the wrong hands. One wonders what the Cap'n hopes to achieve by this maneuvering."

"So one does," agreed Kane.

"Flats, the pair of you!" Julie pulled away from Ned. "The world's made up of sharps ready to take a man on all occasions, and flats waiting to be taken, and Cap'n Jack is the sharpest of them all. He doesn't go easy on those who get in his way. I'm surprised that Mother Yarwood..." She broke off.

"What about Mother Yarwood?" Ned asked.

"It was her as let me out of that locked room. I wonder why she did it, because she has no more true liking for me than I have for her."

"Which is another reason why you must stay here," Ned said grimly. "You know too much. The Cap'n can't be sure you'll keep your mouth shut."

"If he thinks I haven't, he'll hurt Rose."

"That wouldn't serve his purpose. He'll expect you to get in touch with her."

Kane interrupted. "Rose is the person who passed on the things you stole?"

He sounded censorious. Julie swung round to glare. "She didn't have any more choice than I did. The Cap'n threatens his victims with what they fear most."

Rose feared her lovers would be shamed. Tony feared his true nature would be revealed. Julie wondered if Lady Georgiana and Tony had realized she was missing, or if they had arranged for her to be taken away. If not, they might be worried to learn she wasn't in the house.

More likely, they were both limp with relief. "You fear being sent back to Newgate," Clea guessed.

"No." Julie studied the toe of her shoe. "I fear being hanged."

"A fair consideration," observed the baron. "However, I must point out that it's unlikely you would have hanged for stealing your first set of teaspoons."

"That's not what I was told when I was taken out of Newgate." Julie raised her gaze, emotions back under control. "'Death or transportation is the punishment for theft of property worth more than five shillings from a shop.' And that's a quote."

Kane's gaze narrowed. "If Cap'n Jack took you out of Newgate, how is it you never saw his face before last night?"

"Arch coves like the Cap'n don't do things for themselves. They have people like Pritchett to do for them."

Three sets of eyes fixed on Julie—four including Cerberus, wakened irritably from his nap. "Who is Pritchett?" asked Ned, speaking for them all.

Chapter Thirty-Two

The man who has experienced shipwreck
shudders even at a calm sea. — Ovid

The conference underway in Wakely Court was not the sole parlay to take place this day. In a more exclusive area of town, Tony sat plucking his harp as his mama heaped censure on his head. Since his mama hadn't forgiven him for calling her a flap-dragon, they were barely on speaking terms, which made no difference so far as he could see to her ripping up at him. Many more peals rung in his ears and he would be stone deaf.

Tony revenged himself by thinking of maternal appellations. Prattle-box, clack-dish and harridan leapt immediately to mind. At the moment Georgiana was scolding him for eating too much bread and jam, and said his new waistcoat made him look fat.

Fat! Tony tucked in his chin to look down at his belly, currently encased in contrasting shades of Evening Primrose and Periwinkle Green. "Weston fashioned this waistcoat," he protested.

"No doubt it made Weston as bilious as it makes me," retorted his mama, who was herself dressed this morning in—what else?— her favorite lilac.

If his waistcoat made his mama bilious, it was no more than fair, because Georgiana affected Tony the same way. He played an arpeggio and wished he might have a cherry tart. No, he wished he might have *ten* tarts, and eat them all in front of Maman, and watch her gasp and turn pale from the shock of it, and maybe expire, at which point he might regain control of his pocketbook and his life.

He didn't really want his mama to pop off, Tony amended. Even if she was a sneaksby. A crosspatch. An archwife.

"And where is Julie?" demanded Lady Georgiana. "The morning is too advanced for her to be lolling about in bed."

Tony wished that he might loll about somewhere. Elsewhere. His mama continued for several moments in this vein, miffed that Julie was taking advantage of her new status as a blackmailer to sleep in and neglect her morning duties, which mainly consisted —in Tony's opinion—of coaxing her employer down out of the boughs.

Maman, that was, not Tony. Tony might be Julie's employer, but no one humored him. This reflection cast a further blight upon his spirits. He struck a dissonant chord.

Lady Georgiana grimaced. "Try to hit the right notes, if you will. I don't know why we wasted all that money on music lessons if that's all the better you can play."

Fortunately for Tony's temper, because his grip on its reins was weakening, the butler chose that moment to scratch on the door. "A person to see you, my lord."

To say that the butler displayed disapproval of the caller was to grossly overstate the case. Willets would never by so much as a twitch of a nostril do something so vulgar as indicate distaste. Still, Tony had no doubt that Willets *did* disapprove. There was a distinct chill in the air.

On Willet's silver tray lay a calling card. Tony picked up the pasteboard square and immediately regretted he hadn't left that last kipper on his breakfast plate.

Lady Georgiana broke off in mid-complaint. "What is it now?"

Pritchett is what it was, or who, and how Tony was to explain a Bow Street Runner to his mama greatly exercised his mind. "Show him to the study," he said to Willets. "I'll be right along."

"Very good, my lord."

"Tony!" Lady Georgiana repeated, ominously, after the butler left the room. "*Whom* is Willets showing to the study?"

Tony brushed a stray breadcrumb off his waistcoat and strove for nonchalance. "It's gentleman's business. Nothing to bother your head about."

Gentleman's business, was it? Georgiana went on the alert. "If you have been gambling again…"

For every bucket there is a drop that makes the container overflow. For Tony, this was his. "Gamble? With what? You have the purse strings knotted up as tight as if you was one of those old Greek fellows, but you ain't King Midas, and I ain't a minotaur!"

His mama's mouth dropped open. Before she could succumb to the vapors, or alternately hurl her teacup at him, Tony whisked himself out of the room.

There would be a reckoning. Already Tony regretted his rash words. But if he was going to be hauled over the coals in any event, it might as well be for a good cause. Heaven only knew what Maman would say if she knew they had a Bow Street Runner in the house. Heaven only knew what Tony would say by way of explanation if she happened to find out.

If? Of course she would find out. Maman insisted on knowing the minutest detail of everything that went on in her house. *His* house, in point of fact, though nobody would think so from all the say he had about anything. Tony spied his image in a pier glass and paused to give his coat a twitch. And furthermore his new waistcoat did *not* make him look fat.

Pritchett was indeed in the study, contemplating the china figures perched on the marble chimneypiece. Not that Tony had any reason to think Pritchett *wouldn't* be in the study, but one could always hope. The Runner turned as Tony entered the room.

"I said I'd get it!" protested Tony, once the door was securely closed. "I have to find the thing first. Can't just go walking into Julie's room, can I? Look what happened the last time."

Pritchett turned away from the chimneypiece. "What the devil are you talking about?" he inquired.

"What *would* I be talking about? Head of a hippo, legs of a lion, tail of a crocodile: does that ring a bell? And now that I think on it —which I don't *want* to do, by the bye, though what I want don't seem to signify!—it's your fault I'm in such a pickle with Maman, because it was you as told me I should search Julie's rooms in the first place."

Pritchett knew a little French. The term *'bête noire'* sprang to mind. "You searched? What did you find?"

"I found her corset, that's what." Tony seated himself at the organ. "And Maman found me."

Pritchett didn't want to know. He truly didn't. But he couldn't help himself. "Corset?"

"It's not as if I was wearing it! But I might as well have been, for the fit Maman threw." Tony fiddled with the stop knobs, pumped the organ pedals, and placed his hands on the keys.

Pritchett blinked. It was difficult to startle a Bow Street Runner, but Tony had managed to do just that. Before he could ask for further enlightenment, which at any rate he wasn't certain that he wanted, the mellow tones of the organ rolled through the room.

Tony picked his way through a Bach fugue. The organ might not resonate with him as did the harp, but on the other hand it was loud.

He paused. "Julie says her bruises are result of her walking into a door when it's plain as the nose on her face that she did nothing of the sort. Tell you what, I don't think much of this Cap'n of yours if he goes around bruising females."

Pritchett didn't think much of Tony's chances of survival, the way he was going on. "Bruises?" he asked.

"Bruises." Tony tapped his chin. "And then she tumbled out in front of that carriage. I thought it was all over with her. It was an accident. Had to be. A lucky thing Saxe was passing by."

Unlikely that Jules had tripped, thought Pritchett; no matter how much the viscount might wish to think it so. A lass nimble enough to traverse a city by way of its rooftops wasn't likely to stumble into the path of an oncoming carriage. Someone had given her a push.

This, he hadn't known about. Pritchett didn't like it one bit. "It's about Miss Wynne that I'm here," he said.

Tony executed a complicated passage. "What about Miss Wynne?"

That was an excellent question. Julie's disappearance had put the Cap'n in a towering rage. As if he'd misplaced more than a quick-fingered street urchin who could pass as what she was not.

The library door swung open. A woman walked into the room. That this was Tony's mama, Pritchett had no doubt. The family resemblance could not be denied.

Her sharp eyes fixed on her son. "Willets informs me that Julie is nowhere in the house. Her bed looks scarce slept in."

Tony took offense. "Well, she didn't sleep in mine."

"Perhaps," said Georgiana, awfully, "it would better if she had. Better a scheming little nobody than—"

Pritchett cleared his throat. "It's about Miss Wynne that I'm here."

Recalled to the presence of a stranger, Georgiana fixed him with a haughty eye. "I am Lady Georgiana Ashcroft. And you are—"

"Pritchett," Tony offered gloomily. "He's a Bow Street Runner, Maman."

"Bow Street? In your study?" Lady Georgiana wavered between a faint and a frown.

The frown won out. "What about Miss Wynne, pray?"

"There are those who wish to speak with her, my lady." Pritchett had already made a polite bow. "As to why, that must remain private, I'm afraid."

Georgiana elevated her vinaigrette to the vicinity of her nose. "I knew that baggage was up to nothing good."

"You think everyone's up to no good, Maman. It would serve you right if you was to encounter someone who truly is." Tony surveyed Pritchett, his forehead puckered in thought. "If we didn't know Julie was missing, how did *you*?"

Lady Georgiana contemplated the Runner over the top of her vinaigrette. "That is an excellent question, son."

"Let us simply say that a certain party considers it a matter of grave urgency that Miss Wynne should be found." Pritchett didn't know how he could make things more clear to Tony unless he spelled it out. "He will be *extremely* disappointed if she is not."

"Um." The viscount had taken Pritchett's meaning, judging from the stricken expression on his face.

His mama looked suspicious. "I demand to know what is going on. Since I will get it out of you eventually, Tony, you might as well confess."

He might as well go drown himself in the Serpentine. "There must be some good reason Julie ran off," Tony said. "If run off she did, which I for one find too smoky by half, because her new dresses ain't come yet. If she meant to take French leave, she would have waited until after they arrived."

Pritchett wondered if he would ever become accustomed to the viscount's logic, or his lack thereof. "Maybe dresses aren't that important to Miss Wynne."

"That shows all you know! Dresses are important to every female. Just ask Maman." Since it was obvious the maternal suspicions hadn't been allayed, Tony went on the attack. "Mildred went to Oxford Street to match a length of ribbon and never came back. Now Julie's disappeared. I wouldn't be surprised if Maman didn't drive both of them off with her crotchets and megrims. She didn't used to be so nasty-tempered. I think it's her dotage coming on."

"My—" Georgiana clapped a hand to her chest. "It's *you* who are acting like a loony. If you had a grain of proper feeling—"

Tony slammed down his hands on the organ keys. "Well, I don't!"

"Heartless boy! You'll regret this mistreatment when I am no longer here." Georgiana drooped gracefully into a chair.

Tony eyed her blankly. "Are you going somewhere?"

"Gudgeon!" said his mama, in failing tones.

Pritchett edged toward the door. "You have my card."

Tony waved his hand. Despite his mama's theatrics, the viscount was the one who looked ill.

Pritchett sympathized.

At least Julie had escaped the brothel, and for that Dorset's batman must be thanked.

Willets handed the Runner his hat. Pritchett handed the butler a coin. "The least hint of news, I expect to be informed."

Said Willets, in tones never heard by Lady Georgiana, "Aye."

Pritchett tucked his baton beneath his arm and descended the entry steps. None of his numerous sources of information had been able to provide him any clue to what the Cap'n was about, nor any indication of where Jules might be found. If Pritchett were a betting man, which he wasn't, as result of having seen too many bad examples, he would wager that a certain earl had her tucked away somewhere.

In which case, good luck to them both. Pritchett's own next stop was Russell Street, there to warn Rose matters were coming quickly to a head.

Chapter Thirty-Three

No cavalry or infantry has the gall to maneuver
as coolly as a woman can. — Plautus

Everyone who was anybody, a couple thousand strong, jostled for invitations to the subscription ball being given by members of White's Club in honor of the Royal Guests. Ticket-holders—some of whom had paid eighty to one hundred guineas for the privilege— had queued in their carriages from five in the afternoon, in hope of arriving between nine and ten o'clock. People pushed and shoved each other to gain entrance to rooms packed with four times as many bodies as the walls were meant to hold.

The Illustrious Visitors were present *en masse,* the Czar of Russia and the Emperor of Prussia and a bevy of lesser foreign princes, statesmen and generals. As well as, of course, the Grand Duchess of Oldenburg. The gentlemen were in full dress uniform or formal evening wear; the women in beautiful gowns of every color and fabric known under moon and sun. This would be remembered as one of the most handsome assemblies London had ever seen.

And one of the most gay. An estimated nine hundred pounds had been spent on wine alone.

Lord Dorset was among those few attendees who were not enchanted. Ned was impatient to return to Wakely Court, where he had left Clea teaching Julie to play marbles, after which Julie had promised to show Clea how to pick a lock, the both of them under Bates' watchful eye.

Ned was keeping up appearances. If Cap'n Jack had eyes everywhere, those eyes would see the Earl of Dorset acting unconcerned with anything beyond procuring a glass of more potent beverage.

And acting, it was. Ned was worried half to death. He couldn't imagine what Julie had done to bring the villain's wrath down on her; if she had done anything at all. Kidnapping and imprisonment in a brothel seemed overly harsh retribution for a misstolen codebook, especially when any error was due to the Cap'n's miscalculation and not Julie's lack of skill.

The Cap'n had known Ned had a codebook in his possession. Therefore he must also know about Ned's clandestine career. There might have been grist for further blackmail in that knowledge, had Ned been a different man. Espionage agents were not held in high regard, the general feeling being that whereas it was noble to risk one's neck on the field of battle, it was considerably less so to go skulking about behind enemy lines.

The Cap'n was interested in Sandoval's statue. Why?

That statue, along with the knife Ned had given Julie, remained at Ashcroft House. Ned supposed he should make an effort to get them back. And if the Cap'n wasn't responsible for Julie nearly being crushed beneath the wheels of an oncoming carriage, who was?

All this pondering had given Ned a headache, which was being compounded by the perfume of too many bodies, the din of countless conversations, the music of the orchestra. He wanted nothing more than to go home and sleep with Julie in the turret room again, this time without his clothes. Without *her* clothes. With the door locked against interference from friend and foe alike.

"Prussia is aggressive," said Sabine, who had been talking throughout these reflections; "Russia perverse, and Austria devious. Each is in daily dread of being outmaneuvered by the others. Are you listening to me, Ned?"

"Hmm."

"Then you'll be interested to know that Prinny has stripped down to his drawers."

Ned returned abruptly to his surroundings. The dance floor was as crowded as the reception rooms. Among the twirling throng he saw Kane waltzing with the Grand Duchess, and the Czar with Lady Jersey. He did *not* see Prinny exhibiting the royal underpinnings to all the guests.

Sabine smiled. "Admit it. You haven't heard a word I've said."

Ned swung her into a turn. "I was thinking about our arch-rogue. Wondering how he knows the things he does. He may be here tonight."

"And he may not." In pale grey silk and diamonds, Sabine was as elegant as any lady present. And as slender. Ned thought she had lost more weight.

"You look tired," he said. "It's all this racketing around. You should take better care of yourself."

"Time enough to take care later. There are too many things going on just now. Miss Wynne is safe for the moment. You care for her, I think."

Ned did. The world would consider it a most unsuitable affection. If only he were not an earl...

But he was. To his regret.

The waltz ended. Kane relinquished his partner to another of her admirers, joined Ned and Sabine in a stroll through the crowded rooms. "Miss Wynne's 'Mother Yarwood' is Mrs. Lilah Kingston. The 'Mrs.' is an unearned honorific, I expect. She manages a number of businesses, acting as a buffer between the real owner and the law. She was forced to pay several large bribes to avoid imprisonment as result of the recent incident."

"Ah," said Ned. Several things were beginning to make sense. "I hadn't realized that Julie was taken to the Academy. Bates merely said the brothel was in King's Place. So when Julie said Mother Yarwood released her from her bonds, she meant that Lilah did."

"Lilah?" echoed Sabine. "You know the woman?"

"Not well enough, apparently," Kane observed, "to be aware of her various *noms de guerre*. Is there anything else you care to tell us, Ned?"

"That one should never underestimate the value of old friend-ships. Did Lilah tell you who her employer is?"

Kane removed a glass of champagne from a passing waiter's tray. "Her loyalty to you does not extend that far. She did let drop an item of interest, however: in addition to her other enterprises, Mrs. Kingston is involved with an establishment dedicated solely to the gratification of gentlewomen whose sexual preferences are of an uncommon bent. She accepts no responsibility regarding subsequent events, but Amélie Morel visited the premises more than once."

Sabine's fingers tightened on Ned's arm. "The stained glove."

"Also interesting is the fact that Julie didn't come to Mrs. Kingston in the usual manner, but was brought to her. By whom, Mrs. Kingston couldn't be persuaded to say, even under threat of imprisonment. She never heard the girl had a last name."

A shadow flitted over Sabine's face. "Poor child."

Kane regarded Ned. "I'm aware you would have had it otherwise."

"You're the one who would have it otherwise," retorted Ned.

"My primary concern—"

"Ned!" Hannah plowed through the crowd like a warship cresting ocean waves. She wore an Oriental turban and a gold-banded black velvet gown. "I have been searching for you. Come with me."

Kane looked sardonic. Sabine removed her hand from Ned's arm. "Our cue to exit, I believe."

Ignoring them, Hannah grasped Ned's sleeve and tugged. Resistance seeming futile, he followed in her wake.

"So your sister has a cold," continued Hannah; Clea had sent that excuse to beg off from morning calls, music lessons, and the like. "Scant wonder. You should have that drafty house torn down."

His cousin was in an excellent mood. Ned distrusted it, and her. "Clea likes Wakely Court. As do I."

Hannah sniffed. "That old pile is well enough for a Wakely—or *was*, for your grandmother was the last of the line, which is just as well, for the Wakelys were a reckless, feckless lot—but not for the earl of Dorset. However, that will soon change. Your wife will require you to take up your rightful place at the Hall. I shall remain in residence, as my dear William wished it, but there is more than room enough for all."

Ned shuddered at thought of sharing a roof with Hannah. He wondered how much his cousin's high spirits had to do with her rival's fall from grace. Lady Georgiana was the focus of spiteful speculation now that the second of her companions had apparently taken flight.

Gossip. The *ton's* lifeblood. Ned was aware of the glances and whispers that followed in their wake.

Was Hannah up to further mischief, in spite of his warning? "I've told you I'm not going to marry Madalyn Tate."

Hannah tittered. "Why should you think such a thing? You are behind-hand with the news. It is no more than you deserve for ignoring your correspondence. Since it has given us a chance to further our acquaintance, however, I will not scold."

What acquaintance had been furthered? Certainly not Ned's. He thought of Julie, bundled up in nothing but a nightgown and a two-hundred-year-old cloak; and wished he might have unwrapped her like a pretty package, inch by tantalizing inch.

There *was* a pile of correspondence sitting unread on his desk, which Hannah was unlikely to realize unless she had stolen into his house. "Are you deliberately posing me a puzzle?" Ned asked.

Hannah whisked him down a hallway, paused in front of a closed door. "I have a surprise for you, although it wouldn't *be* a surprise if you had been dwelling where you should, because Dorset Hall is where one might reasonably expect to find the earl! But all has worked out for the best, and I make no doubt you will be both astounded and pleased." Without further ado, she opened the door.

Astounded? Unlikely. Ned was equally doubtful about his pleasure, having learned during his acquaintance with his cousin that what pleased her and what pleased him seldom marched apace. He let her nudge him into the room. Behind him, the door clicked firmly shut.

The small parlor was done up in shades of green and white, including the window curtains and the upholstery on the sopha and chairs. The walls were wainscoted. On one hung a circular convex mirror topped by a carved eagle, on either side a girandole. A fitted carpet covered the floor.

A breath of movement, the hint of a sigh, and Ned swung round. He was not alone in the room. A young woman stepped out of the shadows. A beautiful young woman with porcelain skin and glossy dark hair and sleepy eyes. Her gown was fashioned from white mull with silver embroidery all over it, most intensely at the hem, its sleeves set low to display her shoulders. The waist was high, the neckline low. Around her throat hung a simple cross.

That cross was deuced familiar. So was the young woman. Ned had never expected to see her again.

He certainly had never expected to see her looking so virginal. "Bianca. What are you doing here?"

She walked—swayed—toward him. "You left your heart in the Peninsula, *querido*. I have brought it back to you."

Ned took a step backward. "What nonsense is this?"

"Nonsense? Dearest Ned, you need not pretend. We can be together now. All has changed."

There had been a time when Ned wished more than anything to be with Bianca. That time, however, was long past. "I came into a title, you mean. I take it you attempted to contact me at Dorset Hall."

"*Sim!* And spoke with your cousin. She and I have become great together, after talking you over by the hour." Having backed Ned into a corner, Bianca stroked a fingertip down his lapel. "*Papai* has reconsidered our union. He has come to London and is expecting you to call."

Ned caught her caressing hand and set it firmly aside. "Why should I do that?"

"There are matters to be discussed. Dowries. Settlements. We must decide where we will reside after we are wed. From what your cousin tells me, I do not think I would care for where you are living now."

"I couldn't care less where you reside." Ned edged away from her, skirted a rosewood revolving book stand with brass retaining bars. "You broke off our betrothal, as I recall."

Bianca followed him. "It is understandable that I did so; you are a very aggravating man. But I have a great capacity for adjusting myself to facts, and the fact is that I wish to be your countess. You might try and act happy to see me, *caro*. I have traveled a great distance to join you here." She raised a graceful hand to her hair.

He had given her a ring; a ring that she had not returned. With something akin to horror, Ned saw the damned thing gleaming on her hand. "The religious differences remain."

"They are no longer of significance." Bianca pulled the pins from her hair. "Ah, you hesitate. Do not tell me I was merely an amusement. Surely the fifteenth Earl of Dorset is not a seducer of innocent females."

"You were hardly innocent." Ned doubted she had ever been. He experienced profound annoyance that Fate had seen fit to plop down another boulder in his path.

"*Como?* To be assured I was." Bianca reached behind her back and unhooked her gown. It slipped over her shoulders, revealing a great deal of lovely fair flesh. She raised her hands to the ribbons of her chemise.

Ned placed himself prudently behind the sopha. "This will avail you nothing. You need not proceed."

The chemise gaped open. Bianca tugged it lower as she advanced. "My poor darling, try not to look like you are facing a firing squad. It was always good between us. A delicately nurtured English lady would not do for you."

"Neither would a Portuguese *puta*." Ned folded his arms across his chest.

Bianca hurled herself at him. "*Assistência, por favor!*" she cried.

Ned stepped aside. Bianca overshot her target, tumbled over the sopha, and landed on her backside. Unlike the Prince Regent, she was not wearing drawers. The door swung abruptly open, as Ned had anticipated that it would.

Sabine stepped into the room, closed the door behind her and leaned against it. "We thought your cousin might have been planning something of this nature. Kane has intervened. There will be no scandal and no hasty wedding. Bianca, get up off the floor."

"You, I remember from the Peninsula. I did not like you then, and I do not like you now." Bianca climbed to her feet, reclaimed her hairpins, and began setting herself to rights. "Your intervention is for nothing, Senhora Viccars. The lieutenant and I are betrothed. I mean, the earl."

"Indeed?" inquired Sabine.

Ned roused from his appalled fascination. "Indeed we are not."

"But of course we are betrothed!" Bianca held up her hand, the better to display her ring. "You are a man of honor, *caro*. You would not wish the world to think that you are not."

"And if I refuse?"

Bianca's dark eyes flashed. "Then you may look forward to a breach-of-promise suit."

Chapter Thirty-Four

When you have just climbed out of a deep well and are perched on top, you are in the greatest danger of falling in again. — Plautus

"Kane isn't the greatest beast in nature," said Clea, "even if at the moment he's acting like he is. I blame the Allied Sovereigns. Or perhaps I should blame Lord Castlereagh, for he's the one who dropped them in Kane's lap! The Grand Duchess told Kane that she briefly considered marrying Napoleon, after his divorce from Josephine; but then she chose her cousin and Napoleon went on to wed Marie-Louise of Austria. Kane thinks it was the Grand Duchess who persuaded Princess Charlotte against marrying the Prince of Orange, because she is contemplating the Prince as a possible husband for herself due to Holland's wealth. I asked Kane if she was considering *him* as a husband. He said that he lacked royal connections, thank God."

Clea paused to take a breath. She still sported the plumed hat. When Julie refused to don a dress, feeling safer in masculine attire, Clea had changed into the clothes she'd worn for riding in the Peninsula, breeches and boots and a shirt.

She held her lantern high, illuminating one of the passages that wound through the house's old walls. "Kane is a libertine, like Francis Wakely was. Kane isn't half so dissolute as Francis, but we won't tell him that."

Hidden staircases and secret rooms and sliding panels: Julie was impressed. Clea explained that a number of these hidden crannies had likely been devised during the latter part of the sixteenth century, when priest-hunting was a sport; had seen additional use during the Gunpowder Plot, Charles II's escape from Worcester, the

Jacobite uprisings and the Civil War, any of which would have been sufficient cause for gentlemen who backed the wrong party to seek out a hiding-place.

"Francis was one of Lord Rochester's set." Clea was determined to demonstrate that her forebears, and Ned's, had blood less blue than red. "*The* Lord Rochester who died of alcoholism and the pox at age three-and-thirty. He was a favorite of King Charles II who nonetheless exiled him numerous times for his libelous poetry and scandalous behavior at court. My favorite of his poems is 'Love A Woman? You're An Ass'. Kane might have written that."

"The baron writes poetry?" inquired Julie. Having found someone new to chatter to—or at—Miss Clea seldom paused to draw breath.

"To his mistresses, maybe. I wouldn't know. Gentlemen do write poems to their inamoratas, don't they? I think I would like having poems written to me."

This particular passage emptied out by way of a false fireplace into the gardens, which were overgrown and neglected and eerie in the foggy moonlight. Stone paths meandered off in various directions, through weed-filled flowerbeds. Marble statues hid in niches in the old wisteria-covered stone wall.

"Frances held orgies here." Clea contemplated Venus bathing, minus a nose. "My brother prefers to think I don't know what an orgy is."

Julie preferred not to think of Clea's brother in connection with orgies. There was no doubt in her mind that Ned knew exactly what such activities involved. Julie thought none the less of him for it. She thought a great deal less of him for not sharing what he'd learned.

"This is my latest discovery." Clea shone her lantern on a section of the wall where, behind the wisteria, the outline of a doorway could be seen. She picked up the pruning-saw that she'd left lying nearby on the ground.

Her curiosity aroused, Julie made good use of her smallsword. The old wisteria put up a good fight but at last gave way.

The gate squeaked reluctantly open, into a narrow service

street that led off the mews at the back of the house. The stables were dark, equine and human occupants alike asleep.

Reluctant as the gate had been to open, it was equally reluctant to remain so, and swung shut with a rusty thud. Clea tugged, to no avail. Muttered Julie, "Bloody hell."

Clea was disappointed at her companion's tone. Someone with Julie's background should have a better-developed sense of adventure. She kicked the gate. It remained firmly stuck.

Julie hissed, "The lantern. Put it out."

Without the lantern they wouldn't be able to see a foot in front of their noses. As Clea turned to stare at Julie, two rough-looking men headed straight toward them. A third man emerged from the direction of the mews.

Clea blew out the lantern. Julie took firmer hold of her smallsword. "Get ready to run."

The men came closer, closer; close enough to touch. "Now!" Julie cried, and slashed out with her sword. One man stumbled back, clutching his forearm. Clea smacked the other in the face with the lantern. He howled, victim of hot oil and broken glass. The third man was tripped up by his flailing comrades, and the three of them tumbled in a tangle on the ground.

Julie tugged Clea's arm. "Come on!" Already the men were scrambling to their feet. Clea got in one last good thwack before she dropped the pruning-saw.

They ran, this way and that, zigged and zagged through streets that quickly changed from broad and spacious to narrow and mean; passed between two rotting tenements into a small badly paved court. Julie snatched up a handful of grime, rubbed it on her face and clothes; mixed soot with stagnant water and smeared it through her hair; artfully rent her clothing with the blade of her sword. Clea cried out in protest when Julie grasped her precious hat and plucked out the plumes, crushed it and rolled it in the dirt.

Julie led her up an ancient drainpipe and onto a roof. Clea peered over the roof's edge. Below them sprawled a rabbit warren of courts and alleys and covered passages.

Houses in one narrow street connected with those in other

streets by roof and yard. They descended from the rooftops some several streets over by means of back windows that led one to another by a series of large spike nails, one row for hands to grasp and another for feet to rest upon.

A drunken young gentleman stumbled out of a gin-shop, right into their path; tripped over Julie's out-thrust foot and fell flat on his arse. She helped him up from the garbage-strewn pavement and brushed him off, apologizing for bumping into him, scolding him for venturing into so rough a part of town. The gentleman closed one eye, as if by so doing he might improve his vision, and staggered off into the fog.

They slipped down a back alley; passed through a shattered door with rotting hinges into a tiny room where the walls bulged in some places and in others had collapsed. Dim light filtered in through broken windows obstructed by the bits of this-and-that which replaced the fractured glass. Clea made out an iron chair and straw pallets on the floor. In one corner was the sort of apparatus used by a baked-potato man, in another a cage filled with sleepy songbirds, beside it a pile of rags.

The pile stirred. A lean wolfish-looking dog emerged from the shadows with a snarl. "Stow it," Julie snapped. A brief conversation followed, the piles of rags turning out to have people underneath; a conversation conducted in what might as well have been a foreign language, for the only word Clea recognized was 'Jules'. At its conclusion, Julie retrieved a candle from behind a thicket of broken boards and struck a light.

Clea trailed Julie down a rickety staircase. "What if they hadn't known you?"

"We wouldn't have been allowed to pass."

The staircase ended with a closed door. Julie knocked. The door swung open a scant inch, and then a foot. Beyond it lay a low apartment, all rotting wood and broken stone. The room was crowded with ragged filthy children aged six years to fourteen. Some were seated at benches by a long deal table. Others sprawled before the hearth. "Ain't seen you in a while, Jules," the oldest boy drawled.

"You ain't seen me now." Julie tossed the stolen handkerchief and Francis Wakely's plumes onto the table, along with a handful of the coins that had made their way from the drunken gentleman's pocket into her own. Clea kept close to her side as they crossed the small room and crawled through a half-hidden portal in the opposite wall.

The atmosphere was stagnant, mildewy, dank. Julie held the candle higher so as to get the most benefit from its light. From deep in the darkness, rats' eyes glowed red.

They plunged into a maze of damp, gloomy stone vaults. Beneath London lay a fascinating other world. Clea saw arches and corridors and disappearing staircases; ancient bones and tombs and crypts dating back to Roman times. Plague pits. A Saxon cross of powdered sandstone. Remnants of the Great Fire. Julie urged her through a hole two feet square in a cellar wall , even while admitting this act required a considerable amount of trust on Clea's part, for only a beetle-headed half-wit would creep on his hands and knees through an unknown opening in the bowels of the Rookery. As they skirted a large cesspool camouflaged so that anyone who put his foot on the covering would fall into a vat of sewage, the sound of running water grew louder. Julie explained that they were hearing the Fleet River as it made its way alongside London's other buried waterways to dump its filthy contents into the Thames. The air grew fresher as they passed through an opening in another shattered wall and climbed up a narrow staircase with broken steps and rotten rails. At the top stood an ancient door reinforced with mismatched pieces of wood, and a stout lock.

Julie inserted a key. The door was barred from the inside. She knocked, paused, knocked again. A code, concluded Clea, who was relieved to find herself once more above ground.

Sounds of movement came from within. The door edged open and Julie slipped inside. Clea followed. Julie closed the door and turned the lock.

Clea looked curiously around. This room was ten feet by twelve, the ceiling and parts of the wall green and mildewed, the floor dry but bare. Near a small utilitarian fireplace stood a narrow bed. On a rickety wooden table sat a lantern and a book, a loaf of bread and a chunk of cheese, a gin bottle and a teacup.

An old woman wrapped in a shapeless dark gown and shawl shuffled over to the bed. As soon as she was seated, a black cat sprang into her lap. Julie blew out her candle and placed it with her smallsword on the table; removed a battered tin from behind a chink in the wall, and tucked the remainder of her stolen coins inside. Clea glimpsed faded scraps of ribbon, a deck of torn stained playing cards.

Julie tucked the tin back in its hiding place. "Rose, say hello to Lord Dorset's sister. Clea, meet my friend Rose from Drury Lane."

Against one wall leaned a basket filled with wilted flowers. A single sad posy drooped in a cracked vase on the windowsill. "That is an excellent disguise," Clea politely remarked.

Rose eyed the girl with interest. This was her first acquaintance with the sister of an earl. "Thank you," she said.

"I especially like the wart on your chin," Clea added. "However did you get your skin to wrinkle so? I think I would like to tread the boards."

"No, you wouldn't." Fresh cucumber juice, Rose thought glumly. Oil of cacao. "There's always some ambitious youngster waiting in the wings to step on stage in your place. Such as now, when my understudy will take a turn as Lady Macbeth."

"Pritchett warned you?" Julie sank down beside her on the bed.

Pritchett had told Rose enough to turn her hair whiter than her wig. "What have you done, you foolish girl?" Gently, she touched Julie's bruised chin.

What had she done? Aimed above herself, that's what. Julie explained how she had visited Astley's in company with Clea and her brother. "We saw the Flemish Hercules," Clea put in.

Julie stroked Ophelia's soft fur. "I was given a note that Mother Yarwood wished to meet with me. But I met Pego and Mick instead. Ned rescued me from them."

"I wasn't supposed to know about it, but of course I did," Clea put in.

Julie finished, in a rush: "Someone tried to push me under a carriage, and I was snatched out of Tony's house and carried to a brothel and ended up at Wakely Court."

"I hid her in the turret." Clea picked up the deck of cards and sat down on the floor to lay out a game of patience, or as Napoleon called it, *solitaire.* "But then I decided to show her the other secret rooms—Wakely Court has a great many secret rooms—and we went out through the hidden gate."

Rose poured more gin in her teacup. "The house was being watched?"

Julie nodded. "I should have guessed it was."

Quickly, Clea continued: "We couldn't get back inside because the gate was stuck and the other entrances weren't within reach. So I hit one of them with my lantern, and Julie stuck another with her sword—or Francis Wakely's sword, not that I imagine he'd begrudge us the use of it—and we ran away."

Julie flopped back on the bed and stared up at the ceiling. "He said I'd be an old hand at it soon enough."

"Francis Wakely?" Who was Francis Wakely? Rose was having trouble following this account.

"Cap'n Jack. At the nunnery. I saw his face." Julie closed her eyes. "He was going to give me to Mick and Pego when he was done with me. Said Ned would no longer want me then."

Clea looked up from her playing cards. "I probably shouldn't be hearing this."

"You probably shouldn't be having anything to do with the likes of me," Julie muttered.

"Why not?"

"Are you daft? Because if you hadn't, you wouldn't be here."

"*We* wouldn't be here if *I* hadn't been daft enough to force open that gate." Clea uncovered an ace, and placed it in position. "Anyway, this isn't so bad."

Julie propped herself up on an elbow. Rose contemplated Clea over the rim of her teacup. Both looked skeptical.

Clea shrugged. "I spent a few days in a cow shed in Portugal. Along with the cows. That was a great deal less comfortable than this. Ned's not like that, you know."

"Like what?" Julie asked.

"Like the Cap'n said he'd be. Ned truly likes you. I don't think I've ever seen him like anyone so much before."

Julie liked Ned, too. Liking Ned had complicated both her life and his. Now that she had left his house, it would be best for both of them if she never returned.

Arse over teakettle, reflected Rose. She recognized the signs. Her own young lover had proven no less faithless than the ones who came before him, alas.

Clea uncovered another card. "I had an admirer once. Don Miguel Sanchez, one of the Portuguese *guerrilha* chiefs. His idea of a romantic gesture was to present me with a captured Frenchman."

Julie stared at her, distracted. Rose asked, "What happened to Don Miguel?"

"I broke his heart." Clea grinned. "Or so he claimed. Don Miguel already had a wife, as well as a sweetheart in every village he passed through." Furthermore, Don Miguel had been almost as old as Bates.

Her smile faded as she wondered how long it would be before Bates realized they were gone.

Ned would worry. Clea hated the thought. Maybe Kane might also worry, which she wouldn't mind. "This is like one of the priest holes in Wakely Court, isn't it? We will hide here until the danger has passed."

"Or until we can figure how to get you safely home," said Julie. "Snug as three bugs in a rug."

Get 'you' home safely, Clea noted; not 'us'. Rose raised the bottle to pour more gin into her teacup.

Suddenly, the door burst open, with a great crack of breaking wood. Julie grabbed for her sword. Rose froze with the gin bottle hoisted in mid-air.

In the doorway stood a tall dark-haired, dark-eyed man. "Surely you didn't think you would so easily escape me," said Cap'n Jack.

Chapter Thirty-Five

He who would not be idle, let him fall in love.
— Ovid

At last, peace was to be proclaimed in London. The day dawned clear and bright. Early in the morning persons from every walk of life congregated on Hyde Park, not to satisfy their curiosity concerning the Royal Visitors, for the novelty of those dignitaries had long since passed, but to observe the great military review. By nine o'clock the entire area from Tyburn to Hyde Park Gate was covered with soldiers dressed in their finest regimentals. By almost eleven the various corps were at last satisfactorily arranged. Throughout the morning, military bands played brisk martial airs.

The trees were laden down with people; as were every balcony, window and roof with a view. All eyes were fixed on Hyde Park Gate, where the Distinguished Personages were to make their grand *entrée.*

All eyes, that is, save those of Lord Saxe, who would have been more pleased than not to never again espy the Notable Pests. His attention was fixed on his companion, who was wearing a dark blue velvet riding habit with long tight sleeves and a black top hat. "How much longer will you stay in London, do you think?"

"Who knows?" Sabine's own attention was on the Hyde Park Gate. "It is almost morning, darling. You wouldn't want to wake and find me in your bed."

Hubris, Kane reflected. His arrogance had caught the attention of the gods, who as punishment had sentenced him to wanting Sabine in his bed morning, noon, and night.

A salute of twenty-one cannons announced that the Royal

Party was en route. Another discharge heralded their arrival at Hyde Park Gate. A detachment of the Greys moved forward to meet the newcomers, who were received with cheers and shouts. The Prince Regent—accompanied on one side by the Emperor of Prussia, and on the other by the Russian Czar—removed his hat and bowed respectfully to his subjects, who for the most part ignored him, but at least did not hurl rotten fruit. Count Platoff, who was accompanied by a small detachment of his Cossacks, and Field Marshal Blücher received the loudest applause.

Kane glanced down at Sabine. The bright sunlight was unkind, revealing fine lines around her eyes, and flesh at her jaw line that was not so firm as once it would have been.

Her skin was so pale that he could see the veins beneath. Kane sometimes thought he knew her no better now than ever, despite the nights they shared a bed.

She caught him watching her. "You're thinking that I look my age."

Kane was thinking Sabine was older than he was, and that he didn't give a damn. "Nonsense. You are ageless as well as beautiful."

"And you are the consummate diplomat." She turned away to watch the regiments passing in review. At this rate the heralds, who had assembled at eleven to read the peace proclamation, wouldn't be able to start their tour of the city until after four.

Kane wondered what had really prompted Sabine's return to London. Castlereagh seldom acquainted his left hand with the workings of his right.

Tomorrow the Illustrious Irritations were scheduled to depart for Portsmouth, there to disembark from England's shores. Later in the year the struggle to determine the new boundaries of France would resume in Vienna, little progress having thus far been made.

Kane would also travel to Venice, to witness firsthand the scramble for land and influence and power. He wondered if Sabine would be there.

She nudged her dappled mare closer to his black. "Who do you think pushed Miss Wynne?"

Kane wasn't surprised by the change of subject. Sooner or later,

Sabine's conversation always came back to Julie Wynne. "My money is on Lady Georgiana. She was the only one who was close enough."

"Why would Lady Georgiana do such a thing?"

Kane withheld comment. He had, after all, been tempted to push Julie in front of a carriage himself.

Sabine's expression was ironic. "You haven't shared your suspicion with Ned."

"I can't be sure."

"You mean you don't want to see Ned stand his trial for murder. Why do you disapprove of his feelings for the girl?"

"He deserves better."

"Piffle. You're jealous."

He was nothing of the sort. Was he? Kane reminded himself of stolen jewelry, and codebooks. Taweret. Blackmail. Women who hanged themselves.

None of which, if Miss Wynne could be believed, was entirely her fault. Kane recalled being told he'd been born with a silver teaspoon shoved up his arse. The accusation stung.

He paused to watch as the regimental review culminated in the firing of a *feu-du-joie*. Bands played "God Save the King" as the Royals passed by.

"Tell me more about Julian Faulkner," Kane said, when the hubbub had subsided sufficiently to hear another person's voice.

"What do you want to know?"

"Were you in love with him?" Kane asked, then scowled. That wasn't what he'd meant to say.

Sabine looked amused, which irritated him more. "I told you: Julian was my friend."

"Why do you keep his miniature? If he was merely your friend."

"Why does one keep anything? Have you no mementos?"

Kane opened his mouth, then closed it, uncomfortable with what a lack of mementos might reveal about him. He was uncomfortable with any number of the things he was discovering about himself.

Sabine unpinned the cameo from her high-necked habit shirt and fastened it to his lapel. "Now you have something by which to remember me."

The lady was in a deuced odd mood. Kane wondered why. Before he could ask her, if he had dared to ask her, further tumult swept through the crowd. Ned rode toward them, scattering bystanders before him like ninepins.

His face was as grim as if he'd been assigned to redesign the map of Europe himself. "How nice that you could bring yourself to join us," Kane greeted him. "Castlereagh wishes to speak with you. Perhaps he wishes to tender his congratulations. Having read the account of your betrothal this morning in *The Times*."

Sabine had not read the newspapers. She drew in a breath.

"Congratulations are *not* in order," snapped Ned, who had woke up to find himself of even greater interest than the royal visitors; next to a good scandal, the ladies of the *ton* adored to hear that another gentleman had got caught in parson's mousetrap. "And that's not important now."

"How is it not important?" protested Sabine. "If Bianca follows through on her threat to bring a breach-of-promise suit..."

"This is Hannah's doing. I've already told her that it won't serve." Ned had in fact dragged his cousin from her bed, and the wretched woman had been gloating even as she protested she'd merely lent a hand. All Hannah had ever wanted (she said) was for Ned to get himself a proper heir. After meeting Bianca, she saw that in comparison no ordinary young female would do.

Hannah had no longer been triumphant after Ned finished making his displeasure known, along with the circumstance that he would not be taking Bianca as his bride and residing at Dorset Hall, breach-of-promise suit or no; and furthermore announcing that he seriously questioned further exposing his sister to the influence of someone so wanting in wit as to think the mistress of a notorious Portuguese *bandido* would make him a suitable bride. Ned had left his cousin as overset as ever Lady Georgiana had pretended, and it hadn't improved his spirits one whit.

"None of that matters," he repeated.

"Then what *does* matter?" inquired Kane.

They were interrupted by another burst of applause and music.

Ned stroked Soldier's neck and wished someone might similarly soothe him. Specifically, he wished Julie might do so, but he must find her first.

"What matters is that Julie and Clea are missing. You may tell Castlereagh that I'll do anything he wishes if you turn your resources to finding them."

"What do you mean, they're missing?" demanded Sabine.

"I mean they're not at Wakely Court." Ned could still feel Julie sprawled atop him. Draped across him like a blanket. Weeping in his arms. He shouldn't have let her out of his sight. Hadn't meant to, certainly. Now he was terrified she was lost.

After his encounter with Bianca, Ned had got deliberately cupshot. On his return to Wakely Court, he'd avoided the turret room, feeling Julie deserved far better than that he go to her foxed. When he finally climbed the stair to the attics, upon his return from browbeating Hannah and setting in motion numerous other attempts at damage control, he'd discovered that both Julie and Clea were nowhere in the house.

"Bates doesn't know how long they've been gone. He thinks they may have been exploring and something caused them to run off. We found a broken lantern and a pruning saw in the street outside the old garden wall."

Francis Wakely's smallsword was missing. Ned hoped Julie was putting it to good use. What had Clea been thinking, to take her out the midden gate?

Ned daren't dwell on Clea, or the disservice he had done his sister by allowing her to run wild. Had he made the slightest effort to curb Clea's adventurous nature—or to rein in his own reckless infatuation with Julie—she would be snug and safe at Wakely Court. "I've already been to the Academy. According to the servants, Lilah left town on an emergency of some sort two days past." Ned could hardly blame her for saving her own neck. In releasing Julie, Lilah had defied Cap'n Jack.

Kane was unusually silent. Ned had anticipated a scathing denouncement, which would have been another waste of time, since Kane could say nothing Ned hadn't already said to himself. "You're too calm about this."

"I have a certain Bow Street Runner in my keeping." Kane took up his reins. "One who's prepared to talk in return for preventing his neck from being stretched. You might care to join me in hearing what he has to say." He looked around, and frowned. Odd that in the midst of all Ned's trouble, Sabine should have stolen away.

Chapter Thirty-Six

Heavens! What thick darkness pervades the minds of men.
— Ovid

The nursery was bleak and dusty, furnished with cast-off bits and pieces. The windows were barred. Julie said it felt like a prison. She should know.

Rose's wig resembled a frizzed bird's nest, and her ugly dress was torn. She had lost much of the putty from her face, as well as the wart from her chin. Twenty pounds of strawberries and two of raspberries, she promised herself, as she shifted uncomfortably on the narrow iron cot and waited for the door to open; berries crushed and thrown into a bath from which she would emerge with her skin freshly perfumed, soft as velvet, and tinged with a delicate pink. This event, if unlikely to occur in her near future, was considerably more pleasant to contemplate than a recent conversation concerning the popularity of Englishwomen in foreign brothels, even Englishwomen of her advanced age. Clea stood atop a wooden chair on one side of the door, a broken slate in her hand. Julie waited on the other, clutching a length of splintered wood. Desperate times called for desperate measures. Rose wished they could have kept the sword.

Jules had gotten in several good thrusts before the weapon was taken from her. While Rose had cast about with her gin bottle and Clea had shrieked at the top of her lungs. And then the Cap'n wrenched the sword from Julie and bent her damaged arm behind her back; and promised if the nonsense didn't cease he would twist that arm right off.

Rose listened for the sound of the bolt being drawn. She didn't care to think about the reasons a nursery door might be barred from the outside.

How long had the Cap'n known of their secret room? Had he been aware all along? More likely someone had betrayed them, honor among thieves being as great a myth as the Holy Grail.

Came the sound she had been dreading, and the creaking of a hinge. "I cannot imagine," said an irritated male voice, "what is of such importance that I had to come all the way to London. You know I don't travel well. Nor do I see why we must visit the old nursery."

Replied Cap'n Jack, "You will." An older gentleman stumbled through the doorway, as if he'd pushed. He caught his balance and righted himself, leaning heavily on his cane. A startled expression crossed his face as he spied Clea with her slate.

Before the gentleman could speak, Rose groaned. She conjured up visions of foreign brothels, and emptied her belly of a small amount of bread and cheese, and a considerable quantity of gin.

The stranger stared at her. "Help me. I'm dying," Rose moaned, and retched again.

"You're overacting," said the Cap'n, as he entered the room. "If you don't cease chewing up the scenery I'll see you removed permanently from the stage."

Overacting, was she? Insulted by this slur, Rose sat up and wiped her mouth. Ophelia slunk from beneath the cot to jump onto her lap. Rose regretted the selfish impulse that had caused her to bring the cat with her from Drury Lane.

The Cap'n's left hand was bandaged. In his right, he held a pistol pointed unwavering at Rose. "I left them chained. Remember the chains, Father? I thought you might. Come out, Jules, or I will shoot your friend where she sits."

'Father'? Rose took a closer look at the older man. He might have in his youth been handsome, though his body was twisted with arthritis, his face etched with passing time and pain. His hair was a faded gold.

The Cap'n's hair and eyes were dark, his features unremarkable, if cold. Rose might have passed him by countless times and never noticed, at the theater and elsewhere, for he was indistinguishable from his peers.

She wished she could not distinguish him now. How unfair that, if she were to die, she could not be costumed as Desdemona, or even Lady Macbeth, instead of an old crone. "I'm counting, Jules," the Cap'n said. "One. Two…"

Julie stepped out from behind the door. Cap'n Jack cocked his gun. Julie let the long jagged piece of wood fall to the floor.

"Enterprising, isn't she?" said the Cap'n. "I believe that was once part of a crib. One almost feels a degree of family pride. I see your shadow, Miss Fairchild. Step down off that chair."

Reluctantly, Clea obeyed. The Cap'n turned his pistol on her. She dropped her slate. He gestured toward the cot.

Clea dropped down on the cot, nudged Rose, who immediately moaned.

"She's sick, poor thing, and no wonder." What with one thing and another, Clea was feeling ill herself. "I don't know who you are, sir, but this man with you is a lunatic who has locked us up for no good reason. You should make him let us go."

The older man's attention was fixed on Julie, as she followed Clea to the cot. "Boy, what have you done?"

"Already she is of more interest to you than I am. A chit you didn't know existed until moments past." Sounds of protest came from the hall outside. The Cap'n turned toward the doorway as Sabine walked into the room.

"It's that sorry I am, sir," said the servant who trailed after her. "I told her you weren't in."

The Cap'n dismissed the man, closed the nursery door. "Mrs. Viccars. I had expected more of you."

Sabine smiled faintly. "People often do."

Clea pressed closer to Rose. "Hello, Sabine. We've been playing at quotations to pass the time. 'See that you promise: what harm is there in promise? In promises anyone can be rich.' Ovid."

"'And thus I clothe my naked villainy with old odds and ends'. Shakespeare," added Rose, as she simultaneously wondered why Jules was important, and tried not to inhale Clea's ripe scent.

Julie leaned up against Rose's other side, completing the olfactory assault, and spoke for the first time since Cap'n Jack had come into the room. "'Naked villainy' is good. I personally like 'and the vile squealing of the wry-necked fife'."

"They've not been a good influence on each other," remarked Cap'n Jack. "I'm not sure Jules is to blame. *I* am not to blame for them looking like pigs who have been rooting in the mud."

He was, however, to blame for the fact they both sported fresh bruises, and that Rose again felt like casting up her accounts.

Had Mrs. Viccars ridden to their rescue? Rose would have preferred the arrival of a troop of Hussars. Nothing against the lady, but she looked frail.

She had nerve enough, however. Mrs. Viccars regarded the Cap'n's bandaged hand and said, "Was it Julie who damaged you? Her father would have been proud."

The older man's gaze lingered on Julie's bruises, which were evident through her grime. "She has Julian's eyes. Faulkners breed true."

"And so I am a by-blow?" said Cap'n Jack. "If that's what you believed, better you should have thrown me out into the street."

"As in effect, you threw out Julie." Ignoring the pistol that was trained on her, Mrs. Viccars walked toward the barred windows, thereby placing herself between the Cap'n and the cot.

She turned to look at Julie. "The letter I received said Julian had left a child. I traveled to London, unconvinced. I was more curious to discover who could, would, attempt such a blatant manipulation than from any conviction it was true. One look at you changed my mind. I regret that it's taken me so long to discover what Jonathan meant to do."

Julie said, "You mean Cap'n Jack."

"Ah."

The older man roused from his abstraction. "Who is Cap'n Jack?"

At the same time, Clea protested, "I don't understand."

Rose had the benefit of Pritchett's deductions. "Cap'n Jack's true name is Jonathan Faulkner, and he is the sole surviving son of the Marquess of Carlyle. That would be this older gentleman."

"Cap'n Jack is an individual of considerable influence," put in Jonathan Faulkner. "Not, Father, that I expect you to be impressed. It will amuse me to reveal Julie's identity to all the world, before she's hanged. No question that she *will* hang. A large amount of evidence has been amassed against her. Which was the primary purpose for the thefts I had her commit."

Lord Carlyle blanched. "You would do such a thing?"

"This from the man who sent me to Dunkard? I have been planning it for years."

Almost, briefly, Rose pitied Jonathan Faulkner. Dunkard had been a school notorious for the brutal measures with which it subdued hitherto unmanageable boys. Due to an outcry following the death of a student, it had been closed down.

The older man sank down on a wooden chair. "There was bad blood between you from the cradle. Everything was a competition. Julian always won."

"Or so you chose to see it." The Cap'n moved closer to the cot. "Julian was your golden boy, while I could do nothing right. How odd to recall that I once wished your approval. To continue: Julian told me honor demanded he marry his light o' love. However, it didn't suit me that he should. You must have wondered why Julian didn't return to you, Mrs. Viccars. Did you think he had run off? You were so ill after the child was born that I expected you would die. I paid off the midwife and left you to get on with it; placed the brat where I could lay hands on her again if and when I wished." In a mockery of fondness, the Cap'n stroked Julie's hair. "As she grew older, I realized her resemblance to my brother might prove useful."

"Useful as a weapon," said Sabine, dispassionately. "You've been setting up your father to take a devastating fall. My awareness of the business was merely an additional fillip. You wanted us to know, when it was too late, exactly what you'd done."

Julie was related to a lordship? Who looked like he might at any moment pop off in an apoplexy? She said, "When was I born?"

"May 25, 1795. Your father and I were secretly married, though both of us were underage." Sabine studied the Cap'n. "You really think no one can stop you?"

"You really think *you* can? I have in my possession documents that show certain of your recent activities in, shall we say, a less than loyal light."

"I see."

A diversion was called for, lest Cap'n Jack notice Mrs. Viccars was inching her hand toward the pocket of her riding habit. Rose elbowed Julie and then Clea; grasped Ophelia's tail and yanked.

The cat yowled and shot straight up in the air. Julie and Clea both dove for the Cap'n's knees.

Caught off balance, Cap'n Jack stumbled. Sabine pulled her pistol from her pocket and shot him pointblank. His body jerked from the impact.

As he fell, the Cap'n's gun discharged. His bullet caught Sabine in the chest. Footsteps pounded up the stairs. Kane and Ned burst into the room.

Julie sprang to her feet. Lord Carlyle caught her arms and held her fast.

She felt like kicking him. Julie wanted Ned. Who had moved to block his sister's view.

Kane knelt beside Sabine. Her riding habit was already soaked with blood. Desperately, he tried to staunch the flow.

Her eyelids fluttered open. "'*Amare et sapere vix deo conceditur.*'" And then she was gone.

"Syrus," sobbed Clea, against Ned's chest. "The gods never let us love and be wise at the same time."

Chapter Thirty-Seven

I believe love first devised
the torturer's profession for mankind. — Plautus

Lord Carlyle's townhouse was located in a fashionable part of London. Brook Street extended westward from Hanover Square to the northeast corner of Grosvenor Square. Ned wondered if, like many a young miss before her, Sabine had once dreamed of being married in St George's, Hanover Square. Instead she had eloped with Francis Viccars and led the life of a soldier's wife. In memory's eye, Ned saw her in the small two-story house in Frenada, curled up in a chair, watching Wellington pore over his maps, laughing at something Francis said, savoring the inner warmth of the fine claret they all shared.

Gallant Francis Viccars, renowned for his coolness under fire. In the end, Sabine had been no less brave.

Two days had passed since her death and that of Jonathan Faulkner in what was being termed, due to his father's influence, a 'tragic accident', because after all one wouldn't care to have a stigma attached to so old and venerable a name; two busy days during which Ned had diligently presented himself in Brook Street, and as diligently been turned away. This afternoon he had made it as far as the entrance hall with its marble floor and wooden chairs and seven-day clock.

The butler returned. "If you will follow me, my lord." He led the way up the staircase and to a parlor at the front of the house.

Gold-striped paper covered the walls. Wilton carpets lay upon the floor. Lord Carlyle stood by the fireplace, leaning heavily on a cane. Julie was seated primly on a scroll-footed rosewood settee.

In a far corner of the room, a brown-haired woman bent over her needlework. Julie had gone from being a companion to having one herself.

The butler announced him. Julie rose quickly to her feet. "Sit down, child," said Lord Carlyle. "It isn't seemly to so eagerly greet a gentleman." From the companion's corner came what sounded suspiciously like a snort.

The bruises on Julie's face had begun to fade. She still favored one arm. Ned crossed the room, and took her other hand in his. "Are you all right?"

"Of course she is all right," said the marquess. "Overwhelmed by all that has befallen her, and rightly so, but Faulkners have never wanted for backbone."

Nor for excessive self-assurance. "I'm sorry I was unable to come to you sooner, buttercup. The butler had instructions to turn me away at the door."

Julie cast a startled glance at the marquess, who had the grace to look embarrassed. She demanded, "Why?"

"We are in mourning, and not receiving visitors. Moreover, you could not be seen until you were properly attired."

She was that, in as severe a black as Ned's cousin had ever worn. Ned preferred her in Frances Wakely's cloak. Better still, in nothing but his velvet drapery. "I'm more concerned with how you feel."

"I'd feel a great deal better if I wasn't wearing this corset," she retorted. "I can barely breathe."

"Julia!" Lord Carlyle thumped his cane.

She scowled. "'Julia' is not my name."

"You are the Lady Julia Faulkner, daughter of my eldest son, Julian. It may be strange to you now, but you will grow accustomed. I believe, Dorset, that I read recently of your upcoming nuptials."

Lord Carlyle and at least half the world had read of it, not including Julie, who snatched back her hand. In her corner, the older woman broke off a thread.

Ned was growing short of patience. "Had you perused today's newspapers you would have seen both a retraction and an apology.

Senhorita Fernandes is on her way back to Portugal." As result of a private conversation between Lord Castlereagh and the Portuguese ambassador.

"I told you her nose would be out of joint," said Julie. "She was probably even crosser when you sent her away."

"Certain unkind words were said."

Lord Carlyle disliked being excluded from the conversation. "I've never heard of such a thing. Betrothals made and broken within a matter of days. Moreover, Faulkners do not gossip. I am certain, Julia, that you have a general wish of doing right."

Ned had a general wish of bidding his lordship to Hades. "A gentleman can't be seated while a lady remains standing," he said softly, for Julie's ears alone. She rolled her eyes, and sank down on the settee.

Ned seated himself beside her. "I have information for you, Carlyle. About your son."

"Julian?"

"Jonathan."

The marquess lowered himself awkwardly into an armchair. "Jonathan believed I came to town at his bidding. I did not explain that a correspondence from Mrs. Viccars influenced me."

Sabine had been busy. "She wished to speak to you of Julian?" Ned asked.

"I realized she was the chit he once wanted to marry. When Mrs. Viccars showed me the letter that had been sent her, I recognized Jonathan's handwriting, though it was some time before I would admit it to myself. " Lord Carlyle rested his crippled hands atop his cane. "One of the many lowering realizations of advancing age is that one has been more often in error than not. In retrospect I may have been too strict with the boy, but wrong-headedness ran in his mother's family, and he was a difficult child. Still, I find it hard to comprehend the monster he became."

"He wasn't wholly a monster." Ned felt Julie's gaze on him, but his own attention was for the marquess. "Your son—Jonathan— worked for the Home Office. He was deeply involved in Sidmouth's efforts to suppress manifestations of disaffection and discontent.

Which is how 'Cap'n Jack' came to have the network of informants that he did."

Julie so forgot herself as to clutch Ned's arm. "Cap'n Jack worked for the *government*?"

Ned placed his hand over hers. "He started out that way, at any rate."

"Is that why he wanted your statue, and the notebook?"

"Perhaps."

Lord Carlyle's eyebrows beetled. "Sidmouth is too severe. Seventeen convicted Luddites hanged at York, by God, despite numerous pleas for lenience. Julia, you will unhand Dorset at once."

Julie removed her hand, reluctantly Ned thought. Hoped. It was damned difficult to sit here like a proper gentlemen when he wanted nothing more than to pull her onto his lap.

She looked quizzically at him. Ned hoped his thoughts weren't writ clear on his face. "I was wool-gathering. What did you say?"

"I said, the Cap'n didn't know I peached on him." Julie stole a wary look at Lord Carlyle. "Er, told you his name."

"He did not. Have you been blaming yourself? None of this was your fault."

She didn't look convinced. More time must pass before Julie realized that she was truly safe. Impossible that Ned hadn't guessed that she was Sabine's daughter. Yet, how could he have known?

He had promised Julie the Cap'n wouldn't touch her again, he had said he'd keep her safe. Ned wasn't worthy to kiss her smallest toe.

Julie edged her hand forward until it touched his, under cover of her skirts. "I think it's you that's out of curl," she said. "What will happen to Pritchett? He was kind to me, in his way."

"Kane and Pritchett came to an agreement. So long as Pritchett keeps his end of the bargain, he won't be called to account." Kane would find it beneficial to have a villain in his pocket—or in Lord Castlereagh's pocket—especially when said villain operated under the banner of Bow Street.

Julie's companion stirred. Unless Ned's eyes deceived him,

curled up in her sewing basket, amid a tangle of multi-colored silks, was a large black cat.

He returned his attention to the marquess. "Pritchett is the Bow Street Runner who removed Julie from Newgate. After your son arranged for her to be put there."

Julie searched Ned's face. "So it wasn't my fault either that I was pinched?"

"Not a bit of it."

"Julia tells me you are aware of her background, Dorset," put in the marquess. "I must request that you keep that knowledge to yourself."

Julie stared at Lord Carlyle. As did Ned. The older man flushed. "I have no wish for us to be at odds. From what my granddaughter tells me, I am in your debt. However, you must see that under the circumstances the least said is soonest mended. I trust I make myself clear."

Clear, indeed. Ned said stiffly, "With your permission, Carlyle, I would like to speak with Julie alone."

"Most certainly not. The proprieties must be observed."

To the devil with the proprieties. Ned marveled that Julie sat so quietly while her grandfather preached and prosed.

He shifted sideways on the settee, his back to the marquess. "I wished to talk to you about Sabine."

"*Was* she a traitor?" Julie asked.

"Wellington would tell you no. The Corsican might not agree."

Julie sighed. "I've never had a family. Except for Rose and Pritchett; and they were related to me by circumstance, not blood. Now I find out I had a real father and a mother, but both of them are dead."

One had died in front of her, thought Ned.. "You have a grandfather," put in Lord Carlyle.

She'd had as well an uncle who threatened to see her hanged, and worse. Ned glanced at the marquess. "Julie's father died in a riding accident?"

"So we believed. I now suspect that Jonathan took a hand."

Julie said, quietly, "Mrs. Viccars didn't wish to know me."

"I think she wished it more than anything," Ned responded gently, "but she feared a closer acquaintance would make things more difficult. Sabine knew she was dying of a cancer, and that she had little time left. I imagine she thought it would be kinder to remain a stranger than subject you to another loss."

He didn't know that he agreed with Sabine's reasoning. Julie had lost her anyway.

Carlyle put in, with gruff kindness, "I don't think Mrs. Viccars was certain of her suspicions until Jonathan confessed."

Julie narrowed her eyes at Ned. "How long did you know?"

He thought he'd known from their first meeting. Ah, but she wasn't asking about *that*. "There are items among Sabine's effects that you may wish to have. A miniature portrait of your father, for one. I'll keep them until you decide what you want done."

Lord Carlyle interrupted. "You will send them here."

"I will do whatever Julie asks of me." Ned rose and made his bow. "And now it's time I take my leave. Carlyle. Miss Wynne."

"You mean Miss Faulkner."

"No. I mean Miss Wynne."

After the earl's departure, silence fell on the room. Abruptly, Julie stood. "If you will excuse me…"

Her grandfather frowned. "You're not to go after him."

"I'm going to my room."

The marquess rang for a footman. "Escort Miss Faulkner to her chamber." Julie departed, muttering under her breath.

Lord Carlyle didn't care to know precisely what she'd said. This unexpected granddaughter left the marquess bemused, bewildered, even bedazzled, and feeling as a hedge sparrow might upon finding a yellow-billed cuckoo in its nest. He hadn't yet recovered from the shock of being told that appropriating Lady Willoughby's amethyst cross had been as easy as pissing the bed. A subsequent demonstration of pocket-picking had left him overwhelmed.

Rose gave Ophelia a stroke as she set aside her stitchery, which consisted primarily of misshapen knots and snarls interspersed with the occasional spot of blood. She was much better suited to the footlights than the drawing room, but thus far Julie had refused to let her go. And so she would bathe in strawberries and alternately lime-flowers, and anoint her skin with lemon juice and rainwater enriched with roses; rinse her hair with quinine and rum and coddle her face with milk and lemon juice; perfume herself with violets—in short, pamper herself with every luxury until her understudy proved so hugely unsatisfactory that Mr. Kean himself demanded Rose's return to Drury Lane.

Pritchett had brought back her precious letters, with a warning they might be better destroyed. But when had Rose ever been wise? There were her memoirs to consider. And, were romance to ultimately fail her, the comfort of her old age.

She rose and walked toward Lord Carlyle. He roused from contemplation of sparrows and cuckoos to regard her warily.

"You don't remember me," Rose said, without rancor; it had taken her some time to recognize the marquess. He had been a handsome rogue, twenty-odd years before. "I was playing Mrs. Teazle in *The School for Scandal.* You gave me a painting, a Gainsborough village scene. I treasure it still."

Chapter Thirty-Eight

When a woman is openly bad, she at last is good.
— Pubilius Syrus

Lady Georgiana was arrayed in a great deal of purplish pink, a shade that she called puce; and plumage that wouldn't have been out of place on Francis Wakely's hat. Clea regretted the loss of that hat, as well as the smallsword. Further explorations of Wakely House, however, had unearthed a great many other treasures, including horse pistols richly ornamented with tarnished silver; a green leather case containing a 17th century silver and ivory pocket knife and fork; several old manuscripts, a handful of sovereigns dated 1662, a flask of rum, and the bones of a small bird. She hoped this latter had been someone's dinner, and not a pet.

The precise shade of Lord Ashcroft's satin waistcoat, he informed her, was Evening Primrose. His cravat—*blanc d'innocence virginale*, the purest white—was tied in the Trone d'amour. He broke off, uncomfortably, as if unsure that he should be speaking of such things to her, despite the fact Clea was wearing *blanc d'innocence virginale* herself. While the viscount was in excellent spirits, his mama was subdued.

Lady Georgiana was talking, nonetheless, to Clea's cousin. Or, in this particular moment, listening, because Hannah held the stage. "Why, if the gel is Carlyle's granddaughter, was she acting as your companion? That's what *I'd* like to know."

So would have Georgiana liked to know, although she would hardly share that circumstance with her old foe. "It was a way for dear Julie to get her toes damp before she determined whether she wished to take the plunge. Odd as it may seem, Polite Society is not to everybody's taste. And who better than I to show a young woman how to go on?"

Who, indeed? Hannah sniffed at this further example of Lady Georgiana's exalted opinion of herself. The aggravating creature had once again managed to garner a fair amount of attention, for the *ton* was all a-twitter over the intelligence that a child had resulted from the hitherto-unacknowledged marriage of Lord Carlyle's eldest son.

Hannah understood perfectly why the matter had remained secret. The boy had married a nobody. One disliked to admit such a *mésalliance*.

One also disliked admitting one was less well informed than one's archenemy, but curiosity won out. "And does she? Wish to take the plunge?"

She almost *had* taken the plunge. Georgiana shuddered to recall a certain nigh-fateful shove. "Now that Jonathan Faulkner's sudden death has sunk the family into mourning, Julie will be making no social appearances for some time. A strange business, that. No one knows exactly what had happened. Rumor has it all tangled up with Home Office affairs."

Hannah could have cared less about the Home Office, or Jonathan Faulkner, for that matter. There was an earl to get married off. Ned had shown a partiality for Lady Georgiana's companion. Who had turned out, to Hannah's astonishment (and Lady Georgiana's, she would wager), to be the perfectly appropriate granddaughter of a marquess.

Not that Hannah would dream of interfering. She'd given her word.

Clea could almost hear the cogs clanking in her cousin's brain. She had quite naturally been eavesdropping on the conversation, not ladylike conduct admittedly but nigh unavoidable since Lady Georgiana and Hannah hadn't bothered to lower their voices in the slightest, which had earned them several annoyed glances: the musical part of the evening had begun, and various ladies were assassinating Clementi, Pleyel and Haydn by means of pianoforte and harp.

At the moment, Madalyn Tate was singing. She had a surprisingly pleasant voice.

Sabine had spoken kindly of Mrs. Tate. If not *to* her, from all accounts. Clea wondered if Madalyn knew Sabine was gone.

It didn't matter. Clea knew. Therefore, she had dressed up in her finery and insisted on going out into the world, because she had lived through a war and realized that life is short and precious, and should be enjoyed while one can.

She glanced at Lord Ashcroft, seated beside her. He caught her eye, and winked.

Tony felt as if the troubles of the world had been lifted from his shoulders. His vowels had been restored to him, accompanied by some stern advice, as result of which he had told his mama he was taking control of the purse strings.

He had been very firm. Maman hadn't recovered from it yet.

Her displeasure didn't signify. No matter how many crows she plucked, or peals she rang, he wasn't going to change his mind.

Tony had moreover, on further good advice, hired a man of business to instruct him regarding the wise and unwise uses of his funds, and only a little bit regretted that worthy's stern injunction against gaming hells. The clever fellow had managed to track down his mama's previous companion, and discovered she had been given a goodly amount of money to leave town. Tony had offered her even more money to return. Mildred had thus far refused, but he hadn't given up hope.

Things *had* been fixed up all right and tight.

Lady Georgiana and Hannah were currently arguing over the recent conduct of Princess Charlotte, who had fallen out with her mother, who had decided to live abroad. Clea had minimal interest in Princess Charlotte, and less in Wolfgang Mozart's *Rondo Alla Turca*. She watched Kane make his way toward her.

His hair was much too long, and tousled. His handsome features were drawn. He looked angry, and impatient, and there wasn't a lady present who didn't turn her head to wistfully watch the rakish Lord Saxe pass by.

Even Lady Georgiana and Hannah briefly broke off squabbling.

Kane greeted them, as he settled into the empty seat on Clea's far side. "You are looking remarkably grown-up tonight," he said.

Clea *was* more grown-up than she had been mere days past. Kane, on his part, looked as though he had aged overnight.

She was old enough to know some things were better left unstated, and so Clea gave him a quotation.

"Elsie Marley's grown so fair
She won't get up to feed the swine
But lies in bed til eight or nine."

Kane raised an eyebrow. "Nursery rhymes?"

"We had to do something to pass the time in that horrid place. I have added to my vocabulary. A rum duke is a queer unaccountable fellow. Like Cap'n Jack. And going to rest in a horse's night-cap is to be hanged."

Clea would have posed a problem for Cap'n Jack, thought Kane. Rose and Julie were expendable. The sister of an earl was not. "I wish that you didn't know such people existed, brat."

Clea wished he would stop calling her 'brat'. She didn't scold, however, because he was so sad. "The Cap'n called me a hellcat. After I kicked him in the gingambobs."

Kane contemplated her.

"Or twiddle-diddles, if you prefer."

Kane's laugh was infectious. Heads turned. He noticed, and his amusement fled. Clea wondered if Kane would notice when she finished growing up. If necessary, she would place herself naked in his bed. After she had grown bosoms. "'The wild boar is often held by a small dog.' Ovid," she said.

Kane smiled at her. "'I only spout poetry when my feet hurt.' Ennius."

Now it was Clea who chuckled.

She was well on her way to being a beauty already, with her mahogany hair and green eyes and dimples, her irrepressible spirits and unquenchable curiosity. Some young buck would be lucky to win her. Kane felt very old.

He had accompanied the Royal Visitors to Portsmouth, where they surveyed dockyards and barges and men of war, were cheered by ships' companies and entertained with grand cannon salutes, all of which the Grand Duchess bore with surprising fortitude. Indeed, she went so far as to drink grog with the crew of the *Impregnable*. Kane had no stomach for the grand banquet that the Regent was hosting tonight at the Government House, for a select one hundred and fifty persons, and so returned to town.

Castlereagh had made no attempt to discourage him. The Foreign Secretary would also, if for different reasons, mourn Sabine.

A smatter of polite applause interrupted Kane's reflections. The young lady who had been abusing Mozart removed her hands from the piano keys.

Another young woman approached the harp. She sat down and plucked a timid chord.

"Oh, for heaven's sake!" Tony could tolerate no more. He stalked across the room, shoo'd away the startled young lady, took up a position at the harp and placed his hands on the strings.

The richly brilliant strains of Louis Spohr's *Fantasie in C minor* filled the room. Even Lady Georgiana and Hannah fell mute. By the time he finished playing, not a person present doubted that Lord Ashcroft possessed a tremendous musical ability. In the midst of the ensuing adulation, few (and of those, all were ladies) noticed the departure of Lord Saxe.

Kane gave his coachman instructions. The night was young, and he had no desire to be alone.

Had he loved Sabine, or she him? Kane didn't know. He suspected they would have wearied of each other, in time. But that time had been cut short, and Kane felt a profound sense of loss.

Candles beckoned from behind plate glass windows. Soft music and seductive voices whispered through briefly opened doors. The Academy was doing a good business. Kane handed his hat and coat to a liveried servant.

Mrs. Kingston walked down the hallway toward him. "I left instructions that I was to be informed immediately if you returned."

She'd said 'if', but had meant 'when'. "May we speak privately?"

Kane asked.

"Of course." She led him into a small, excellently furnished sitting room, poured brandy in two glasses, and handed one to him. "I was sorry to hear about Mrs. Viccars. I know she was Ned's friend."

Kane sampled his own brandy, found it excellent. "You won't mourn Cap'n Jack."

"Hardly. Pray be seated." Lilah arranged herself gracefully on a satin-upholstered love seat. "I shan't pretend he didn't make me a wealthy woman. Or that I don't have some concern about who may take his place."

Kane reached into his pocket and withdrew the document that had brought him here. "Ned asked me to give you this."

She took the paper, read it, set it carefully aside. Had Kane not been watching closely, he might have missed her trembling hand.

It didn't surprise him. He had just given her the deed to this house.

She didn't ask why Ned hadn't brought the thing himself.

Lilah's lavender eyes had seen a great deal of the world. Saw more, indeed, than her caller might have wished. "If you're not in a hurry to take your leave, perhaps you would care to inspect the supper rooms, my lord. I have an excellent French chef."

Chapter Thirty-Nine

There's no point in seeking a remedy for a thunderbolt.
— Pubilius Syrus

It was close on midnight when Julie arrived at Wakely House, one of her grandfather's servants trailing at her heels. James the footman opened the front door. Tidcombe hovered at his shoulder, curious about who was calling at this odd hour. "The master is in the library, miss. I daresay you would prefer to find your own way."

Julie shrugged out of her cloak. "No, Tidcombe, I would prefer that you announce me. Please have William taken to the kitchen for a spot of something to keep him warm, because I expect I'm going to keep him out late."

Tidcombe had long since accepted that he would never be able to anticipate what unusual circumstance he might next encounter at Wakely Court; but high among those various excitements must surely rank the night when she-who-not-so-long-ago-had-been-a-housebreaker presented herself at the front door, dressed in poppy red no less, and requested to be announced as Lady Julia Faulkner.

Announce her, Tidcombe did, with all due pomp, whereupon the earl's feet thudded off the desk where he had propped them, and his batman's jaw fell open so wide it almost hit the floor. The young lady smiled graciously at the pair of them as she swept into the room. What happened next, Tidcombe couldn't say, because the door closed in his face. It being beneath the dignity of a butler to eavesdrop, Tidcombe descended to the kitchen, there to quiz Lord Carlyle's servant, the gossip that went on below-stairs being no less energetic than above.

Julie held out her hand to Bates. "I have never properly thanked you for taking such good care of me."

Bates flushed. "I was only doing my job, miss. Um, my lady, that is."

"Odd, is it not? I haven't gotten used to it myself."

Ned was looking quizzical. Suddenly uncertain, Julie moved to the hearth where Cerberus was enjoying a snooze. Clea's old muff lay on the floor nearby. Julie leaned down to pick it up.

The dog leapt to attention, with a snarl and a snap and a fine display of his numerous sharp teeth. Julie stepped quickly back. Bates said, "I'll just be leaving," and did.

"Cerberus has developed a tendre," explained Ned. Julie eyed the muff, which had not benefited from being the recipient of canine *l'amour.* Cerberus dragged the thing toward him, lay his head upon it, and went back to sleep.

Julie moved toward the desk, where the earl was seated. He was in his shirtsleeves. Pretty Ned the buccaneer. She said, "Do you like my dress?"

His eyes moved slowly over her. "It is very red."

It was also very low-cut in the bosom. "Lady Georgiana had it made. I think she meant me to seduce someone."

Ned contemplated the gown's plunging neckline. "And why would she wish that?"

"She thought I had designs on Tony." Julie circled the desk. "That's why she pushed me in front of that carriage. What are you looking at?"

Ned nudged the miniature toward her. Julie took it in her hand. She might have been staring at a male version of herself.

"That, sunshine, is Julian Faulkner. Your father," Ned explained.

He had been so young. Julie gazed again at the portrait, then set it aside. Tonight wasn't for feeling sad. "I told my grandfather that if he means to claim me, he must take me as I am. I wondered for a time if you knew the truth all along."

Ned frowned, which made him look even more piratical and handsome. "You thought I was interested in you because I knew you were the granddaughter of a marquess and therefore suitable to rub shoulders with an earl?"

"It made me cross."

The earl felt a little cross himself. "May I hope you've changed your mind?"

"Rose said I was a peagoose. And anyway, you couldn't have known any of that when we first met."

"When you broke into my house, you mean."

"When I stole your statue." Which now sat primly on a bookshelf. Pritchett had returned the thing, along with Ned's knife. "I have my blade back also. It was among the Cap'n's things." Julie flicked up her skirt so that Ned might see the blade strapped to her thigh.

Ned looked, and looked again. Julie was sufficiently encouraged by his expression to slide off the desk and onto his lap. "I'm trying to behave like a gentleman," he sighed, as she nuzzled his ear.

Julie slipped one hand beneath his shirt to rest it against his smooth, warm skin. "Why?"

"Because I thought I should." He caught her hand in his and held it flat against his chest. "I've been worried about you, buttercup."

"I've been worried about me, too." Julie fingered the fabric of his shirt. "But it has all worked out, if not for the best, maybe as it was meant to, and I don't want to talk about that now."

Ned didn't either, truth be told. "What, then?"

"You promised me pleasure, if you will recall. You're not going to spoil everything, are you, by saying this is the wrong time?"

"I wouldn't dare refuse you. Not when you're carrying that knife." Ned plucked her hand from his chest and pressed a kiss into her palm. "Are you absolutely certain this is what you want?"

She gave him a look. He swept her up into his arms and carried her to the bookshelves; pressed the hidden mechanism that caused a section to swing out from the wall. Cerberus opened one mildly curious dark eye, then went back to dreaming on, about, his muff.

The passage was lighted with candles, the bedroom ablaze with light. Ned set Julie on her feet.

She spun around in wonder. The tapestries were as she had last seen them, and the Turkey carpets, but now flowers were strewn everywhere.

The coverlet on the four-post bed was turned invitingly back. "You were so certain that I'd come?"

"I hoped you would." Ned pulled off his shirt and tossed it aside. All that lovely golden skin was beyond tempting. Julie placed her hands on his chest, felt the muscles ripple beneath his flesh. Felt his own hands make short work of the fastenings of her dress.

She was having trouble concentrating. "What if I had not?"

"I would have come to fetch you." Ned eased the gown over her shoulders, paused for a good look.

She hadn't worn a corset. His fingers tangled in the ribbons of her shift. "Bates informed me that there is a tree outside your bedroom window at your grandfather's house."

"You would have climbed a tree?"

"I would have swum an ocean." A few deft movements, and her clothing puddled at her feet. Julie stood in the middle of the bedroom naked, save for her shoes and stockings and knife.

Ned knelt before her. His breath was warm against her belly as his hands slid down her hips. Julie clasped his shoulders, for her knees had turned to jelly and she feared she might altogether melt. He peeled away the knife, her garters and her stockings, all the time kissing and stroking and touching until she couldn't decide if she wanted him to be done teasing her, or never to stop. As she was struggling with these possibilities, Ned picked her up and deposited her gently in the middle of his great carved bed.

Julie smoothed her hand over the sheets. They were the softest she had ever lain upon. She would have lain upon straw, and happily, if she could lie with Ned.

He stood beside the bed, looking down at her. There was no need for the fire burning on the hearth; Julie could have toasted herself in the heat of his emerald gaze. She trailed her fingers along one of his scars. "Trifling, remember? With me?" she said.

He'd made her uncomfortable. He truly was an oaf. She was

absolute perfection, and Ned would tell her so, just as soon as he regained the use of his tongue.

His hands moved to the placket of his breeches. The remainder of his clothing joined the other discards on the floor. There was nothing for Julie's curiosity then but that she must crawl forward to take a closer look. Ned groaned to find his manly appendage in close proximity with her nose.

She extended one finger to give it a little poke. As male organs are wont to do, it swelled. All the more intrigued, Julie reached out. Ned caught her wrists and bore her down beneath him on the bed.

"You didn't like that? Then what about this?" Playfully, Julie wriggled her hips.

Ned was a doomed man. And felt damned cheerful about it, furthermore. He set about exploring bit by bit, starting with that lusciously provocative lower lip.

Julie's amusement fled, and with it all coherent thought. She was aware, vaguely, that she murmured, and gasped, and moaned; but she was overwhelmed with the sensation of Ned's hands and mouth, his hands moving all over her, his mouth burning a trail of pure sensation along her skin. He found each bruise and hurt and healed it with a caress; pleasured her, treasured her, from the arch of her eyebrows to the tips of her toes, not leaving out her bellybutton or the inside of her elbows or the back of her knees, his lips against her breast, his fingers moving between her legs, his manhood hot and heavy against her thigh.

She was drunk with the taste and touch and feel of him. They tumbled amid the silken sheets, at his whim and then hers, because it was her desire to in turn learn his flesh, to touch him every place she could, nip his shoulder and smooth her fingers through his silky hair—it was more than flesh, it was spirit, too, Ned moving over, against, and at long last, into her. There was pain, but not much, and an incredible pleasure that built and built until she tumbled right off the edge of the world.

It was a space out of time. An interval of sheer bliss. When the present caught up with them again, Ned was sprawled spread-eagled on the rumpled sheets, Julie's warm body atop him, her legs tangled with his.

She was gently snoring. Ned caught one of her bright curls and tugged. "In case you don't know it, I am *very* partial to you, buttercup," he said.

Julie yawned and stretched. "I fancy you, too."

There was no help for it. Ned had to kiss her again.

At length he paused, so that both of them might catch their breath. "I've been asked to travel to Vienna when the Allied Sovereigns resume their negotiations later in the year."

Julie didn't ask who had invited him, as he'd thought she might, in which case Ned was prepared to explain his complicated relationship with Lord Castlereagh, even though that gentleman would doubtless prefer he did not. She trailed a lazy finger across his lower lip and said, "Take me with you."

Ah, the places he could take her. Ned caught her finger and nibbled on its tip. "Anywhere you wish. But you must first marry me."

Julie pulled back, to stare at him. Her eyes filled with tears.

Ned's heart cracked a little. "Is it so terrible a notion? I've wanted you from the start." He recalled his first sight of her, damp and furious, wrapped in his drapery, tied up in his chair.

She smiled, also remembering. "I was hoping for a slip on the shoulder. Plain pickpocket Julie couldn't marry the Earl of Dorset."

"*I* was wondering if I might get rid of the title." Julie's nose had reddened with emotion, and Ned gave it a tweak. "You will have to act the lady sometimes. I promise to make it up to you."

She swatted at his hand. "Like you have to act the earl. I suppose I'm to make that up to you. It doesn't matter, does it? That's what I've realized. It doesn't matter how the world may see us, or whose blood runs in our veins; we're still who we are. But you must be certain. Granddaughter of a marquess or no, I was clapped in Newgate for pilfering teaspoons."

"So? They weren't my teaspoons. If you find yourself with an urge to pilfer others, I'll tuck them in my barrow until it's safe to pass them on to an angling cove. Say yes, sweetheart. I don't know how ordinary we shall be, but I very much want to share your life."

"Arse over teakettle." Julie propped her chin on her fist.

Lord, but he adored her. "Why are you looking like the cat that's got into the cream?"

"I was thinking how your cousin Hannah will dislike hearing that the Earl of Dorset has eloped to Gretna Green."

The End

Author's Note

History is a fluid thing. Primary sources frequently don't agree. I have tried to be as true as possible to actual events while rearranging some minor details to better suit the story.

A partial bibliography follows:

In The Absence of the Emperor, London-Paris 1814-1815, written by Simona Pakenham, published by Cresset Press, London, 1968.

The Age of Elegance, written by Arthur Bryant, published by Harper and Brothers Publisher, New York, 1950.

The Prince of Pleasure and his Regency, J. B. Priestley, Harper and Row, 1969

George IV, Christopher Hibbert, Palgrave Macmillan, 2007

Wellington, The Years of the Sword, Elizabeth Longford, Harper and Row, 1969

Napoleon on Elba, Sir Neal Campbell, edited by Jonathan North, Ravenhall Books, 2004

England's Triumph: Being An Account Of The Rejoicings, Etc., Which Have Lately Taken Place In London And Elsewhere (1814), printed for J. Hatchard Bookseller to the Queen

I was also fortunate enough to come into possession of the June 1814 issue of *The Gentleman's Magazine*, which included "Diary of the Proceedings of the Allied Sovereigns".

Another excellent source of information is British History Online: www.british_history.ac.uk/

Made in the USA
Monee, IL
07 July 2026